Love And Liaisons

Quills

CONTENTS

MISTAKEN MISTRESS 7
Margaret McPhee

THE VENETIAN'S MISTRESS 337
Ann Elizabeth Cree

MARGARET MCPHEE
Mistaken Mistress

> DID YOU PURCHASE THIS BOOK WITHOUT A COVER?
> If you did, you should be aware it is **stolen property** as it was
> reported 'unsold and destroyed' by a retailer.
> Neither the author nor the publisher has received any payment
> for this book.

First Published 2006
First Australian Paperback Edition 2006
ISBN 0 733 57276 6

MISTAKEN MISTRESS © 2006 by Margaret McPhee
Philippine Copyright 2006
Australian Copyright 2006
New Zealand Copyright 2006
Except for use in any review, the reproduction or utilisation of this work in
whole or in part in any form by any electronic, mechanical or other means,
now known or hereafter invented, including xerography, photocopying and
recording, or in any information storage or retrieval system, is forbidden without the permission of the publisher, Harlequin Mills & Boon, Locked Bag 7002,
Chatswood D.C. N.S.W., Australia 2067.

All the characters in this book have no existence outside the imagination of
the author, and have no relation whatsoever to anyone bearing the same
name or names. They are not even distantly inspired by any individual known
or unknown to the author, and all the incidents are pure invention.

This book is sold subject to the condition that it shall not, by way of trade or
otherwise, be lent, resold, hired out or otherwise circulated without the prior
consent of the publisher in any form of binding or cover other than that in
which it is published and without a similar condition including this condition
being imposed on the subsequent purchaser.

All rights reserved including the right of reproduction in whole or in part in
any form. This edition is published by arrangement with Harlequin Books
S.A.

Published by
Harlequin Mills & Boon
3 Gibbes Street
CHATSWOOD NSW 2067
AUSTRALIA

HARLEQUIN MILLS & BOON and the Rose Device are trademarks used
under license and registered in Australia, New Zealand, Philippines, United
States Patent & Trademark Office and in other countries.

Printed and bound in Australia by
McPherson's Printing Group

Chapter One

May 1815

'*Kathryn, my sweet dove, you're the only woman for me. Say that you'll be my wife, I beg of you!' Lord Ravensmede plucked her svelte figure into his arms and placed an ardent kiss of love upon her perfect pouting lips. His glossy dark hair mixed with the rich red-brown ringlets dancing temptingly at the sides of her beautiful face. He moved back to stare into her eyes, eyes that were of a serene silver coloration and not at all a bland grey. 'I love you, Kathryn Marchant!' he declared with passion and kissed her again, mindful not to spoil the arrangement of her new and highly fashionable lemon silk dress.*

'Kathryn, Kathryn! Stop wool-gathering and attend to me at once! Are you deaf that you cannot hear me calling you?' Lottie stared at her cousin with narrowed eyes. 'For heaven's sake,' she whispered loudly, 'you're here to assist me, not gawk around like an imbecile.' Her voice resumed its normal tone and with one white and perfectly manicured hand she gestured vaguely in the direction of the floor. 'The hem of my dress has caught on the buckle of Miss Dawson's slipper. Disengage it before any damage is done.'

As Kathryn stooped to free the offending article, which proved to be more difficult than anticipated, she listened to Lottie's conversation. *Dear Lord*, she thought. *The pair of them are as vainly empty-headed as ever!* Then had the grace to blush when she remembered the content of her own sweet daydream.

'Jane, I declare they're both prodigiously handsome. I couldn't pick which man is the better of the two.'

'Well, they're rakes, both of them. My mama has warned me to stay clear of their sort.'

'Tush, Jane, you're such a ninnyhammer at times. They may be rakes, but they're titled and wealthy to boot…and so devilishly good looking. Would your mama say no to you landing a lord?'

'They're looking over here, Lottie.'

'No!'

'Yes, indeed, it's true.'

'Look away, quickly! Don't let them see that we've noticed them.'

Not only did Miss Dawson avert her head but, in a moment of preoccupation, which can only be supposed to have resulted from her excitement over the gentlemen in question, she also stepped back.

Kathryn gasped as Miss Dawson's large foot inadvertently trod on her fingers. The good that resulted from this was that Lottie's dress was freed in an instant. The bad, aside from Kathryn's bruised digits, was that a small tear appeared in the hem.

'Dear Lord, I don't believe it! My dress is ruined. This is the first time I've worn it and, thanks to Kathryn, it's ruined. I may as well go home this instant.' Tears pricked at Lottie's blue eyes, rendering them brighter and bluer, if that were at all possible. The tiniest flush of pink crept into her cheeks, completing, in Kathryn's mind at least, the perfection of her beauty.

'No, dear Lottie. It's scarcely noticeable. A small stitch will soon have that remedied,' Miss Dawson soothed her friend.

Lottie's pale eyebrows arched in irritation as she peered down at Kathryn, who was trying her best to conceal the damage. 'You did that on purpose, just to ruin my evening!' Then she turned to Miss Dawson once more. 'Kathryn's such a spiteful cat. You'd think she'd be grateful, wouldn't you? Saved from destitution by the kindness of *my* family.'

Miss Dawson's eyes opened wider. She tried to speak. 'Lottie—'

But Lottie was in full rant as she warmed to one of her favourite subjects. 'And what does she give in return? Humble gratitude? Most certainly not.'

Miss Dawson tried again. 'Lott—'

'If you would be so kind as to let me finish, Jane. As I was saying, all she gives is jealousy and stupidity!'

'Indeed, life can be so tedious sometimes, Miss Marchant, don't you think?'

The deep masculine drawl caused Lottie to jump. She turned startled eyes in the direction from which it had sounded. Her expression of spiteful fury transformed instantly to one of demure innocence. 'Lord Ravensmede,' she uttered faintly. And looking beyond the breadth of his shoulder, 'Lord Cadmount.' Belatedly, and with a countenance that had stained ruddy, she made her devoirs.

Kathryn looked up from her knees and saw Lord Ravensmede so very far above her. *Not like this. Please, don't let him see me like this!* She swallowed her embarrassment and rose swiftly to her feet, allowing the two quizzical glances to wash over her. The thumping of her heart was so loud that she feared the whole ballroom would hear it. On either side of her were the taller forms of Miss Dawson and Cousin Lottie in all their finery. And not three feet in front stood the subject of her daydreams—the Viscount of Ravensmede. This time there was no lemon silk dress for Kathryn, no pretty dancing ringlets. The reality of their meeting stood in stark contrast to her dream. Still, she mustered a stiff little smile.

Ravensmede's gaze did not linger, returning instead to Lottie, who was frantically fanning herself to remove the scalded heat from her cheeks. She batted her eyelashes, looked coy, and did not offer to introduce her cousin. Neither did his lordship request an introduction. Indeed, he had looked at her, in Kathryn's own view, as if she were no more than a crumb upon the floor.

Attraction retreated. Indignation rallied. Anger advanced. Quite clearly Lord Ravensmede's handsome looks were not matched by a handsome temperament. Why, he was possibly one of the rudest men Kathryn had ever met. And then it dawned on her exactly why Lottie had made no introduction. Lord Ravensmede thought her a servant, and Lottie, dear Cousin Lottie, wanted it to appear so to excuse the chastisement he had interrupted. Two fiery patches erupted on Kathryn's cheeks. She might be an orphan, and poor. She might live under the name of companion and work as a servant. But through all her shabby misery she still had her good name, and that knowledge lent her courage. Might well they talk of a breach of manners! She set a stubborn tilt to her jaw and in a frosty tone uttered their given names. 'Lottie, Jane, gentlemen—' she eyed Lord Ravensmede with special dislike '—please do excuse me.' She saw the arrogant arch of his eyebrow. With a degree of satisfaction and her head held high, she turned on her heel and walked away.

Ravensmede noticed her then, the small sparrow of a girl with her ancient grey gown and her ruffled dignity. The look that she shot him from those stunning silver eyes was not one the Viscount was used to seeing in women: disapproval, dislike and disappointment all wrapped up into one. A spark of interest ignited. Ravensmede followed the retreat of the girl's straight back until she disappeared into the crowd. Even then, he continued to trace her steady progress weaving through the crush of guests until he heard Cadmount say with the glimmer of a laugh, 'One just can't get the staff these days.'

He watched while Miss Dawson creased with embarrassment and glanced nervously at Miss Marchant, whose bland prettiness seemed only mildly perturbed. Neither replied. Ravensmede tucked the matter away for later consideration and idled away a little more of his time before announcing, 'Ladies, please excuse me. I have a rather pressing engagement.' Then he headed off on the real purpose behind his attendance at so dull an affair as Lady Finlay's ball.

Kathryn had almost made it out of the ballroom when she was halted by a woman's haughty voice.

'Just where do you think you're going?' Aunt Anna loomed behind her, reticule in hand, resplendent in a cream-and-rose creation.

'The ladies' retiring room.' Kathryn forced a politeness to the words that she did not feel. It was the only way of dealing with Aunt Anna. Every other means only worsened the situation. That she was reliant on her aunt and uncle's charity for the roof over her head and the food in her belly was something that she never forgot. Neither, for that matter, did they.

'You've left Lottie alone?' The question was in her aunt's usual imperious tone. Kathryn could have sworn that it was edged with accusation.

'No. She's with Miss Dawson.' Kathryn looked at her tall well-dressed relative and waited. She omitted to mention the conditions under which she had abandoned the younger women. No doubt Aunt Anna would find out soon enough.

Mrs Marchant frowned, as was her habit when addressing her niece, and averted her gaze. 'Then you had best be quick about your business. You're here as Lottie's companion, try to remember that. My patience wears thin with reminding you.'

Still Kathryn stood, betraying nothing, her face a mask of polite indifference.

'Well, what are you waiting for? Get on with it.' Mrs Marchant waved her hand in a dismissive gesture.

Kathryn turned and walked away.

She sighed and rubbed at her brow to ease the knot of tension. In truth Kathryn had no need to visit the retiring room; it was merely an excuse to avoid the loathsome Lottie. No matter the cost, Kathryn knew that she needed some little time away from the spoiled spite of her cousin and the arrogant disregard of Lord Ravensmede. She'd already done quite enough damage on the Lottie front, the repercussions of which would no doubt be reaped in the very near future. And as for Lord Ravensmede…

Walking as briskly as she could, she passed unnoticed through the throng of hot, perfumed bodies and escaped into the hall. Quite where she was going she did not know—anywhere would do as long as it gave her the respite she sought. Just five minutes to cool the splurge of temper that had risen too readily. Over the past three years she had learned to school such reactions, to bear all with a stoic countenance. It was better, after all, to show nothing. And now, despite all of that practice, she had almost lost her temper.

Five minutes. It surely wasn't too much to ask. Five paltry

minutes, and then she'd turn her feet around and return to face it all once more, as if she had never been away. No one need notice. Indeed, no one ever did notice plain Kathryn Marchant, which is why Aunt Anna and Uncle Henry had agreed to have her to live with them after her papa's death. She was the perfect backdrop against which to exhibit their own sweet Lottie, and, of course, it saved on the expense of employing another servant. It was something that Kathryn had firmly resolved not to dwell upon, as such thoughts could do nothing except produce a bitterness that was unworthy of all that her dear departed mama and papa had instilled in her.

The hallway had become a corridor, which continued through a set of doors towards the rear of Lady Finlay's large mansion house. Not another soul was to be seen. Evidently Lady Finlay had the servants engaged elsewhere and no other guest would be so rude or so bold as to wander so freely. The corridor became a gallery and Kathryn paused to examine the paintings that lined the walls. Faces, some faintly reminiscent of the elderly Lord Finlay, peered down at her. Just as she was examining a lofty-looking young man's features, footsteps sounded in the distance.

Lord above, she could not be found here! Why, just imagine Aunt Anna's reaction to the news that her niece had taken it upon herself to inspect her ladyship's family portraits. Glancing around in panic, she spied a single door at the end of the gallery, just at the point where the corridor turned and led away to the right. The footsteps grew louder.

Kathryn did not wait to hear any more. Within the blink of an eye she ran towards the door, and, finding it to be unlocked, whipped into the room beyond. Just in time, for the footsteps, large and plodding, passed her hiding place and continued off into the distance. She heaved a sigh of relief and turned to look at the place in which she now stood.

It appeared to be a large room with a few items of dustsheet-covered furniture clustered around its periphery. There were no candles burning and no fire within the blackened grate. Yet the centre of the room was bathed in a silver light that flooded in through a pair of glass doors. The magical illumination drew Kathryn like a moth. Lottie and Aunt Anna were no more. All else was forgotten as the moonlight lulled her under its spell. Through the panes of glass she could see the deep darkness of the night sky studded with the glitter of distant stars. But the moon itself was what held her attention—huge and white, a glowing orb amidst the darkness. Kathryn stared with increasing fascination. Such a feeling of peace. Within the silent silver room anger ebbed, indignation crumbled.

There had been nothing unusual in Lottie's behaviour; Kathryn had long since grown used to her cousin's high-handed ways. What was it, then, that had instigated her outburst? The question perhaps should have been *who* rather than *what*. And the answer, to Kathryn's chagrin, was patently obvious: Lord Ravensmede.

It was one thing to escape the reality of her life by daydreaming, but quite another when those dreams involved a particular nobleman. Unfortunately, she had been thus affected since first seeing the arrogant man across the floor at Almack's Assembly Rooms a month ago. It was just an imagining, a game that she played inside her head, nothing more. Harmless, or at least it had been until now. But she had reckoned without this evening. She knew that no man of quality would look twice at such a plain penniless creature as herself. Witnessing the obvious disdain in which Lord Ravensmede held her was humiliating, as if the cloth had been torn from the mirror and she had been forced to stand exposed before it. Kathryn's life did not make for a pretty picture.

She thought of the past eight years, of the deaths of her parents and her sister. Nothing of Aunt Anna's dislike or Lottie's tantrums could compare with the pain that those losses had wrought. At first she had thought it intolerable, but as the weeks became months, and the months, years, Kathryn had learned to live with the ache buried deep in her heart. She could take whatever Aunt Anna wished to throw at her. Wasn't that what daydreams were for? To make life bearable? To make one impervious to hurt? Lord Ravensmede could not be allowed to change that. His behaviour was an abomination of all that was gentlemanly. He was as arrogant a scoundrel as his reputation told. For certain his place in her dreams was now forfeit. She would not think of him again. Most definitely not. And all the while the cool silver light stroked her with its comforting caress.

Kathryn could never be sure of what it was that made her suddenly draw back into the darkness of the shadows, but barely had she done so when the door creaked open and a large figure slipped inside. The door closed with a quiet click.

'Amanda?' The whisper was clearly that of a man.

She stood quiet and motionless, hoping to hide her presence from the stranger.

The soft tread of his footsteps sounded against the floor.

Her back hugged the floral-print wallpaper. *Please stay where you are and come no further.*

'Amanda?' the voice whispered again and a figure advanced into the moonlight.

The breath caught in Kathryn's throat as the light illuminated his face. *Dear Lord, no! It cannot be.* As if summoned by her thoughts, there stood the stark figure of the Viscount of Ravensmede.

His head lifted, as a hound that scents the hare, and it seemed that he could see through the darkness to look right at her.

Do not see me. Pray, do not know that I'm here. Kathryn tried to quieten her ragged breathing.

'Amanda, what game are you playing? Have you forgotten our little arrangement?' He walked slowly, determinedly towards her.

A meeting with his inamorata, except that it isn't Amanda, whomever she may be, who is here. She swallowed hard, and heard the smile in his voice.

'Very well, we'll proceed as you prefer. I must agree that it is a rather entertaining novelty…for now.'

There is nothing else for it; I will have to own my identity. Kathryn was just about to step forward when his fingers touched to her wrist. A short sharp intake of breath. She made to warn him of his mistake, only to find herself in the Viscount's arms and her would-be protestations silenced by the warm touch of his lips. She stiffened and tried to pull away.

But Lord Ravensmede clearly had other ideas. His hands stroked sensuously against her back, imprisoning her with their caress. His heat burned through the fabric of her bodice.

She pushed hard against his chest, her fingers all too aware of the unyielding muscle beneath. Panic gripped her. She struggled. Opened her mouth to scream.

Slowly, deliberately, he intensified the kiss, his tongue tracing a spell against her lips before it probed within.

Something fluttered deep within her, and all her good intentions disappeared in a warm fuzzy haze. Kathryn moaned and gave up all semblance of resistance as reality and daydream merged within the passion of the moment.

She didn't understand what was happening to her. Knew that her behaviour was reprehensible. But her blood surged wild and strong, and the sensations assailing her would not be denied. Taste of nectar on her tongue. Touch of lips that slid against hers—demanding, enticing. Smell of clean masculinity mixed with the subtle undertones of bergamot. Even when every rational thought screamed out that she should stop she could not. Common sense fled. Kathryn answered the call of Lord Ravensmede's body. She relaxed into his arms, her rigidity shed like a cloak upon the floor. So warm, so comfortable. She sighed and nestled closer. For that one brief moment in time Kathryn was the woman of her dreams, neither poor nor dowdy, but desirable and loved. Dewy breath caressed her cheek. A soft whisper tickled her ear.

'Amanda.' The name rolled lazily off his tongue.

Kathryn descended back down to earth with a crash, all her dreams shattered in an instant. *What am I doing letting him kiss me? It's not Kathryn Marchant that he holds so tenderly, but another woman altogether. If he knew the truth...* 'No!' Her whisper was loud and urgent. She thrust herself back from him.

'What the...?' His puzzlement was palpable.

'No!' she said again, louder this time and with quiet determination. She tried to move away. But she had reckoned without Lord Ravensmede.

He stepped closer, backing her up against the wall. 'What's wrong? Was the diamond bracelet not to your liking?' One large thumb drizzled slowly down her cheek to brush against the soft cushion of her mouth. 'Come, Amanda, we're both hardened players of this game.'

Kathryn's heart thundered in her chest, her pulse leaping at her throat. Her whisper was loud against the hiss of silence. 'You're mistaken, my lord. I am not...'

Ravensmede halted her words with an ardent kiss. 'Am I

then mistaken in that? Or in the fact that your kisses are the sweetest I've ever tasted?' His hands slid over her shoulders as he pulled her to him. 'Trembling like a virgin, Mrs White? Did I not know just how determinedly you had courted my attention, your timidity might be believable.' He made to kiss her again, but was thwarted by Kathryn's wriggles and succeeded only in planting a chaste kiss upon the tip of her nose.

The time for speaking was past. Kathryn knew she had but one opportunity for escape and she created it with a sudden exclamation. 'My lord, there's someone at the window!' When Ravensmede turned to look over his shoulder, she bolted and ran for the door. Blood pounded in her temples and her breath shortened. Movement sounded behind her, but she did not look back, just kept running. Her fingers reached forward, the tips touching to the cool brass of the doorknob before their contact was severed. A strong arm wound around her waist and yanked her back against a wall of solid muscle.

'What the hell is this about, Amanda? You've been flirting with me for months, practically begging me to visit your bed, and when finally I agree you flee as if the very devil is on your heels. Let's resolve this matter once and for all, madam.' He waited with patience, but did not loosen his grip.

A thousand thoughts whirled through Kathryn's brain. Plans to escape, words of excuse, fear and panic, but through them all she knew her time had come. There was no alternative other than to let him see the truth and await his reaction. Dear Lord, if there was any other way! She steeled herself to the task, to the revulsion and anger she knew that she would see in his face. There could be no further prevarication. She ceased her struggle.

'An explanation, please, if you would be so good, Mrs White.'

'I did not mean for this to happen, my lord.'

She allowed Lord Ravensmede to turn her in his arms, knowing full well it would be the last time ever she would feel his touch. The shadow had lightened a little, but as she looked up she could see nothing more than the dark outline of his face, and was thankful that it was so. 'I am not Mrs White,' she said simply.

Silence stretched between them.

Abruptly he pulled her across the room to stand before the glass doors. Moonlight captured his stunned features, proclaiming the perfection of each contour, every plane. Dark eyes glittered incredulously, raking every fibre of her being until she thought she could stand his silent scrutiny no more. She stood stiff and erect, her pride holding all else in check.

'I am Miss Kathryn Marchant, the cousin of Miss Lottie Marchant.'

No reply, just the soft sound of his breathing, and the continued pressure of his hands around her upper arms.

A tremble set up in her legs. 'I only sought some…somewhere where I could be alone.' The words were stilted, awkward. 'I did not know that…that the room was to be used by another…others,' she corrected.

Still he did not speak.

'What has occurred here has been a mistake. I beg that you'll speak of it to no one. If my aunt was to hear…' She could not finish what she had started.

His voice rumbled low, little more than a whisper. 'Why did you not speak earlier? Inform me of my…error?'

A hot blush flooded her cheeks. 'I tried—'

He raised an eyebrow. 'Not very convincingly.'

'I could not, my lord.'

'Could not, or would not, Miss Marchant?'

She quailed beneath the intensity of his stare.

'You play a very foolish game...a downright dangerous game.'

The touch of his fingers burned where they contacted the bare skin of her arms.

'Don't tell me you have not heard of my reputation?' he mocked, then glanced away as if there was something he could not quite fathom. When his gaze slid back to hers there was something in it that caused her heart to race even faster.

She did not answer. Aridity threatened to close her throat. When finally her words came they were nothing but a hoarse whisper. 'Please excuse me, my lord, I must return to my cousin.'

'Really?' There was a lazy drawl in Ravensmede's voice that did not match the glint in his eye.

'Indeed, my lord.'

His lordship showed not the slightest inclination to withdraw his hands.

Beneath the magical glow of the moonlight her skin was pale and smooth as alabaster. Her hair was still pinned back, but some of the curls had escaped to dangle enticingly against her cheek and throat. One finger lifted a curl from her cheek, then slid down to trace the delicate line of her jaw. His gaze followed where his finger led, then meandered back to her eyes that appeared opalescent in the moonlight. Fringed with long dark lashes, glittering with unshed moisture, her eyes were quite simply beautiful. And contained in the stare that she returned him Ravensmede could see shock and guilt...and passion. She was playing with fire. Already the heat within him kindled.

'Miss Marchant, someone should teach you...' deliberately he leaned down and allowed his breath to caress her ear

'…the perils…' his lips hovered by the side of her face, so close yet not touching '…of allowing yourself…' he closed the last small space that divided them until he felt his thighs brush against her skirts '…to be kissed by a rake.' Her clean feminine fragrance filled his nose. Where their legs touched he could feel the slight tremor running through her. He watched her eyes widen, but she did not try to pull away. 'Shall I, Kathryn?' he exhaled the question in a soft breath. He looked at her a moment longer, then gently, insistently, covered her mouth with his, massaging her lips in a slow, sensual motion.

She tasted sweet and innocent…and completely alluring. Desire leapt. Their first kisses had not lied. He wanted nothing more than to deepen the kiss, to drink in every last drop of her. Attraction scorched as hot as if he were the greenest of lads. He wanted to reach in and touch her as she had touched him. Temptation loomed large. And Nicholas Maybury, Viscount of Ravensmede, had never been a man to deny himself.

'By the heavens, Ravensmede! You arrange an assignation with me then fill my place with another before I arrive!' A woman's shrill voice shrieked at full volume from the doorway. 'You, sir, are a damnable scoundrel!'

He felt the girl jump within his arms, heard her sudden shocked gasp. It was with a great degree of reticence that he removed his embrace. 'Mrs White, how very good of you to join us,' he said.

The voluptuous young widow's eyes slid towards Miss Marchant and narrowed further.

He sensed rather than saw the girl's withdrawal. 'Miss Marchant and I were just admiring the night sky.'

A derisive snort sounded from the beauty. She stepped

fully into the room, leaving the door gaping wide behind her. 'I know full well exactly what you and…Miss Marchant… were doing and it had nothing to do with the stars! Don't take me for a fool, Ravensmede!'

'I must insist that you're mistaken, my dear Mrs White.' He moved to stand between the two women, shielding Kathryn from the other's view. Mrs White's abundant bosom expanded before his very eyes, rising and falling with alarming speed. There was about her face a slyness that he had not observed before. He wondered that he ever could have mistaken one woman for the other, for in the clear moonlight there was certainly nothing of a similarity between them. Amanda White was tall with a curvaceous figure. Kathryn Marchant was not. And yet it was the smaller, slimmer woman in the unfashionable plain gown that he wanted; the woman whose eyes were cool silver, and whose lips were hot with untapped passion.

'I know what I saw, sir,' Mrs White said harshly. 'Miss Marchant, indeed.' Her head bobbed to look down upon Kathryn's pale face. 'My, how your standards have dropped if you have taken up with such a plain little specimen. You know, of course, that she's nothing but a poor companion.' Her pretty face hardened into malice as she stared. 'But then gentlemen will be gentlemen and have *whatever* they can from *whoever* will give it. It signifies nothing other than the perfidy of men in general. You, my lord, are no exception to the rule.'

Kathryn skirted Lord Ravensmede's large frame and made for the door, but not before Mrs White had moved to block her exit.

'You're a trifle late in leaving, Miss Marchant. In fact, you never should have arrived. Scuttle back to your aunt, I'm sure she'll be very interested in this evening's activities.' The widow laughed, a cruel and petty sound.

Through the dimness Ravensmede could see Kathryn's face, white as a ghost, her eyes huge and round, staring with a horror that even her controlled façade could not disguise. Such vulnerability, such innocence. In one fleeting moment her life had been ruined…and he was not without blame in the matter. It was one thing to have a little fun, quite another to allow the woman to suffer. He knew what would happen if Mrs White's gossip was allowed to spread. Guilt flickered. It was not a familiar feeling for Lord Ravensmede, and it led to contrariness.

'Miss Marchant,' he said with more asperity in his tone than was necessary, 'return to your family.' It sounded cold and imperious even to his own ear. She walked towards the door as if heading to her own execution. 'We shall continue our study in astronomy another time.' And he meant it. Kathryn Marchant's kisses had shattered the monotony of his boredom and awakened a long-forgotten part of him. Ravensmede had no intention of just letting her walk out of his life. But first, and more importantly, he had to deal with Amanda White. He waited until he heard the soft click of the closing door.

'Mrs White, I apologise for the misunderstanding this evening. The situation, as I said, was one of complete innocence, even if it may have appeared otherwise.'

The widow said nothing, just looked at him with her heavy-lidded eyes and an expression of smug irritation.

Rose-scented perfume wafted to greet his nostrils. Overstated, cloying, like its wearer. Strangely he had not noticed it before. 'You're a woman of some standing—' that was certainly one way of putting it '—with a compassionate nature.' There was nothing of those traits in the look she returned him, but Amanda White was above all a vain woman, and it was to this weakness that Ravensmede played. 'I know that when I ask that you make no mention of this affair, you will indulge my request.'

'Of course, Lord Ravensmede. Your request is my pleasure.' Her pale eyes glittered coldly; a veil of insincerity covered her. She stepped closer, arranging her posture to exemplify the voluptuous curves of her figure. Rosebud lips parted as if in invitation. 'But, first, have we not unfinished business to attend to?'

Lord Ravensmede looked at the woman before him, at the artfully arranged hair, and the costly silver-and-blue dress. Her generous bosom swelled, tempting, teasing in design. And then her cruel derisive words to Kathryn Marchant rang clearly in his mind, dampening any interest he may have had. Revulsion rippled down his spine.

'I'm afraid that that can no longer be the case.'

The pale eyes narrowed.

'This evening's...incident...has no bearing on the matter. Circumstances have changed.'

The pouting lips narrowed to a thin line.

'You're welcome to retain the gift that I sent.'

'Of course.'

Ravensmede said nothing, just allowed the silence to stretch to discomfort, and watched the widow's anger and irritation grow.

Mrs White's gaze broke first. 'If that is all, Lord Ravensmede, I shall bid you good evening. There is suddenly a matter that I simply must discuss with the ladies.' She turned to leave.

'Not quite all, Mrs White.'

Her movement checked. Hope leapt. 'My lord?'

Ravensmede could hear the deliberate reversion in her

tone: from shrill annoyance to husky enticement. The ghost of a curve touched at his lips. 'Gossip is such a vulgar pastime, don't you think?'

She hesitated. 'I cannot agree, sir.' There was a furtiveness to her expression.

'Allow me to persuade you otherwise—a banker's draft for two thousand guineas to be delivered to your address tomorrow morning in exchange for your silence.'

Two thousand guineas! Mrs White's eyes bulged. And then she recovered herself. 'I might consider it…' she sniffed '…if the sum were perhaps three thousand.'

Ravensmede's smiled a chilling smile. It was enough to make the hairs on the back of Amanda White's pretty white neck stand on end. 'Two thousand guineas,' he said, 'take it or leave it. Make your choice before the offer is withdrawn.' He stepped towards her. 'And should you choose wrongly, Mrs White, let's just say you may find your own reputation a little the worse for wear.'

'Are you threatening me?'

'Would I do such a thing?' He raised an arrogant eyebrow as if the very suggestion amused him. 'I'm merely illustrating the rule of cause and effect. Gossip about Kathryn Marchant and you'll not find a welcome at any decent house in London.'

Anger flashed in her eyes. 'Don't be ridiculous! You know nothing, Ravensmede, nothing that you could use against me.'

He shrugged his shoulders in a nonchalant manner. 'Perhaps, but everyone has something to hide, a secret. Consider yours very carefully. For should I have reason, I would discover it.'

'You could not!' she exclaimed, but there was a definite echo of fear in her voice.

'My wealth and power are considerable. And everybody has a price. You of all people should know that, Amanda.'

She paled and took a few steps back.

He slipped his watch from his pocket and glanced down at the face. 'Time's up, Mrs White. What is it to be?'

She cleared her throat. 'I'll accept the money.'

'Bravo.' He looked at her a little longer with that same lazy expression. 'Might I be so bold as to suggest that you would benefit from a sojourn in the country. A few weeks away from the heat of the town…'

'I'll think about it,' she ground out from between gritted teeth.

'Please do,' he said as if they were having the politest of conversations.

They stared at one another with barely concealed dislike across the small distance.

'Good evening, my lord.'

She turned and was gone, leaving Ravensmede to ponder on what he had just done to one of London's most coveted women…and all for the sake of Miss Kathryn Marchant.

Chapter Two

Kathryn sat composedly watching her cousin being whirled around the dance floor by a young gentleman whose features bore a startling resemblance to a horse. On the other side of Lottie's empty chair Mrs Marchant was chatting to Mrs Brown, the tinkle of her laughter ringing out into the ballroom.

Kathryn concentrated on the music and tried to disguise her mounting worry. As the minutes ticked slowly by without a sign of either Lord Ravensmede or Mrs White, she began to hope that they had left the ball. But that would mean only one thing, and, despite everything, it was not a pleasing thought. She heard again the echo of his parting words: *We shall continue our study in astronomy another time.* Surely he did not think... But hadn't she given him every reason to believe so? So caught up in her remembrances was she that she did not at first notice the arrival of the beautiful woman accompanying Lady Spey. Only the overpowering scent of roses alerted her.

'Mrs Marchant, may I present Mrs White, who is a friend of mine.'

Kathryn senses reeled. *No!*

'Mrs Marchant!' the husky voice gushed. 'How very pleased I am to meet you. I've heard only good things about you.'

'Mrs White, the pleasure is mine.' Mrs Marchant puffed out her chest in a self-important manner.

The widow turned to view Kathryn. 'And this must be your—'

'Niece,' supplied Mrs Marchant in a rush.

'Ah,' Mrs White uttered softly, 'this must then be Miss Kathryn Marchant.' She sauntered closer and inclined a regal head. And never once did her pale ice eyes leave Kathryn's face. 'Such a delight.'

'Mrs White.' Kathryn bobbed a curtsy and forced her face to a mask of politeness. For the briefest of moments her eyes met the scrutiny, and held. Amanda White's sly smile widened.

'Please say that you won't object to my being seated with you, my dear Mrs Marchant.' It was not so much a question as an assumption. Amanda sat down with a show of elegance and proceeded to monopolise Mrs Marchant.

Kathryn sat rigid. Perspiration prickled beneath her arms. The length of her back had adhered to the grey silk of her dress. Even her palms were cold and clammy. And still she waited, while Mrs White played her cat-and-mouse game. Each time those pale eyes slanted her way, each time that husky voice lowered conspiratorially to utter, *My dear Mrs Marchant*, Kathryn's heart lurched. Every nerve in her body was stretched taut, vibrating with expectation.

'But Kathryn—' the widow broke off to pat Kathryn's cold white hand '—you don't mind if I call you that, do you?' and without waiting for an answer rushed on, 'You look so pale. Are you ill?'

Kathryn licked the dryness from her lips. 'I'm quite well, thank you.' And all the while she wanted to scream, *Tell her, if that's what you mean to do, and be done with it*.

But Mrs White had no intention of ending her game, not

when her humiliation still burned so painfully. Ravensmede might have bought her silence, but Kathryn was ignorant of the fact. The widow fully intended to exact a measure of revenge upon the girl for the remainder of the evening. A slow, delicious torture, and one that would not leave Ravensmede unaffected. Amanda White relished the prospect. She drew Kathryn a malevolent smile and turned her attention back to Anna Marchant.

Kathryn's overstretched nerves began to fray.

'That woman has the cheek of the devil.'

Cadmount followed Ravensmede's focus and smiled lazily. 'The Winsome Widow White, I perceive. I thought you and the lady had reached an arrangement?'

Lord Ravensmede bestowed a withering look upon his friend. 'Not the kind of arrangement that you think. Matters have altered.'

'What are you not telling of the Winsome Widow?' Cadmount studied his friend for a moment. When no answer was forthcoming, he added, 'Or rather, should I ask which new face has captured your interest?'

Ravensmede lifted one haughty eyebrow.

'I know you too well, my friend.' Cadmount chuckled. 'You don't fool me for an instant.'

'Perhaps.'

'Come on, let's head to Brooks's. I've a mind to enjoy a turn at the tables and a drink or two. This place is so full of blasted chits and tabbies as to wear a man's soul.'

Ravensmede smiled at that, but his eyes soon drifted back to where Kathryn Marchant sat drained and rigid. Her chestnut hair was scraped back in a chignon from which the escaped curls still hung defiantly. Despite the pallor of her cheeks her back was straight and her head held up. She was afraid, but she was fighting it with courage. And courage was something that Lord Ravensmede had ever respected.

He thought of the harangue he had interrupted between pampered Miss Lottie Marchant and her cousin; thought too of how hard Lottie had tried to portray Kathryn as her servant. He remembered the feel of Kathryn's lips beneath his, and how slender her body was within his arms. Just the memory brought a stirring in his nether regions. Finally he allowed his thoughts to turn to Amanda White. The widow was no fool; she was unlikely to jeopardise the little agreement they had just reached. But a warning shot wouldn't go amiss. As he stood there, beneath the bright glow of the chandeliers, surrounded by the crowd and the melodic strains of the band, he knew just what to do.

Cadmount's perceptive gaze lit upon Kathryn. He decided to test his theory. 'Drab little chit.'

Ravensmede glanced up.

'Miss Marchant's cousin. The one she would have us believe is her servant.'

Ravensmede donned a slightly amused expression. 'Only to those with a less discerning eye. The only drab thing about Miss Kathryn Marchant is her dress. Clothing is easily replaced.'

'It's like that, then? I'm impressed. One would hardly have guessed it from the look she gave you earlier this evening. Were you a military man, you would surely have made Commander-in-Chief for your ability to claim victory from the most hopeless of situations.' Cadmount widened his eyes in feigned surprise and tried not to appear smug.

Ravensmede resumed his watch. 'You're making assumptions, dear boy.'

'Afraid it's what I must do if you won't spill the beans, old man.' Cadmount looked at the awkward little group. Their tension was palpable even across the room. 'It's rather interesting that the Winsome Widow is so friendly with Mrs Marchant. Didn't think they'd get on. Wonder what she's up to?'

'Baiting Miss Marchant, I should guess.' As if to confirm Ravensmede's words, Mrs White's gaze flitted to meet his. The widow looked pointedly at Miss Marchant, then back to the Viscount before delivering a nasty smile.

None of it was missed by Cadmount. 'Now what could the very respectable Miss Marchant have done to so upset the widow?' he mused, and looked speculatively at his friend.

The flicker of a smile crossed the Viscount's face. He said nothing.

'Care to enlighten me?'

'No.' Ravensmede didn't even look round. 'What do you know of her?'

'The Winsome Widow?' Cadmount's forehead wrinkled in mock puzzlement.

One dark brow raised in sarcastic denial. 'I was referring to Miss Marchant, as well you know.'

Cadmount scratched at the dark blond of his curls, sniffed knowingly and reeled off the information. 'Family lost their money in some confounded investment venture that went awry. Poor as church mice. Father shot himself little over three years past, the mother and sister died about eight or nine years ago; Miss Marchant must have been little more than a child at the time. Henry Marchant is the father's brother. The girl's lived with his family ever since. Have it from the best sources that she's little more than a domestic in that household. Anna Marchant doesn't take to her too well. That's as much as I know.'

'Caddie, I'm the one who's impressed. Should you wish to purchase another commission, consider military intelligence. Undoubtedly you'd go far.'

They laughed.

Then Cadmount said knowingly, 'So Brooks's will have to wait?'

'For now.'

Cadmount picked distractedly at his nails and deliberately yawned. 'Shouldn't take too long, damned chit looks as if she's about to keel over any minute now.'

The corner of Ravensmede's mouth twitched. 'Not if I have anything to do with it. How are your dance steps these days?'

They shared a look of mutual understanding. No need for further explanation between old friends.

'It'll cost you a bottle of your finest brandy.'

'Done!'

'You do know that you'll be delivering a monumental snub to the widow, don't you? I mean, the whole town is aware that she's been chasing you for months and what do you do? Head straight in the direction of the good lady and ask the plainest chit in the room, who just happens to be sitting by her side, to waltz. No denying that it don't look too good for Mrs White.'

'How very perceptive of you, Caddie,' drawled Ravensmede. 'Mrs White will soon learn the wisdom of good advice, and her departure from London might suddenly seem rather more urgent.'

The pair set off at a sedentary saunter in their deep-blue fitted tail-coats.

'Now to really set the cat amidst the pigeons!' Cadmount said under his breath. 'I hope the chit's worth it, my friend, I sincerely do.'

***

'It's so unusual to meet a young lady with an interest in astronomy, don't you agree?' Mrs White's voice grated against Kathryn's ear. 'I was just telling your aunt, it's such a curious trait to observe in a female.'

Kathryn gritted her teeth and looked round. The widow was enjoying herself immensely. Beyond the gleam of Amanda White's dark curls Aunt Anna's face was scowling in perplexity. It was time that things came to a head. Temptation beckoned. 'Perhaps, but I understand it to be a most enjoyable pastime.' She was relieved to hear that her voice held no trace of fear. Indeed it was positively calm. The words acted, as Kathryn knew they would, as a burr to Mrs White.

The lady's face contorted to a sour grimace before she recollected herself. 'For those of a certain set. Hardly a fitting activity for a young lady. Wouldn't you say, Mrs Marchant?'

Aunt Anna might not have understood to what Mrs White was alluding, but she definitely detected an underlying current of dislike aimed at her niece. She smiled and shifted a little closer to the widow. 'Completely, Mrs White. Please do call me Anna.'

'Thank you, Anna. And you must call me Amanda.'

The two women smiled in unity.

'There is a rather delicate matter which I'm not fully at liberty to discuss.' Mrs White held her fan over her mouth. 'You must think me foolish not to know how to proceed, but, with your valuable experience of raising such a beautiful daughter, and then your great kindness in inviting your niece into your home as a member of your family, there's no one better I can think to ask.'

Anna Marchant patted her hair and tried not to look superior. 'I've always tried to set an example. Lottie has just to make a match and my job will be complete.'

'Miss Marchant...that is, Miss *Lottie* Marchant, will have no lack of interest from *suitable* gentlemen.' Mrs White shot a glance at Kathryn. 'She's a credit to her mother,' she said. 'Which is why I must ask for your help on behalf of a friend whose charge has just been discovered to have behaved in a most improper manner with a gentleman. I declare the guardian to be quite distraught.'

'Is the girl known to me?' Mrs Marchant's curiosity got the better of her.

Mrs White nodded her beautiful ebony head. 'Most definitely. But do not press me to tell you. I'm sworn to secrecy.' She batted her fan, then added, 'It does so prey upon my mind. I'm in such a quandary as to what to do for the best. Will you trust me as I trust you, dearest Anna?'

'Of course, Amanda.'

'In that case I feel I may speak of it to you.'

Ruined. Cast out, penniless and in shame. There would be little hope for the future. Kathryn waited for the life-changing words. Stared at the floor, wishing it would open up and swallow her whole, and waited. Waited, and waited some more. And then she heard them.

'Miss Marchant, may I enquire whether your card is marked for this dance?' The deep timbre of the voice sent a shiver down Kathryn's spine. She looked up into the moss green eyes of Lord Ravensmede.

'I'm afraid I don't have a dance card. I'm here as a companion to my cousin.'

'Then I'll take it that you're free to accompany me on to the floor.' And with that he took one of her hands in his and pulled. Glancing over at the two older women, he inclined his head. 'Always a pleasure, ladies.'

Kathryn had only the briefest moment to revel in the slack-jawed gawking expressions of her aunt and Mrs White before she found herself clamped firmly in Lord Ravensmede's arms and waltzing across to the other side of the room. It all happened with such speed that she did not know whether to laugh or cry. The former won.

Lord Ravensmede raised a wry eyebrow. 'My dancing is a source of amusement?'

'Not at all.' The vestige of a smile remained upon her face. 'I was merely thinking that your timing is impeccable, my lord. Mrs White is on the brink of revealing all to my aunt. The question is whether she'll await my return before she delivers her denouement.'

'I fancy that Mrs White may have suffered a change of heart,' he said softly and glanced directly down into her eyes.

Kathryn suddenly felt acutely conscious of the touch of one of his hands upon her waist and the other encompassing the fingers of her right hand. 'I can only hope that you're right, my lord.'

His head gestured subtly in the direction of a couple some distance away.

'Mrs White and Lord Cadmount! How very clever. But you only defer the inevitable, my lord. That lady won't be quieted for long.' For someone so perilously close to doom she felt rather light-hearted.

He was still looking at her in that strange way. 'Are you quite recovered?'

A warmth swept into her cheeks and her voice became a little gruff. 'Yes, thank you. I'm concerned only that…' She paused, and glanced towards Amanda White.

'That Mrs White will seek to destroy your reputation?'

'Yes.'

His hand gently squeezed her fingers. 'You have nothing to worry about.'

'I think, my lord, that you underestimate just how much I've heated Mrs White's ire; it will be a long time in the cooling.'

'I underestimate nothing,' he said softly. 'As I said, you need not worry. I shall see that Mrs White holds her tongue.'

Kathryn's heart kicked to a gallop. 'And how do you propose to do that, my lord?'

He smiled a devastatingly wicked smile.

Kathryn did not remain unaffected; the pulse leapt to a fury in her neck, she missed a step, and almost trod on Lord Ravensmede's toes.

His smile deepened.

Kathryn grew even more flustered. 'I'm sorry, but it's a long time since I've danced.' Her cheeks grew warm and pink. 'I didn't mean to embarrass you by my mistake.' And then she realised just how her words could equally well apply to her earlier misdemeanour in the moonlit room, and her blush intensified.

There was a twinkle in his eye. 'I assure you that I'm not in the least embarrassed.'

She looked away. The music filled the small silence between them.

'Do you enjoy waltzing, Miss Marchant?'

Her eyes flitted back to find his gaze upon her. At least the conversation had turned to safer ground, or so she thought. 'Yes, very much so, my lord.'

'Good. Then we'll waltz the next time we meet.'

Their eyes met, and held. 'I did not mean…' Kathryn's

words trailed off unfinished. 'There's really no need. My aunt would not approve.' Her teeth nipped at her bottom lip.

Lord Ravensmede gave a short dry laugh. 'And you, of course, would never do anything of which your relative would not approve?'

The colour staining her cheeks deepened. She knew exactly to what he was referring.

'Then it's settled.'

The regulatory inches between them seemed to shrink. 'I don't think that...' She swallowed hard.

Lord Ravensmede's focus did not waver for a moment.

Kathryn's words of refusal remained unspoken. The final bars of 'Ach! Du lieber Augustine' sounded and she noticed the stares and whispers behind fans. Hardly surprising given that the heir to the Earl of Maybury had just danced with a woman little better than a servant, and it was the waltz of all dances. Despite the attention, and her shabby clothes, and worst of all the prospect of what awaited her back at the seats, Kathryn felt neither shame nor embarrassment, nor even apprehension. She smiled at his lordship, thanked him and allowed him to lead her back to her grim-faced relatives.

Mrs White seemed to have disappeared. So too had Lord Cadmount. And it wasn't long before Ravensmede followed suit. Only Aunt Anna and Lottie remained to scowl their disbelief at Kathryn.

'Whatever have you done to make Lord Ravensmede dance with you?' Lottie was incredulous. 'It's quite unheard of, a man of his calibre dancing with someone like you.' Her lower lip pouted to a petted curl. 'It should have been me that he asked.' She ground her slipper against the floor. 'Say it's so, Mama, say it.'

'Of course, my dearest.' Aunt Anna shot a foul look at her

niece. 'It was probably the result of some wager or joke at Kathryn's expense.'

Kathryn said nothing. At least their preoccupation with Lottie told her one thing: that Mrs White had not made her revelation...yet. She supposed she ought to smooth things over or life in the Marchant household would be miserable for the rest of the week...as if it were ever anything other. A smile tickled the edges of her mouth. 'Lottie, I'm sure that his lordship approached us with the intention of asking you to dance. As you were already on the floor with Mr Richardson, he asked me, but only out of courtesy.'

Lottie's eyes flashed a hard, bright blue. 'I wasn't dancing when he returned you to us. Why did he not ask me then?'

'He had an urgent appointment, or so he told me upon the dance floor.' Beneath Kathryn's demurely folded hands her fingers were firmly crossed. 'Otherwise I'm sure he would have sought you as partner for this quadrille.'

Lottie appeared temporarily placated, but had seemingly developed the most frightful headache.

For this reason, or so it was said, the Marchant ladies bid a hasty departure from Lady Finlay's ball.

From where she stood, Kathryn could see almost the whole of the drawing room in the house in Green Street, as well as herself, reflected in the large gilt overmantel mirror. She was a drab grey figure against the yellow painted walls. The room seemed loud and gaudy, even beneath the subdued lighting of the candles flickering in the drop-crystal chandelier and ormolu cherubim wall sconces. A large group portrait of Mr and Mrs Marchant with Lottie seated demurely between them hung proudly between the two large Palladian windows opposite the fireplace. It had been painted two months previously by Mr Jackson. Kathryn's gaze alighted briefly on the cosy Marchant family captured on canvas before moving on to the lavish sets of curtains. Fringed and tasselled gold-and-yellow damask curtains festooned either side of each window. Not one of them was closed. A thin blind of cream material had been pulled down to create the illusion of privacy. Kathryn could feel the press of the sofa at the back of her knees. Its cream covering decorated with mulberry-coloured roses seemed too cheerful for a house that was so lacking in that sentiment. She shifted her feet uneasily, and was thankful for the cushion of the gold-and-burgundy patterned Oriental rug through her thin worn slippers.

'It has been one of the worst evenings of my entire life,' sobbed Lottie and flung herself into the nearest chair. 'And the blame rests entirely with Kathryn!'

'Now, now, Lottie,' cajoled her mother. 'I have told you already. Lord Ravensmede cannot possibly be interested in your cousin. I dare say it's all part of some jest the gentlemen were playing.'

'It d-didn't look like a jest.' Lottie's eyes were red and swollen from the sobbing and the feigned headache was fast becoming a reality. 'No one would have realised that it w-was.'

'Of course they did, my angel.' Mrs Marchant touched a gentle hand to Lottie's wet cheek. 'If you don't cease this weeping, your looks will be quite spoiled for tomorrow and then what will Mr Dalton say when he calls to collect you for your carriage ride?'

A suitably mollified Lottie turned to Kathryn and sniffed. 'Mama is right. You're such a spiteful cat that it serves you right that you are long on the shelf. When did a gentleman ever call for you to take you driving in the park? Never! And they never will because you look positively ghastly, and everyone hates you!'

Kathryn should have let the comments go; they were not worthy of a reply. But she did not. Although she had long since reconciled herself to a life with neither husband nor children, it still hurt to have the fact rubbed in her face. So for the third time that night Kathryn succumbed to impulse. 'And you, Lottie, are behaving little better than a spoiled and pampered brat,' she said wearily.

Lottie set up a wail. 'Mama, but hear what she's saying to me! Will you let her get away with such insolence?'

'Kathryn Marchant!' exclaimed Mrs Marchant. 'Close your mouth this instant! Do not dare to presume that you can insult Lottie before my very eyes! Haven't you caused enough damage for one night?'

'Aunt Anna—'

'Be quiet!' said Mrs Marchant. 'It's my job to instruct you in the ways of polite society as your papa would have wanted, Kathryn. It would be remiss of me not to do so.' The pink feathers in her bandeau quivered as she shook her head with mock sorrow. 'It's for your own good.' The feathers positively swayed in delight. 'As a punishment, all social outings shall be forbidden.' She looked for a response on Kathryn's face.

Kathryn gave none.

'In addition you'll have no dinner for a fortnight.'

Still no hint of emotion registered on Kathryn's face.

'And…you shall assist cook in the kitchen for the same duration. Mrs Moultrie will, of course, be under strict instructions that dinner is prohibited to you.' She smiled at the ingenuity of her little plan.

'As you wish, Aunt.' Still her gaze held steady.

'When not required by Mrs Moultrie you shall help with the laundry. That, at least, might teach you to know your place. You are here to help Lottie, not attempt to spoil her evening in a fit of jealous spite. Such malice cannot be allowed to go unchecked.'

Kathryn's eyes flickered to some point in the distance, knowing full well the game that her aunt played. What matter if Aunt Anna punished her a thousand times, as long as Lord Ravensmede and Mrs White held their tongues? It was not a hope in which she trusted.

'And you will apologise to Lottie for the foulness of your tongue.'

'She was unkind in her words to me,' said Kathryn.

'She is upset. And little wonder! This season is about making a match for Charlotte, not about you making an exhibition of yourself by dancing with the most libidinous nobleman you can find!'

Lottie looked smugly on.

'I did not—'

'And the waltz of all dances! For heaven's sake, girl, if you have not a care for your own reputation then at least have some consideration for your cousin. Through the goodness of his heart Mr Marchant has taken you into his home, fed and clothed you. And what thanks do you give him? None save to plague his own daughter with spite.'

'No, that isn't true. I merely—'

'You merely tried to steal a better match for yourself. Did you think to catch yourself a viscount, miss?'

Kathryn frowned her indignation. 'Of course not!'

'I have tried my best to see that you dress demurely and behave in a modest and sober manner, but bad blood will out.'

'What do you mean?'

'I mean, my dear, that your mother was the exactly the same: wanton.'

The word seemed to echo between them. The blood drained from Kathryn's face. 'You go too far, Aunt. My mother was not wanton. How can you cast such an unfair slur upon her name?'

'Why else did she run off with Robert Marchant? She was little better than a bitch in heat. It was hardly surprising that her family disowned her!'

'Take that back! You know nothing of my mother. She was a good and kind woman. She eloped with my father because they were in love.'

'Of course that's what she would have told you,' Anna Marchant sneered.

'My mother spoke the truth, unlike you. I won't believe your lies!'

The older woman's eyes narrowed with malevolent intent. 'You are a foul little trollop just as she was.' She advanced quickly and captured Kathryn's upper arms in a cruel grip. 'But if you think that I will allow you to ruin things for Lottie, then you're sadly mistaken.' Her fingers tightened, biting into Kathryn's flesh. 'I tolerate you here as Lottie's companion, nothing more.' The vice-like grip began to shake Kathryn. 'Start behaving with a modicum of decorum and modesty if you don't want to find yourself out on the street. How long do you think you'd last out there?' screeched her aunt. 'You'd be in a bordello or have your throat slit before a single day was out.' The rough shaking intensified.

'Take your hands off me!'

With no warning whatsoever Kathryn found herself thrust down against the sofa. 'Oh, I haven't even started with you, miss,' said Anna Marchant in a voice that chilled Kathryn to the bone.

* * *

A week later the Viscount of Ravensmede still had not forgotten Kathryn Marchant. Indeed, she was the topic of his conversation with Cadmount, and not for the first time.

'The girl's avoiding me. Why else have we seen Mrs Marchant and Miss Lottie Marchant, but no sign of Kathryn? I have endured three balls, an evening at Almack's and two routs! Imagine what this is doing to my reputation.' Ravensmede's long legs stretched out before him as he lounged back in the wing chair.

'And mine.' Cadmount loosened his neckcloth and, in a flippant gesture, dropped it over the side of his chair. 'Sir,' he slurred, 'you obviously haven't looked in the betting book in Brooks's of late.'

One dark eyebrow quirked. 'Enlighten me, Cadmount.' Despite the languor of his manner, there was a darkening of his eye and a quickening of his heart. Surely Amanda White had not reneged on their agreement so soon? Two thousand guineas should have silenced her for good. Money well spent...if she stayed silent. And she shouldn't even still be in London. He carefully refilled each glass and sat back, waiting.

'A fine drop of brandy, I do declare.' Cadmount's lips smacked with pleasure. 'I'd dance all night with the Winsome Widow for a case of this. Are you sure it was just the one bottle you promised me?'

A green gimlet eye stared back at him. 'The betting book?'

Cadmount took another gulp of brandy. 'Yes, the betting book.' He stopped and rubbed his fingers over the golden stubble upon his chin. 'Should shave more often. Wingham says the ladies prefer a smoother approach.' He guffawed at his own joke.

'Hell's teeth, man, spit it out! What does the damnable

book say about Kathryn Marchant?' For once, Ravensmede's usual aplomb had deserted him.

Cadmount blinked in confusion. ''Bout the chit...why, nothing.' He took another a drink and then looked knowledgeable all at once. Tapping the side of his nose, he leaned forward to his friend and said, 'Say no more, old man, understand it perfectly. Li'l Kathryn is your ladybird.' One wavering forefinger pressed to his lips. 'Sshh! Won't say a word.'

The amber liquid swirled around Ravensmede's balloon glass. 'Sorry to disappoint you, but there's no such understanding between Miss Marchant and myself.'

'Absolutely not.' An enormous grin erupted on Cadmount's face.

Ravensmede smiled in return. 'You are the most infuriating man when you're in your cups.

Cadmount's grin deepened, and he hiccuped.

'Brooks's betting book—what does it say with regard to me?' There was no hint in Lord Ravensmede's voice that he had drunk the same quantity of brandy as his friend.

A smile. 'That you'll be wed before the summer is out.'

Ravensmede laughed as a wave of relief swept through him. 'They think I'm on the hunt for a bride because of my attendance at Almack's? Seeking some precious chit just out of the schoolroom? I think not. You know me better than that, Caddie.'

'Indeed I do, sir,' avowed Lord Cadmount. 'Thirty-two years old, heir to an earldom, no wife, no nursery, old man breathing down your neck. Thank God I'm only a younger son. No such pressure.'

'Are you always this philosophical when you're foxed?' Ravensmede demanded somewhat sourly.

'Always.' Another gulp of brandy. 'If Kathryn Marchant's not your girl, then why have we been trailing round one blasted place after the other in search of the little lady, and all the while missing out on the finer things in life? Beats me why you're behaving like a green lad over her. She's not your type at all!' Even the worse for several glasses of brandy, Archibald Cadmount knew exactly how to nettle Ravensmede.

In return, Ravensmede slowly and deliberately set his glass aside. 'You're quite right in thinking that I would like to make Miss Marchant my mistress.' He recollected vividly those soft supple lips beneath his, the gentle swell of her hips, and the sound of her wicked chuckle of laughter when he plucked her from beneath Amanda White's nose. 'However, she's an innocent and,' he added drolly, 'I haven't stooped quite so low as to start deflowering virgins.'

'You could always make an exception in her case.'

Silence followed the scandalous suggestion.

Cadmount waited to see if things were bad enough for Ravensmede to take the bait.

'Perhaps…' Ravensmede's eyes flicked shut. A vision of Kathryn Marchant's pale face arose. His mind meandered to imaginings of just how soft and white her skin would be beneath that hideous grey dress. Temptation loomed large. He quelled it with impatience. 'But then again, maybe not. She's made her feelings quite clear: a no-show at any of her cousin's outings this week. I've never forced a woman, and I don't intend to start now.'

'Glad to hear it, old man. Had you made an arrangement with her?'

Ravensmede thought of his promise to dance with Miss Marchant, and of her conspicuous absence from her cousin's side. 'Of sorts.'

Cadmount looked impressed. 'By Jove, this must be a first. A lady that turns you down. She won't have you. Hah!

Well, it's about bloody time!' A snort of merriment resounded throughout the library. His eyes closed, but not before they had alighted on Lord Ravensmede's wry smile.

The clock ticked upon the mantel. Logs crackled within the grate.

A flicker of Cadmount's heavy-lidded eyes. 'Are you for Lady Campbell's gathering tonight?'

'I think not. I've other fish to fry.'

This time Cadmount's eyes remained shut and within a few minutes the soft sound of a snore was upon his lips. Ravensmede rose without a noise and left the library.

A sleepy whisper murmured behind him, 'Chit might as well as thrown down the gauntlet. Twenty guineas he'll have her in his bed before the month is out, whatever the right or wrong of it.'

But had Archibald Cadmount known Miss Kathryn Marchant, he would have wagered very differently.

Chapter Three

The street was thronging with bodies as Kathryn wove a path through the crowds. Although the afternoon was well advanced, the street vendors were still plying their trade, which was fortuitous, as it was on an errand of procurement that she was employed. Despite the dusty heat and the overpowering smells arising from the pigs and piles of rotting rubbish nearby, she was glad to be free of the house in Green Street, no matter how short the duration. The week had passed slowly, with Aunt Anna and Lottie taking delight in meting out Kathryn's punishment. No doubt it somehow acted to salve the snub that Lottie felt Ravensmede had dealt her at the ball. Kathryn had endured without complaint, and indeed had striven to appear positively cheerful. There was nothing like it for irritating Lottie, or Aunt Anna for that matter. Little did they know how she enjoyed her brief excursions from the house. It was only twenty minutes since Lottie, on overhearing that there were no potatoes left, had demanded a dish of potato pudding for dinner. Upon Lottie's insistence, Kathryn had been dispatched to fetch some more. It was supposed to be a degrading experience, and one that would teach her a lesson.

* * *

A while later, and overhead the dazzling sun still shone down from a cloudless blue sky. A soft humming sounded from Kathryn's lips as the notes of the music danced through her head. Her feet neatly avoided a pile of fresh horse manure and, as the tempo increased, she skipped over the stream of bloodied water running down from a nearby butcher's shop. *The noisy street had vanished. A cooling breeze fanned her face as she breathed in the fresh country air. She was beautifully composed as the gentleman swept her into his arms and they began to glide with effortless grace across the neat lawns of the country mansion. One two three, one two three, she counted the beats as her delicately embroidered slippers scarcely touched the ground. Lord Ravensmede was smiling, his green eyes twinkling in the sunlight... Ravensmede!* Kathryn banished the thought and the noisy bustle of London reappeared. She adjusted the sack of potatoes balanced on her hip and continued her steady pace.

Ahead she could see the golden glint of the railings surrounding St James's Park. The green grass and the cool sparkle of the canal beckoned enticingly. It wouldn't take long, just to shelter beneath the cool dapple shade of the trees, to feel some little sense of space. Without a moment's hesitation her dusty feet padded up the street and into the park. Carriages containing fine ladies rolled by. Smartly dressed gentlemen astride their horses trotted past. The grass was fresh and springy beneath Kathryn's shoes. Ahead the air rippled with a heat haze.

She had just paused to watch two swans upon the water when a small family group passed close by. A familiar voice caught her attention. Glancing round, she saw, with some consternation, Miss Dawson walking arm in arm with her younger sister. Kathryn became suddenly all too aware of her situation. There could be no hiding the large and conspicuous sack of potatoes, and Miss Dawson was sure to mention any such meeting to Lottie. And then Lottie would know exactly what Kathryn had been up to during her errand. Quite deliberately Kathryn averted her face and walked in the opposite direction. She needn't have worried. With half her hair escaping from her bonnet, a smear of dust on her chin, a soil-stained dress, and the presence of the exceedingly dirty sack on her hip, she appeared more like one of the inhabitants of St Giles's Rookery, and not anyone connected to the respectable household of Mr Henry Marchant.

A close shave. Without further ado she disappeared behind the breadth of a large oak tree. It was only here that she laid down her burden. Hidden quite well as she was from view, she not only sat herself comfortably on the grass and leaned her back against the gnarled bark, but also dispensed with her bonnet and set about repairing the worst of her hair.

Lord Ravensmede reined his horse to a standstill, unable to quite believe his eyes. Surely that could not have been Miss Marchant he had just witnessed vanishing behind that oak? The slight figure certainly bore a striking resemblance to her graceful form, even bowed as it was with some large and weighty object. Perdition, he was becoming obsessed with the chit. First, she had been in his thoughts for the past week. Now, he was imagining that he saw her at every turn. It did not sit well with his lordship. His hand moved to twitch Rollo's rein, then stilled. What if it really was Miss Marchant? He had a thing or two to say to that young lady. No matter how much Ravensmede might deny it, he felt aggrieved by her snub, especially in view of the effort he had made to silence Amanda White. His leg slid over the saddle and he jumped down to the ground.

Having securely tethered the gelding to a nearby tree, Ravensmede proceeded on foot with some caution. Thus, he walked directly to the opposite side of the massive oak without the slightest noise. He heard the hushed melody from her lips before he saw her: 'Ach! Du lieber Augustine.' It had been playing when he danced with her at Lady Finlay's ball. The memory tugged a smile at his mouth. He moved leisurely around the trunk.

She was sitting on the grass, her legs drawn up beneath her, intent on scraping her mass of red-brown hair up into a chignon. The hairpins were held at the ready between her lips. And all the while her soft humming filled the air. At her side lay a lumpy and rather grubby sack. Ravensmede stared, intrigued with the sight. What an earth was the girl up to?

He stepped forward. 'Miss Marchant, a pleasure to make your acquaintance once again.'

Kathryn jumped, dropped the hank of hair she was attempting to secure, and almost inhaled one of the hairpins. The remainder of the pins scattered on the ground as she exclaimed with undisguised horror, 'Lord Ravensmede!'

Ravensmede watched while she scrambled unceremoniously to her feet, brushing any remnants of grass from her skirt. In one glance he took in the worn shoes caked in dust, the soiled dress, and the fatigue in her eyes. The bridge of her nose and cheeks were smattered with freckles that had not been there a week ago, and dirt streaked her chin. He held out his hand to take hers. Kathryn stared at it as if it held a dagger. 'Miss Marchant,' he said with the utmost politeness, and with slow deliberation touched her bare fingers to his lips. Not only was she gloveless, but her hands were reddened and rough, almost as if she had been scrubbing floors or laundering. A frown flitted across his brow at the thought.

Kathryn saw the look and, snatching her fingers away, clasped her hands behind her back. 'What are you doing here?' she blurted, then, remembering her manners, 'I mean...I didn't expect to meet you here.'

'Apparently not.' Ravensmede's gaze dropped to the sack and wandered back to her face. Crimson washed her cheeks and he thought he saw a flash of anger in her eyes before it was masked.

She held his gaze boldly. 'Please don't allow me to interrupt your walk, my lord.' Her cheeks burned hotter.

Ravensmede smiled lazily. He was not to be dismissed so easily. 'I assure you it's no interruption. Perhaps I could join you.'

The girl seemed speechless for a moment at the audacity of his suggestion. He was fully aware that it was rather inappropriate. 'I'm afraid that's not possible, my lord.' As he knew it would not be. Her voice was firm, her body poised for flight. 'Indeed, I must be getting back to Green Street. I've been away too long as it is.' Her eyes scanned for the pins, and, having located them in the soil by an exposed tree root, she bent to retrieve them.

Ravensmede saw her purpose and, with surprising agility for a gentleman wearing such tight-fitting buckskins, stooped to reach them first. Their fingers brushed; an intense awareness tingled in the air between them. He stared into the widening clear grey eyes. Realised that he wanted her, even dressed as she was in the guise of a servant. A determined interest stirred. Jaded boredom faded. His gaze dropped to her lips.

Kathryn withdrew her hand as if she had been burned. 'I do b-beg your pardon,' she stuttered, and rose swiftly to her feet.

Ravensmede followed, his eyes still trained on her face. The pins lay forgotten in the dirt. He closed the distance between them and reached out for her.

A woman's laugh sounded from the other side of the oak. 'Come along, Mary, we mustn't be late.'

It was enough to burst the growing bubble of tension.

Lord Ravensmede recovered first, dropping his hand to his side, and did not move. He was so close he could see the dark sweep of her eyelashes and the glitter of perspiration on her cheekbones.

One step back and then she halted, an expression of confusion on her face. 'I should leave.'

Ravensmede was not fooled by the small gruff voice.

She stepped aside and bent to retrieve the sack.

'Wait.' His hand stilled her outstretched arm. Neither the material of her dress nor his fine leather gloves dampened the arc of excitement that sparked between them.

She looked pointedly at his fingers; only when he removed the offending articles did she raise her gaze to meet his. 'My lord?'

'May I be so bold as to enquire the nature of your burden?' His horsewhip flicked towards the sack.

Her eyes lowered only momentarily before her chin raised a notch, as if in challenge. 'Potatoes.'

'Potatoes!' That would explain the preponderance of sandy soil about her person. 'You've been sent to buy them?' His lordship asked the question with a nonchalant air, as if lugging a huge sack of the damn things was an everyday occurrence for a gently bred companion.

She nodded once, that fierce little gaze never faltering for a minute.

'I see,' murmured Ravensmede with a sudden clarity of

perception. The sinister hand of Mrs Marchant loomed large.

'And this is one of your usual chores?'

'No.' Her fingers plucked nervously at the material of her skirt.

Ravensmede waited in silence, a look of expectation upon his face.

'I'm assisting Mrs Moultrie in the kitchen this week.'

'And last week too?' he asked in a gentle tone. He suddenly understood why Kathryn had not accompanied her cousin and aunt on any of their recent outings.

More plucking at the material. 'Yes.'

'Surely Henry Marchant is not so strapped for cash that he cannot employ a kitchen maid?'

She said nothing, just looked at him.

'It seems that you are out of favour with your aunt of late.'

Her eyes held his for a moment longer before glancing away.

'Kathryn?'

She shivered.

The tips of his fingers brushed against hers. 'Why might that be?'

She shook her head in denial.

'Kathryn,' he said again, more gently this time. 'Will you not tell me the reason?'

A soft sigh sounded in the air. 'Please, Lord Ravensmede, I must—'

'You have not told her of our study in astronomy at Lady Finlay's ball?'

Her cheeks reddened. 'Of course not!' Indignation flashed in her eyes. 'I don't wish to sound rude, my lord, but the reason that I'm assisting in the kitchen is none of your consideration.'

Ravensmede looked at her with growing intensity. 'On the

contrary, Miss Marchant,' he said quietly, 'it is everything of my consideration.'

Miss Marchant ignored his remark and continued, 'Now, if you will please excuse me, my lord.'

'No,' he said with a wicked glint in his eye.

The poor girl paled.

'How long is this…punishment to endure?'

A guarded look closed over Miss Marchant's face. 'I didn't say anything about a punishment.'

His eyes held hers. 'How long?'

Her gaze flickered away. She made to step back.

Ravensmede touched his fingers to her chin, guiding her focus to his. 'Let me help you, Kathryn.'

For an instant, just one fleeting moment, he saw the softening of her expression, the hope that shone in her eyes. 'Help me?'

'If you were to be under my protection…'

A pause, followed by a dawning realisation. And then it was gone, replaced instead with hurt disbelief, and finally furious humiliation. 'Certainly not!'

He had never had such an offer so adamantly refused.

She jerked away, leaving his fingers suspended in mid-air. 'I don't need your *help,* Lord Ravensmede.' Her voice was cool, her words clipped. 'I bid you good day, my lord.' She bent to retrieve the sack of potatoes.

But Ravensmede was there first. He watched her cheeks blanch and her eyes widen.

'My offer stands, Miss Marchant. If you should change your mind, you need only send me a message. Perhaps in time you will view matters differently.'

Her nostrils flared with fury. Her small breasts rose and

fell with the quickening of her breathing. 'I will never accept such an offer!' Her hand tugged at the sack.

But Lord Ravensmede held firm. In one easy motion he tucked the sack neatly beneath his arm. 'My horse is tethered close by. We'd best fasten this to Rollo's saddle and make our way smartly to Green Street if these potatoes are on this evening's menu.' There was a teasing note in his voice, and the suggestion of a smile. Then off he sauntered towards the gelding, leaving Kathryn staring after him.

The sack was securely attached to the horse when he heard the rustle of her skirt behind him.

'Lord Ravensmede, surely you cannot seriously mean to accompany me home?' The glorious spread of hair had disappeared beneath a bonnet that matched the unfashionable brown coloration of her dress. The glare of sunlight exposed the fragility of her face, highlighting the smudges below her eyes.

A muscle twitched in Ravensmede's jaw. 'But of course, Miss Marchant. It would not be gentlemanly to do otherwise.' He'd be damned if he let her struggle beneath the weight of that load.

Panic rose in her voice. 'No, it won't do. You mustn't! Please pass me the potatoes at once.'

Ravensmede turned to face her, a twinkling in his clear green eyes. 'Have no fear, they're fixed firmly in place and shall not dislodge.'

'My lord,' she said in a stage whisper, 'I must insist that you return my potatoes and cease this…this…' she plucked the word from the air '…madness, at once!'

The corners of Ravensmede's mouth twisted upwards. 'I believe that I've already explained my position, Miss Marchant.' He tried not to laugh. 'The potatoes are quite safe.'

One dark eyebrow arched. 'Now, if you wish to avoid a scene I suggest that you take my arm and let us be on our way.'

Several murmurs alerted Miss Marchant to the interest growing around their conversation. At least two ladies were staring. She sighed and tentatively touched her fingers to his sleeve, only to find them firmly tucked within the crook of his arm.

With Miss Marchant secured on one side, and Rollo and the precious cargo on the other, Lord Ravensmede made his way towards Green Street.

Blast the confounded man! How dare he take such a liberty! She'd have rather balanced the potatoes on her hip to Stepney and back than endure this. What could he be thinking of? His offer of help? Help, indeed! Like a fool she had thought it an honest offer until the truth of his meaning had dawned. What kind of woman did he take her for? Well, he would soon learn that Kathryn Marchant had no need of his sort of help, not now, not ever!

She sneaked a look up at his face. His strong handsome features showed not the slightest hint of discomfort. In fact, if she hadn't known better, she could almost have sworn that he was actually enjoying himself. Such behaviour was only to be expected from a man with Ravensmede's reputation. Not that she knew exactly what it was that he was actually guilty of, only that there were many pursed lips and raised eyebrows at his arrival, and that he had a penchant for women, gaming and drink…in that order.

Her eyes dropped to the burgundy coat, the matching waistcoat and immaculately arranged neckcloth. And lower still to the buff-coloured pantaloons that hugged the muscles of his thighs in a quite indecent fashion. The pristine condition and expensive cut of his clothing only served to emphasise the tawdry state of her own. Realising that she was staring at his lordship's thighs brought her gaze rapidly up, only to meet with an amused pair of green eyes.

'Do I meet with your approval, Miss Marchant?' His voice was a slow delicious drawl.

'Most certainly not,' she snapped, feeling her cheeks begin to burn. Then, realising just how rude she sounded, added, 'I appreciate that your intention to relieve me of my burden is one of kindness. It is, however, quite unnecessary.'

That slightly mocking gaze found hers once more. 'On the contrary, Miss Marchant, I assure you that I'm never kind.' Emerald lights danced in his eyes, rendering them such an unusual colour that it took the immense application of Kathryn's will-power not to stare.

Not trusting herself not to deliver him a sharp retort, she bit her tongue. They strolled along in silence and all the while she took care to keep her face turned from him.

It was some minutes before he spoke again. 'It appears that I've unwittingly offended you, Miss Marchant. Or have you just a natural aversion to my company?'

Her head swung round with surprise at the directness of his question. It was a big mistake. Those alluring eyes were on her again. A tingling sensation crept across her skin. Her tongue tied itself into knots and she quickly glanced away. 'I…I'm…'

His voice lowered, so that the words would reach her ears alone. 'It did not seem so at Lady Finlay's ball.'

She stared at him aghast. 'You appear to be labouring under some false impression of my character, my lord.' Her hand tried to wriggle free of Ravensmede's arm.

He did not release her. 'Where precisely have I erred?'

As an elderly lady peered down at her from a passing carriage, Kathryn ceased her struggle.

Keeping her expression carefully bland as if they were discussing the weather, or other such matters, she whispered, 'How can you ask such a thing?' She glanced around and recognised that they were close to Green Street. 'Please hurry, my lord. I have kept Mrs Moultrie waiting some considerable time.'

If anything, Ravensmede's feet dragged.

'My lord, I'm very late.' Agitation raised her voice, and she tugged at his arm to propel him faster.

His lordship stopped stock-still. 'What are you so afraid of?'

'Nothing.'

A cynical brow raised. 'I'll speak to your uncle. The situation may change if he realises that your shoddy treatment has not gone unnoticed.'

Kathryn paled at the very thought. Heaven forbid that he should do such a thing! 'No!' She licked her suddenly dry lips. 'Thank you, but no. It would serve only to make matters worse.'

Ravensmede looked at her, then slowly resumed walking towards Green Street. Once they reached the Marchant residence he loosened Rollo's load and made to mount the steps up to the front door.

'Lord Ravensmede.' Kathryn gently pulled at his arm.

'I won't see you struggle beneath this weight.'

Her fingers tightened around the broad band of muscle. She looked up into his face and bit at her bottom lip. 'Very well. Then please come this way.' She made to walk around the side of the house.

The Viscount of Ravensmede showed no sign of moving. 'I find I have a preference for the front door. I've never used a servants' entrance in my life, and I don't intend to do so now.

Kathryn's heart missed a beat. The blood drained from her face. She composed a breath. 'Please, my lord.'

The green eyes held hers, and in his gaze was understanding and determination. 'It's better this way,' he said softly, and, tucking her hand into his arm, walked up the steps.

The bell rang. And in that moment of waiting, Kathryn was never more aware of the absurdity of her situation. The tall handsome aristocrat by her side, a sack of potatoes under one arm, her own hand tucked in the other, standing at the front door of the house in Green Street for all the world to see. Footsteps sounded from within. The trickle of fear surged and she felt suddenly that she might be sick. She tried to remove her hand from Lord Ravensmede's arm.

His lordship's hold tightened.

The door opened.

Kathryn swallowed hard.

'I'm here to call upon Mr Marchant,' said Lord Ravensmede and thrust the sack into the unsuspecting manservant's hands. The sack was followed by Ravensmede's card.

The manservant stared first at the potatoes, then at Lord Ravensmede, and finally at Kathryn. He blinked once or twice, seemingly unable to find words.

Ravensmede gestured Kathryn in ahead of him. 'After you, Miss Marchant.' Once within the hallway he raised Kathryn's hand to his lips. 'So fortuitous to have met you again,' he said gallantly, and finally released her.

'Lord Ravensmede,' she said, and gave a small curtsy. Even her breath was shaky.

'Ever your servant,' he said and bowed.

With a very straight back, and very precise steps, Kathryn walked away…while she still could.

Only then did the manservant remember himself enough to stop gaping and fetch the master of the house.

Lord Ravensmede was wiping his hands on a pristine white handkerchief when Henry Marchant entered the drawing room.

'Lord Ravensmede! What an unexpected pleasure.' Mr Marchant bustled forward, unable to believe just who had called upon him. His lordship might be considered one of the worst rake-hells in London, but, as the current Viscount of Ravensmede, heir to an exceptionally wealthy earldom, and in receipt of a considerable allowance, he was not a man that Henry Marchant felt any inclination to snub. Ravensmede made the Marchant monies look like a pile of pennies, and he was what Henry for all his hard work could never hope to become—an aristocrat. As the initial surprise waned Henry began to calculate just how advantageous Lord Ravensmede's visit might prove. Mr Marchant was, after all, in possession of a young and attractive daughter, and his lordship had ever been known to have an eye for a beautiful woman. The possibilities danced before him. 'Please take a seat. Would you care for a drink?'

'Brandy, if you have any.'

'Most certainly,' said Mr Marchant. He poured the brandy into two crystal glasses and passed one to Lord Ravensmede.

Ravensmede made himself comfortable in the chair and leisurely perused the surrounding room before turning his attention to Henry Marchant. 'Perhaps you may be able to assist me, Mr Marchant.'

Mr Marchant's chins wobbled in delight. 'Of course, my lord, in any way that I can.'

'It is the most peculiar of situations.'

'Indeed?' The older man leaned forward.

'I chanced upon your niece while I was out. She was carrying a sack of potatoes.'

There was the smallest silence before Mr Marchant spoke. '*Potatoes*, you say?'

'Most definitely potatoes,' said Ravensmede, and waited.

A subtle pink coloration crept into Henry Marchant's complexion. 'I don't understand. What on earth would Kathryn be doing with potatoes?'

'My question precisely, sir. Naturally no gentleman would allow a lady to carry such a burden.'

'No, no, of course not,' Mr Marchant added in bluff agreement.

'I therefore carried the potatoes in her stead.'

'You?' said Mr Marchant weakly.

'Me,' said the Viscount of Ravensmede, and smiled grimly.

'Good God!' came the whispered reply.

'Financial straits are always embarrassing, sir, but it is a gentleman's duty to spare his womenfolk.'

The colour of Mr Marchant's cheeks deepened to puce. He stuttered so much as to almost choke on the words. 'M-m-my finances are all in order. You are mistaken, sir, in your thoughts. I employ a house full of servants.'

'Indeed?' Ravensmede paused. 'Then why was Miss Marchant sent to do a servant's job?'

'I've no idea, but rest assured, my lord, I shall discover what this business is about.'

'I'm glad to hear it.'

'Kathryn is very grateful for my family's charity and tries to make herself useful in return. Perhaps that was her intention in this instance—well meant, but poorly judged. There is, after all, no fathoming the workings of the female mind!' Mr Marchant laughed. It sounded false and uneasy in the room.

Ravensmede raised a single eyebrow.

Mr Marchant hurriedly cleared his throat. 'As I was saying, I mean to get to the bottom of the matter. Kathryn came to us when my brother tragically died some number of years ago. She has been welcomed into the bosom of my family. I've never been one to flout my duty, my lord, and I trust that no one would suggest otherwise.'

'Heaven forbid, sir.' Ravensmede took a swig of brandy and stood to leave. 'You stock a fine brandy, Mr Marchant.'

Soothed by Lord Ravensmede's response, Mr Marchant sought to redeem something of the situation. The thought of a match between the Viscount and Lottie was still rather tantalising. 'If you would like to call again, my lord, under more auspicious circumstances, I have some rather splendid cigars.'

'How very kind,' said Ravensmede with an irony that was lost on Henry Marchant, and departed.

Lord Cadmount attacked the game pie with obvious exuberance. 'Nothing like an afternoon practising the pugilistic arts to fire up a man's appetite. Didn't mean to land you such a planter.'

'You got lucky. It was a very respectable left hook, and my mind was elsewhere.' Three hours' boxing had not taken the edge off Ravensmede's disgruntlement. It was a sentiment that had failed to shift since his earlier encounter with Miss Kathryn Marchant.

'So I noticed.' Cadmount forked a great mound of meat into his mouth. There was nothing but the sound of cutlery scraping against plates and noisy mastication coming from Cadmount. He licked a smear of gravy from his lip. 'Ain't been happy for a while. Can see it in your face. Been winning at the card tables; cellar is stocked with the best of bottles; plenty of luck with the ladies too. But something ain't right. Known you too long for you to pull the wool over my eyes.' Cadmount resumed his attack on the enormous piece of pie before him. 'Pressure from the old man getting too much? Is he still trying to force that heiress upon you—what's her name—Pitten?'

'Francesca Paton.' Had it been anyone else sitting across the table, Ravensmede would have quelled them with an arrogant stare. Archie Cadmount was different. He was one of the few people that Ravensmede trusted. The two men were as dissimilar in temperament as they were in looks. But since their youthful days at Eton they had remained true friends. And because it was Cadmount, Ravensmede spoke the truth. 'And, no, things are no worse than usual. My father can say what he will, but I'll be damned if I'll let him dictate my life.'

'Still sore about him forbidding your commission?'

'While you were risking your life in the Peninsula to put a halt to Boney's forces, I was here doing what I've been doing for the last twelve years, what I'm still doing. Men are dying for England and I'm here drinking, gambling, whoring... What's the bloody point?'

'Ain't your fault that you're heir to the earldom. Ain't your father's fault either. Maybury just wants to ensure things are safe for the future. Only son and all that. Can't have you going off and getting yourself killed. Can't blame the old man for that.'

'Maybe not,' said Ravensmede. 'But tell me this, Caddie—if you hadn't been obliged to come home because of your brother, would you choose to still be out there fighting, or sitting here in London leading a comfortable existence?'

'Point taken. But if you ain't happy with things as they are, perhaps it's time for a change. Perhaps Maybury is right, perhaps it *is* time for a wife and a nursery.'

'Hell's teeth, Caddie, not you too! I'll marry when I'm good and ready and not before.'

'Stubborn to the bone,' murmured his friend. 'Always were, always will be. Stubborn and wilful.'

Ravensmede gave him a crooked smile. 'You know me so well.'

A little pie remained on Cadmount's plate. He set about remedying that with one final flourish of his fork and pondered on his friend's unhappiness. Clearly a change of subject was required. Something to cheer Ravensmede. Something with which the Viscount was enamoured. He paused to savour the richly flavoured gravy. 'By God, but that was good. If you ever tire of Lamont's cooking, send him to me.' The claret was drained in one gulp and he eyed Ravensmede. Inspiration came to him. 'Made any progress with the Marchant chit?'

Ravensmede sipped his wine with a nonchalance that he did not feel. 'I happened to chance upon Miss Marchant while I was out this afternoon. She's not treated well within the Marchant household, but refuses to consider possible ways out.' He looked away to conceal the depth of his emotion. 'Blasted girl's pride will be her downfall.'

A snort of laughter sounded in the dining room. 'Turned you down again, did she?'

The blue-shadowed jaw-line tightened. 'Something like that.'

Cadmount snorted again. 'Good for her.'

Ravensmede did not want to reveal the full extent of his encounter with Kathryn Marchant. He knew full well what he had offered the girl. Could still taste the sourness that the ignoble offer left upon his tongue. And yet he wanted her, even here, even now, knowing all that he did. Any mention of what she had been doing or her tired appearance would be an act of betrayal. Instinctively he knew that Kathryn would not want others to know of her circumstance. Living as she did could not be pleasant. He thought of her lugging the sack of potatoes across St James's Park, of her seeking refuge behind the old oak tree, ashamed to be seen. Despite her dusty worn clothes and her red chapped hands she had been happy, humming that tune, with a faraway look in her eyes. Happy, at least until he had arrived. He set his fork down upon his plate.

Cadmount eyed him with interest.

Ravensmede's finger tapped thoughtfully against the stem of the glass. 'There must be something I can do, Archie. I'll be damned if I'll just leave her to that family's devices.'

Lord Cadmount knew things must be serious. Ravensmede never, but never, used his given name. It looked as if Kathryn Marchant might be just the tonic that Ravensmede needed. 'She turned you down, old man, and if she ain't under your protection then there's nothing you can do. Unmarried lady and all that. And she *is* a lady,' he said. 'Wouldn't look too good for li'l Miss Marchant if you start charging in there, pistols blazing. Not to put too fine a point on it, Ravensmede, any association with you is likely to leave a lady's reputation a little the worse for wear. No offence intended.'

Ravensmede thought grimly of his meeting with Mr Marchant. Hardly charging in with pistols blazing, rather a case of letting the man know that his treatment of the girl hadn't gone unnoticed.

'Best thing you could do is to stay away.' A large dollop of puréed potato was scooped into Cadmount's mouth. It did not prevent his continued conversation. 'Unless, of course, you're prepared to contemplate a more respectable alternative.' The adroit blue gaze slid to Ravensmede.

Lord Ravensmede picked at the fillet of sole, before pushing his plate away.

'Stands to reason,' Cadmount released a loud and resonant burp, 'why did you turn down the splendid Mrs White if your interest in Miss Marchant isn't in earnest? I mean, the Winsome Widow's practically offering herself on a platter. Don't think that I'd send *her* packing. And from where I was standing, it looked like you were about to devour the Marchant chit on the dance floor. If it ain't serious, why else did you waltz with her?'

Ravensmede's eyes glowered in the candlelight. 'Why indeed?'

Cadmount affected not to notice. 'I know you'll go your own way, you always do. But for what my humble opinion is worth, if you've any regard for the girl you'll stop sniffing round her skirts and leave well alone. There's no family to hush a scandal, and no man waiting in the wings to salvage her reputation. Don't ruin her life, Nick…unless you mean to offer her marriage.'

One haughty eyebrow cocked. 'Still on that old theme? I'm beginning to think that you're in league with m'father.' He savoured the taste of the claret against his palate. 'I've no intention of marrying Miss Kathryn Marchant or anyone else.'

'Good thing you'll be leaving her alone then. Besides…' he looked pointedly at Ravensmede '…I don't suppose the chit is quite what Maybury has in mind for your bride.'

'Don't push it, Caddie,' Ravensmede said quietly.

Cadmount laughed, and shrugged off his serious garb. 'Then it's to Brooks's this evening and the faro tables.' He slapped the table and belched again, grinning all the while. 'It's not as though Henry Marchant will starve or beat the girl.' And with that parting comment Lord Cadmount went to relieve himself.

Ravensmede remained alone at the dining table. Starvation. Beatings. For some reason the thoughts weighed uneasy on his mind. He rubbed at his chin and tried to banish the image of a small heart-shaped face. His dark brows puckered. Damn Kathryn Marchant's pride, and damn Archibald Cadmount's warnings. He could no sooner leave the girl to her fate than he could pluck out his own eyes. Whether she wanted it or not, Miss Marchant was about to become the recipient of his help…whatever guise that it might come in.

Chapter Four

It was ten o'clock and Kathryn was busy helping Nancy wash the linen. The coarse soap stung at their hands as they scrubbed within the cold water, but neither woman complained. They chatted about Nancy's young man and her sister's new baby boy.

"E's as bright as a button, miss, truly 'e is. All downy black 'air and big blue eyes, and such a big smile for a little fella.' The front door bell sounded. 'Wonder who that could be?'

Kathryn tucked a stray curl back up into her cap with a soapy finger. 'It's rather early for visitors. Unless, of course, there was some scandalous affair last night at Lady Campbell's after Aunt Anna and Lottie left. Just think what they might have missed!'

The scullery filled with their chuckles.

'You ain't 'alf a laugh, miss.'

A delicious aroma of eggs and chops and toast wafted through from the kitchen. Kathryn's stomach growled so loudly that Nancy pulled a face.

'Lawk! Sounds like someone ain't had no breakfast!'

Kathryn just shrugged and carried on with the scrubbing. Her stomach protested at being ignored.

Nancy peered suspiciously at the other girl's pale face. "Ave you ate somethin' this mornin', miss?'

'There was a to-do over the potatoes yesterday that displeased my aunt. Breakfast is forbidden for the next week.'

Nancy knew exactly what the 'to-do' was about. Indeed, the servants had talked of little else since that fancy lord had brought Kathryn and the potatoes home. But Nancy was wise enough to make no mention of it.

'Don't worry. I'm not really hungry. It's just that smell causing all the rumbling down there.' Kathryn's eyes dropped down to indicate her stomach.

'But you didn't 'ave no dinner last night neither. Let me get you somethin'.'

Kathryn's soapy hand reached out towards the maidservant's, and squeezed it affectionately. 'Thank you, but no. I don't want you getting into trouble on my behalf, and it would be just like Mrs Moultrie to spot what you were about. She seems to inform my aunt of every detail. No, Nancy, kind as your offer is, I shall last very well until lunch.'

'She's a bloody bitch, that one,' came the sharp reply. 'Sorry, miss. I know I shouldn't be swearin' in front of you, but I couldn't help myself. She's a mean-hearted woman.'

Kathryn smiled at what a shock it would cause if she were to ask Nancy to which woman precisely the maid was referring. Swallowing down her bad grace, which she feared was getting out of hand, she changed the subject. 'When will you visit your sister again?'

The maid was just about to reply when the clatter of footsteps sounded from the kitchen. Mrs Moultrie's scowling jowls appeared in the doorway.

'The master and mistress are up early this morning so you best get upstairs and strip the beds. It's a fine day, so don't be dallying.' A jaundiced eye stared smugly at Kathryn. 'No outdoor chores today, miss. Mrs Marchant says as there's plenty to keep you busy in here.'

'I'm sure that my aunt is quite correct.'

Mrs Moultrie sniffed and waddled back to her kitchen.

Upstairs the visitor was being shown into the dining room by a somewhat awed footman.

Even the master of the house had lost his normal staid countenance and was eyeing the doorway of the dining room in a rather apprehensive manner. The *Morning Post* lay discarded upon the table.

Anna Marchant recovered from the shock first and greeted their guest with a feigned smile and a nod of her golden head. 'Lord Ravensmede, what a pleasant surprise and so early in the morning. Please do join us for breakfast.'

'Indeed,' agreed her husband a tad too heartily. 'Make yourself comfortable, my lord.'

Ravensmede passed his beaver and gloves to the footman and sat himself down at the table. The dark ruffle of his hair and colour in his cheeks bespoke a man who had been up since the crack of dawn. He wore an aura of strength and vitality, quite unlike his host and hostess, who had not long crawled from their beds and were still feeling not quite up to scratch.

'Sorry to trouble you at such an unearthly hour,' he drawled with absolutely no hint of sincerity. An invisible speck of dust on the sleeve of his impeccable dark green coat required his attention, leaving Mr and Mrs Marchant perched on the edge of their seats.

'Will you take something to eat, my lord?' Mr Marchant's chins stretched into a smile.

Ravensmede's waved his hand in a dismissive gesture. 'No, thank you, sir. I've already broken my fast.' He watched the shadow of anxiety cloud Henry Marchant's face.

Mr Marchant cleared his throat. 'Regarding the matter you brought to my attention yesterday, my lord, it was a silly misunderstanding and shall not happen again.' His gaze flickered to Mrs Marchant, then back to the Viscount.

His wife looked on coldly, dislike bristling beneath her pleasant veneer.

'Good,' said Ravensmede, 'But I'm here for quite a different purpose, sir. I wondered if I might call upon Miss Marchant this afternoon to accompany me for a drive in Hyde Park.'

'Yes, indeed you may, sir.' The words were out before Ravensmede had even finished his sentence. 'Lottie's the apple of my eye. A darling girl. And a diamond of the first water, even if I do say so myself.'

His lordship did not immediately correct the man's mistake. He thought of Lottie Marchant and her bland prettiness, so like a hundred other young women. He checked the twitch at his lips.

'My daughter will be more than happy to accompany you, won't she, my dear?'

Anna Marchant inclined her head in agreement.

Lord Ravensmede's haughty brow raised just a little. 'But, sir, you misunderstand me. I was speaking of Miss Kathryn Marchant.' He paused to watch the shot go home.

Henry Marchant's countenance coloured and his wife was staring as if the very devil had just appeared.

'My niece?' The words ground slowly from Mr Marchant's mouth.

'I take it you have no problem with my request.'

Unless he had gauged the Marchants wrongly, then they would do nothing other than comply.

Mr Marchant nodded once. 'Fine by me, sir.'

Anna Marchant's top lip curled with disdain before she forced it once more to the semblance of a smile. 'Unfortunately, my niece is indisposed with a chill. It will take some days before she's fully recovered, and I doubt that the outdoor air would be advisable for her state of health.'

Ravensmede's expression did not alter from unassailable boredom. It was the one he used when engaged in card play and it had never failed him yet. 'Indeed, madam, I send my condolences. In that case, I won't waste any more of your time.' He executed the tiniest of bows and made to leave.

Mr Marchant made haste to repair any damage. 'I'm sure she will be recovered by next week, if you would care to call then.'

If looks could kill, Henry Marchant would have been a bloodied corpse upon the rug, a victim of his wife's malice.

'Perhaps,' said his lordship ambiguously and strolled out into the hallway just in time to see Kathryn Marchant running down the stairs with a basket full of crumpled sheets between her hands.

'Miss Marchant,' said Lord Ravensmede, in a tone of absolute correctness. 'I trust you're feeling well enough to be out of bed?'

Kathryn stared at the tall athletic figure that had just emerged from the dining room. 'Lord Ravensmede?' Was she dreaming? Her fingers loosed their grip on the wicker strands, leaving Anna Marchant's dirty sheets to tumble out in full display down the staircase before her.

The lady screeched in the background. 'Kathryn, what are you doing up there? No doubt she has developed a fever to make her behave in such an obscure manner. I cannot begin to think what on earth she is doing with that linen. Leave it at once and return to your room.' As Nancy appeared over Kathryn's shoulder she added, 'You, girl, why are you using the main stairs? Get this mess sorted out at once! I'll speak to you later.'

Aunt Anna's harsh words pulled Kathryn's attention from the Viscount. 'Aunt, please do not be cross with Nancy. I insisted that we come this way. These baskets are so wide it makes the servants' stairwell difficult to squeeze down. I did not think…' The words trailed off and she glanced apologetically in the direction of Lord Ravensmede.

'You never do,' came her aunt's withering reply.

Ravensmede looked directly from the sheets to Mr Marchant.

A flush appeared on the older man's cheeks.

Ravensmede allowed a small awkward silence before turning his attention back to Kathryn. 'You appear to have recovered from your chill, Miss Marchant,' he said in a voice that was silky smooth.

Kathryn's brow wrinkled in bewilderment. 'I'm quite well, thank you, my lord. Whatever made you think that I was not?'

Ravensmede cocked an eyebrow in Mrs Marchant's direction.

'Kathryn, you silly girl, you don't know what you're saying! It must be the fever.' Anna attempted to shoo her niece back up the stairs. 'And have a care not to waken Lottie.'

'Shall I send my own physician to attend Miss Marchant?' The deep voice arrested the ladies' progress. He stepped forward, extending his hand to touch his fingers against Kathryn's forehead. 'How strange, no heat at all. A miraculous recovery wouldn't you say, Mrs Marchant?'

Anna Marchant's mouth compressed with fury.

Her husband tugged helplessly at his neckcloth. 'Just as you say, sir, a speedy and fortuitous recovery.'

Ravensmede stepped back, fixed his beaver hat on his head and carefully donned his gloves. 'Then I shall call at four.' The piercing gaze rested on Mr Marchant, 'Good morning, sir', flitted to his wife, 'madam', and finally alighted on Kathryn, 'Miss Marchant.'

The three stood slack-jawed and silent as Lord Ravensmede sauntered from the house in Green Street.

Kathryn had changed into her best walking dress: a slightly faded blue muslin purchased five years ago. It was dated in appearance, but clean, and she knew that the colour suited her well. Her hair was caught back in a knot at the nape of her neck and was well hidden beneath the mud-brown bonnet, which had been a gift from Aunt Anna when her own had fallen apart. A fichu, a rather tight spencer, sturdy walking shoes, darned gloves, and a small home-made reticule, all in a matching shade of greyish brown, completed the ensemble. Standing in front of the mirror, Kathryn surveyed her reflection with a critical eye. Her face was so pale that even her lips had lost their rosy hue. She looked exactly like she felt: tired and washed out. And she had yet to face an afternoon in Lord Ravensmede's company. The prospect was really rather daunting. Why would a man like him be interested in a woman like her? The answer was plainly evident. He had made his intent very clear. Raising her chin a notch, she determined to set his lordship firmly in his place with regard to that. A noise sounded behind her.

'Ah, Kathryn, getting ready for Lord Ravensmede?' Lottie swept an appraising gaze over her cousin. 'You look…like someone far past her last prayers.'

Kathryn said nothing, just watched while Lottie flounced into the bedchamber and sat herself down upon the single battered chair.

'There's only one reason that Ravensmede would be taking the likes of you for a drive, and we all know what that is.' One pretty slippered foot swung repetitively. 'Let's just say that it's certainly not marriage he has on his mind.' A snigger escaped her. 'What have you been up to with his lordship, Kathryn?' Lottie leaned forward, a smug gloating look upon her face.

'Stop it, Lottie. I didn't ask Lord Ravensmede to take me driving. Indeed, I would much prefer not to spend any time in his company. I was as surprised as you to hear that he had made such an offer.'

'And is that the only offer he has made you?'

On seeing the barb hit home and two patches of colour flow into her cousin's cheeks, Lottie continued, 'That night at Lady Finlay's, when he waltzed with you, where were you when you stormed off out of the ball room? In the retiring room? I don't think so. More like reaching an agreement with the Viscount of Ravensmede!'

Kathryn turned, eyes flashing, fists clenched to control her fury. 'Lottie, how can you make such wicked allegations? You know very well that it's nonsense.'

Lottie did not reply, just smiled knowingly.

'Please excuse me, Cousin.' Kathryn could not bear to stay in the room a minute longer.

A snide laugh followed her. 'You may run, Kathryn, but you won't get very far. Mama has a little surprise planned for you.'

She sat alone and tense in the drawing room awaiting the sound of the bell. If Lottie thought such a thing, then the rest of the world was likely to view it in much the same vein. She would have to deter Lord Ravensmede in no uncertain terms. Her gaze fixed on the blackened fireplace. She forced herself to relax, to breathe deeply. In, and out. Tension ebbed. *The fireplace disappeared. Her mother's face smiled kindly. A soft hand reached out to softly stroke her hair. The wind whipped at her face, sea air inhaled deep into her lungs. Mama was laughing and pointing to the shimmering water and the rolling white waves. Lottie's cruel words receded into oblivion. Meaningless. Gentle fingers stroked her cheek. 'Kathryn,' Mama whispered. Kathryn smiled beneath the caress. 'Kathryn.' The voice was deeper, slightly more insistent, not like Mama's at all. She touched her hand to Mama's.* Her eyelids fluttered open, and she looked up into the clear green eyes of Lord Ravensmede. A gasp sounded, her own, and she was up and out of the chair, breathless with confusion. 'Lord Ravensmede, you startled me!'

'My apologies, Miss Marchant. I did not mean to.' He was regarding her with such scrutiny as to set Kathryn's cheeks aflame.

'Good afternoon, Lord Ravensmede.' Mrs Marchant breezed into the room. 'We seem to have found Kathryn at last. I shall tell Lottie she can call off the search.' The bright blue eyes narrowed as they flicked over Kathryn's reddened face.

Ravensmede extended his arm in Kathryn's direction. 'I shall return your niece safely before six. Try not to concern yourself, ma'am. I shall see to it personally that there's no deterioration in her health.'

'Indeed, Lord Ravensmede, I don't doubt it. But I will, of course, be present myself to witness your attentions. Lottie and I will accompany Kathryn this afternoon.' Mrs Marchant almost cackled at the deliverance of her cunning plan. 'It would be unseemly to allow my niece out without a chaperon.' She did not add the words 'and in your company'. She did not need to.

Lord Ravensmede delivered the woman a glare of such glacial proportions that she actually stumbled back. 'Such a thought is anathema to my sensibilities. Which is why I've brought my grandmother in just such a capacity. She preferred to wait in the barouche while I came in to collect Miss Marchant.' The inferred insult was obvious. 'Perhaps you would care to step outside to meet her?'

Anna Marchant moved swiftly to the window and looked out at Lord Ravensmede's barouche complete with an elderly lady dressed entirely in gaudy purple.

Kathryn looked from her aunt to Ravensmede and back again.

'But of course, Lord Ravensmede,' Mrs Marchant uttered between gritted teeth. 'How very thoughtful of you.' Every step those daintily clad feet took on their way out to the barouche warned of a mounting violence. 'I shall await Kathryn's return with impatience.' She slid a meaningful look at her niece.

Kathryn did not miss the promise held so clearly in those cold blue eyes.

The day was warm, but that had not prevented the frail little lady being almost hidden beneath the thickest pile of blankets.

'Grandmama, may I introduce Mrs Marchant, Miss Kathryn Marchant, and…' he indicated the sullen-faced young woman who refused to leave the doorway '…Miss Charlotte Marchant.'

Anna Marchant dropped a graceful curtsy, hid the malice from her face and smiled charmingly. 'Such a pleasure to meet you, Lady Maybury.'

The old lady subjected each of the offered females to a

piercing stare from eyes that were a faded version of Ravensmede's own, and let out a cackle. 'The little chit looks nothing like the other two. I fancy Mr Marchant may have been cuckolded there.' Then, as if she hadn't just dropped a monumental insult, she dabbed a lilac lace handkerchief to her nose and declared in an imperious tone, 'Nicholas, how much longer do you intend to keep me waiting? Even the greys are getting bored.'

For the first time since meeting her Ravensmede bestowed a smile upon Mrs Marchant, then he took his leave of her, lifting Kathryn neatly into the barouche and bowling off down the road at what could only be described as a reckless pace.

The entirety of London's *ton* had decided to partake of the afternoon air within the green surround of Hyde Park, or so it seemed to Kathryn when they entered. So many pairs of curious eyes turned upon her, so many hushed whispers and veiled finger pointings. She hid her discomfort well and smiled at Ravensmede's eagle-eyed grandmother. The old lady fussed around with her blankets, oblivious to the heat of the day, raised a withered hand in the direction of a distant carriage and then turned her attentions to Kathryn.

'Well, let me have a good look at you, gel.' A quizzing glass appeared from beneath the blankets. One greatly enlarged faded eye gave a close scrutiny, missing nothing of the worn attire or the way Miss Kathryn Marchant kept her head averted from her grandson's person. 'Not got the fair locks or the silly prettiness of the other two,' came the succinct observation.

Kathryn heard the sharpness in Lady Maybury's voice. Those unused to her ladyship's company had been known to quail under her blunt comments, but Kathryn sensed no malice beneath the harsh veneer. 'No, my lady. Mrs Marchant is my aunt, and Charlotte, my cousin. I've lived with them since my father died.'

'And your father was…Robert Marchant?'

Kathryn's eyes opened wide. Forgetting her reserve, she twisted round to face Lady Maybury. 'You knew him?'

'No. When you've been alive for as long as I have, there's not much you don't eventually get to hear of. Refresh my memory.'

'Grandmama!' said Ravensmede, remembering Archie Cadmount's brief account of Kathryn's history, 'Miss Marchant may not wish to speak of her family.'

'Tush and nonsense, Nick!' exclaimed the old lady heatedly. She then bestowed a look of obvious affection upon her favourite grandson.

For the first time since leaving Green Street Kathryn looked directly at his lordship. 'Really, I don't mind, my lord.'

Ravensmede kept his eyes upon her. And in his breast rose that same inexplicable feeling that had enveloped him on seeing Kathryn Marchant seated all alone in the drawing room with her mind a thousand miles away. Who was it that she saw behind those closed eyes? Someone who had the power to make her smile, someone she was happy to have caress her cheek. A suitor from the past, or some secret lover? The thought did not please him. That velvet-smooth skin washed with the merest hint of colour as she turned once more to his grandmother.

'As you said, my father was Robert Marchant, the elder brother of Uncle Henry. My mother was Elizabeth Thornley, from Overton. She died of consumption almost eight years ago. Soon after, my sister died too, of the same illness. My father…' Her voice wavered. 'My father suffered an accident.' She couldn't bring herself to tell them the exact nature of the 'accident', or how she had spent the time since his death trying to forget the horrendous image that seemed branded on her memory. 'He's been dead for just over three years. Uncle Henry and Aunt Anna were kind enough to offer me a home.' Her fingers tightened against the seat.

'What of your mother's relatives? Have you no contact with them?' the Dowager Countess demanded, but there was a distinct mellowing in the sharpness of her tone.

Kathryn's fingers plucked at the muslin of her skirt, and her lashes swept low before she answered, 'They didn't approve of my parents' marriage. I've never met them.'

'I see.' Lady Maybury raised her quizzing glass once more. 'And why are you not yet married?'

Kathryn blushed. 'There was never time for that.' She did not speak of the pain of nursing her mother and sister, nor of the years of caring for her grief-stricken father. Neither did she mention the torment of her father's death. 'And now I'm my cousin's companion.'

A tutting sound escaped the crinkled lips. 'Stuff and nonsense! No time indeed!'

On seeing the deepening hue of Kathryn's cheeks, Ravensmede came to her rescue. 'You mustn't tease Miss Marchant so, Grandmama. It really is quite cruel of you.' Besides he didn't want his relative getting ideas about arranging a marriage for the girl with the first convenient man; not when he had other plans for Kathryn Marchant.

Of all his family Ravensmede was closest to his paternal grandmother. Even so, that did not mean he was blind to her tendency for bossy dominance and interfering in matters that did not concern her. Not that it was a family trait by any means, or so he told himself. He made a mental note to have a word with her at a more opportune moment.

The dowager snorted, but changed the subject all the same.

They stopped on several occasions to allow Lady Maybury to converse with other ladies, to all of whom she insisted on introducing Miss Marchant. The afternoon was progressing splendidly and even Kathryn had begun to relax and enjoy the bright sunshine and wonderful cooling breeze when the unfortunate incident occurred.

The tiny ragged figure appeared as if from thin air to materialise directly in front of Lord Ravensmede's barouche. Even with the wealth of his driving experience and his renowned skill with the ribbons, there was little that Ravensmede could do to stop the team in time. As it was, his expertise allowed him to pull the team hard to the right-hand side of the path and, in all probability, it was this reflex that prevented the collision and saved the child's life. As the horses ground to a halt, he glanced round to check that his passengers had not been dislodged by the abruptness of his stopping. Kathryn was tucking the blanket around his grandmother, who was complaining in a most querulous tone of voice. Her gaze met his as he heard the soft murmur of her voice reassure the old lady.

He moved quickly, reaching the child in a matter of seconds. With firm but gentle hands he examined the body lying so still upon the ground before him. She was a small girl, three or four years of age at the most. Her hair was dark and matted; her clothes dirty and ragged. There was no blood, and no lacerations of the skin. Neither were her limbs twisted. She looked unhurt, as if she were just sleeping. He heard the commotion as his grandmother struggled to climb down from the carriage. 'Stay where you are, Grandmama. The child does not appear badly injured, but I don't yet know the extent of the damage caused. You may find it distressing.'

Lady Maybury spluttered her indignation. 'Fiddlesticks! If you're bent on shaking me around this carriage as if I'm a bowl of dried peas, then at least have the decency to allow my curiosity!'

Ravensmede recognised the stubborn tone of her voice. Resistance would be futile, and more to the point, a waste of time. With a barely stifled sigh of frustration he ignored her comments and turned his attention once more to the child, only to find Miss Marchant crouched on the opposite side of the poor motionless body. And the concern clear in the gaze that met his caused a peculiar sensation within his chest.

Her darned gloves were unceremoniously cast aside and two little work-worn hands were engaged in feeling the length of the child's body to measure the extent of the hurts, just as he had done. Upon her face was a look of such focused intensity of which Ravensmede had never seen the like. He heard the movement of his grandmother behind him; felt her hand touch briefly to his arm.

'Is the child...?'

Kathryn glanced up for the briefest of moments. 'Thank the Lord, she's not dead. But I fear that she may have broken her leg.' She raised the little girl's skirts to expose her ankles and shins. 'See how swollen and red it is below her knee. Mercifully she's fainted and so cannot feel the pain.'

'It's fortunate indeed that she was thrown clear. She ran straight in front of me. There wasn't much I could do.' A frown wrinkled Ravensmede's brow. 'She should be seen by a doctor. Let's hope that the leg is not broken.'

A moan escaped the little girl's lips.

'Hush, child. You're safe now.' Kathryn rubbed the child's dirty, scrawny arms. 'You've had an accident and hurt your leg, but everything is going to be fine. Can you tell me your name?'

'Maggie,' the child whispered, scarcely loud enough to be heard.

'Well, Maggie, just you lie still until we can get your leg mended. Be a brave girl.'

Ravensmede watched in amazement while Kathryn gently stroked the child's filthy hair, her voice crooning softly to calm the little girl's panic. That a grubby, unknown street child could engender such a tender, caring response! Most young ladies of the *ton* would have run a mile rather than touch such an offensive specimen of the lower classes. But then, again, why should he expect Miss Kathryn Marchant to be like most young ladies, when she had so far proven herself quite dissimilar in every aspect? It seemed she was determined to provide him with further evidence of her rather unique qualities as she began to strip off first her spencer, then her fichu.

He felt the flicker of the familiar hunger that he'd come to associate with her. Without thinking, he licked his lips. Anticipation hardened the angles of his face. And then he remembered where he was, and that his grandmother was at his shoulder. 'Miss Marchant, what do you think you're…?' The question trailed off unfinished as he watched her wrap the garments around the child's body.

'No doubt it's the shock that has chased the warmth from her. We mustn't allow her to become chilled.' Kathryn appeared to be so completely focused upon the little girl that she betrayed not the slightest inhibition at her partially disrobed state and spoke as if tending an injured child was an everyday occurrence in her life.

Lord Ravensmede stared at what had been exposed by the missing fichu. He stared at the tender skin above the shabby dress's neckline. He stared as he had never stared at any woman before. And the expression on his face was not one of lust or desire; rather, shock more aptly described the sensation. Shock that was rapidly progressing to anger. For Kathryn Marchant's skin bore marks that should adorn no woman.

'Nicholas.' A firm hand touched to his shoulder. Elderly green eyes gazed down into his, and he saw in them the reflection of what he felt. Lady Maybury gave a barely perceptible nod of her head before subtly drawing her grandson's attention to the rapidly massing crowd.

An indefinable curse growled from the Viscount of Ravensmede before he hastily shrugged off his coat and swept it around Kathryn's shoulders.

Wide grey eyes met his with blatant surprise. 'My lord? There is no—'

Ravensmede smoothly cut her off. 'It would not do for *you* to catch a chill, Miss Marchant.'

'But it's a warm day and…'

The full force of his powerful gaze turned upon her. Anger spurred his actions and hardened his voice. Those marks, in faded hues of blue and purple, green and yellow, were still vivid enough against the white of her skin. Bruising. Made perhaps a week or so ago. Made by cruel fingers, if the patterning was anything to go by. What the hell had happened to her? Who was the scoundrel that had hit her? He slammed the brakes on the route his thoughts were taking. Hyde Park was neither the time nor the place.

He was brought back to reality by his grandmother's voice. 'Wrap the child in one of my travelling blankets. There's plenty warmth in those.'

His eyes fleetingly met Kathryn Marchant's once more, before he gathered up the urchin in his arms, complete with Miss Marchant's draping clothing, and walked to the carriage. 'I'll have Dr Porter treat the child at the house.' And, so saying, he deposited the small bundle into one of his grandmother's travelling blankets, ensured that both ladies were safely aboard, and set off for Berkeley Square.

Kathryn's eyes opened wide at the magnificent mansion before her. Ravensmede House was quite the grandest abode she had ever seen. And this was only one of his lordship's properties. She did not dare to think of all of his other houses. The image of one of London's most infamous rake-hells carrying the swaddled bundle with such care up the grand stone stairs would stay with her for ever. In that moment it seemed that the summer breeze had stilled, and her breathing too. The liquid warmth of tenderness erupted in her heart. It was obvious that there was very much more to Lord Ravensmede than his reputation suggested.

Ravensmede withdrew the toe of his boot from the fender and his elbow from the mantelpiece, and turned to face the drawing room chairs in which both Kathryn Marchant and his grandmother were seated. 'Dr Porter has been up there for some considerable time. I hope that the child's injuries are not worse than we thought.'

The dowager arched a quizzical eyebrow at her grandson.

Ravensmede seemed not to notice. 'Little Maggie seemed most reassured by Miss Marchant. Perhaps if Miss Marchant were to go to her… But no, I'm being too presumptuous…'

Kathryn carefully replaced the fine china cup upon the ornate saucer. 'No, not at all, Lord Ravensmede. I should have thought of such a thing myself. It was very kind of your housekeeper to sit with Maggie, but the poor child will be feeling frightened and alone.' She brushed down her skirts and rose, all the while remembering similar feelings from the years following her mother and sister's deaths. It was not something that she was content to let any child suffer. She pushed the memories away and concentrated on the child lying up in one of Lord Ravensmede's guest bedchambers. 'If you do not mind, I will stay with her until the doctor is finished.'

'Of course, Miss Marchant,' Ravensmede said politely. 'It's for the best.'

He reached over and rang the bell.

He did not speak again until the maid had arrived and escorted Kathryn from the drawing room.

'Well?' the dowager enquired of her grandson.

Ravensmede moved to sit on the sofa close by his grandmother's chair. 'Well,' he threw back at her. 'Judging from the bruises covering her neck and chest, I think that someone has tried to throttle Miss Marchant.'

'I'm not blind, boy!' she snorted. 'I saw them all right. I'm quite sure half of London did too when she whipped off her spencer and fichu in the middle of Hyde Park!'

'She was trying to help the child.'

'And exposing herself in the process.'

'She was unaware of what she was doing.' Ravensmede's eyes darkened. 'It would seem that I'm required once more to call upon Henry Marchant. The man is in need of guidance when it comes to his treatment of Miss Marchant.' He cracked his knuckles and balled one hand to a fist.'

'And have the whole of London gossip as to why the

bachelor Viscount of Ravensmede is intervening in that man's treatment of his niece. Damn it, Nick, you don't even know if Henry Marchant's your man. She might have got the bruises elsewhere.' Lady Maybury drained the tea from her cup and swiftly refilled it.

'Indeed she might have. But as her uncle, it's his responsibility to ensure her safety. Whether he lifted his hands to her or not, the blame still lies with him.'

The dowager watched her grandson closely.

'I'll be damned if I just deliver her back into his hands. I suspect that his wife lies behind the problem. Mrs Marchant had her niece in the kitchen and laundering the bed-linen, as if she were a blasted maid of all.' Belatedly he remembered to whom he was talking. 'Please excuse my language,' he muttered.

Nothing had stirred Nicholas to such a passion in a very long time. Lady Maybury's focus sharpened. 'You seem to have developed rather a concern with Miss Marchant.'

Ravensmede lay back languidly and stretched his legs out before him. 'What I'm concerned with is righting an injustice,' he said in a lazy tone. 'Hitting a woman goes far beyond the pale for any man, least of all the most charitable Mr Henry Marchant.'

'I agree entirely, but you had no notion of Kathryn's bruises when you asked me to act as chaperon.'

'I enjoy her company. She's an interesting woman.'

'And an attractive one.'

'A very attractive one.' Ravensmede met his grandmother's gaze.

'Her mother was a Thornley of Overton,' she said. 'Kathryn Marchant is a lady. And a young, unmarried lady at that.'

Ravensmede knew the turn the dowager's thoughts were

taking. 'She is indeed. I do not mean to ruin her, if that's what you're thinking.'

'Then what exactly is your interest in the gel? Marriage?'

A dark eyebrow quirked in disbelief. 'Certainly not. I like Miss Marchant, and suspected her situation was unhappy, although I had no notion of the extent of her mistreatment. My interest in the girl, as you so aptly put it, is purely philanthropic. Would you have me turn a blind eye to her suffering?'

They looked at one another for a moment longer, before Lady Maybury finally said, 'So what exactly is it that you are proposing?'

Ravensmede's mouth formed a charming smile, and then he proceeded to explain his plan in full.

Chapter Five

A soft knock at the door heralded Kathryn's return.

Lord Ravensmede slipped from the room to speak with the physician.

Lady Maybury patted the empty chair by her side. 'Come and sit here, Miss Marchant. Tell me how the child fares.'

'Thank you,' said Kathryn, and sat down where the dowager indicated. 'The doctor says that Maggie's leg is not broken, only bruised. As Lord Ravensmede said, she's had a very lucky escape.'

'Lucky, indeed,' said her ladyship.

'She doesn't seem too distressed, but the poor little thing is exhausted. The doctor says that she needs rest. She was dozing off as I came away.'

'Excellent.' The dowager beamed. 'The child could not be in better hands. Dr Porter attends all our family and is one of the best physicians in London. Treated Nicholas when he was a boy. I remember twenty years ago when…' She went on to reminisce over her grandchildren's childhood ailments and the antics that caused them, much to Kathryn's amusement. In light of Lady Maybury's stories her aristocratic family did not seem quite so daunting. They were still laughing when Lord Ravensmede returned.

The clock on the mantel chimed six. 'I hadn't thought it so late,' said Kathryn. 'I must return home. My aunt was expecting me before now.'

'Oh, but we have not even begun to discuss the other matter.' The Dowager Countess's small eyes brightened.

Kathryn did not miss the conspiratorial look exchanged between Lady Maybury and her grandson. She felt herself stiffen involuntarily and eyed the elderly lady with suspicion. 'What other matter?'

Lady Maybury crowed a small sharp chuckle. 'Well, my dear, you're nothing if not blunt!'

'Please do forgive me, my lady.' Kathryn looked away awkwardly at her sudden lapse in manners.

'It's a trait I admire,' declared Ravensmede's grandmother. 'Can't stand these milk-and-water misses who are scared to say what they think. Would agree with anything I say. Faugh!' The sunburst of wrinkles deepened as the top lip curled with contempt. 'Much prefer a gel who'll tell me the truth!' A smile replaced the frown. 'So, Miss Marchant, how do you find me?'

The grey eyes widened and she stared at the dowager. 'How do I find you?' she repeated with rising incredulity.

'That, indeed, is the question,' affirmed Lady Maybury with a twinkle in her eye, and the same mischievous look that Kathryn had seen cross her grandson's face on occasion.

A short pause sufficed to frame Kathryn's reply. 'Why, I find you to be very nice, and I've enjoyed your company greatly this afternoon.' It was the truth no less.

'Splendid!' her ladyship returned in increasingly exuberant tones. 'Then you'll have no objection to accepting my offer.'

'Your offer?' Kathryn said slowly, aware that she sounded rather like a simpleton who could do nothing other than repeat the questions asked of her.

The faded green gaze locked on to hers. 'To become my companion for the next two months of my visit.'

'Oh, no, my lady. I'm afraid that would be quite impossible. My aunt and uncle—'

'Nonsense!' chirped the grandam. 'I've already made my mind up and I don't mean to take no for an answer.'

'But—' She tried again, to no avail.

'I've a need for a companion. Can't stay in London with only Nick for company. He'll drive me mad before the week is out.' She snorted in the direction of her grandson.

Kathryn glanced over to see a smile curve Lord Ravensmede's lips.

'I'm afraid that my grandmother is quite right. All those wild card parties, the brandy, the gambling… She needs someone to keep her on the straight and narrow. I confess it's a job beyond my capabilities. Why, just look at the shocking influence she's already had on me.' The straight white teeth flashed and one dark eyebrow raised in a crooked gesture.

For all that she tried to resist, Kathryn felt the smile tug at her lips and looked abruptly away from temptation. Was it possible? Could she really just leave the torment of her life within the Marchant household? A brief flame of hope flickered…and then expired. Uncle Henry and Aunt Anna were her relatives, had offered her a home, albeit a miserable one, for the last three years. Wasn't it her duty to act as Lottie's companion until her cousin was successfully married? And if Aunt Anna had her way, a husband for Lottie would be netted before the Season was over. Perhaps then she could… Such thoughts were futile. Lady Maybury desired her as a temporary companion only during her visit to London. And afterwards? It was quite beyond question. She raised her eyes once more to Lady Maybury. 'I thank you for your generous offer, my lady. Indeed, it's most kind of you to even consider asking me, but I'm afraid that I'm forced to decline. It's my duty to act as Lottie's companion until she's—'

'Surely Mrs Marchant attends all of the society events along with her daughter?' The elderly voice was severe in the extreme.

'Yes, but—'

'Then, what does the chit need a companion for? As an unmarried and young lady you can hardly be expected to act as her chaperon can you?'

Kathryn felt the net closing around her. 'No, but—'

'I suppose I should not be surprised that you prefer to accompany a pretty, young chit to dances than spend your time assisting an old woman who is not much longer for this earth.'

The dowager seemed to shrink before Kathryn's very eyes, her narrow shoulders closing in, her velvet cheeks growing gaunt. A hollow cough rent the air.

Guilt stabbed at Kathryn's breast. 'No, it isn't—'

'Do not worry yourself, Miss Marchant.' A blue-veined hand dabbed a delicate lace handkerchief to each faded eye. A sad little sniff...and then the dowager played her trump card. 'I shall contrive my best to attend the injured child upstairs, but at my age...' The words trailed off. 'Such a strain on my health, the worry of it all...' Lady Maybury sniffed again and a tremor quivered upon her lips.

Dear Lord, but the old woman was clearly distraught and in danger of working herself into a fit of the vapours! Kathryn leapt forward and took one frail old hand within her own.

'That poor urchin...' There was what sounded to be a definite sob in her ladyship's voice.

Kathryn gently rubbed the paper-thin skin covering the back of Lady Maybury's hand. How could she make her understand that it really was not her choice at all? That she would much rather leave behind the house in Green Street and live her life as the dowager's companion? But it was not a matter of want. 'Dear Lady Maybury, please do not think that I don't want to accept your kind offer, or help little Maggie. There's nothing I would rather do, but—'

The old lady clung to her, her eyes brightening of a sudden. 'Oh my dearest gel! I knew that you would see sense; that you wouldn't be so heartless as to sentence an old lady to a season of loneliness and ill health. I cannot tell you the relief!' Ravensmede's grandmother's smile was wonderful to see.

'But—' started Kathryn uselessly, and stopped. The old lady was looking at her with such expectation that she could not correct the mistake. It would be a cruel and heartless woman that could shatter such joy. Who knew the effect such a shock would have on the lady's health? Kathryn swallowed down that sinking feeling and forced a smile to her face. And not once did she allow herself to look in the direction of the lady's grandson standing so tall and silent by the fireplace.

The small girl lay still within the great bed, her brown pansy eyes trained upon Kathryn's face.

'How old are you, Maggie?'

'Four,' the little voice whispered back.

'And do you remember where it is that you live?'

'Whitecross Road, the top room in Number Sixteen.'

'Good girl! You're really very clever. I'll send a message to your mama and papa so that they know where you are and aren't worried about you.'

Two fat tears rolled down the cheeks that Kathryn had just cleaned. 'Want to go home. Want me ma.' A hiccup sounded.

Kathryn wiped the tears away. 'Of course you do, moppet. And when you're better, so you shall. The doctor's looked at your leg and do you know what he said?'

The question distracted Maggie away from the sobbing she was poised to commence. 'What?'

'He said that it isn't broken at all, only bruised, and that it will get better very soon. But until then you're to rest in bed and eat lots of food.'

Maggie's eyes opened wide at the prospect. 'Lots an' lots of food?'

'Lots and lots and *lots*!' confirmed Kathryn with a grin. 'And I'll be here to tell you stories and talk to you, so you won't be lonely at all.'

Maggie smiled up into the kind face that hovered above hers.

A creaking of the door and Lord Ravensmede materialised by the bed. Kathryn struggled to get to her feet, but was stayed by a warm hand touched to her elbow.

'No need to get up on my account.' His voice was both deep and melodic, without a hint of the practised drawl he used when he was out.

She raised her eyes to his and felt a shimmer of excitement ripple down her spine. Just his proximity caused her heart to race. Her fingers fluttered to rearrange the fichu that she had recently replaced. Averting her face, she sought to turn her mind from inappropriate thoughts of the Viscount of Ravensmede. 'Maggie is a very clever girl and has told me where she lives.' With great gentleness she stroked the child's forehead.

Ravensmede smiled. 'Very good.'

Whether this remark was addressed to herself or Maggie, Kathryn remained unsure.

Maggie was regarding the tall dark-haired man solemnly. 'Are you the pa?' she asked quite suddenly.

'The pa?' Ravensmede looked rather bemused.

'Are you?' The round dark eyes had not wavered from his face.

Ravensmede glanced with amusement at Miss Marchant.

'You *must* be.' The strands of black hair so carefully combed out by Kathryn bobbed up and down as the child nodded. 'And you must be the ma,' added Maggie with certainty to Kathryn. 'Where are your little girls an' boys?'

Crimson flooded Kathryn's cheeks. 'Hush now, Maggie, you're tired and need to sleep. I'll come back and see you later.' A small kiss was dropped to the little girl's forehead.

'Promise?' the baby voice queried.

'I promise,' vowed Kathryn and rose to her feet, casting the child's previous innocently uttered questions from her mind.

Ravensmede opened the door and waited for her to pass through, before following her out into the passageway.

A throaty laugh sounded. 'Ma and pa!' And the look that smouldered from those green eyes caused a dancing sensation deep in Kathryn's belly.

She kept her gaze straight ahead, concentrating on each step, the pink-and-gold patterned carpet, the pale gold-coloured walls with their wall sconces and elaborate gilt-framed paintings, anything other than the man walking by her side. He was so close she could almost feel his heat scorching the full length of her left-hand side. Living in the same house as Lord Ravensmede was going to prove difficult in more ways than one.

Firstly, there was the simple fact that he was a bachelor, coupled with the not-so-small problem of his reputation.

Secondly, Aunt Anna and Uncle Henry were not likely to receive the news of her move well. Finally, and perhaps most importantly, was the strength of her own inappropriate reaction to the Viscount. From their first encounter over Miss Dawson's shoe, to that unwitting kiss and the subsequent calamity with the potatoes in St James's Park, Kathryn was well aware of the trouble resulting from that very reaction. The more she thought on it, the more she came to realise that, even as Lady Maybury's companion, living under the same roof as Lord Ravensmede was likely to prove a dangerous pastime—and one that she could not afford to risk, even if it did mean an escape from Aunt Anna's cruel treatment. All she had left was her reputation, and that wasn't something that she was prepared to jeopardise. She did not want to hurt Lady Maybury, or leave Maggie for that matter, but the alternative was far too threatening to contemplate. The decision made, she pressed her lips firmly together and stopped abruptly.

Ravensmede had stepped past her before reacting to her halt. 'Miss Marchant?' He sauntered back to stand beside her.

'My lord, I...' The words were rushed before her fragile resolve could fail. 'I know that I agreed to your grandmother's most kind offer, but upon further reflection I'm afraid that it is—'

Ravensmede took her hand within his and raised it lightly to his lips. 'For your kindness to my grandmother you have my gratitude. She's very dear to me and I would not like to see her ill or distressed. Her heart is weak and the family have been advised that she must be spared all that we can. Any shocking news, any great disappointment is to be avoided. That's why I'm so relieved that you have the generosity of spirit, Miss Marchant, to indulge an old lady's whim.' Warm lips pressed against the roughened red skin of her hand.

Kathryn felt the breath catch in her throat. She blinked several times to clear her head. And stifled the groan.

'Grandmama is rather set in her ways. As you may already have noticed, she's very much determined to do things in her own style, even if it does rather fly in the face of what is deemed convention.' He smiled. 'She often takes irrational sets against people, but rarely have I seen her warm to someone as she has to you. My grandmother likes you, Miss Marchant, and that really is quite an achievement.'

It seemed that there was no way to extricate herself from the agreement. *But surely the Viscount himself can see the position in which I would be placed?* Kathryn's thoughts flitted back and forth. 'My lord—'

'Please, call me Nicholas.'

Kathryn recoiled as if he'd slapped her. Call him by his given name? Indeed she would not!

The smile deepened. 'Or Ravensmede, if that is your preference.'

She gritted her teeth and started again. 'Lord Ravensmede...' Confound the man, but he was laughing at her. Anger flushed her cheeks and she raised steely eyes to his. 'This is a serious matter, not some tomfoolery for your amusement.'

His mouth straightened but those mesmerising green eyes were still brimful of laughter. 'Indeed, Miss Marchant, I assure you that I had no such thought.'

With a tug she rescued her hand from within his. 'You cannot be unaware that living here as your grandmother's companion would place me in a somewhat awkward position.'

The green eyes opened wide and innocent. 'Whatever can you mean, Miss Marchant?'

Her anger deserted her of a sudden and she sighed. 'Just that you are a bachelor and that, as an unmarried lady, perhaps I'm not best placed to accept the position offered.' There, she had said it. She found sudden fascination in the patterned carpet.

'How old are you, Miss Marchant?'

She looked up in surprise. Of all the answers she had expected this had not been one. 'Four and twenty, my lord.'

'Ravensmede,' he corrected.

Two spots of colour burned high in her cheeks. 'Ravensmede,' she repeated softly.

The corner of his mouth squinted up in a boyish gesture. 'Then you're hardly a schoolroom miss, and quite old enough to be considered suitable as a lady's companion. That, coupled with my grandmother's lineage, will ensure that no disadvantage attaches itself to your reputation.'

Her cheeks were glowing with all the subtlety of two blazing beacons. 'I'm well aware that I'm considered to be left on the shelf, but that has no bearing on the concern that I've raised.' The thump of her heart echoed throughout her body and she wished that she were anywhere but here, standing beside Lord Ravensmede, listening to him confirm his notion of her as an old maid.

He watched her closely. 'That was not my meaning, Miss Marchant. I'm sure that there's many a gentleman who would be only too happy to make you his wife.'

Kathryn swallowed her embarrassment well and attempted to force the conversation towards safer ground. 'You mentioned your grandmother's lineage?' she said demurely, as if her face were not aflame.

That not-quite-serious expression was back on his face. 'She's the daughter of a duke, and the widow of one of the wealthiest earls in the country. If Grandmama is for you, Miss Marchant, no one will dare be against you.'

She digested this information in silence for some minutes. It seemed that Lord Ravensmede had just removed the last of her reasons to refuse Lady Maybury's request. 'Then I hope I may prove useful in my new position.' Quite deliberately she turned and walked slowly towards the staircase, throwing the words over her shoulder as she went. 'When does Lady Maybury wish me to start?'

'Immediately.'

She nodded once. 'Then, I shall return first thing tomorrow morning.'

'I fear you misunderstand me, Miss Marchant. My grandmother needs your assistance *now*.' His gaze held hers.

'Very well. I'll return to my uncle's house to inform him of what has happened and pack up my clothes.'

'There's no need. I will dispatch a letter to Mr Marchant. Your clothes may be sent over later.' There was a determination in his voice that she did not understand.

'I cannot just leave for a drive in the park one afternoon and not return! It's a preposterous suggestion!'

A hand on her shoulder spun her round, and she found herself imprisoned by his grip on her upper arms. 'And what of your aunt and uncle, what of your cousin—is their treatment of you not equally preposterous?' His eyes stared down into hers.

Her skin scorched beneath the touch of his hands. 'I...I've never said so.'

'You don't need to.'

Surely he could not know? She had spoken to no one. Her heart was beating wildly within her chest. 'I won't renege on my agreement with Lady Maybury, if that's what you're afraid of.'

'I know you would not hurt an old lady's feelings, Kathryn.'

Her eyes widened at his use of her name.

'Nevertheless, I cannot permit you to return alone to Green Street. As I said, I will write to Mr Marchant with a full explanation.'

His confident assertion pricked at her pride. *'Cannot permit?'* Her tone was incredulous. 'I don't think that it's your place to say such a thing, Lord Ravensmede.'

The green eyes did not betray their surprise by as much as a flicker. 'If you're bent on such a journey, then I must insist on accompanying you. My grandmother is quite fatigued by the drive and subsequent incident with the child. Trailing her back across town is quite out of the question. Therefore, we should ready ourselves immediately, Miss Marchant, unless you would prefer to wait until it is dark…'

Kathryn knew very well what his lordship was saying. Arriving alone with Lord Ravensmede to take her leave of them, no matter Ravensmede's assertions as to Lady Maybury's influence, there could be no doubt what it would look like. Aunt Anna and Uncle Henry would have an apoplectic fit. She ground her teeth. 'I have no need of your escort. I'm perfectly happy to go alone.'

'No.' The single word was decidedly emphatic.

'Lord Ravensmede, you're behaving most unreasonably.'

A dark eyebrow raised. 'Are you so very eager to return there? Do they treat you so well that you're loath to leave them?' There was an undercurrent to his words that made her shiver.

'It's not so strange a request.'

'You haven't answered the question, Miss Marchant.'

There was silence.

'It seems that you leave me little option, my lord. Write the letter if you must.'

And this time he did not chide her for the use of his title.

It had been several hours since a letter had been dispatched from the Viscount of Ravensmede to Mr Henry Marchant and still there had been no reply. Kathryn eyed the soft white cotton of the borrowed nightdress with some reticence. She was still uneasy about her sudden new-found position and the means by which it had been effected. Ravensmede's refusal to allow her to return alone to Green Street worried her. Undoubtedly he was stubborn and arrogant and used to getting his own way, but she had never thought him to be so downright unreasonable. It flew in the face of all she knew of him. But then she had to concede that her knowledge of Lord Ravensmede was remarkably scant. And he *had* made her a most indecent proposal in St James's Park.

Her fingers reached out and lifted the garment to her lap. Lady Maybury had seemed to think nothing remarkable in her grandson's overbearing attitude; indeed, the old lady appeared to positively encourage Ravensmede. She was still half-expecting Uncle Henry to come charging over, demanding to know what precisely was going on. But hadn't her uncle always been too keen to court the favour of the aristocracy? If she knew Uncle Henry, he'd be carefully weighing up the best response to further advance his own schemes. She sighed just as a light knock sounded at the door and a young maid entered.

'I'm Jean, miss. Come to help you undress for bed.' She bobbed a little curtsy.

'Thank you, Jean, but I'm used to dressing and undressing myself.' Kathryn watched the crestfallen face and suddenly realised why. 'Are you an abigail?'

The thin face flushed. 'No, miss, I'm a chambermaid, but I'm a quick learner and...' The maid waited to be dismissed.

'Perhaps it would be nice not to have to struggle round to reach the buttons on this dress,' Kathryn said with a smile. 'Do you mind if I change my answer?'

'Oh, no, miss, not at all.' And Jean bounded across the bedchamber to begin work in the lofty realms of a lady's maid. She started with the careful removal of Miss Marchant's fichu, folding the worn length of material into a neat pile before turning to tackle the buttons of the faded blue afternoon dress. It was only then that the smile dropped from her face, replaced instead with a look of shock. The narrow brow wrinkled in consternation and the brown eyes rounded as two new pennies.

'Is something wrong?' Kathryn eyed the maid with some concern.

The gaze dropped to the floor and two small spots of colour mounted in the thin cheeks. 'No, miss.' She skirted round to release the back buttons that secured Miss Marchant's dress, taking care not to meet the lady's eyes. The dress, petticoats and stays were removed in a matter of minutes. 'Shall I help you into your nightdress, miss, before brushing your hair?' The slender hands strayed towards the folded nightdress.

'No thank you, I can manage from here myself. Thank you, Jean, I shall see you in the morning.'

The maid bobbed a curtsy and almost ran from the room, leaving a rather puzzled Miss Marchant looking after her.

Still clad in her threadbare shift, Kathryn unpinned the heavy coil of her curls, sat down at the dressing table, and began to brush her hair using the silver-backed hairbrush from the set laid out on the mahogany surface. The golden glow from the fireplace illuminated the room, and the candle still sat where she had left it on the small table beside the bed. Her eyes glanced up to the oval looking-glass and froze. The brush ceased its action, hovered in mid-air and quickly resumed its position upon the dressing table. And all the while Kathryn's gaze did not waver.

From the mirrored glass a pale thin figure stared back, a ghost of the woman she had once been. Her stomach tightened and sank at the sight. For there, in front of her very eyes, was the obvious reason for the maid's strange behaviour. How could she have so easily forgotten? Reddened fingers reached up and cautiously traced the large purple black smudges adorning the skin around her collarbone, then shifted down to touch each and every one of the bruises peppering her thin arms. Beneath each eye was the faintest trace of shadow and her cheeks had about them a slight gauntness, lending her whole face a look of worn fatigue. Indeed, she looked little better than the poor child recovering in the bedchamber further along the passageway. Little Maggie, who had lain so still and cold on the ground in Hyde Park as to chase every thought from Kathryn's head save for those concerned with the child's welfare. Little Maggie, over whom Kathryn had so readily draped her fichu and spencer. And, by removing her fichu, she had unwittingly exposed her shame for all to see. Dear Lord! The bruises could not be missed. Not by Lady Maybury. And certainly not by Lord Ravensmede. So absorbed had she been in the accident and all that ensued that not once had she remembered the presence of those ugly telling bruises. A groan escaped her at her own ineptitude. She knew now why the Viscount had been so downright stubborn in his refusal to allow her to return to Green Street. He had seen the bruises and drawn his own conclusions.

Humiliation scalded her cheeks and caused an aching in her heart. Her fingers kneaded at the worn linen of her shift. But Kathryn did not cry, even though Ravensmede had viewed the shameful marks upon her body, even though she now knew herself to be an object of pity and curiosity. Jean's eyes had been telling enough and she did not doubt that by tomorrow morning the story of her darned underclothing and smattering of bruises would be the main topic of conversation below stairs. Her chin jutted out as she held her head high. Let them talk. She had survived worse than a little tittle-tattle, much worse. Gossip would not touch her, as nothing had ever touched her since her father had placed the muzzle of a Manton in his mouth and pulled the trigger.

She had cried then, for days—or was it weeks? When the tears had finally stopped she had vowed they would never come again. That was when she had discovered the power of daydreams. Dreams that took her away from the pain of reality. Dreams that made life bearable. And the worse things got, the more Kathryn dreamed. Resolutely she raised the brush to the thick hank of chestnut hair curling over her shoulder and began slowly, steadily, to brush.

'I like this toast. Is there more?' Maggie demanded as she sat plumped up in the big bed. Sunshine shimmered on her black locks, coating them with a blue sheen and bleaching her small elfin face white.

Kathryn laughed. 'Of course, moppet, but first you have your ham and eggs to eat. Let's see what room you have left when they're gone.'

The brown pansy eyes widened in awe. 'Ham *and* eggs *and* toast?'

'Most definitely.' Kathryn positioned the full plate on the child's tray.

A large grin spread across Maggie's face and soon she was too busy eating to manage more than the odd unintelligible word uttered through a mouthful of half-chewed food.

Kathryn sat in the chair beside the bed. Sipping the hot coffee chased away the thick-headed feeling that had troubled her since waking. The bed had been both warm and comfortable, a far cry from the hard, lumpy truckle bed in her room at Green Street. But she had slept poorly, tormented by worries, and nightmares from the past. Her escape from the bosom of Henry Marchant's family was not likely to be that simple. She nibbled at the toast, finding that the previous week's starvation rations had rendered her unable to eat much before her stomach protested its fullness. A crumb was displaced from the bodice of her blue muslin dress with the flick of a finger before she caught sight of Maggie's little face looking at her with a rather guilty expression. 'Is something wrong? You seem to have stopped eating?'

The black head shook in denial. The dark eyes peeped up through long lashes. 'You ain't got no eggs or ham. You can have some of mine if you want.'

Kathryn knew what it had cost the child to make such a generous offer. A child who was no doubt used to going hungry. 'It's very kind of you to offer, Maggie, but I've already eaten some eggs before I came to see you,' she lied. 'I'm afraid you'll have to eat them all yourself!'

Maggie wasted no time in complying. 'Where's the pa?' she questioned between mouthfuls of egg.

The thought of Ravensmede in the role of a father brought a wry smile to Kathryn's face. 'Lord Ravensmede is probably still sleeping.' She had no idea when he had returned, or, indeed, if he had returned at all. 'He was out late last night and is bound to be very tired this morning.'

The gentleman in question chose this precise minute to make his entry. 'Good morning, Miss Marchant, Miss Maggie.'

Maggie giggled, spluttering a piece of half-chewed ham down her chin.

Kathryn remedied the accident with a starched white napkin while returning the greeting. For someone who'd been up half the night, he was looking bright-eyed and refreshed.

'The ma said you was in bed 'cos you was out last night. But she was wrong, 'cos you're here.' Maggie smiled up at the tall dark-haired man, not intimidated by his lordship in the slightest. 'Where was you?' she asked sweetly.

'Maggie!' Kathryn admonished. 'You mustn't ask Lord Ravensmede such questions.' But her cheeks glowed and not just because the child had unwittingly revealed that the 'ma' had noticed his absence the previous evening.

Ravensmede sat himself down on the bed and tousled Maggie's hair. 'I was very busy, but now I'm back to check whether you're eating up all of your breakfast.'

If the Viscount's reputation was true, Kathryn had a very good idea exactly what Lord Ravensmede had been 'very busy' doing throughout the night. She sought to change the subject. 'Maggie's leg is much better this morning. Dr Porter will be pleased when he calls again this afternoon to decide whether she may go home.'

'Home to *my* ma and pa,' declared Maggie in a cheerful tone.

'Indeed so. They were very worried when I told them about your sore leg. If you're to stay here much longer, they'll come and visit you.' The Viscount's eyes twinkled.

Kathryn could not prevent herself exclaiming, 'You've spoken to them yourself?'

His gaze met with her incredulous stare. 'But of course. What else did you expect?'

She smiled. 'From what I've heard, certainly not that.'

'Then you should not believe everything that you hear, Kathryn.' He said her name like a caress.

'And you should not seek to encourage an unwarranted reputation, sir!' The smile deepened to a most unladylike grin.

His lordship arched a dark eyebrow and said, 'I assure you that my reputation is most deserved, Miss Marchant.'

If it had not been for the glimmer of the smile that lurked too readily behind his lips, she would have withdrawn. As it was, Miss Kathryn Marchant, who had for the past three years striven to be as quiet and unnoticeable as could be, was engaging in what could only be described as a rather flirtatious conversation with a notorious rake. But he was so damnably arrogant that he deserved to be taken down a peg or two. 'Indeed, sir? Perhaps it is rather overrated.' Had she just said such a comment? It barely seemed possible. Surely she must be in the grip of some madness. She most certainly knew she was when she saw his lips slide into a sensual curve.

'Would you care to put it to the test?' The suggestion in his gaze caused the heat to rise in her cheeks.

Standing up abruptly, she smoothed her skirts down with the palms of her hands. 'Certainly not. Now, if you'll excuse me, I had better get on.' And, so saying, she gathered up Maggie's tray containing the emptied plates and cups.

A pair of strong arms reached across the bed and deftly lifted the tray away. The teasing sensuality had vanished. Instead, the stark contours of his face contained what looked to be anger. 'You are a guest in this house, Miss Marchant, along with my grandmother. I pay my servants well to do such things.' The tray was deposited unceremoniously on an occasional table and the bell pulled. 'If you would be kind enough to attend the library in ten minutes, there is something which we must discuss.'

A shiver stole down Kathryn's spine. Clear grey eyes raised to meet green. 'My lord?'

'My name is Nicholas, Kathryn, I would that you used it,' he said soberly and softly closed the door.

Chapter Six

Ravensmede was about to ignore his grandmother's advice. The source of the foul markings on Kathryn Marchant's skin was like a needle that pricked at him constantly. Even during last night's journey to Whitecross Road to call upon little Maggie's parents he could scarcely concentrate on what he had to say because of the blasted matter. Hitting a woman, any woman, was something that sickened Ravensmede to the pit of his stomach. The fact that it had been Kathryn on the receiving end of someone's vicious temper exacerbated that response a hundredfold. He controlled his mounting fury admirably.

Someone had been liberal with their fists, that much was evident, and there was no point in meeting Henry Marchant until he knew the truth of it. No matter what Lady Maybury said, Ravensmede had every intention of getting to the bottom of the sickening assault…and today. Waiting for Kathryn to tell them in her own time was simply not soon enough. The brandy hit the back of his throat like a brand. He swallowed it down. Too damn early in the day, but he needed something to dampen his temper.

A quiet tap at the door sounded and the subject of his

concern presented herself. She was still dressed in the shabby muslin gown that she had worn yesterday. He noticed that the periwinkle blue coloration brought out the creamy white hue of her skin, and the red lights in her hair. The fichu had been arranged to cover every trace of the bruising. She was so slender as to appear fragile, something he had no memory of either on that first night at Lady Finlay's ball, or later in St James's Park. No doubt the bastard had been starving her as well. The thought of Henry Marchant curled his fingers into fists. With calm deliberation he forced his hands to relax. A deep breath, and he was ready to face her.

'Kathryn.' He smiled and gestured towards one of the two large wing chairs around the fireplace. 'Sit down.' As the day was fine and warm, and showed every promise to continue as such, the hearth was empty. Sunshine flooded in through the large bow window, highlighting a halo of red around the rich brown of her hair. He positioned himself in the opposite chair, stretching out his long, pantaloon-clad legs before him.

She sat demurely, hands folded motionless in her lap, as if she were a model of relaxed serenity...as if she had not been beaten and starved by her so-called family. Her eyes glanced up, but the question in them remained unasked. He would have to tread very carefully. 'Would you like some tea?'

'No, thank you, my lor...Ravensmede.' Her fingers gripped tighter and then relaxed.

'Then I will come straight to the point. Mr Marchant has arranged to call here at three o'clock to discuss your new position. My grandmother will explain the urgency of her need for a companion. In view of her age and the injured child upstairs, I'm sure that your uncle will understand why it was imperative that you commence as Lady Maybury's companion with immediate effect.' And if Henry Marchant dared to raise the slightest objection he'd see to it that the man was put firmly in his place.

Her gaze was trained on the blackened grate. The rigid tension across her narrow shoulders tightened at his words. 'Will he be accompanied by my aunt?'

Now why should that matter so much to her? For suddenly he knew that to be very much the case. 'In truth, I do not know. Do you wish to take your leave of her?'

There was a pause, just long enough to be obvious. 'Naturally. They are my family. It's only polite, after all that they've done, that I take my leave of them all.' And still her focus did not waver from the grate.

'And what have they done, Kathryn?' The question slipped softly from his lips.

Startled eyes raised to his and quickly looked away again. A whisper of pink touched to her cheeks, before the small chin was thrust defiantly up. 'Why, they took me in and offered me a home when my father died. I...I'm very grateful for their charity.'

The time had come to say what must be said, to discover the truth. He leaned forward by the smallest fraction. 'But it wasn't charity they had in mind when they dealt you your bruises, was it? And I would hazard a guess that it wasn't gratitude you felt in receipt of those markings.' His voice rumbled low and quiet, each word enunciated clearly, no hint of the practised rakish drawl.

The chestnut-coloured head whipped round to face him, her breast rising and falling dramatically beneath the outmoded gown. Within her eyes flashed anger and something else that had gone in an instant. She faced him with her fear concealed. It seemed for a moment that his words had rendered her speechless, but she recovered herself well, forcing her emotions back under control. When her voice finally sounded it was quiet and careful, as if she were attending to his grandmother or the child that lay upstairs. 'Lord Ravensmede,' she began, 'you are mistaken. The… bruises…that you happened to see upon my person are the result of a small accident, nothing more. Through my own clumsiness I tripped and fell. The blame rests entirely on my own head and no one else.' The slender fingers began to twist themselves together.

His eyes flitted to her hands, saw more than he was meant to see, and returned once more to her face and the darkened gaze that had been rapidly averted while she told her story. 'You make a very poor liar, Kathryn.'

The colour heightened in her cheeks and she shot him one brief infuriated glance. 'I'm telling you the truth, sir. You've drawn the wrong conclusion.'

'I don't think so.' He watched the small white teeth nibble delicately on the fullness of her lower lip and did not speak again until those stormy grey eyes slowly dragged round, as if not quite of their own accord, to meet his.

'We have nothing further to discuss, sir. I shall be ready to meet my uncle at three o'clock.' With that she rose and made to step away.

But Ravensmede had no intention of letting Miss Marchant evade him quite so easily. Within an instant he was towering over her. 'On the contrary, we've only just begun. Is that your best effort? I would not have thought your imagination to be so lacking.'

A slight gasp escaped her lips before they pressed firmly together with annoyance.

Before she could retaliate he pressed a hand to hers. 'Do

you always cross your fingers when you lie? Who told you that it saved you from the sin? Your nurse?'

Rosy stain flooded her face and the fingers encased beneath his straightened themselves. She shifted her feet uneasily. 'How did you know?'

'Mine said the same, much to my father's disgust!'

She smiled a small smile at that.

It seemed a shame to destroy the sudden rapport that had developed between them, but he could do nothing else if he meant to know just who was responsible for her hurts. A suspect loomed large in his mind, but he would not confront the man without first hearing Kathryn's side of the story. He lowered his head to hers. She was so close that his breath fanned a ripple across the curls framing her face, so close that the sweet scent of her filled his nostrils. One finger moved to tilt her chin, until her eyes were looking up into his. Ravensmede swallowed hard and resisted the urge to place his lips upon hers, to kiss her as thoroughly as he'd kissed her that night in the moonlit room. Temptation pulled him closer, beckoned him down a path he knew he had no right to tread. So close, so sweet. It seemed that her lips parted in invitation. He felt the stirrings of other interests and reined himself back with a self-denying hand. She was here for his protection, not the practised art of his seduction. But when he looked into Kathryn Marchant's face there was nothing practised about the erratic thud of his heart or the overwhelming urge to take her in his arms and never let her go.

He wondered as to his assertion to his grandmother. *I do not mean to ruin her*, he had said. But the woman standing so close that he could have plucked a sweet kiss from her lips stirred his blood like no one else. He wanted her. Had wanted her since that night at Lady Finlay's ball. A woman he could not allow himself to have; a woman who deserved better than the hand life had dealt her; a woman he had just made his grandmother's companion. Mentally he dowsed himself with cold water and focused on the matter in hand. And that was confirming Henry Marchant's guilt in the abuse of his niece. She was still looking up at him with such trust that it quite smote his jaded heart. With the gentlest of movements he touched his lips to the coolness of her forehead, before scanning her eyes once more.

'Will you not trust me with the truth?' he said softly.

For the beat of a heart he thought she would do just that. Her mouth opened to speak and then closed again. Her gaze dropped and the moment was gone. 'I cannot,' she whispered.

At least there were no more lies.

'What happened is in the past and will not happen again. I know that you only mean to help me…Nicholas… but…please, just let the matter go.'

His stomach somersaulted at the sound of his name upon her lips. What a glorious sound it was. 'I cannot do that, Kathryn. You've been treated most cruelly and I cannot let any man get away with such injustice.' Beneath his fingers her hand trembled and she sighed a sigh of such fatigue and sadness and disappointment. 'Kathryn?' The word held an intimacy that he had no right to.

Slowly she shook her head and stepped back. 'No.' Her shoulders straightened and her face was filled with firm resolve.

He made no move to reclaim her. Just watched, and waited.

'No,' she said again with increasing determination.

There was nothing else for it. 'Then you leave me with no other option.' He waited for her response. Knew that it would come.

Her voice was small and tight. 'What do you mean to do?'

The slightest pause. 'I will speak with Henry Marchant until I know the whole of it. And then I'll decide what to do with him. Perhaps I should call him out.'

'No!' Her eyes widened in horror. 'You must not!'

'He does not deserve your sympathy, Kathryn.'

'No, please!' Her hands grasped at his arms, tightening, enforcing her will. 'You're wrong. It wasn't him...he's done nothing!'

Not Henry Marchant? His focus narrowed. 'Then who?'

Nothing, just the pressure of those slight fingers.

'Hell's teeth, Kathryn, tell me!' he growled with more force than he intended.

'Aunt Anna.' A faint whisper, barely more than the expiration of a breath. Cheeks so pale he thought she would swoon.

He moved to take her arms, unmindful that she still held his. A mirror of her stance, unnoticed in the incredulity that enveloped him. 'Are you telling me that Anna Marchant inflicted those bruises upon you?' His voice sounded cold and hard and distant even to his own ears.

'Yes.' Her body recoiled from his, and she stepped back until the chair was between them. 'You have what you wanted. Are you happy now?' The slight figure turned and fled, leaving Ravensmede staring at the library door that had just been slammed so adamantly in his face.

Kathryn stood still as a statue and stared down from the window of her bedchamber, although quite what made it hers she could not be sure since there was nothing of her own in it. A calm, light-filled room that was furnished with the finest furniture, or so it seemed to the woman who had made do for as many years as she could remember. It was as close to a sanctuary as she had come, even if it was owned by the man who had just caused her to reveal that which she had promised never to. But she could not have allowed him to meet Uncle Henry thinking what he did. The thought of exactly what Ravensmede had threatened to do twisted in her gut. Call him out. There was no doubt in her mind that he would have done just that...and more.

Her fingers kneaded at the tight spot developing behind her forehead, trying to forestall the headache she knew it would become. What would the Viscount do with the knowledge? *Oh, Lord, please do not let him speak of it, not to Uncle Henry, and certainly not to Aunt Anna herself. It would only make matters worse. Aunt Anna will deny all, cast me as a liar. I have no proof and they have provided me with a home all this time. And the scandal! Perhaps I should speak with Nicholas... Dear Lord, have I so quickly come to think upon him in such familiar terms?* The thought was really rather shocking. She pressed the cooling palms of her hands to her eyes. *Think, Kathryn, think!* She willed herself. *I have created this problem and therefore I can solve it.* So engrossed in her task was she that she did not hear the chamber door brush against the rug as it was pushed hesitantly open. Indeed, it was not until something tugged at her skirts that she jumped and gave a small exclamation of surprise.

'Why are you crying?' The pansy brown eyes were regarding her with concern.

One slender hand pressed to her breast before Kathryn bent and clutched the child to her. 'Maggie! You startled me. I didn't hear you come in.' She rearranged the locks of hair around the girl's forehead and kissed her. 'You were as quiet as a little mouse.'

Maggie smiled and touched small fingers softly to the shadowed areas beneath Kathryn's eyes. 'Why was you crying?' she repeated.

'I wasn't crying, moppet, just thinking.'

But the child persisted. 'But you was sad, wasn't you?'

'Just a little, but I'm not any more. Now, Miss Maggie, what are you doing out of bed?' Kathryn chided in a voice of mock severity.

Maggie was not fooled for one minute. 'Looking for you to tell me another story.'

Kathryn placed her hands on her hips and looked stern.

Maggie laughed.

'Oh, very well then, but only if you get back into bed. You must not get up until Dr Porter has checked your leg this afternoon.' Secretly Kathryn was pleased that the child felt well enough to wander. And, from the way she was jumping rather excitedly up and down, it appeared that the injury to her leg was perhaps not as bad as they had first thought. With one arm cupped protectively round Maggie's shoulders, Kathryn guided the small girl back along to the room from whence she had come.

The day passed quickly for Kathryn in her new role as Lady Maybury's companion, and she did have to admit that her first impression of that employment found it to be infinitely preferable to anything she had experienced in the house at Green Street. Ravensmede's grandmother was loud, opinionated and had evidently taken rather a shine to Kathryn. Beneath the old lady's harsh exterior was a heart of gold. She brooked no nonsense and did not suffer fools gladly, but when it came to her grandson it was quite clear to Kathryn that he held a special place in the lady's heart. It was just before three o'clock when the doorbell sounded. Miss Marchant was still seated at the lady's writing desk situated within Lady Maybury's rooms. With pen poised in hand and rather ink-stained fingers, she was waiting patiently for the dowager to dictate the next line of the letter. Her ladyship showed no sign of having heard the bell.

'Lady Harriet sounds to me to be indolent in the extreme. You must not hesitate to chastise her as such, my dear Frances, else you will never get her married off.' Lady Maybury was seated comfortably upon a pink chair. She paused to allow Kathryn to copy down her words, her head cocked to one side like a small lively robin.

Kathryn finished the sentence and glanced up. The clock on the mantel chimed three.

Lady Maybury ignored it. 'Lady Gardiner's daughter was quite the same, and look what became of her.'

The grey eyes drifted to the clock face.

'No, Frances, you must stand firm. It's the best advice I can offer.' Lady Maybury nodded her white curls forcefully. 'Do not pen the next words,' she instructed. 'They are for your ears alone. Harriet Kiddleby was an indolent child and she's now an indolent young woman. I blame Frances, of course. She always was too soft with the gel. If she doesn't act quickly, she'll be saddled with the wretched gel for the rest of her days. Frances never did have much sense.' A tap at the door interrupted Lady Maybury's tirade.

A footman entered and addressed himself to the dowager. 'Mr Marchant has arrived, my lady. He's in the drawing room with Lord Ravensmede.'

The snowy head graciously inclined. Only when the door had closed did she resume her conversation. 'Now, what was I saying? Ah, that's right, I remember now.'

'Should we not…?' Kathryn looked tentatively at the old lady.

'Make them wait!' came the abrupt reply. And so she did.

It was some considerable time later and with a degree of mounting agitation that Kathryn came finally to pen the words, *remember me to Lady Augusta. Adieu—Yours ever, Eleanor Maybury.*

Ravensmede's grandmother offered no apologies for her tardiness. Rather, she cast a piercing eye in Henry Marchant's direction as if it were he who was making unfair demands upon her time. Kathryn sat at the old lady's side on the sofa and prayed fervently that the Viscount had not made any mention of her bruising. Her uncle looked distinctly uncomfortable, a sign that did not bode well. The tension in the room was thick and suffocating. No one spoke. She forced a smile to her face. 'Uncle Henry, how good of you to come. My aunt is not with you?'

'No.' He did not return the smile. 'Unfortunately she is otherwise engaged.'

Another awkward silence.

Her eyes sought Ravensmede's. His face was stern, forbidding even, but she thought she saw a softening in that shared moment. It was gone before she could be sure. His attention returned to the man sitting uneasily in the chair with his back to the door.

'Mr Marchant. As I explained in my letter, Miss Marchant has been kind enough to agree to become my grandmother's companion. You understand, of course, the honour that Lady Maybury is conferring upon your family with such an appointment?' Ravensmede had resumed the habitual arrogant drawl that had been missing for the past two days. A dark eyebrow winged as if daring Henry Marchant to disagree.

Henry cleared his throat and looked away. 'Quite. I have no objection to my niece accepting such a position *per se*.'

The gruff throat cleared again and the large hands gripped the chair arms. 'However...' Henry looked at the marbled fireplace. 'My wife and I are concerned with the manner and speed with which the offer and acceptance have been made. Kathryn is like a daughter to us and naturally we can only be greatly concerned when she leaves our home for a drive around Hyde Park, and fails to return.'

'I understand your...*concern*.' The stress was on Ravensmede's last word. There was an iciness to his tone that Kathryn had never heard before. 'Indeed, it really is most commendable.'

Mr Marchant's gaze shifted uncomfortably.

Ravensmede's drawl intensified. 'The accident involving the child that occurred during the drive has left my grandmother quite exhausted. At her age, I hardly expect her to oversee the child's care amidst all of her other activities. Thus, the immediate requirement for a companion to assist her arose. Miss Marchant was the ideal candidate.'

Henry Marchant gave a little cough. 'And Lady Maybury will be staying here with you?' The question dropped dangerously into the air.

Kathryn's stomach tensed. The unspoken inference was obvious. And, if her uncle thought it, then so would everyone else, despite all of Lord Ravensmede's persuasion. The Viscount turned a glacial focus upon Mr Marchant.

Mr Marchant drew back against his chair.

'My grandmother has taken a house in Upper Grosvenor Street for the Season,' said Lord Ravensmede.

Kathryn could not suppress a surprised glance in his lordship's direction. Hadn't Lord Ravensmede led her to believe that they would be living here in Ravensmede House? His face betrayed nothing.

'In that case, I can raise no objection. My niece is four and twenty, and many years beyond the age at which she would require my permission.' For the first time since entering the room Henry Marchant looked at Kathryn. 'I hope that you'll be happy in your new position.' His gaze skittered away. 'I'll have your trunk sent round.'

'Thank you.' Kathryn had never been one to shirk her duty and she did not do so now. 'I will call upon my aunt and Lottie tomorrow to take my leave of them.' Belatedly she consulted her new employer, 'If that is acceptable to you, my lady.'

A scowl flitted over Lord Ravensmede's face, and disappeared.

Before Lady Maybury could reply, Henry Marchant cleared his throat and repeated the words that his wife had instructed, 'Regrettably, both your aunt and cousin will be out tomorrow.'

A small silence followed.

'Then the day after, perhaps?' Kathryn suggested.

'I believe them to be engaged on that day also,' he said awkwardly, and shifted in his chair.

Kathryn made to reply but Ravensmede was there first. 'How good of your family to be so understanding of the situation.'

Confusion clouded Mr Marchant's face.

The Viscount leaned forward towards the older man in a confiding manner. 'Some people are embarrassed by class differences, but clearly your lady wife is not one of them. Now that Miss Marchant is companion to my grandmother, she must exercise more discernment in her choice of those with whom she associates. It is well that Mrs Marchant understands that.'

Henry Marchant's cheeks stained a ruddy red at the insult, but he said nothing.

Seeking to alleviate the growing tension, Kathryn spoke to her uncle. 'Please send Aunt Anna and Cousin Lottie my regards and my thanks for all their kindness over the years.' From the corner of her eye she saw Lord Ravensmede's jaw twitch, and she almost smiled. Then Kathryn remembered Aunt Anna. If she had thought her aunt to be an enemy before, she had best have a care and watch her back from now on. Anna Marchant was not a woman to forgive or forget.

Henry Marchant nodded once. 'Of course.' He cleared his throat again and looked uneasy.

It was Ravensmede who finally brought an end to the charade. 'Then we bid you good day, Mr Marchant.' He stood over a head taller than Henry Marchant and looked down into the man's small eyes. 'Your niece will be safe with my grandmother, Mr Marchant. Have no doubt of that.' And beneath the polite reassurance was the veiled threat of something dark and dangerous. Henry Marchant felt it too and scuttled from the room with a speed surprising for a man of his girth.

Sunshine flooded the breakfast room the next morning as Ravensmede sipped his coffee. A plate containing the remains of kedgeree lay abandoned before him.

'It's quite impossible, Nicholas. I barely slept a wink last night, most probably as a result of that infernal Marchant rat. What kind of man stands by and allows his wife to beat his niece? He's despicable! Little wonder I was tossing and turning throughout the night!'

'Grandmama,' the Viscount admonished gently, 'you promised that you wouldn't speak of it. Kathryn did not want us to know of her aunt's guilt.'

'Fustian!' exclaimed his grandmother. 'The gel's still up

with Maggie. She'll not hear me from there!' She winced. 'It's no good. I'm really not myself this morning. You and Kathryn will have to take the child home.'

Ravensmede's eyes narrowed. 'I'll send for Dr Porter.'

'No! There's nothing wrong with me that a few hours' sleep won't cure. Stop fussing, Nick. I'm not dead yet!' The old lady drew him a fierce stare. 'Just make sure you look after my companion.'

Ravensmede's mood lightened at the thought of Kathryn and a closed carriage. He quirked a smile. 'As you wish, Grandmama.' A small bow and he turned to leave.

'And Nick—' Her voice stopped him at the door. The faded green eyes glared a warning. 'Remember that Miss Marchant is under *my* protection.'

He raised an ironic brow and was gone.

Kathryn's arm tightened around the child sitting by her side. 'I promise I shall come and see you again very soon.' The carriage rumbled through the streets leading them to the rookeries in Whitecross Street and the little girl's home.

Maggie eyed her hopefully before looking over at Lord Ravensmede on the opposite seat. 'And will the pa come too?'

'I don't know about that.' She laughed. Somehow she could not imagine the Viscount of Ravensmede visiting a four-year-old girl in a street of overcrowded slums. But, come to that, she had not thought he would have paid for Maggie to have the best of medical treatments, cared for her within his own house and then personally delivered her to her parents.

Ravensmede leaned forward. 'Of course I will.'

'Good.' Maggie snuggled closer into Kathryn's side, feeling in the pockets of her new apron. The pretty white frills around its edge contrasted nicely with the matching pink-and-white high-waisted frock worn beneath it. An apple was produced and the carriage soon reverberated with the sound of Maggie's crunches.

'That's what I like to see, a good healthy appetite.' Kathryn stroked the little girl's clean, shiny hair, fixing the pink satin ribbons as she did.

She felt Ravensmede's gaze upon her and looked up to meet it. His mouth was not quite in a smile, and there was a solemnity about his eyes that made her feel peculiar.

The rest of the journey continued with Kathryn pointing out landmarks and shops to Maggie. Ravensmede made no effort to join in, just sat back and watched the woman and the child. Once they had arrived, Kathryn did not miss the purse that he pressed into Maggie's father's hand, or the kind words that he uttered to the child's poor work-worn mother. A kiss on Maggie's cheek and they were gone. Kathryn waved until the little girl and her family were just a speck in the distance, and wondered at what she could never hope to have. A child of her own. A family. She thrust the thought aside and looked at Lord Ravensmede. He had not spoken since their return to the carriage, just sat looking from the window as if his thoughts were elsewhere.

'You should not have said that you would visit her. She'll look for you and be disappointed when you don't come.' Kathryn spoke the words gently, not to chastise but merely to show him the error of his ways. What did a man like Ravensmede know of a child's fragile trust?

Then his eyes were on her, casting a spiral of excitement into her breast and down deeper into her stomach as they ever did. She ignored her body's response as best she could. 'What makes you think that I would lie to the child? Do you think so little of me?'

She felt the colour rise to her face at his continued scrutiny and the accusation in his voice. 'No, I just thought…'

'I know what you thought, Kathryn,' he said.

Anger flared. 'On the contrary, Lord Ravensmede, you know nothing of what I think! Don't presume to do so!'

He smiled at that. 'Ouch,' he said. 'The kitten has claws.'

He really was the most infuriating man alive. Deliberately she turned her face to watch the passing houses. And ignored him.

'You think me infuriating,' he said with unnerving accuracy.

'I didn't say so.'

'You didn't have to. And you think that I make promises I won't keep.'

'No.'

A cynical eyebrow raised.

'Very well, yes.'

His eyes did not leave her face and a sensual tone crept into his voice. 'I always keep my promises, Kathryn.'

Her blood tingled.

Anticipation grew in the punctuating silence.

'It seems that you have much to learn of me.'

Kathryn's heart thudded in her chest. Blood surged through her veins, visibly throbbing at the pulse-point in her neck. 'Lest you had forgotten, Lord Ravensmede, I'm companion to your grandmother. There is no need for us to know anything of each other.'

He did not appear in the least discomposed, just stayed leaning back against the seat with his legs stretched out before him. 'On the contrary, I care for my grandmother, and, as such, it's only natural that I take an interest in her health, in her life and…in any companion that she may have. Indeed, I would be failing in my duty if I did not undertake a thorough appraisal of your character, Miss Marchant.'

Her cheeks scorched scarlet. 'I do not think that is necessary, my lord.'

'Oh, but I assure you that it is. I am most determined to know you.' The words were low and mellow, scarcely audible over the rumble of the wheels and the passing shouts from the street.

She faced him defiantly. 'I do not care for the turn this conversation is taking, sir.'

He shrugged his shoulders as if to say that her consideration did not matter.

The balance of Kathryn's temper tipped. With one hand gripping the travelling strap, she reached up and banged twice upon the carriage roof. 'Stop!' she shouted loud enough for the coachman to hear. Her fingers tugged at the window. Her head whipped round in Ravensmede's direction. 'I'll walk the rest of the way.'

The carriage showed no sign of slowing.

'Perdition, Kathryn! Are you trying to kill yourself?' He grabbed at her hands, pulling them away from the glass. The carriage bounced over some bumps. She staggered, striving to keep her balance, and toppled over straight on to Ravensmede's knee.

'Dear Lord!' she gasped and tried to escape. But Ravensmede's arms had already closed around her. 'Unhand me at once!'

'And let you fall out of a moving carriage? I do not think so, Kathryn.'

'I was going to wait for it to stop,' she said with indignation.

'Really?' he said drolly.

'I refuse to stay in here a moment longer with you!'

No reply, just that nearly smile upon his face.

'Lord Ravensmede!' she gasped.

'Miss Marchant,' he replied.

He held her gently but firmly throughout her struggles until at last she realised their futility and relaxed against the hard muscle of his body. Still his arms wound around her, barring any route of possible escape. His clean scent of bergamot surrounded her and she was growing increasingly aware of the muscular thighs on which she was sitting and the tautness of his stomach and chest hugging the contours of her back. The pulse still leapt in her throat, throbbing with a speed that made her ragged breathing seem slow in comparison. It was no longer anger that drove her reactions, but something quite different, something that she most definitely should not feel.

He was a rake! He would take what he could, and cast her aside. To a man like Ravensmede she was easy prey, a nothing, a nobody. If his grandmother found out, then Kathryn knew that she would lose her new home and position…not to mention her reputation. And then where would she be? The thought gave her the strength she needed. Quite suddenly she pulled away from him and attempted to break free. At first she thought she would succeed. It seemed her stillness had lulled him into a false sense of security. But even as her body made to rise the large arms clamped her back down. The breath shuddered in her throat.

'Keep still, Kathryn. I would not have you hurt yourself.'

The words were so close as to tickle her ear. The sensation shuddered down through her core. Whatever she knew of Nicholas Maybury, it was not enough to still her traitorous body's response. She could have cried aloud. Instead, she forced herself to calmness, letting the seconds become minutes. When at last she had some semblance of control she spoke. 'Lord Ravensmede, you may release me now. I give you my word that I won't try to leave the carriage.'

Only the sound of his breath whispered past her ear.

'My lord?'

He did not speak. Slowly his arms relaxed and opened in a gesture of release.

Kathryn knew she should leap across to the opposite seat, but she stayed quite still, only swung her legs round to the side and moved her head so that she might look into his face. His gaze was trained on her, glittering with a force that made the breath catch in her throat. For in those eyes, those alluring green eyes, was a look of such tenderness as to shatter every belief Kathryn had of the man. A large hand moved to cup the back of her head, his fingers untied the ribbons of her bonnet and, casting it aside, threaded into the silkiness of her hair. She knew what he was going to do and still she did nothing to stop him.

With calm deliberation he manoeuvred her until their lips met. And in their caress was the escalation of passionate need. His mouth moved with slow sensuality, sliding and sucking, coaxing and nipping, until she found her lips lapping against his, giving as much as receiving. Just when she thought she was melting in the heat of his embrace she felt the tantalising tease of his tongue, sliding against her lips, invading her mouth, seeking her own. Tongue touched tongue in warm and moist intimacy.

A long low groan issued deep in his throat and his hands moved to stroke her back, sweeping down to cover the swell of her hip, pulling her closer against him. Breast against breast. Even through the layers of clothing that separated their two bodies Kathryn felt the strong steady beat of his heart. Her skin warmed and blossomed against his until there was an aching tightness in her breasts. Not knowing what she did, she rose against him, arching instinctively until their hardened peaks thrust against the firm muscle of his chest. His roughened jawline rasped at the scorch marks left by his lips.

'Kathryn!' The whisper was a shuddering caress, full of desire. His fingers wove their magic through the muslin of her dress, sliding round to move against the flatness of her stomach, and up, further, until they reached their goal. He groaned again, a low guttural sound. 'God, but you're beautiful.'

She touched her lips to his.

The coach ground to a halt. The thump of footsteps sounded and, not a moment after Kathryn found herself dumped unceremoniously on to the opposite seat, the door swung open. Ravensmede House loomed large in the background. A footman positioned the steps and stood back to await his lordship's descent.

The green eyes raised to hers. 'Kathryn…'

She didn't wait to hear the words. She didn't need to. Before Ravensmede could stop her she had clambered out of the carriage and was fleeing up the stone stairs to the front door.

Chapter Seven

If Lady Maybury noticed that her new companion's colour was rather high, or that the girl's lips were swollen from being thoroughly kissed, she kept such observations to herself. There was much work to be done with organising the packing and arrangement of her ladyship's luggage for the move to Upper Grosvenor Street. And the dowager seemed to be in a rather cantankerous mood with everyone except Kathryn. It was somewhat surprising that the lady's favourite grandson was also being included under this edict. The dowager's disposition had not improved by the time both she and Miss Marchant came to take their leave of the Viscount.

'Nicholas.' Lady Maybury presented a small withered hand to be kissed. 'You may call upon me next week and not before. I will be busy ensuring that all is in order and have no desire for a distraction. Do I make myself clear?' A rather chilly focus fixed itself upon her grandson.

Ravensmede was not indifferent to his grandmother's mood, but, not trusting exactly what that perceptive gaze of hers had fathomed, he did not enquire as to its cause. 'Perfectly clear, Grandmama. Never fear, I shall not disturb you before the appointed time.' He pressed a kiss to the papery hand and moved to face Miss Marchant, who to all intent and purpose was attempting to hide herself behind the tiny frame of his grandmother. 'Miss Marchant,' he said politely, 'I trust that you have found your stay to be comfortable?'

'Yes, thank you, my lord.' There was nothing in her manner to suggest that all was not as it should be, apart from the slight tremor in her fingers when he pressed them briefly to his lips. Ravensmede felt it keenly, but could do nothing as she withdrew her hand and stepped away.

He suffered the baleful stare of a faded green eye and then the two women were walking down the steps to the heavily laden carriage and the journey that would remove them from the house in Berkeley Square. The door closed with a thump, leaving Ravensmede alone, save for the creeping sense of loss.

'Heard Lady Maybury has taken li'l Miss Marchant on as her companion. Rather convenient for you, I'd say.' If Lord Cadmount lounged any lower in the chair he would be in danger of slipping out of it. The brandy glass balanced delicately on one thigh as he gave his friend a knowing wink.

Ravensmede grunted and loosened the neckcloth that his valet had spent twenty minutes in tying. 'Then you'd be wrong.'

The pale eyebrows raised as high as they could. 'How so? Could it be that you've already bedded her and found her not to your taste?'

A dry laugh. 'Hell, Caddie! You know that I haven't.' The memory of her slender body pressed against his, the softness of those pink lips, the sweetness of her tentative response, intruded all too readily. He felt a stirring in his lower regions and clamped it down with frustrated determination. A gulp of brandy warmed his throat before he continued. 'As my grandmother's companion, she should be safe from any such speculation.' He made no mention of the vile family from whom Kathryn was also now safe.

'Not quite,' argued his friend. 'There's always room for that wherever the woman is placed.'

'Not when my grandmother is involved,' replied Ravensmede.

'I agree that Lady Maybury would make a most formidable foe.' Cadmount sipped his drink and mulled his thoughts. 'Strange that Henry Marchant never looked to make a marriage for the girl. I know she's no schoolroom miss, but neither has she reached her dotage. Must have been keen to keep her in the bosom of his family. A charitable chap, wouldn't you say?'

Ravensmede's eyes darkened. 'Hardly that. Marchant lacks a backbone; he does little more than dance to his wife's tune. A less charitable couple I've yet to meet.' Something of the darkness lifted from his mood. 'Neither was their home a suitable place for a woman like Miss Marchant.'

Cadmount smiled. 'Ah,' he said softly. 'I think I begin to understand.'

The green eyes raised to his. One corner of his mouth flickered up. 'I doubt very much that you do, my dear Caddie.'

'And therein lies the rub.' A finger stroked thoughtfully at his chin. 'You still want her.' It was a statement rather than a question.

Ravensmede did not deny it. 'She's my grandmother's companion now, and even if she wasn't…'

'It would take a rake of the lowest order to seduce a woman who lost her mother and sister and found her father with half his head blown off.'

'Hell, I didn't realise that Kathryn saw her father after he shot himself.' Ravensmede's brows drew together.

'The chit found him all right. Couldn't have been a pretty sight. Had an interesting chat with Bertie Devon. He remembers the whole thing.'

'No woman should have to suffer that.'

Cadmount paused, then asked in a stolid tone, 'Do you mean to seduce her?'

Ravensmede blew a languid sigh. Seduce her? He had come damn near to doing so a week ago in his carriage. He gave Cadmount a cynical look. 'Do you think that I will?'

'I honestly don't know.'

A wry smile. 'My grandmother will take good care of her. She'll be safe there.' Safe from Anna Marchant, but was she truly safe from him?

Cadmount leaned over the chair and, catching his somewhat wrinkled coat up from the floor, set about rummaging in the pockets. 'Strikes me that the girl brings out the protective streak in you.'

Ravensmede crooked an eyebrow. 'Too much brandy, Caddie. Your imaginings run wild. Next you'll have me attending lectures by the Humane Society.'

'Now that would be something worth seeing.' Cadmount laughed. 'Are you telling me that you have no care for Miss Marchant?'

'I'm saying that the woman's suffered enough. She deserves to have some little happiness.'

The two men looked at one another.

'Undoubtedly we need another drink.' The Viscount walked without a hint of unsteadiness to retrieve the decanter.

'Won't help, old man.' Lord Cadmount shook his head sagely. 'Happens to us all sooner or later.'

Ravensmede rubbed at the darkening shadow of stubble on his chin as he refilled their glasses. 'Enlighten me.'

The finely painted miniature box nestled on Cadmount's palm as he regarded it with a knowing expression. 'Love.'

'You're most definitely foxed, Caddie.'

'Indeed I am,' said his friend, helping himself to a generous helping of snuff. 'But it doesn't mean I'm not right. Fancy a pinch?' The box was dangled enticingly towards Ravensmede.

'Why not?' He helped himself to some snuff and snapped the lid shut again.

Golden flames leapt high in the hearth, causing the logs to crackle and spit. The two men sat in comfortable silence, Cadmount knowing when he had pushed far enough, Ravensmede brooding on the growing fascination that he felt for Kathryn Marchant.

'Read me the last verse again,' Lady Maybury instructed.

Kathryn glanced up at the dowager's smiling countenance and then, lowering her eyes once more to the book, began to read.

> Whate'er the theme, the Maiden sang
> As if her song could have no ending;
> I saw her singing at her work,
> And o'er the sickle bending—
> I listened, motionless and still;
> And, as I mounted up the hill,
> The music in my heart I bore,
> Long after it was heard no more.

'No poet is quite as lyrical as Mr Wordsworth, and no lady reads poetry quite so well as you, my dear gel. You have a wonderful voice.'

Kathryn blushed at Lady Maybury's generous praise and

lowered the book to her lap. 'Thank you, my lady. My father always liked to hear my sister and me reading, and we did so most nights in the parlour. Poems, essays, novels, anything would do, even the newspaper. Papa would listen as if he had never heard anything so interesting in all the day.' She paused and smiled, before adding quietly, 'They're happy memories.' She did not think of the bad ones.

'And did you read to your aunt and uncle when you came to London?' the old lady asked.

The rich brown curls swayed as she slowly shook her head. 'Oh, no, Uncle Henry reads the *Morning Post* and Aunt Anna does not much care for reading at all.'

'And the cousin? What did you say her name was—Lettie?' The ancient tone had sharpened imperceptibly.

'Lottie. I'm afraid my cousin finds reading rather irksome. She's of a more musical disposition, being very fond of singing and with a voice that's lovely to hear.' Kathryn carefully turned the page in the book nestled upon her lap. 'Indeed, my aunt is holding a musical evening very soon at which Lottie will be singing to Mr Dalton's piano accompaniment. Lottie has been practising for weeks.'

Lady Maybury showed not the slightest interest. 'I've just remembered our appointment with Madame Dupont. Come, we had best ready ourselves. She's rather high in the instep for a dressmaker, but I've never patronised anyone else in the last thirty years. Her designs are very much to my liking.'

Thus it was that, precisely two hours later, Kathryn and Lady Maybury came to be sitting within the tiny backroom of Madame Dupont's elegant establishment in highly fashionable Bond Street.

'But, my lady, it is such a colour as to bring out the fire in your eyes. A dark green silk will make the gown, damask is not at all right for this style.' The tall thin woman with the severe white chignon spoke passionately in an accent that still held the lilt of her Gallic origins. 'Most definitely *non!*' She shook her head defiantly.

For the first time since their meeting Kathryn saw Lady Maybury capitulate. 'Very well, Marie. I'll allow you to have your way in this one respect. A small turban in green and black should go very well, don't you think?'

'Indeed, my lady, very well indeed. And I shall add a few small ebony plumes as the finishing touch, yes?'

'Yes. Now that's enough for me at present, Marie. My companion Miss Marchant requires an evening dress for the same event. And we had better have a couple of afternoon dresses and another evening dress while we're at it.' Lady Maybury's small veined hand was pushing Kathryn forward in no uncertain terms.

Her companion, on the other hand, had very different ideas. 'My lady, it's really not necessary, I have a very serviceable evening gown and several other dresses too. I must insist that there is no need for anything more.' Kathryn thought of the few outmoded shabby dresses that had arrived in her old trunk from Green Street. She thought too of the six shillings hidden at the bottom of the trunk, next to the small battered bible that had belonged to her mother. The sum of her worldly savings would not suffice to pay for one of Madame Dupont's gowns, let alone four. 'Thank you for thinking of me,' she added hastily lest Lady Maybury think her rude.

The dressmaker's dark eyes swung back to the dowager.

'Kathryn,' Lady Maybury began, and Kathryn recognised it as her most autocratic tone. 'It is in the role of my companion that you require several new items of clothing. The choice is mine as is the reckoning of the account.' There was definitely more than a hint of the same imperious tone Kathryn had witnessed in the old lady's grandson.

Kathryn's cheeks flushed at the barely veiled implication. Lady Maybury did not care to be seen in the company of someone dressed so poorly. It was also evident that the dowager knew something of her companion's meagre means and thus felt compelled to pay for the clothing. Kathryn could not dispute that her dresses were probably of a state to cause her employer some degree of embarrassment, but she was also very aware of the pride that was lodged stubbornly in her throat. 'Thank you, my lady, but, kind as your offer is, you must know that I cannot possibly accept it. I will pay for the dresses myself.' The defiant little chin thrust up as she waited for Lady Maybury's reaction.

'Very well, my dear. It seems that you have your mind set over the matter.'

With a calm demeanour Kathryn nodded her gratitude and turned to face the dressmaker. She would worry over how to obtain the money later, when she knew the full sum owing.

If Lady Maybury felt any irritation towards her companion's insistence she hid it well and thus, at the end of the afternoon, they finally departed Madame Dupont's on very good terms with the promise of two completed evening gowns for the following week, and the rest to follow later.

The days passed with an easiness and speed that Kathryn had not experienced for many a year. Life with Lady Maybury was pleasant indeed. The old lady could be demanding in the extreme, but she was also kind, interesting and in possession of a rather wicked sense of humour, as her companion quickly discovered. Even Lord Ravensmede's visits to his grandparent failed to blight Kathryn's growing happiness. From the time of his arrival until his eventual departure she kept herself busily employed in tasks well away from the drawing room where Lady Maybury entertained. There was, after all, no point is jeopardising the harmonious existence into which she had fallen within the dowager's rented townhouse.

As Kathryn found contentment in her new life, her daydreaming diminished. There were still times when, in her mind, she was the sole recipient of a certain nobleman's heart—a nobleman who did not want her as his mistress, but as his wife and the mother of his children. But this time, she kept the tall, handsome Viscount strictly confined to her dreams. Kathryn had learned her lesson well. Neither Lord Ravensmede, nor anyone else for that matter, would be allowed to ruin the chance she now had for happiness.

Warm golden sunlight spilled across the deep rosewood table in the parlour of the house in Green Street, highlighting a patch of dust that had escaped the maid's cloth and beeswax. Under ordinary circumstances such an omission would have been enough to earn the poor girl a clout round the ear and a thorough tongue lashing from the lady of the house. But, fortunately for the maid, matters within the Marchant household that afternoon were anything but ordinary. For Anna Marchant, sitting alone and bolt upright in the comfortable armchair beside the unlit fireplace, was reading the contents of a letter that had just been delivered by the letter carrier. A small gasp erupted into the emptiness of the room. The colour drained from her complexion. Her mouth gaped liked a landed fish. 'No!' she whispered aloud. 'It cannot be...' She smoothed the paper out upon her lap and then, grasping the sheet so tightly that her nails dug into her palms, made to read the small, neatly formed script once more.

> 26 May 1815
> Amersham
> Buckinghamshire
>
> Dear Mrs Marchant
>
> I beg that you will forgive the nature of the tidings that I write to impart, but I have just heard such news that renders me, in good conscience, unable to remain silent.
>
> I was very pleased to make your acquaintance at Lady Finlay's recent ball, and I do not think that I was mistaken in finding that you are a lady of impeccable taste and judgement. However, word has just reached me here at my sister's residence that your niece, Miss Kathryn Marchant, has accepted the offer of a position as the dowager Lady Maybury's companion. As you will be well aware, Lady Maybury is the grandmother of the Viscount of Ravensmede, a nobleman of renowned repute. For reasons that I dare not put into writing, my dear Mrs Marchant, I am compelled to warn you against allowing your niece to take up Lady Maybury's offer. Suffice to say, I have evidence that, were it to become public knowledge, would most certainly jeopardise her reputation. I fear that Kathryn is not of the same genteel mould as you and your sweet daughter Lottie, but of that I will say no more lest this letter falls into the wrong hands and risks your family's embarrassment. It is unfortunate that I am forced to remain here in the country for a few days longer on account of my sister's confinement, but I assure you that I will re-

turn to London with haste and call upon you as soon as is possible.

With all good intentions
Your friend
Amanda White

By the time Mrs Marchant finished reading her mouth was quite dry and her heart rate had kicked to a canter. What on earth had that little bitch Kathryn been up to? Making a fool of the family that had saved her from destitution on the streets, if Amanda White's insinuations were to be believed. Mrs Marchant folded the letter up and went to hide it in a safe place, all the while musing on why she disliked Kathryn so very much. The deed was done: Kathryn was already installed in the dowager's house in Upper Grosvenor Street. Nothing in Mrs White's letter could undo that, not without serving the entire Marchant family up to the gossipmongers. And that was something that could not be risked. A sneer contorted her mouth, and her eyes were filled with spite. Anna Marchant had no intention of meekly awaiting the return of the widow to discover just what was going on with Kathryn, no intention at all.

Kathryn stared at her reflection in disbelief. She tried to speak, her mouth even shaped to say the words, but none were forthcoming. Her delicately shaped eyebrows rose and fell expressively and when still she could not speak she whirled around and in three steps had gathered Lady Maybury into a spontaneous embrace.

'I take it you're pleased with Madame Dupont's creation!' chuckled the old lady.

Kathryn finally found her tongue. 'Indeed, my lady, it's

quite the most beautiful dress I've ever seen. When I look in the mirror I see a stranger looking back at me. I'm nothing like myself!' A slender hand patted the dowager's arm once more. 'Thank you for allowing me to repay your loan with such reasonable terms.' As Lady Maybury's companion she was not entitled to a wage as such, but her ladyship had insisted on giving her a generous sum, all of which would now be consumed in paying for the outfit in which she was now attired.

'You are very welcome, child.' Lady Maybury smiled. 'I do believe Marie was right when she insisted upon this colour. It complements your eyes.' Her head perched to one side in contemplation. "Yes, Kathryn, you shall do very well.' One snowy eyebrow arched, mimicking the gesture so often used by her grandson. 'Very well indeed.'

For once in her life, Kathryn Marchant thought that perhaps that might just be true. The dress was of a sheer violet silk, high-waisted and cut so that the skirt draped enticingly to the floor with the merest suggestion of the curves hidden beneath. With a low décolletage it revealed rather more of Kathryn's other assets than she was used to, but her bruises were gone; when she suggested the addition of her fichu, Lady Maybury snorted and turned a more-than-querulous eye in her direction.

'There's no need for any such thing.'

Sprinkled liberally over the bodice were the tiniest cream pearls, which led the eye down to the broad cream satin ribbon that adorned Kathryn's waist as well as the edge of her short puffed sleeves. On her hands she wore an elegant new pair of cream gloves that reached up and over her arms to past her elbows. Her neck was bare save for the few chestnut tendrils that nestled about it. The mass of her curls had been gathered up high on the back of her head and fixed in place with pins and cream-and-violet coloured ribbons. A matching cream shawl and reticule completed the elegant ensemble. Little wonder that she scarcely recognised the woman looking back at her from the dressing mirror. Suddenly aware that she had been entirely absorbed in her own appearance, Kathryn turned to the dowager, who was resplendent in the forest green silk. 'You look lovely, my lady. Madame Dupont has truly worked her magic here tonight. We shall be quite the finest dressed ladies at Lady Cooper's ball.'

'I never doubted it for a moment,' said her ladyship in reply.

The ballroom was glowing with the light of a multitude of candles balanced in four enormous crystal chandeliers. Lady Cooper's affair was proving to be quite a success judging from the mass of people squashed within the confines of her ballroom. Kathryn and Lady Maybury had been fortuitous in finding seats close by the floor-length windows, which were opened in an attempt to remedy the stifling heat. Mrs Lee and Lady Hadstone soon arrived to monopolise the dowager's attention, leaving Kathryn to watch the proceedings upon the dance floor and around its periphery. She sipped her lemonade and enjoyed her contemplation. *The oppressive heat of the ballroom vanished, the air grew cool and sweet, scented with the freshness of grass and earth and blue sky. Instead of the press of sweat-drenched bodies were spacious marble chequered floor tiles and a flood of sunlight. Across the floor stood one large figure, immaculate in full evening dress, his green eyes light like tender young leaves, smiling his heart-rending smile... for her alone.*

'Kathryn!' The dowager's hand touched to her arm, and the spell was broken.

She looked at Lady Maybury, an expression of guilt blazoned across her face. 'I do beg your pardon, my lady. I'm afraid my thoughts had wandered a little.'

But the dowager's focus had shifted and was fixed quite firmly on someone else, someone that stood directly before Kathryn, someone of whom Kathryn was becoming rapidly aware.

'Miss Marchant,' he said. The deep melodic tone teased a shiver down her spine. 'A pleasure to see you again.' His bow was superbly executed.

'Lord Ravensmede.' She made her devoirs and tried to ignore the warmth that had suddenly pervaded her cheeks. *Distant and polite, stay distant and polite at all times*, she reminded herself. But it did not slow the thrumming of her heart or the acrobatic antics of the butterflies massing in her stomach.

He was dressed as if he had stepped straight out of her daydream: a finely tailored black coat worn with pale pantaloons that clung rather revealingly to his long muscular thighs. Well-shaped calves and ankles were encased in white stockings, leading down to a pair of highly polished black buckle slippers. A white satin waistcoat overlaid a snow-white shirt and neckcloth, beneath which it was clear that there had been no need for padding of any description. Nicholas Maybury was indeed a man of impressive physique. He turned to his grandmother and smiled. 'I trust this evening finds you in good health?'

'Never better, my boy. I have the constitution of an ox, as well you know.' Aside to her cronies she added, 'He's ever hopeful that I will shuffle off this mortal coil, but I do not intend to accommodate him for quite some time.'

Kathryn listened to the conversation continue for some little time, with Ravensmede politely exchanging small talk with all three elderly ladies. Notably he did not attempt the same with her. Indeed, his neglect was rather marked. Two strangers in a ballroom. Their kisses had never been. Respectable. The Viscount and his grandmother's companion—a class apart. It was what she wanted, after all, so why did it bring a heaviness to her heart? And then, at last, Lord Ravensmede's attention was upon her, and it was as if they were the only two people there.

His eyes met hers.

Her heart skipped a beat. It was her dream becoming a reality. She wetted her suddenly dry lips. Tried to shake off the enchantment in danger of overcoming her. Knew that she was staring at him in a highly inappropriate fashion. None of it made any difference. Kathryn glanced around, looking for a way to extricate herself from such temptation.

'Miss Marchant,' he said, and her name sounded like a caress upon his lips.

His lips... Her eyes were on them, tracing their outline. Firm, chiselled, with a hint of sensual fullness. Lips that had kissed her with such expertise. Her own mouth parted at the memory. Anticipation fluttered in her stomach. The breath trembled within her throat. She swallowed hard. Fought to regain some semblance of self-control. 'Lord Ravensmede.' How could she sound so calm, so unaffected, when she wanted so desperately to feel the press of his mouth against hers, the strength of his arms around her?

'The next dance is the waltz. I understand it to be a favourite of yours.' He did not appear to be in the grip of any such torrent of emotion. But there was something in his gaze that made the hairs on the back of her neck stand upright.

Kathryn's cheeks warmed. 'I…um…that is…' Her fingers slid to twist at the violet silk of her skirt. 'I do not think that…'

A corner of his mouth twitched. 'Grandmama, may I borrow Miss Marchant for the next dance? I promise to return her safely and I'm sure that these two beautiful ladies…' he turned the full force of his rakish good looks upon Lady Hadstone and Mrs Lee '…will engage you in such interesting and witty conversation that you shall not note her absence.'

Lady Hadstone and Mrs Lee giggled girlishly and fanned themselves with fervour.

Lady Maybury knew better. The tone of her voice was harsh, but the look in her eye was one of endearment. 'Why the blazes should I object?' And she turned her attention back to her friends.

Ravensmede smiled at that, then faced Kathryn again. 'Miss Marchant, would you do me the honour of partnering me for the waltz?' His eyes lingered at her lips before rising to meet her gaze.

Her throat was in danger of sticking together. The pulse at the side of her neck throbbed wildly. She prayed fervently that it would not show. 'Thank you, Lord Ravensmede,' she uttered weakly. From the corner of her eye she could see Mrs Lee and Lady Hadstone positively agog. For the sake of good manners she could not refuse him, and neither did she want to. 'I would be delighted.' And in her heart she knew it was the truth.

A large hand extended, closed around hers and tucked it securely into his arm. He did not speak until the music started and they were gliding effortlessly around the room. 'Are you happy with my grandmother?'

Her lashes swept up and she regarded him with surprise

that he could ask such a question. 'Of course, my lord. Lady Maybury is very kind to me.' He smelled of soap and bergamot and something else that was uniquely him.

'It seems you have a short memory, Kathryn.'

She swallowed hard, aware that she remembered all too well a moonlit room and the dimmed interior of a coach. 'I don't know to what you are referring, sir.'

His eyes glinted with emerald lights. 'My lord? Sir? I think we know each other rather better than that would suggest.'

Her cheeks grew hotter. Did he know what he was doing to her? From the look on his face, most probably so. 'On the contrary, Lord Ravensmede, I'm companion to your grandmother. Any other mode of address would be quite inappropriate.' Despite the traitorous reaction of her body to his proximity, she was determined not to let her mask of polite indifference slip. Such a path was the rocky descent to ruin, nothing more.

'Do you deny then, *Miss Marchant*—' he stressed the use of her formal address '—that which has passed between us on two separate occasions?' His eyes held hers with an intimacy to which he had no right.

She bit uneasily at her lower lip, unsure of where his words were leading.

'Surely you do not forget that as well? Shall I remind you of the kisses that we've shared?' he teased.

She gasped and glanced self-consciously around. 'Ssh! Someone might hear you!'

'Then you do remember, after all.'

'Of course I remember,' she snapped. 'I'm unlikely ever to forget!'

'Why? Do my kisses affect you like no other's?' Ravensmede laughed.

She could do nothing to prevent the intensifying rosy stain that scalded the fairness of her skin.

'Your face betrays you, Kathryn.' And for some reason he looked extraordinarily pleased about it.

'You are no gentleman to say such things!' she said, afraid of what she had revealed.

'I assure you, Kathryn, I'm no gentleman at all.' A wicked twinkle set in the green eyes. 'But that is something of which you are, no doubt, already aware.'

'Lord Ravens—'

A dark eyebrow arched. 'Tut tut, Kathryn, what must I do to make you use my given name?' His gaze dropped pointedly to her lips.

'Nicholas!' the whisper ejected with alacrity.

He smiled. 'Much better. So now that we've sorted one small problem, let us deal with another. Why have you been avoiding me?'

Her denial was too quick. 'You're mistaken.' The chestnut tendrils cascading around her neck shook. She was not wanton. No matter the strength of his left hand surrounding hers, or the undeniable heat that emanated from the touch of his right against her waist. No matter that she quivered with the hope that he would kiss her, as he had before. She must strive to show him that he erred in his opinion.

'I've visited my grandmother on five occasions and not once have you been present. Do you mean to tell me that she sent you away when she knew I had arrived?'

'No. I was simply engaged with other chores.'

'I've told you before, Kathryn Marchant, you make a poor liar.'

Her eyes met his at the shared memory of the last time he had uttered those words.

His hand tightened upon her waist.

She trembled beneath it.

'I owe you an apology, Kathryn. That day in the carriage, I should not have taken advantage of you. Forgive me.' The edge of his thumb delicately caressed her fingers.

Right at this moment in time she would have forgiven him anything. 'I was not entirely blameless in the situation,' she admitted. 'I should not have…' She glanced away. 'I ought not to have…' Was there any polite way of saying what had to be said? Silver eyes met smouldering green once more. 'You know very well what I'm trying to say, Nicholas.'

A knowing smile was her only answer.

She cleared her throat nervously. 'No such thing must happen again. I'm Lady Maybury's companion, and even if that were not the case…' Anxiety widened her eyes. 'I would not have you think me anything other than respectable.' There, she had said it.

The music filled the silence between them.

'I do not think anything else,' he said, and a strange expression came over his face. 'And as you rightly said, you're my grandmother's companion. Do you think that I would do anything to dishonour her?'

'No.' It was the truth. There seemed to be a genuine bond of affection between the Viscount and his grandparent.

He was still looking at her in that peculiar way. 'Are you truly so averse to my company, Kathryn?'

She sighed. The lie refused to form upon her lips. 'I'm averse to any impropriety that might blight my reputation. My good name is all that I have left.'

'I do not seek to damage it,' he said softly.

She should treat him with the cool distance that propriety demanded, but she could not. 'If we are agreed that no such thing should happen again between us, then there is no reason that we cannot be friends.'

'Friends?' He rolled the word around his tongue in careful consideration. It would certainly be a novelty. 'Friends do not avoid one another, Kathryn.'

'No, they do not,' she said quietly.

'Well, in that case…' the side of his mouth quirked '…we shall be friends.'

The last bars of 'Ach! Du lieber Augustine' sounded in the ballroom.

Kathryn had no opportunity to speak further with Lord Ravensmede that evening. It seemed that his taking her on to the floor had acted as a signal as to her availability as a dancing partner, for no sooner had she taken her seat once more than she was approached by first one young man and then another. She tried to decline as politely as possible, knowing that she was present only in the capacity of a companion, but Lady Maybury was having none of it and, at her insistence, Kathryn was forced to accept each and every one of the flood of dance invitations. While partnering Captain Brent for the quadrille she became aware of Lord Ravensmede's scrutiny and during the Scottish reel with Mr Parket she saw that he had stood up with an elegant young blonde lady. After that he disappeared and Kathryn focused her attentions on remembering her dance steps.

Chapter Eight

Ravensmede carelessly dropped the neckcloth on to the chair and massaged the knot of tension at the back of his neck that had been growing all night since witnessing Kathryn in the arms of another man, or several other men to be precise. He sighed and loosened his shirt, glad that he had instructed his valet not to wait up. The night was still young, certainly for someone of the Viscount's lifestyle, but he had no inclination to attend his club, and still less to visit Millicent Miller. He wondered whether he had been a trifle hasty in paying his latest mistress off. He paced around the bedchamber, restless, discontented. Each time he closed his eyes an image appeared—Kathryn smiling at someone, and that someone wasn't him. Little wonder he'd been forced to leave early. He poured himself another large and aromatic brandy and lay back still clothed upon the bed.

Perhaps Millicent was exactly what he needed. A pretty face and willing body to ease his frustration. But the thought went no further. The need that gnawed at him was specific, and he was quite sure that only one woman could remedy it. He had no notion for any of the women that had served as his mistresses. Indeed, he had no notion for anyone or anything other than his grandmother's companion; a woman whom life had treated harshly, who, until he had quite literally stumbled upon her at Lady Finlay's ball with that dreadful blonde cousin, had battled alone through life's trials. The thought of what she had witnessed after her father's suicide, and, worse still, at the hands of the woman who called herself her aunt, nipped at Ravensmede. Yet Kathryn had endured and refused to be either cowed or embittered by her experiences.

Perdition, but she was beautiful. He had known it from the first, when she was hidden behind that monstrosity of a grey garment that passed for a dress. His grandmother's influence had unmasked Kathryn's real beauty for all to see. She was not pretty in the mundane sense of the *ton*. Rather her eyes had a silver sparkle, and that smile... He had scarcely been able to draw his eyes away from the sight of Kathryn, encased in the violet evening dress that emphasised the gentle curves of her figure.

And when he'd first approached her, only to find her with that faraway look in her eyes, he wanted nothing other than to pull her into his arms and kiss that delectable mouth that moved so readily to laughter. It had nigh on been his undoing, causing as it did certain physical reactions that were hardly appropriate at a society ball, least of all in front of his own grandmother. He'd been forced to concentrate his attentions on his grandam's cronies in the hope of preventing what could have been an embarrassing situation for them all.

His fingers raked the dark ruffle of his hair. What was this obsession he felt for Kathryn? A desire to bed her, and yet he recoiled from treating her in such a despicable way. He was growing soft. Never once in all the years of playing the rake had he suffered such a revelation of conscience. And all because he'd developed a fancy for his grandmother's companion. Truth to be told, much more than a fancy.

It was time he took himself in hand. She was just a woman, like any other. The brandy trickled down his throat, soothing the edge from his emptiness. A smile crooked across his face. Yes, Kathryn Marchant was definitely all woman, but she was nothing like any of the others. Maybe, just maybe, Kathryn had already offered him the solution to his problem. It was almost as if he heard again the soft whisper of her words within his bedchamber, *there is no reason that we cannot be friends*.

Slowly and carefully he placed the empty glass upon the bedside table, stripped off the remainder of his clothes and crawled beneath the covers. For the first time in ten years Ravensmede was sound asleep before the clock struck midnight.

The sunshine flooded the breakfast room, basking both Kathryn and Lady Maybury in its golden light. Her ladyship was devouring a plate of chops, her appetite being disproportionately large for so small and frail a person. Her companion was satisfied with a mere egg on toast. Behind Kathryn's plate was propped *The Times*, from which she was reading aloud the announcements, between mouthfuls of breakfast.

'Lord Barclay has the common sense of a flea. Engaged to Wilhelmina Turbet? Mark my words, the girl will bore him rigid in less than a month. Just like her mother—nothing between the ears, I'm afraid.' Lady Maybury helped herself to yet another slice of toast.

Kathryn poked an errant curl behind her ear and smiled mischievously. 'But I thought that's precisely what a gentleman demanded of his wife. Did not Lady Hadstone say there's nothing less attractive than a clever woman?'

'Ho!' screeched her ladyship at the top of her voice. 'Amelia's three daughters couldn't hold a single thought in their heads between them. She's not likely to say anything else! Fortunately for her, their dowries were large. Had them off her hands in no time, even though they each had the brain of a small carp, and the face to match.'

The two ladies were laughing at Lady Maybury's scathing observation when the footman entered to announce the Viscount of Ravensmede, followed closely by the man himself.

'Grandmama, Miss Marchant.' He gave a nonchalant bow. 'Forgive the early hour of my call. I wished to catch you before you made arrangements for the day.'

'Nick,' murmured the dowager with pleasure. 'Come and join us for a spot of breakfast.' She indicated the empty seat to her right-hand side and rammed another mouthful of pork into her mouth. 'I'm sure Miss Marchant will not object.'

Kathryn smiled at both grandmother and grandson. 'Of course not.'

Lord Ravensmede helped himself to a little toast and some coffee.

'What's wrong with you, boy?' The dowager's brow wrinkled. 'Picking at your food like a sparrow. Are you sickening for something?'

Ravensmede took his grandparent's jibes with good nature. 'I've already broken my fast. I'm merely accommodating your hospitality, ma'am.'

Lady Maybury grunted, but the faded green eyes remained unconvinced.

'Have you made plans for today?' Ravensmede sipped his coffee, but abandoned the half-eaten toast.

'Apart from attending the Opera House tonight, we are as yet undecided.'

'Then perhaps you'll allow me to accompany you on a visit to the exhibition of the Society of Painters in Oil and Watercolours. From there we could travel to the British Museum.' His gaze flitted from his grandmother to her companion.

The old lady smiled, a fiery light appearing in her eyes. 'What do you say, Kathryn? Shall we attend?'

Kathryn could barely conceal her surprise in being asked. 'My lady, I'm happy to abide by whatever you should decide,' she said with the utmost diplomacy.

'Don't flannel me, gel! Do you want to go or don't you? It's a simple enough question.'

The heat rose in Kathryn's face, creating two small spots of colour. 'I would very much like to see the paintings.' With calm deliberation she folded the newspaper over and laid it on the table.

'Good,' announced the dowager, and then said to her grandson, 'Come back in an hour, we shall be ready then. Haven't had time to finish m'breakfast,' she grumbled. 'Blasted interruptions aren't good for the digestion. Off with you, then!' And the formidable little lady held her cheek up for Lord Ravensmede's kiss before shooing him from the room.

It was very different from the last journey she had made in this same carriage. Kathryn drew her mind carefully away from that avenue of thought. Seated beside Lady Maybury with a well-behaved Lord Ravensmede opposite, things could not have been more dissimilar. Despite the warmth of the fine summer day and the firmly closed windows, Lady Maybury insisted on being covered with the vast expanse of her favourite travelling rug. Its woollen folds overlapped on to Kathryn's legs, making her feel hot and sticky before they'd even arrived at Spring Gardens. She still wore the shabby blue muslin gown as her new afternoon dresses were yet to be delivered; a fact for which she was grateful, given the coolness of the simple material. Fortunately Lady Maybury had not demanded that her companion wear a spencer, although the mud-brown bonnet was an absolute necessity. They arrived at the exhibition while it was still relatively quiet and so were able to enjoy an unimpeded appreciation of the fine collection of water-colour and oil paintings.

'I simply must sit and have a closer look at these paintings,' said her ladyship, seating herself on one of the green-and-pink painted benches within the gallery.

Kathryn touched a hand to the dowager's arm. 'Are you quite well?'

A snort of disgust greeted her concern. 'You're getting as bad as m'grandson, miss. Can't I enjoy the merits of Mr Fielding's work without those around me becoming fixated on m'health?'

'I beg your pardon, my lady, I didn't mean to—'

'No one ever does, it is—' said the dowager with mounting exasperation.

Ravensmede's voice interrupted smoothly. 'Grandmama, allow me to suggest that I accompany Miss Marchant around the room, while you view Mr Fielding's paintings in more detail.'

Kathryn looked rather uneasily towards Lord Ravensmede. 'I—'

The old lady did not shift her gaze from the paintings on the wall before her. 'Very well, Nick.' And then, as if remembering Kathryn, she turned her head and mumbled, 'Go ahead, gel.'

Without further ado Kathryn felt her hand being tucked

into the Viscount's arm, and then she was quite literally whisked to the other side of the expansive airy room.

His voice was deep and mellow, laced with a hint of amusement. 'Please do forgive my grandmother, Miss Marchant. I'm sure she didn't mean to be so...forthright in her opinion.' Given that they were in such a very public place, he released her arm and stood back to consider the painting before them.

'Your grandmother is honest and always speaks her mind. It's a trait that I much admire,' she said in stout defence of her employer, and stepped likewise to view the same work. With her head perched to one side she studied Mr Robson's watercolour showing a rather sombre scene of a castle on a rock. 'Mmm, it's a very atmospheric scene,' she said. 'Do you like it, my lord?'

'It's well executed and undoubtedly of excellent technical expertise, but as to actually liking it...'

'Can you not feel the sheer rugged rock on which Stirling Castle is built, the bleakness of the vast view, and the humidity of the grey cloud-layered sky?'

A nearly smile hovered at his mouth. 'Enough to make me feel an inkling of gratitude that I'm here instead of there,' he said drolly.

Kathryn's eyes lit with passionate enthusiasm. 'But *there* is freedom unbounded, wildness untamed—see the mountains in the background. And *here* is something altogether different.' Her eyes met his and she smiled. 'Mr Robson has succeeded very well in showing us that. He truly is a great artist.'

'You sound as if you have a real interest in art.'

Her lips curved up in readiness. 'I know very little of the subject, but when I was younger I enjoyed painting very much.'

'And now?'

A shrug of the shoulders. 'And now I have other things to occupy my time. What of you, my lord? Do you paint or sketch?'

Ravensmede laughed. 'Not at all. Let's just say my talents lie elsewhere. But I appreciate good art, especially that depicting the sea.'

'Really?' The genuine surprise was evident in her voice. 'Seascapes are my favourite too. I remember once, many years ago, my father took us to Cornwall to visit his old friend. All those rugged sea views, it was bliss!'

They looked at Mr Robson's painting in companionable silence, each caught in their own thoughts, unaware of the other bodies that drifted by. And by the time Kathryn had been returned to Lady Maybury's side she felt quite sure that beneath the rakish exterior of Nicholas Maybury lurked another man altogether: a man who was infinitely likeable.

'I'm sorry that you didn't get to see more of the museum, Miss Marchant.' Lord Ravensmede's voice dropped in volume. 'My grandmother's constitution is not what it was.' He glanced ahead to where Lady Maybury was tottering down the pathway of Montagu House. 'Perhaps we could return another day.'

'That would be most agreeable, my lord.' Kathryn caught up with the dowager just in time to hear her cursing.

'Where the hell is the blasted carriage?'

'Edwards will be walking the horses. He shall arrive presently,' Lord Ravensmede reassured his grandmother.

'Lady Maybury, Lord Ravensmede,' said a coldly polite voice. And then added, 'And, of course, Kathryn.' Anna Marchant and her daughter stopped before the Viscount and his grandmother.

'Aunt Anna, Lottie.' Kathryn inclined her head in greeting. It had been some weeks since she'd left Green Street and in all that time she had never once set eyes again on any one of her relatives. She was surprised at just how easily their memory had been erased from her life. Now it was as if that miserable time had never been. Both Marchant women were immaculately dressed, their golden-blonde curls peeping from beneath their splendid bonnets. But the perfection of their appearance did little to hide the coolness of their eyes. 'How nice to see you both again.' It was gratifying to find that her time with Lady Maybury had not blunted Kathryn's ability to play a part well.

Unfortunately Anna Marchant was not gifted with such thespian skills. Her narrow lips pursed to a fine line across her face, and the fair eyebrows could not quite prevent their involuntary scowl. 'Indeed, dear Kathryn.'

Young Lottie's gaze was having trouble detaching from Lord Ravensmede's visage. When eventually she managed to prise it away, it flitted back and forth between the Viscount and her pauper cousin. 'We're on our way to the dressmaker. Mama has promised me a new gown for my musical evening and Mrs Thomas wants one final fitting before it will be complete.'

Mrs Marchant looked pointedly at the familiar old gown in which her niece was garbed.

A movement from the Viscount drew her attention, as he stepped forward, partially obscuring her view of Kathryn. 'How very interesting,' he uttered in a voice that would have curdled the freshest of milk.

'Dear Kathryn.' Mrs Marchant ignored him and managed to force a smile to her mouth; it did not extend anywhere near as far as her eyes. 'What good fortune that we've chanced to meet like this.'

Lottie's jaw dropped and she stared with puzzlement at her mama.

'We've missed you so, haven't we, Lottie?'

Lottie looked at her mother as if she had run mad.

'Haven't we, Lottie?' said her mother again and pressed a forceful hand to Lottie's arm.

'Yes, of course,' said Lottie.

Kathryn looked from the false geniality on her aunt's face to the perplexity on that of her cousin.

'We wanted to be sure of your attendance at Lottie's musical evening,' said Mrs Marchant.

Lottie positively scowled at her mama.

'Things just wouldn't be the same without you, dear Kathryn. And your uncle would so like to see you again.'

Her uncle had revealed no such inclination at their last meeting, thought Kathryn grimly. Nor did she relish the thought of spending an evening in the house in Green Street. But there seemed to be no way to decline the invitation graciously. 'Thank you, Aunt, I shall enquire of Lady Maybury if it is permissible.' She prayed that her ladyship would judge otherwise.

Mrs Marchant glanced at the dowager. 'I promise we shall take very good care of your companion,' she said with forced jollity.

Lady Maybury's eyes brightened. 'A musical evening, did you say? They are quite my favourite form of entertainment. We shall be happy to come.'

Kathryn's heart sank.

'How delightful,' said Mrs Marchant weakly, and the smile on her face appeared to be suffering under the strain. 'It shall, of course, be the smallest and most modest of affairs.'

Lady Maybury appeared undeterred.

'Then I shall send you a card with all of the details,' Mrs Marchant said. 'And now we really must rush. We cannot keep Mrs Thomas waiting. Please do excuse us.' With one rapid inclination of the head she placed a hand behind Lottie's back and pushed. 'Goodbye, Lady Maybury, Lord Ravensmede, Kathryn.' And without another word she steered her daughter towards their carriage as fast as she could manage.

Lord Ravensmede raised a cynical eyebrow at his grandparent. 'An interest in musical evenings? I seem to recall that you were afflicted by no such tendency last Season.'

'Fiddlesticks!' declared the old lady. 'Your memory's going, boy. Never missed an invitation to a musical event in m'life.'

'I had not thought you would have included Mrs Marchant in your circle.' His lordship's voice never normally betrayed emotion. But on this occasion Kathryn thought she could detect the subtle undertone of disapproval.

One faded eye glittered rather threateningly in Ravensmede's direction. 'Would you have Kathryn go without me? I have a notion to hear the chit sing, nothing more.' Then fatigue showed in her face. 'Take us home, Nick. I must have my nap in preparation for tonight's outing and time is getting on.'

Anna Marchant was up to something, Ravensmede was certain. Why should the woman suddenly be so eager for Kathryn's attendance…and seemingly on her own? The invitation had been issued to Kathryn alone. His grandmother had taken the liberty of inviting herself. Mrs Marchant's lack of enthusiasm for Lady Maybury's presence had not escaped his attention. For the rest of the day Ravensmede found himself to be pondering the question. It was the foremost matter in his mind as he dispatched the note to Cadmount. He had still not resolved the issue when a footman announced Lord Cadmount's carriage. Five minutes later the two men were *en route* to Haymarket.

It did not take long for Cadmount to become aware that his friend's attention was otherwise engaged. Conversation was scant for the duration of the journey. Cadmount had his suspicions as to the cause of Ravensmede's somewhat brooding mood, but knew better than to test them at that precise moment.

It was only when they had seated themselves within the auditorium that Lord Cadmount understood Ravensmede's sudden urge to attend the opera this evening.

'Isn't that your grandmother with li'l Miss Marchant over there?' The fair brows indicated the direction of the sky-blue box not so very far from Cadmount's own.

'It appears you may be right,' drawled Ravensmede. 'Shall we…?' He did not wait for the answer, but was up and threading his way through the crowds with leisurely determination.

'Lord Ravensmede.' Kathryn could not prevent the sudden gallop of her heart.

'So you decided to join us,' said Lady Maybury quite matter of factly. 'Lord Cadmount.' The snowy white head dipped, sending the deep red plumes balanced thereon into a frenzy.

'Your servant, ma'am,' said Lord Cadmount and bowed. 'You look as exquisite as ever, dear lady.'

'Flatterer!' shrieked her ladyship, but she smiled and fanned herself all the same.

Kathryn tried hard to keep a straight face. It appeared that Lady Maybury had rather a soft spot for her grandson's friend. Her eyes flitted once more to Lord Ravensmede, who was looking devilishly handsome. 'You made no mention, sir, that you planned to attend tonight.'

'No, I did not.' His gaze held hers for a moment longer, raising in Kathryn the peculiar tension she had felt before when he had held her in his arms or pressed his lips to hers. She looked away, unwilling to allow such feelings to resurface.

For the rest of the evening nothing in Lord Ravensmede's manner or speech was anything but formally polite, but she could not dispel the odd sensation that he was, by his very presence, lending her his protection, and not at all in the scandalous way he had once suggested. And when, at the end of the evening, Ravensmede and Cadmount assisted Lady Maybury and herself to her ladyship's carriage, Kathryn was surprised to find that she did not wish to say goodbye.

The next day Kathryn entered the breakfast room to find a parcel and a small box sitting on the breakfast table.

Her ladyship barely raised her eyes from *The Times*. 'Could they print this confounded news any smaller? I can't see a damn thing!' she complained.

'Would you like me to read to you?' Kathryn knew how her ladyship hated to admit just how much her eyesight had deteriorated. It was their usual routine, Kathryn reading aloud, the dowager interrupting with comments, both learning the news of the day, both discussing their subsequent views and opinions. 'I'm sorry I'm late, my lady. I overslept a little. I hope I haven't kept you waiting long.'

For morning time Lady Maybury appeared to be in an unusually good mood. 'It's of little consequence. My stomach can't be kept waiting for breakfast and I knew you would arrive shortly.' She helped herself to another chop and a couple of devilled kidneys. 'Couldn't sleep then, gel?'

Kathryn lifted the coffee pot. 'No. I slept like a top,' she lied. 'I can't think why I didn't waken. It must have been all the excitement of yesterday.' She most certainly was not about to admit that she had lain awake half the night thinking about the lady's grandson.

'What excitement?' asked Lady Maybury between mouthfuls of kidney.

'Why, our visits to the painting exhibition and the museum, and, of course, the opera.'

Lady Maybury smiled. After a few minutes in which Kathryn sipped her coffee and ate some eggs, the elderly voice asked, 'Aren't you going to open them?'

'Open them?' Kathryn asked, rather unsure of herself, and her eyes drifted to the packages sitting across the table.

'It is your birthday, is it not?'

Kathryn let out an exclamation of surprise. 'Yes, but how did you know?'

'We Mayburys have our ways.' The old lady smiled, and pushed the small dark box towards Kathryn. 'A small token of my affection, gel.'

Kathryn stared at the box, her hand touched to her lips.

'Open it.'

The box was shallow and rectangular in shape, with an external covering of blue chinoiserie painted silk. Inside, on a lining of plain white silk, lay a strand of ivory pearls and two matching single-pearl drop earrings. Kathryn gasped. 'They're beautiful!'

Lady Maybury's smile broadened. 'Happy birthday, Kathryn.'

'I...' The words faltered and then she was up out of her seat and throwing her arms around the dowager. 'Thank you,' she whispered in a voice thick with emotion, 'it is a long time since anyone remembered my birthday, and never with such a truly lovely gift.'

Lady Maybury patted Kathryn's hand. 'I'm glad that you like them. Now, open your other present.'

Still standing, Kathryn looked at the large parcel on the table.

'Hurry up, then. My curiosity's getting the better of me.' Lady Maybury resumed her attack on her breakfast. 'When one gets to my age one's family take steps to curtail all excitement. It has the effect of making some ladies, not to put too fine a point on it, overly inquisitive.' One ancient hand removed itself from the cutlery for long enough to push the parcel further in Kathryn's direction.

The brown paper crinkled beneath her fingers as she picked at the knots in the string.

'For heaven's sake, gel,' huffed her ladyship, and, extracting a small, finely crafted pair of scissors from a pocket in her dress, she reached across and snipped the string. 'You'll be there all day with those knots. No point in wasting time.' Lady Maybury attacked her chop once more, but her eyes were trained firmly on the parcel.

Kathryn peeled back the wrapping to reveal a wooden box filled with the brightest range of water-colour pans. Inserted in cunningly designed compartments within the set were small pots for holding water and a narrow drawer containing the finest sable brushes. 'It's wonderful!' Her fingers traced the contours of each and every part, touching with a care that suggested reverence.

'What's that beneath it?' A silver fork stabbed towards the paintbox.

With the box positioned carefully on the tablecloth, Kathryn saw that the parcel also contained a pad of cut paper sheets and a box of sketching pencils. 'Who on earth could have sent me…?' The letter was folded in half and lay at the bottom of the pile. Even before she read the words her heart leapt, for there at the top of the paper was the Viscount of Ravensmede's crest. Fingers fluttered to her cheek as her eyes skimmed the boldly penned script.

Her ladyship laid down her cutlery upon the emptied plate, dabbed a napkin to her lips, and emitted a small burp. 'Do you like m'grandson's gift?'

Kathryn's emotions were in quite a flurry. Abruptly she found her chair, and stared at the pile of art materials before her. 'It's…exquisite! But…' She plucked distractedly at the apron of her dress before running her fingers across the beech paintbox. The clear grey eyes raised to the dowager's. 'I can't accept it.'

'Why ever not?'

'It's not that I'm not grateful, because, of course, I am. It's just…well… not quite appropriate that I receive a gift from a…' She couldn't very well describe Ravensmede as a rake to his own grandmother, so she searched frantically for a suitable word, and found one: '…man.'

'Man!' Lady Maybury's tone cast the word in derision. A cackle rent the air as she seemed to find Kathryn's statement of extreme comic value. When she had stopped laughing long enough to speak, her ladyship helped herself to more coffee and said, 'I thought the fact he's reputed to be one of London's most notorious rake-hells might have influenced you more.'

Kathryn balked at the lady's words and flushed with embarrassment. It seemed that nothing similar affected Lady Maybury's sensibilities.

'It's all a load of stuff and nonsense, of course. Rebelling against his father's hand and the like. Wanted to fight for his country. Tried to buy himself a commission. Charles, m'son, soon put paid to that. The two of them have been at loggerheads ever since. Nick's not cut out to be a rake and a wastrel. He's just bored; there's nothing and no one to tax his mind. Never had a real challenge in his life, errant puppy that he is. Things have fallen too easily into his lap all along.' The distant look in her eyes faded. 'For all of his reputation, Kathryn, I'm certain that, in this at least, Nick is well intentioned. It is a birthday gift, nothing more. I see no impropriety. My advice to you, gel, is to accept the art materials with grace. Besides, I enjoy watching others paint. It soothes m'nerves.'

In all the time Kathryn had known the dowager she had seen no evidence to suggest that the old lady was afflicted with anything that could be remotely described as a nervous condition. The paintbox was very beautiful. She cast a longing look at it.

'So you'll paint for me this afternoon,' coaxed Lady Maybury.

Using the water-colours and brushes and paper that Lord Ravensmede had bought for her? His letter wishing her birthday greetings was still clutched between her fingers. She folded it and placed it on the table. 'Yes, my lady, of course I will.'

A week later Lord Ravensmede was standing in the library of his grandmother's rented townhouse, browsing through the water-colour studies that lay upon the table. The assortment mainly consisted of still-life studies, carefully contrived arrangements of flowers and fruits. All were of a good artistic standard, but what really caught his eye was the single sheet at the very bottom of the pile. Kathryn Marchant had captured every aspect of his grandmother's personality in those few brush strokes. The intelligence and perception within that gaze, the kindness and loyalty beneath that harsh façade, and, most tenderly of all, the hint of vulnerability in the grand demeanour. It was something that Ravensmede guessed few others besides himself had ever glimpsed. It was not a posed portrait of rigid formality, but a natural moment frozen in time. His grandmother looked as if she were watching Kathryn, but without the consciousness so usual in those sitting for a portrait. Ravensmede found it hard to draw his eyes away. A noise at his back signalled Lady Maybury's entry.

'Quite the little artist, isn't she, Nick?' Then, without waiting for an answer, she continued, 'I didn't know my face was so revealing. Seems that our Kathryn has a very real talent when it comes to portraits. Unlike most, she can look beneath the veneer we present to the world.'

Our Kathryn... The expression hit Ravensmede like a bolt from the blue. *Our Kathryn*... It seemed so right that she was one of them, a part of their family. Aware of his grandmother's scrutiny, he shook the thought from his head and looked directly at her. 'Grandmama...you do know what you're about with Anna Marchant tonight, don't you?'

'Of course,' she said. 'Thought I would send her into that viper's nest on her own, did you?'

'No, I thought that you might find an excuse that Kathryn need not endure such a farce,' he said wryly.

The old lady chuckled. 'Doubting your old grandam's wisdom, Nick?' She caught his large hand and held it sandwiched between her own. 'Kathryn's attendance this evening will put paid to any suggestion that all is not well between her and her relatives. We do not want any gossip arising over either that or the haste of her move to Upper Grosvenor Street.'

'Indeed not,' said Ravensmede. 'But Anna Marchant seemed too eager that Kathryn attend Lottie's musical. Given the fact that the woman can barely conceal her dislike for her niece, I wonder why that might be.'

'As I said, it would be commented upon if Kathryn were not present. And the Marchant woman is determined to curry favour with the *ton*.'

'Maybe,' said her grandson, 'but I have the feeling there is more to Mrs Marchant's invitation than meets the eye.' His lips curved in a mocking smile. 'I fancy that I too have a notion to hear the chit sing.'

A voice floated in from the hall.

'That will be Kathryn.' The dowager drew him a strange little look. 'The aim is to stamp out gossip, not start it. Is your presence really necessary?'

'Absolutely,' answered her grandson.

The two moved towards the door.

Kathryn's sense of dread that had fast been escalating over the past week had reached a pinnacle. No matter how many times she told herself that she was being foolish, no matter how much she insisted that Aunt Anna would never behave with anything other than congeniality before the dowager, Kathryn could not rid herself of the fear. She did not want to set one foot back in the house in Green Street. Even just thinking about the place brought a cold nausea to her stomach. The memory of the three long years that she had lived there would not be easily erased. It was one thing meeting Aunt Anna out in the street, quite another venturing back into her aunt's own domain—where all the power was, and always had been, in Mrs Marchant's hands. Nothing bad could happen, not in Lady Maybury's presence, or so Kathryn reassured herself. But despite all of her efforts, she could not quell her mounting apprehension. It was therefore with a considerable amount of relief that Kathryn descended the staircase of the dowager's house to discover that Lord Ravensmede had every intention of accompanying his grandmother and her companion to Miss Lottie Marchant's musical evening.

'Kathryn…and Lady Maybury,' gushed Anna Marchant with a sickly smile plastered across her face. 'So pleased that you could both make it to our little gathering.' The ladies were in the middle of their devoirs when Mrs Marchant spotted the tall dark presence by the doorway. 'Lord Ravensmede!' It was all she could do to prevent the smile slipping from her face. 'What a pleasant surprise.'

'Mrs Marchant,' he said lazily, and watched her through narrowed eyes while she led them across the room to where Lady Finlay was chatting with Lottie.

'Lottie dearest, look, some more guests have arrived to hear you sing. Cousin Kathryn, Lady Maybury, and…and Lord Ravensmede.' Anna Marchant looked up to see his lordship smile. It was something that bore a startling resemblance to one of the great black wild cats in the royal menagerie, being unaccountably menacing. The Viscount's eyes held the suggestion of a threat.

Lady Finlay stared short-sightedly at Kathryn. 'I can't say that I remember meeting you before, Miss Marchant.' She peered long and hard. 'Have we been introduced?'

Kathryn raised her chin a notch and endured the scrutiny. 'No, indeed, my lady, I don't believe I've had the pleasure.'

'My cousin was present at your recent ball as my companion, but that was before she was persuaded into Lady Maybury's establishment.' The words were innocent enough, but no one present was in any doubt as to the intention behind them. Charlotte Marchant intended to set her cousin firmly back in her place.

'Indeed,' drawled Lord Ravensmede from Kathryn's side. He looked at Lottie with an air of utter boredom. 'My grandmother insisted that Miss Marchant is such delightful company that she simply would not hear of anyone else as her companion.'

Kathryn felt her hand being tucked into Lady Maybury's arm. 'Such a lovely gel,' said the dowager.

With such overt championing, who would dare to stand against it? Certainly not Lady Finlay. Especially when Lady Maybury leaned forward and hissed in her loudest stage whisper, 'Her mother was one of the Overton Thornleys.' The snowy white curls nodded knowingly.

Anna Marchant looked as if she would have liked to throttle the dear old dowager there and then. 'Ah, here is Mr Dalton. Now we can all take our seats for tonight's entertainment. I'm sure that no one will be disappointed with my darling girl's performance.'

'I'm sure that young Lettie will not let you down,' said Lady Maybury.

Lottie's baby-blue eyes squinted in displeasure and she looked demandingly at her mama.

'Lottie,' said Mrs Marchant with emphasis.

The dowager's smile contained all the warmth of a hooded cobra. 'Yes, indeed, dear little Lettie. Let us hope she's as talented as her cousin.'

'Her name is Charlotte, which the family shorten to *Lottie*.' Anna Marchant positively snapped the sharp retort.

Aristocratic cheeks were sucked in all round and a knowing look passed between the ladies of the group as they ambled to take their seats in Mrs Marchant's drawing room.

Kathryn found herself seated between Lord Ravensmede and Lady Maybury in the row of chairs furthest back in the room. His lordship sat closest to the door, as if he hoped to make a quick escape should Lottie's musical ability prove not to his taste. Kathryn hoped fervently that he would not leave. Just his presence made her feel safer, allaying the worst of her fears regarding her aunt and the house in Green Street.

She sneaked a look up at him through downcast lashes. He was relaxed in the chair, as if he had not a care in the world, long legs stretched out before him, dark hair worn fashionably short, and an expression of bored indifference upon his face. His attire was immaculate as usual. A deep blue tailcoat, above which showed a white high-pointed collar and a snow-white neckcloth tied in a simple but stylish knot. Her eyes slid lower to where one hand rested on his thigh. A light sprinkling of dark hair showed on the back of the hand. His nails were short and clean, his skin a light honey coloration. It looked to be a strong squarish hand; a hand used to taking what it wanted, and one that Kathryn knew was capable of the most tender caress. Her abdomen gave a little flutter and she swiftly moved her eyes on from his hand to the thigh beneath it. That did not help matters. Not when the thigh, encased in tight buff-coloured buckskin, was so long and muscular, and the front of his coat was so very short. Her cheeks grew warm and she quickly raised her gaze to find herself staring directly into his eyes. Something warm quivered deep inside her. He smiled, and the quiver became a somersault.

'Are you comfortable enough, Miss Marchant?' There was something in his look that made her think that he had more than an inkling of her thoughts.

'Yes, thank you, my lord, quite comfortable.' She nodded and glanced away, unwilling to let him see just how much he affected her.

Fortuitously Mr Dalton sounded the first notes upon the piano and then Lottie began to sing, and Kathryn was saved from any further embarrassment.

Chapter Nine

Lottie had just finished her third rendition to rapturous applause when Anna Marchant threaded her way quietly to the back of the drawing room, to stand beside the Viscount of Ravensmede's chair. She ignored Ravensmede, smiled sweetly at his grandmother and leaned towards Kathryn. 'Dearest niece,' she whispered, 'may I have a minute of your time?'

Kathryn's heart began to thud within her chest and a certain uneasiness started to squirm within. A sense of foreboding rippled down her spine. For one awful moment she was seized by the sudden overwhelming desire to just run through the door and keep on running—far away from Aunt Anna and this house. Her eyes flickered towards the door longingly. And then common sense prevailed. Kathryn knew very well that there was no way out. She could not refuse to speak to her aunt. So she took a deep breath, looked at the dowager, and said quietly, 'Please excuse me, my lady.' Then she nodded and rose to follow Mrs Marchant.

Ravensmede stood to let her leave. As she squeezed past she heard the silk of her skirt slide against his legs, and smelled the clean citrus scent of him. She looked up to read the unspoken question of concern in his eyes, and tried to hide the fear in her own. Then she had passed him and was following Aunt Anna across the floor and out of the drawing room.

Anna Marchant waited until Kathryn was seated in the small room before closing the door behind her. The click of the latch echoed in the silence.

Kathryn recognised it as her aunt and uncle's own personal parlour. It was much smaller than the drawing room and nowhere near as ornate. The décor was a cool combination of duck-egg blue and pale grey, with no hint of warmth or welcome. A small pile of tinder, sticks and coal dross had been set up within the hearth in readiness for a fire. The temperature of the evening outside meant it had not been lit; the chill in the parlour suggested that it should have. Kathryn suppressed a shiver. Nothing of the summer warmth pervaded the little room. The light of the candles in the wall sconces flickered within the gloom. She noticed that the heavy blue curtains had been pulled to shut out the daylight. Everything about the place felt dim and dank and claustrophobic. Her fingers smoothed nervously over the silk of her skirt. 'You wished to speak to me, Aunt?'

'Yes.' Mrs Marchant took the chair between Kathryn and the door. Now that they were alone all pretence of amiability had disappeared. Her eyes were a cold hard blue; her lips pursed to a thin, narrow line. 'I wish to know exactly how matters are between you and Lady Maybury.'

Distrust tutored Kathryn's words. 'Why, they are very well indeed. Lady Maybury is both kind and thoughtful. I could not ask for more.' She waited to see what this game was about.

'And how fares the child?'

'The child?' Kathryn stared at her aunt.

'The child that necessitated such a sudden and immediate move to Ravensmede House.'

Kathryn's fingers pleated the violet silk of her skirt between them. 'Lady Maybury's house is in Upper Grosvenor Street,' she said carefully. 'Maggie, the little girl who was involved in the carriage accident, is recovered and back living with her family.'

'How fortuitous.'

Kathryn said nothing. A horrible suspicion was forming.

'Does Lord Ravensmede spend much time visiting Upper Grosvenor Street?'

'No.' The violet silk twisted tighter in her hands.

'But I've heard he's inordinately fond of his grandmother.'

Kathryn could guess where this was leading. Perspiration beaded cold upon her skin. 'We're missing Lottie's singing.'

'So we are.' Anna Marchant smiled a vicious little smile. 'Then I had best come straight to the point, hadn't I?' The faint strains of music and a high pitched melodic voice drifted through the barrier of the door. 'Certain rumours have come to my ears, Kathryn, rumours involving you and some very improper behaviour.'

The blood rushed in Kathryn's ears. She felt the tripping of her heart. Her eyes widened in shock.

'If you are intent on destroying your reputation then I have a right to know exactly what you are up to.'

Kathryn rose from her chair, her cheeks scalded with embarrassment and anger. 'How could you say such a thing? Any rumours to which you may have listened are false.'

'Don't give me that, you little bitch,' snapped her aunt. 'I know that you're lying; it's written all over your face.'

'I think I should return to Lady Maybury now,' said Kathryn with a great deal more control than she felt.

'Oh, no, I haven't finished with you yet, miss.'

Kathryn hid her growing fear and made to move towards the door, only to find her way blocked by her aunt.

'You're going nowhere until you tell me exactly what's been going on.'

'Aunt Anna—'

'Don't "Aunt Anna" me! You leave here with Ravensmede and his grandmother on the premise of going for a drive in Hyde Park, and the next minute you're installed in the old woman's house as her companion, without so much as a by your leave. The first that your uncle knows of it is a letter from Ravensmede!' Mrs Marchant advanced towards her niece.

Kathryn instinctively backed away.

'Do you think I know nothing of his reputation?' The older woman's mouth twisted to a snarl.

'The child's leg was injured in her fall, and Lady Maybury was in need of immediate assistance,' said Kathryn with force.

'And what of Ravensmede?'

'He could not be expected to look after a four-year-old girl.'

'But he could look after you, miss, very well indeed.'

Kathryn stiffened at the insult. 'You malign both his lordship and me!' She thrust aside the memory of just exactly what she and the Viscount had shared.

Mrs Marchant stepped closer. 'He's the only man to have shown an interest in you, though God knows why he should have taken notice of so plain a creature. And why else would her ladyship have taken you up? It stands to reason, if you're indulging Ravensmede's interest.'

'Lady Maybury would never stoop to such a scandal. Her reputation is beyond reproach.' The eyes that were normally a clear pale grey became dark and stormy.

'Lucky for us all,' said Anna Marchant, 'else your reputation would be in tatters, miss.' She took another step towards her niece.

Kathryn felt the press of the wall against her back. 'My reputation is unblemished.' A sliver of guilt stuck in her throat.

Mrs Marchant stepped closer still. 'That's not what I've heard, and I mean to have the truth from you, you selfish little trollop. You have no thought in your head for anyone other than yourself.'

Kathryn scanned the room for an escape route, but the only way out was the same way through which she had entered.

'If you cast your reputation to the gutter then what of Lottie? Innocent of all blame, yet she'll suffer just the same.'

'Aunt, you're mistaken—'

Anna Marchant's hands closed hard around the tops of Kathryn's arms. 'Tell me what you've been up to, girl, or, so help me, I'll have the truth from you one way or another!'

'Leave me be!' Kathryn struggled to free herself, but her aunt was much larger and stronger.

'Tell me!' Anna Marchant said again and tightened her grip.

Kathryn's ordeal went no further: the door of the parlour swung open.

Anna Marchant spun to face the intruder, her hands dropping to her sides.

'Mrs Marchant,' said the man's voice, but for all its drawl there was in it an unmistakable flint-like quality.

Anna Marchant flushed to the roots of her golden hair. 'Lord Ravensmede,' she said, unsure of quite how much the Viscount had seen or indeed heard.

His expression was one of cold contempt and every line of his face held the promise of retribution. Mrs Marchant surreptitiously backed away towards the corner of the room.

His gaze slid to Kathryn who still stood, as if pinioned,

against the wall. Her face had drained to a powder white. 'Miss Marchant, my grandmother has need of you.' The words were innocent enough, but the tone was loaded with danger. 'You appear to be somewhat distressed. Has someone upset you?' His focus drifted questioningly towards Anna Marchant, and the colour of the woman's cheeks darkened to a deep puce.

Kathryn's hands kneaded at the violet silk. 'No!' she almost shouted, then more calmly, as if regaining control of her emotions, 'No, I am quite well, thank you, my lord. I was just about to return to the drawing room.'

'As I'm sure is Mrs Marchant,' he said smoothly, and waited for the golden-haired woman to cross the floor before them. Anna Marchant did not look back. Only then did he place a supportive hand on the small of Kathryn's back and guide her in her aunt's wake. Lottie was still singing as they quietly settled back into their seats. No one commented on the ladies' short absence.

Kathryn never knew how she made it through the rest of that evening. Certainly the knowledge that Lord Ravensmede was never far from her side gave her strength. She could hazard a very good guess at what would have happened within that horrible little room had he not interrupted. A nausea was rising in her stomach and she longed for nothing more than to flee from the house in Green Street. One look at Lady Maybury's face told her that was not possible. The dowager seemed to be in her element, relaying stories of Kathryn's artistic abilities, introducing her new companion to all and sundry, ensuring that everyone knew just who Kathryn Marchant's mother had been. Through it all Kathryn endured with a smile, a murmur of the right response, and an interested expression as the most trivial of stories were told; and all the while she was conscious of the Viscount standing so very close by, guarding her with his presence.

Strangely enough, at the end of the evening it was not Lottie's musical achievements that were talked of by all the best people. Rather, the sudden emergence of the quietly refined Miss Kathryn Marchant, with her water-colour talents, held that coveted spot, thanks to Lady Maybury.

Anna Marchant had some inkling of the matter and it did not please her. 'It was a mistake to invite your cousin,' she conceded to her daughter in the few quiet minutes they had alone. 'I learned nothing, and, because of that battleaxe dowager, Kathryn has managed to steal your thunder.' She flicked a gaze at her daughter. 'For heaven's sake, don't you dare start crying. Do you want them talking of your hideous red blotchy face instead of tonight's performance?'

Lottie's pouted lips trembled, but she swallowed back the tears that threatened to fall. 'I saw you take her out of the drawing room. And then Lord Ravensmede went and fetched you both back.'

'Interfering villain! I fancy that I must be right in my supposition.'

'Mama?' Lottie's still-watery eyes opened wide and round in bewilderment. 'I don't understand.'

'No, you never do.'

Lottie's lips began to quiver again. 'But that mean cat has ruined my evening.'

'She could ruin a whole lot more than that,' said her mother ominously.

Fortunately the comment was lost upon Lottie, who continued unabated with her complaining. 'Only see how Mr Dalton is looking at her, I'm sure he means to offer for her instead of me. Oh, I shall never forgive her if he does. How I wish she was living back here, then you could box her ears and none of this would ever have happened.' Lottie's voice whined close to hysteria.

'Calm yourself.' Her mother moved a blonde ringlet from across Lottie's cheek. 'Unlike you, my darling, your cousin is a nobody.'

'But Lady Maybury said Kathryn's mother was one of the Overton Thornleys, and everyone was much impressed,' she snuffled.

'Elizabeth Thornley was a strumpet and her family disowned her. The Overton Thornleys wanted nothing more to do with her or her children. Why else do you think we were forced to take Kathryn into our home? Just because Lady Maybury has her in favour does not alter that fact. It was not so long ago that Kathryn was scrubbing floors and washing your linen. Hold that memory close. She may have tried to steal this evening from you, but I don't mean to just stand by and watch that little bitch get away with it, or anything else for that matter, my dear. No. Cousin Kathryn may find she has a little surprise coming to her.' Mrs Marchant's hand turned to stroke her daughter's bright golden locks. 'Just you trust your mama, Lottie. I shall see that Kathryn gets her due, be very assured of that.'

'Such a delightful evening, thank you, Nick. You may call on us tomorrow,' said the dowager when Ravensmede's town-coach halted outside her house in Upper Grosvenor Street.

'I'd rather call on you now.' Lord Ravensmede's eyes flickered towards Kathryn before returning his grandmother's gaze.

'As you will,' she said.

Only once they were all seated within the dowager's drawing room did she speak again. 'Kathryn, my dear, could you go and fetch me a suitably interesting book from the library? I've a mind to hear you read a little before I go to bed—that is, if you're not too tired.'

'Certainly, my lady.'

Lady Maybury waited until the door closed behind Kathryn before turning to her grandson. 'Well, out with it. I take it you want to tell me what went on between Kathryn and her aunt.'

Ravensmede didn't even comment upon his grandparent's bluntness. 'Anna Marchant had her pinned against a wall and was threatening her when I found them.'

'Good gad! Little wonder the gel looked powder white when you brought her back through.'

Ravensmede looked directly at his grandmother. 'I need to talk to her…alone.'

A white eyebrow arched high.

'I would know exactly what Mrs Marchant was up to this evening.'

The faded green eyes held his. 'You know that I should not allow it,' she said quietly.

'And you know I would not ask were it not so important.'

They looked at each other for a moment longer.

'Very well,' Lady Maybury uttered at last. 'I need not say the rest.'

Ravensmede nodded, and dropped a kiss to the lined velvet cheek. 'Thank you.'

When Kathryn returned to the drawing room, complete with book in hand, it was to find Lord Ravensmede standing by the unlit fireplace. Of Lady Maybury there was no sign.

She hesitated halfway across the rug, as if a little unsure of herself. 'My lord…where is Lady Maybury?'

Ravensmede saw the pallor of her cheeks and the signs of fatigue around her eyes. 'Sit down, Kathryn.'

'I think she'll like this one.' She gestured to the small leather-bound book gripped within her hand. 'It's a collection of works by Lord Byron.'

He said nothing, just waited for her to sit down upon the sofa.

'Perhaps I should check if she needs my assistance.'

'Kathryn…' and the word sounded like a sigh on his lips '…my grandmother has retired for the night. I want to speak with you before I leave.'

Her eyes widened. 'I do not think that's a good idea, my lord.'

He shrugged. 'I disagree.'

She was still wearing the violet-and-cream evening dress. He noted how well the colour became her, how enticingly it fitted around her small bosom. The neckline was plain, the violet silk a fine contrast to the exposed smooth white curves of the tops of her breasts that rose and fell at such regular intervals. Suddenly conscious that he was staring, he dropped his gaze lower to where her fingers plucked at her skirt. He knew then the level of her unease. 'You need not be afraid, Kathryn. I only wish to speak to you.'

'What do you wish to discuss?' A note of caution sounded in her voice.

'That which happened this evening at your aunt's.'

Her fingers tightened around the violet material. She swallowed. 'There is nothing to say about that, sir.'

'Oh, but I think there is, Kathryn.' He watched a hint of panic flit across her face.

Silence stretched between them.

'Kathryn.' The word acted as a prompt, as he knew it would.

'We…we had a disagreement, that's all.' Her focus shifted away to study the pattern on the rug.'

'Then it must have been a very heated disagreement; she had you against the wall when I walked in.'

'She was merely making her point, rather forcibly.'

'She was threatening you,' he said succinctly.

'No…she was just—'

'Damnation, Kathryn, why are you trying to protect her?'

She glanced up at him then and he caught a glimpse of guilt and embarrassment in her eyes, before her gaze skittered away again. 'I-I'm not.'

'Then you're hiding something from me.'

'No!' The denial did not ring true, and he knew it.

The violet silk was suffering a thorough pulverisation beneath her fingers.

He leaned back against the mantel, rested his booted foot upon the fender, and watched her. 'Your lying does not improve with practice.'

She rose swiftly from the sofa. 'It's late, Lord Ravensmede, and I have much to do tomorrow. Please excuse me, sir.'

He pushed off from the fender and moved swiftly to stand before her. 'No.'

Indignation stared from the silver eyes. 'I beg your pardon,' she said stiffly. 'It's not seemly that we're here, alone, at this time of night.'

Exasperation rose in Ravensmede's throat. 'It's not seemly that you're lying to me,' he growled.

'Lord Ravensmede,' she said primly.

'Miss Marchant,' he countered.

She made to turn towards the door.

'I did not excuse you.' He saw the slight body stiffen. Felt a scoundrel for what he was doing. Knew he must do it for Kathryn's own sake.

'I can stand here all night, my lord, and there will still be nothing more to say.'

One step, and the distance between them disappeared. 'Tell me,' he said roughly. His hand closed around her arm. He felt her start beneath him, try to pull away. She looked up at him, fear blazoning in her eyes. Shock kicked in his gut at the realisation of just what she thought. 'I'm not going to hurt you!' One by one he uncurled his fingers so that she was free. 'God help me, I could *never* hurt you.' They were standing so close that the hem of her skirt brushed the gleaming toes of his long black riding boots; so close that he could hear the whisper of her breath and smell her sweet scent. 'Don't you know that by now?'

Her eyelids fluttered shut.

Next to him she was so small, so slender. It pained him that she believed he could have struck her. 'Forgive me if I frightened you, Kathryn.'

There was a catch of breath in her throat and then those beautiful eyes raised to his once more. 'I'm sorry,' she said, and her, words were so quiet as to scarcely catch his ears. 'I didn't mean to…'

'Hush.' With great tenderness he cupped one hand against her cheek and stroked a delicate caress across the silken skin. It seemed that there was a great stillness within him and a peculiar ache across his chest. It was a novel sensation for Ravensmede. Beneath his fingers her skin was warm and smooth. And her eyes clung to his like a woman drowning. She made him feel both powerless and omnipotent at the same time. 'You need not tell me if you really do not wish

to. I sought only to save you from the worst of your aunt.'
For all that he wanted to help her, he could not bear her pain.

Her eyes shuttered. 'Oh, Nicholas,' she sighed. 'You, of all people, cannot.'

He touched his lips against her forehead, not kissing, just resting them there, trying desperately to give her some small comfort.

'Aunt Anna said…'

He pulled back, rested his hands loosely, lightly, against her shoulders, and watched the hint of a blush stain those pale cheeks. Kathryn would not meet his gaze. 'What did she say?' he asked as gently as he could.

A deep breath. A tremor of tension beneath his palms. 'She said that there were rumours.'

There was a sudden coldness in the pit of his stomach.

'She implied that I…that we…' Her hand moved to worry at her skirt. But his moved faster, catching her fingers back up and threading them through his own. 'That we?'

'That we have behaved improperly.'

Only the ticking of the clock on the mantel punctuated the silence in the room.

'She wanted to question me on the matter.'

'I see,' said Ravensmede. His fingers pressed a gentle reassurance against hers. He controlled the anger rising within him, didn't want to distress Kathryn any more than she was already.

'And she's right, isn't she?' said Kathryn quietly. 'We haven't behaved as we should.'

'Perhaps I haven't behaved entirely as I should, but you've done nothing wrong.'

Her chin came up and she squared her shoulders. 'I'm every bit as guilty as you, Nicholas. I wasn't unwilling.' Colour flared in her cheeks.

His blood quickened at her bold admission, and his heart gladdened that she was not indifferent to him. 'Your aunt can know nothing for certain; she's fishing for trouble.' But even as he said the words, Ravensmede thought of someone who most definitely knew enough to destroy Kathryn's reputation. The fact that he had parted with a hefty sum to buy the woman's silence did not make him feel any easier. Amanda White's discretion could not to be entirely trusted. He could only be thankful that she had been persuaded to leave London for a while.

Kathryn sighed. 'I only hope that you're right.'

How could he reassure her? He traced his thumb against the inside of her wrist, slowly, intimately. 'We shared a few kisses, Kathryn, nothing more. There's nothing so very wrong in that.' A few kisses…it sounded so innocent, but Ravensmede knew better. Kathryn Marchant's kisses were fit to overwhelm a man's mind. One taste of her lips was enough to snare a fellow for life. And even had that not been the case, even if her mouth had been hard and dry and unyielding so that he never touched her again, he had already done enough to sully her name if the truth were to come out. He thrust the thought aside. 'You said yourself it will not happen again…and now we are just friends.' It was what she wanted, what she *needed,* to hear; or so he told himself.

Hurt flashed in her eyes, and then was gone so quickly that he thought he must have been mistaken. She stared down at her feet.

He squeezed her hands in what he hoped was an encouraging manner; struggled to ignore the smell of her perfume drifting up from her hair, and the tantalising touch of her fingers still entwined within his own. Ruthlessly he quelled the desire to wrap his arms around her and crush her to him.

Loosening his hand, he took her chin between his fingers and gently raised her face so that he could look into her eyes. 'I look after my friends, Kathryn,' he said slowly. 'I won't allow Mrs Marchant to hurt you again.'

She nodded. 'Thank you,' she said softly.

He could resist no more. Sliding his arms round her back, he pulled her into his embrace, and then just held her, with the softness of her curves pressed against him, and the smell of her filling his nose. She made no protest, just clung to him as he clung to her, her breath warm and moist against his chest. He dropped his lips to rest against the top of her head. And they stood there, as if they would merge together as one for all eternity.

In the days that followed Miss Lottie Marchant's musical evening Kathryn heard nothing more from her aunt. It seemed that Ravensmede had been right in his assertion that Mrs Marchant had been untruthful about the existence of injurious rumours, for, from the very next day following the event, it became clear that Kathryn had been taken into the bosom of the *ton*. Invitations to balls and routs and parties arrived at the house in Upper Grosvenor Street by the score, and all were extended to both Lady Maybury and her companion.

For the first time in her life people looked *at* Kathryn instead of *through* her. There was definitely no danger of her being ignored. People who had previously not deigned to notice her were suddenly keen to be seen chatting with Lady Maybury's protégé. She lost count of the number of requests she received from people asking her to paint their portraits. And a number of gentlemen took to calling in the hope of fixing Miss Marchant's attention. It was akin to the past fantasies played out in her head, unreal in every aspect except that when she opened her eyes it did not vanish. Kathryn should have been happy, and, indeed, she was content of sorts. But something was missing, and that something left an emptiness within.

Since that night when he had held her so tenderly in Lady Maybury's drawing room, Lord Ravensmede had been careful to avoid being alone in her company. He was a model of polite consideration. Indeed, Kathryn would have gone as far as to describe him as the very epitome of gentlemanly behaviour. But there was a new distance between them, as if he had withdrawn from her. It was the right thing to do, the proper thing to do. Especially for a viscount to his grandmother's companion. So why did she feel a constant ache in her heart?

We shared a few kisses, he had said, *nothing more*. Was that all it had been to him? Didn't he too feel that the world had turned upside down? Clearly not. But then he was a rake. Everyone said it. A man who was used to taking what he wanted from women and moving on. Just the thought of that was enough to turn her blood cold. She should be glad that he was behaving with the utmost respectability. And then she remembered the dark smoulder in his eyes when he kissed her, the gentle insistence of his lips upon her, and the tenderness of his touch…and she knew that against all rhyme and reason, what she really wanted from Nicholas Maybury was not in the least respectable.

'Oh, it has been an age since I was in Brighthelmstone. Such a good idea of m'grandson. To escape from the infernal smells of the town will be a blessed relief. I only hope the sea air is not too cold. At my time of life one cannot be too careful about catching a chill.' Lady Maybury drew her shawl around her as if she already felt the gusting of the bracing sea air, instead of the stifling heat of London. 'Are you finished, my dear?'

Kathryn was engaged in yet another portrait of the dowager, this time a sketch in charcoal and chalk. She bobbed her head to the side, considered the work carefully, and, after a stroke here and a smudge there pronounced that she was.

The briefest of knocks sounded upon the library door behind Kathryn and then footsteps sounded upon the wooden floor.

'Nick!' Lady Maybury's face illuminated as her grandson came forward to sweep a kiss to her hand.

'Grandmama,' and, turning to the slight figure half-hidden behind the large wooden drawing board, 'Kathryn.' He made to politely lift her hand, but she pulled it back before he could reach it.

A smile lit her face as she set the board down on the floor and wiped her palms on the dark stained apron covering her dress. 'I'm afraid that I'm quite covered in charcoal.' As if to prove her point, she extended one hand and several slender fingers dangled temptingly in front of his face. It was clear to see that Kathryn was telling the truth, for her hands were indeed ingrained with a thick black dust.

'I've seen cleaner hands on a climbing boy,' he laughed and, before she could protest, plucked the dirty little hand into his and kissed it. 'Let it not be said that Lord Ravensmede could be deterred from his manners by a few grains of charcoal.'

'Your manners are quite impeccable, sir. I don't think you need worry that such an accusation could be levelled at you.'

Her grin was less than ladylike, but it smote Ravensmede's heart just the same. Several wild curls had escaped her chignon and were draping artlessly around her throat, the grey eyes were clear and bright, and her skin, beneath the daubs and smudges of black dust, was of a creamy luminescence. There had been too many days of polite formality, too much self-restraint. Before her appeal the Viscount's willpower began to crumble. In a moment of weakness he touched one thumb tenderly to her cheek, and then, suddenly conscious of exactly what he was doing and his grandmother's perceptive gaze, said lazily, 'More charcoal.' A large snow-white handkerchief was produced and he quickly wiped at the offending mark. 'That's better.'

Lady Maybury's mouth shaped as if to catch flies, before she snapped it shut. Kathryn said nothing, but could not prevent the flood of colour that warmed her face. The skin that he had touched with such betraying intimacy burned as if branded.

Ravensmede replaced his handkerchief, unwittingly transferring a small quantity of charcoal dust on to the pocket of his coat in the process, which he then proceeded to inadvertently share between his chin, and his cheek. He wandered away from the faded green scrutiny and feigned an interest in a shelf of books. At the other side of the room he could hear the scrape of Kathryn's chair and the movement of the drawing board upon a table.

'If you would be so kind as to excuse me, my lady, I'll attempt to remove the worst of this mess. A good shake of my apron outside and a hand scrub should suffice. And then I'll wipe the floor in here just in case—'

Lord Ravensmede glanced up from the book he had just extracted from the shelf. 'My grandmother employs servants to do that, Kathryn; you are not one of them. Is that not so, Grandmama?'

Lady Maybury looked from her grandson to her companion. 'Yes, of course.' Then, waving her hand in a dismissive gesture, 'Mary won't mind a little extra dust to sweep in the morning. Don't bother the gel just now.'

'Very well. I'll go and clean myself up. I'll come back later when you have need of me.' Kathryn started towards the door.

'Kathryn.' The single word stopped her progress immediately. 'We plan to discuss our forthcoming trip to Brighthelmstone. I would have you here.'

Kathryn had frozen halfway across the library floor. When she turned around, Ravensmede could see the deepening colour of her cheeks.

'Fustian, Nick! Must you always be so high-handed? I don't know where you get it from. Let the gel tidy herself. We can wait for her return before we start upon the plans for Brighthelmstone.' Lady Maybury peered down the length of her short little nose at her grandson. 'Besides, I can't think of a thing until I've had some Madeira and cake. Be so kind as to ring the bell.' She turned to Kathryn, who was still standing rather awkwardly in the middle of the room, unsure of what to do. 'Well, what are you waiting for, gel? Off you go.'

The door closed quietly behind the slight figure and the dowager and her grandson were left alone. Neither spoke. The slow steady tick of the grandfather clock marked the passing of the seconds.

And then the faded green gaze fixed its focus upon Ravensmede. 'Are you going to tell me what's going on?'

'Nothing's going on.'

'You seem uncommonly concerned with m'companion.'

A dark eyebrow arched. 'I'm merely being polite.'

'Polite, my foot!' sniffed the old lady. 'You fancy the gel!'

Ravensmede laughed. 'You've been reading too many romantic novels, Grandmama.'

'Don't try to flannel me, boy, I'm not so old that I can't see when a young man's ardour is up, even if he is m'own grandson.'

'Whatever I feel about her is irrelevant—she's your companion, nothing more.' The broad shoulders shrugged.

'I'm trusting you to remember that, Nick,' she said and fixed a belligerent eye on her grandson. 'I've put in a lot of effort to establish Kathryn in the eyes of the *ton*. Got plenty of respectable young gentlemen interested in her. Won't be long before one of them makes her an offer.' She sniffed. 'But one whiff of scandal and that will soon change. I don't want you ruining things for Kathryn, or for myself.'

'I've no intention of ruining anything,' Ravensmede drawled. 'As I said before, my interest in Kathryn is purely philanthropic.'

'Then you should take care to remember that until I can find her a husband,' said the dowager.

The thought of Kathryn marrying one of Lady Maybury's young gentlemen did not please the Viscount. His grandmother clearly had the bit between her teeth and was progressing her plan at an all-out gallop. It was time that Ravensmede slowed things down a little. 'Have a care you don't tire both Kathryn and yourself out, Grandmama. I've never seen you attend so many balls and routs as in these last weeks. When was the last time you spent the evening in?'

'Stuff and nonsense!' declared the old lady with a considerable degree of venom. 'I'm not in m'coffin yet. Why should I want to be sitting in here all evening when I can be out enjoying m'self. And as for Kathryn, the gel's as strong as a horse. We'll go out every night if we damn well choose!'

'You already do. But just think, if you make yourself ill what will happen to your plans for Kathryn then? She cannot go out alone.' That made Lady Maybury think; he could tell by the closed look that settled upon her face.

'It won't be for much longer,' she said. 'I'm very close to success. Indeed, if it were not for our holiday to Brighthelmstone I would be expectant of her receiving a proposal in the next few weeks.'

Ravensmede secretly blessed the forthcoming trip.

'Mr Roodley and Mr Williams have both been attentive and I have been warned that Lord Stanfield and Lord Raith have expressed more than a passing interest in my gel. She'll make a good marriage before this Season is out, or I'll eat my hat.'

'Roodley and Williams would bore Kathryn silly within a week of their company. As for Stanfield…the man's one of the biggest lechers in the country. And Raith's old enough to be her father. Are any of them really a suitable match?' Ravensmede flashed a lazy smile. 'I don't think so, and when you think about it, neither will you.'

Her ladyship cast him a determined look. 'I fully intend to catch her a husband, Nick.'

Ravensmede examined his nails, as if the matter was of such little importance to him. 'I fail to see the rush. Couldn't you just take her home to the dower house at Landon Park with you, and bring her back again next year?'

'The gel's four and twenty! Another year shan't be in her favour. I have Kathryn's best interest at heart when I say that I mean to secure her an offer as soon as possible.'

A wave of disgruntlement swept over the Viscount. The thought of Kathryn Marchant married to another man goaded him to irritation. For all that he'd sworn he would not touch her, for all his good intention for friendship and nothing more, he knew them both for the lies they were. Nothing and everything had changed from that moment at Lady Finlay's ball. He wanted her as much as ever—no, if he was honest, even more so. Then, her standing had been little better than a servant, and now, thanks to his grandmother, she was an eligible young lady on the marriage mart. Eligible to everyone other than himself. He gave a dry little smile and continued to sip his Madeira.

Chapter Ten

With a tap at the door, Kathryn walked into the room. She had changed into one of her new afternoon dresses and tidied the wayward curls of her hair. Her hands were still pink from being scrubbed with soap, but all signs of the black dust had disappeared. As soon as she entered she had the feeling that she had just interrupted an awkward silence. 'I hope the Madeira has refreshed you, my lady.'

'Never more so,' replied her ladyship. 'I was tempted by a second slice, but managed to resist.' She passed Kathryn a slice of sponge cake on a delicate painted plate. 'Help yourself to Madeira, my dear.'

Kathryn did as she was bid and then settled herself down in the empty chair next to the table. It was positioned beside the dowager and directly opposite the Viscount, so that she could not help but obtain an excellent view of his face. He certainly looked to be pondering something. She wondered what his grandmother had said to make him so. Perhaps more strikingly, though, he had a faint thumbprint of charcoal dust upon his chin and a smaller but similar mark upon his cheek. Her eyes flitted towards Lady Maybury who seemed to have observed nothing out of the ordinary with her grandson's appearance. Kathryn's fingers twisted at the skirt of her dress. What to do? She couldn't let Nicholas leave the house like that—he'd be a laughing stock within five minutes. But to point it out when his grandmother had failed to do so was to risk embarrassing both the dowager and her grandson. Perhaps Lady Maybury would notice before that time came. True to form, the old lady was suffering none of her grandson's silence.

'Well?' A haughty brow rose. 'We are waiting for your discussions on Brighthelmstone.'

Ravensmede seemed to shake the contemplative mood from him, and started to recount the arrangements he had made. 'My servants shall travel down tomorrow to ensure that all is ready for us upon our arrival. We will leave on Thursday, take a leisurely journey with one overnight stop on the way down, thus arriving on Friday. No point in making the journey uncomfortable for you.'

His grandmother made what sounded to be a snort of disgust at this point, but he ignored it and continued undeterred.

'Once in Brighthelmstone I've rented us a house for the month. I'm told it has a good position with unimpeded views of the sea. It's on The Steyne and not far from the Prince's Pavilion.'

'Sea views?' Kathryn could not keep the excitement from her voice.

Ravensmede's mouth curved into a smile, the first since she had returned to the room. 'They're reported to be most scenic.'

Her face lit with delight. 'I can scarcely wait.'

'You will be taking your sketching and painting materials?' He was looking at her with an unfathomable expression.

She smiled. 'Of course! Nothing could stop me. You know how I treasure them.'

His voice was a low husky murmur. 'Yes.'

Their eyes met across the table and held.

'Kathryn, my dear,' Lady Maybury interrupted. 'Do you think I have enough shawls? I should so hate to catch a chill. They do say that the sea air is rather invigorating.'

'Perhaps we could check this afternoon, and if you're not happy we could go shopping for some more.' Kathryn ignored the flush that had leapt to her cheeks and turned her attentions to the dowager. 'Are you warm enough just now? If not, I could fetch you a thicker shawl.'

'I'm pleasantly warm and cosy,' said the old lady.

A subtle knock at the door and a footman appeared. 'Lady Kiddleby to see you, my lady. I've taken the liberty of showing her to the drawing room.'

The dowager's brow wrinkled. 'Frances here? I wasn't expecting her.' She turned to Kathryn. 'This is not like her at all. I had best go to her at once. Come along, gel.'

The footman gave one delicate cough. 'Lady Kiddleby asked that she see you alone, my lady.' He coughed again. 'Her ladyship appears somewhat distressed.'

'Dear, oh, dear,' muttered Lady Maybury. 'No doubt Harriet has been upsetting her mama again. This shouldn't take long.' She drew her grandson a warning stare. 'I trust Nick shall not make a cake of himself in my absence.' She stared at him a moment longer before rising from her chair and leaving.

A silence.

The moss green eyes were on Kathryn.

'Would you like another glass of Madeira? Some more cake, perhaps?' She lifted the bottle.

'No, thank you.'

Another silence.

'I wondered if I might speak bluntly to you, Kathryn.'

The butterflies flocked within her stomach. She netted them down. 'Certainly, Nicholas.' She saw the tug of his mouth at her use of his name.

He touched a finger to his lips in a gesture that she had not seen him use before. 'I'm concerned about my grandmother's health. You see how much she hates to admit the slightest weakness and would never tell either of us if she were unwell. All these late nights are taking their toll on her. For all her protestations, she's in her eighty-first year with a weak heart, and I fear her hectic lifestyle of late is in danger of making her ill.'

The hand of guilt laid heavy on Kathryn's heart. 'I'm afraid you may be right. I know Lady Maybury enjoys going out but…I cannot help but wonder that she has my interest too much at heart.' She nibbled again at her lip and wondered if she should be confessing such things to her employer's grandson. 'At many events she's insistent that I accept every invitation to dance. Indeed, it's now quite common that I spend the evening upon the dance floor and not in Lady Maybury's company at all.' The grey eyes raised to Lord Ravensmede's with mounting anxiety. 'I have tried to refuse, but she won't have it. I feel that her fatigue is, in part, my fault.'

'My grandmother is forthright in her opinions, and once set upon a course is not easy to dissuade. You must not blame yourself, Kathryn, and, indeed, I did not mean that you should do so.' He reached across the table and gently took one of her hands.

'Is there anything I can do to remedy the situation?' She thought she saw something akin to guilt flicker within his gaze and then it was gone.

'The only way my grandmother would be persuaded to

stay in on an evening is if you, yourself, Kathryn, were to feel unwell.' It was there again, an uneasiness in his eyes.

She understood very well what he was asking her to do. 'Yes. The odd headache…' Her words trailed off and she stared at the charcoal dust smears upon his face. She touched a finger to those imprinted places, but upon her own face instead of his. She couldn't let him leave like that, and the dowager's poor eyesight was unlikely to notice. Her finger tapped very deliberately against her chin. 'You have a little…' The finger tapped harder.

Ravensmede's focus sharpened like that of a starving man shown food.

'And here.' The finger had moved to poke a spot on her own cheek.

'Kathryn?'

'A little charcoal, just here.'

The dark head shook its denial. 'No, your face is quite clean,' he said slowly, and licked his lips. The green eyes had darkened considerably and were watching the movement of her fingers intently.

'But yours is not,' she replied with a wry smile. 'Somehow you must have touched the charcoal dust. And it's now on your face.'

A large hand rubbed ineffectually at a clean patch of skin on his cheek.

'No, it's over some more.'

'Here?' The fingers slid too far to the left.

'No, back a bit.'

Again he missed the mark.

'Move forward a little.' Before she could contemplate and dismiss the impulse she half-rose from her seat, reached across the table and moved her hand to touch his face. Then slowly and with what amounted to a caress she rubbed her thumb against the square edge of his chin until no trace of the charcoal remained. From there her fingers slid to his cheek. She could feel the roughness of the first hint of stubble on his skin, was so close she could smell the bergamot of his scent. With calm deliberation she kept her gaze fixed on the charcoal-shadowed skin. A sharp intake of breath that was not her own made her forget her purpose. His eyes were a deep, dark green, and in them was a hunger that made her forget where she was and just what she was doing.

'Kathryn,' he whispered. And contained in that single word was both pain and longing.

She could not speak, could not move, just stared into those dark mesmerising eyes.

His face crept towards hers until she could feel the warm stir of his breath tickle her cheek.

Chest compressed. Heart expanded. A sudden rush of blood to her head.

The smouldering gaze dropped to her lips.

Yes, she wanted to shout, but no words came. His skin brushed hers. Cheek touched cheek.

'Kathryn,' he said, and it was almost a growl. The need in his voice mirrored that in her soul.

Yes! Please. Did she have to plead? Their noses nestled. Lips so close to imagine their feeling. Touching...almost. Nothing existed outside that single moment. Locked in time, alone. 'Nick!' her voice was hoarse, barely recognisable as her own. She wanted *him,* nothing more.

His mouth claimed hers in sweeping possession.

A sigh and her lips opened in sweet surrender. Wanting all he would give, giving all he would take. Urgent. Demanding. The table jabbed at the front of her thighs as he pulled her into his arms. She felt the press of his hands upon her back, warm, caressing.

Footsteps sounded outside the door. A knock.

Before she could even register what was happening, Kathryn found herself quite suddenly pushed back into her chair.

By the time the footman entered the library it was to find a rather startled-looking Miss Marchant sitting bolt upright in her chair, and Lord Ravensmede lounging rather too comfortably back in his. 'Beggin' your pardon, my lord, but her ladyship has asked if Miss Marchant would be so kind as to come through to the drawing room.'

Kathryn's legs were shaking so badly that, had she not already been seated, she was positive she would have fallen. Her heart pounded in her chest. 'Yes, certainly. I'll come right away.'

Lord Ravensmede gave a nod of his head, and the footman retreated. 'Kathryn.'

A blush coloured her cheeks and her fingers plucked at the material of her skirt. She did not raise her eyes. 'I…I must go.'

Ravensmede stood. 'Until Thursday then,' he said politely and bowed.

Only when she reached the door did Kathryn look back to meet his eyes and see that they held a most determined promise.

Mrs Marchant was busy at her needlework within the drawing room of the house in Green Street when the visitor arrived. No sooner had the maid whispered the lady's name in Mrs Marchant's ear than the lady herself appeared in the doorway.

'My dear Mrs Marchant!' gushed the female voice. 'Anna. I came as quickly as I could. I'm only just returned to town as of last night.'

Anna Marchant's eyes widened momentarily and then she regained her composure. 'Amanda.' She smiled. 'Please do come in and take a seat.'

'Thank you. You're too kind,' said the widow and arranged herself on a stylish gold-covered armchair.

'How was your visit to the country?' enquired Mrs Marchant with politeness. 'I trust your sister is well again.'

'I cannot stand the country,' confided Mrs White. 'The roads are in a terrible state—it takes an age to travel anywhere; there is a dearth of anything remotely interesting; and the assemblies are positively backward in terms of their fashion and the clodhoppers who patronise them. All in all a thoroughly boring experience.' She did not mention that her ennui more specifically arose from the absence of rich young men to fawn over her beauty. The country squires and parsons in the vicinity were all elderly or grossly overweight or both. Amanda White had found much time to brood upon matters in Amersham…and subsequently the insult Ravensmede had dealt her in that little room at Lady Finlay's ball had become honed and magnified in her memory.

'And your sister?' prompted Mrs Marchant again.

'Delivered of a bawling son,' came the curt reply. 'But that is not of what I came to speak. My letter—'

'Came as a great shock to me. I must confess I'd no notion of that which you suggested. My niece has always behaved with the utmost decorum,' Anna lied.

'My dear Mrs Marchant, it pained me to have to be the bearer of such bad tidings; I felt I had little choice but to warn you of the danger.' The afternoon dress was cut to display Amanda White's curvaceous figure to perfection, its deep ruby-red coloration complementing the lush darkness of the widow's elegantly coiffured hair, and the smooth sheen of her pale skin. 'Not long after I'd sent the letter I learned that Lady Maybury has indeed taken the girl up as her companion.'

The accusation hung in the air between them.

'Your letter arrived too late,' said Mrs Marchant crisply. 'Kathryn had already accepted the position, and, whatever you might suggest, Lady Maybury has a lineage without blemish. The Mayburys are not without influence.'

The widow pouted her pretty lips while a sly expression slid across her eyes. 'Indeed, but it makes no difference to what Miss Marchant is about.'

Much as Anna Marchant disliked her niece, she realised full well the consequences of any slur on Kathryn's name. The Marchant family would not escape unscathed. And so it was with this in mind that Mrs Marchant prepared to defend her niece's reputation. 'Kathryn is a young lady of impeccable values. I must insist that your fears as to any improper behaviour are quite mistaken, Mrs White.'

'I saw her with my own eyes, Mrs Marchant, behaving little better than a common whore.'

A sharp inhalation of breath. 'Mrs White! I must protest!'

Both women rose to their feet.

'I thought to tell you only because I know you hold a fine and respectable standing within society; I did not think that you would want your own reputation jeopardised by your niece's scandalous behaviour.' She shrugged her beautiful shoulders. 'But if you are not interested in your niece's dealings…' Mrs White made to leave.

'There is no need for such haste,' said Anna Marchant with feigned sweetness, as she moved swiftly to block her visitor's exit path. 'Your concern for my family is admirable.' It was a lie, of course. The pretty young widow had no concern for anyone other than herself. Anna knew quite clearly that Amanda White's world revolved singularly around herself and her pretty looks. Not that it made one blind bit of difference to Mrs Marchant. But it did make her wonder as to exactly what game Amanda White was playing with her letter and her visit. A smile moved across Mrs Marchant's lips. 'Sit down again, Amanda,' she said. 'I would hear what you have to say.' Before the afternoon was out Anna Marchant intended to have the answer to all of her questions in full.

Mrs White swished her skirts and sat back down before the words were even out of her hostess's mouth. It was clear that she had had no intention of going anywhere. Mrs Marchant's smile stretched wider. 'If you can bring yourself to tell me all, my dear,' she added.

'Dearest Anna,' simpered Amanda White. 'I shall strive to do what is right.' And proceeded to describe the scene she had interrupted between Lord Ravensmede and Kathryn Marchant at Lady Finlay's ball. Every possible embellishment was added, so that not only was Ravensmede kissing Miss Marchant with a passion (which of course was true) but he was kneading upon her breast and clutching her against him in the most carnal of manners. Mrs White gave no mention as to her own assignation with the Viscount and said she had wandered into the room quite mistakenly.

'Why did you not tell me at the ball?' asked Mrs Marchant, barely able to hide the rise in her temper.

'Lord Cadmount whisked me away just as I was about to. And then Ravensmede practically bullied me into going to the country. I was fearful to do anything other than he bid.'

Anna Marchant had trouble in believing that. The young widow was a woman more used to controlling men than being controlled by them.

'You must have enough influence over the girl to bring her to her senses before it is too late. Surely you can make her give up this ridiculous affair and move back here with you? You're her aunt; she'll listen to you. Forbid the girl any further contact with Ravensmede. It's not too late to salvage some semblance of her reputation. The fact that she's his mistress has not yet become common knowledge. There's still time, if you act now.'

So that was what Amanda White wanted: Ravensmede… for herself. Mrs Marchant said somewhat coldly, 'Kathryn has always been disobedient and stubborn. There is, and always has been, little love lost between us.'

'Oh, dear,' said Amanda without the slightest emotion. 'It would be such a shame if anyone else was to learn of your niece's indiscretion. Especially now that she's Lady Maybury's companion, it wouldn't take much for the whole town to deduce that she's Ravensmede's mistress. Poor Lottie, I suppose she shall not remain unaffected by Kathryn's shame.' Mrs White looked slyly at the older woman. 'And you had such hopes of a good match for your daughter.'

Anna Marchant's teeth clamped tightly shut. Her top lip curled with unconcealed contempt. She knew very well exactly what Mrs White was about: blackmail. Get Kathryn back to Green Street, or the widow would spread her gossip. And the thought that Kathryn had allowed her to be put into such a position fuelled the hatred already burning in Mrs Marchant's breast. 'Very well, Amanda. Since you place me in an untenable position, I will do as you ask, but I must warn you it may take some little time.'

'The longer you take, dear Anna, the more chance there is that I may inadvertently let something slip. I can be such a forgetful puss at times.'

'Then the sooner I start, the better,' said Mrs Marchant.

Mrs White took the hint and soon only Anna Marchant sat alone in the drawing room, cursing the widow, trying to think how she could lure Kathryn back from Lady Maybury, planning just what she would do to her when she did.

The journey to Brighthelmstone was pleasantly uneventful. Although the road appeared to be dreadfully busy with carriages and carts, Ravensmede assured both Kathryn and his grandmother that the level of traffic was quite normal. The journey, having been designed not to tire Lady Maybury, was conducted at a leisurely pace. Ravensmede's large closed carriage was well sprung and he had ensured not only a mountain of travelling rugs for his grandmother's warmth but also a basket of provisions including the most refreshing lemonade Kathryn had ever tasted. Lady Maybury alternated between watching the passing countryside, chatting and napping, the latter activity occupying the greater part of her time, thus leaving her companion to fill her own time as best she could. As far as Kathryn was concerned, it was fortuitous indeed that Lord Ravensmede had chosen to ride alongside the carriage rather than travel within its small interior.

Following what had flared between them in the library, being alone in the Viscount's presence was not something with which Kathryn trusted herself. And she had only herself to blame. It was true that he had kissed her, but she was well aware that her own actions had precipitated such a response. Touching her fingers to his face…whatever would he think of her? Kathryn gritted her teeth at the all-too-obvious answer to that question. How could she repay the dowager's kindness by encouraging her grandson, for there was no doubt that that was what her behaviour amounted to? It was behaviour in keeping with Aunt Anna and Cousin Lottie's taunts. Tired fingers kneaded against her forehead, and she sighed. The passing hedges and fields became nothing more than a distant green blur.

'Kathryn? What's wrong? Are you sickening for something?' Lady Maybury's voice interrupted her reverie.

She glanced up in surprise, thinking the dowager to have still been sleeping. 'No, my lady. I have the slightest of headaches, nothing more.'

'Then we must make a stop at the next inn and allow you to wander and stretch your legs. Perhaps it's being cooped up in here that has brought it on.'

'Oh, no, please do not.' The thought of having to face Lord Ravensmede again so soon was not something with which she felt comfortable.

The faded green eyes narrowed in their focus and lingered upon Kathryn's anxiety-ridden countenance.

Blood scalded her cheeks under the scrutiny. 'I mean… please don't stop for me. I would rather press on with our journey.' She plucked at the material of her skirts. 'I'm so looking forward to arriving in Brighthelmstone,' she said with false brightness.

Lady Maybury remained singularly unconvinced. 'Indeed,' she said drily. 'We've first to spend the night at Horley Common.' Not once had that relentless green gaze faltered.

'Yes.' Kathryn did not know what else to say. The old lady was looking at her as if she could see her innermost thoughts. If that were indeed true, Miss Kathryn Marchant would find herself turned off without so much as a reference, and then what would she do? Half of London's bachelors would not be dangling after her then!

Neither woman spoke and the dowager had not shifted her attention.

'Has Nick done something to upset you?' The question fired out of the silence.

Kathryn's heart missed a beat. She forced herself to stay calm. 'No. Lord Ravensmede has been nothing but polite at all times.' She chewed at her lip. 'What makes you think so?'

'An idle thought, nothing more.' The dowager tucked the blanket higher, so that it almost reached her chin. 'Still, if you say there's nothing in it…' One white brow raised in enquiry.

'Nothing at all, my lady,' Kathryn speedily replied. 'I… I'm very happy as your companion, Lady Maybury. Indeed, I've never been happier, and hope that nothing will jeopardise my position.'

The snow white curls nodded once. 'And I'm very happy to have you as my friend.' Lady Maybury relaxed back against the seat and snuggled beneath her blankets. Within a matter of minutes her eyelids had shuttered and the gentle wheeze of her snoring filled the carriage.

That night in the King's Arms coaching inn and for the entirety of the journey Ravensmede behaved with the utmost propriety. Nothing in his speech or manner betrayed in the slightest that he felt anything other than the appropriate civil concern for his grandmother's companion. Neither did he suggest at any time that he should share the carriage, even when he was subjected to a rather heavy rain shower. So by the time the small party arrived in Brighthelmstone to take up residence within their rented accommodation, Kathryn had managed to rein her wayward emotions under sensible control once more.

The episode in Lady Maybury's library was banished far

from her thoughts, and she was able to relax, firm in the belief that she would not tempt fate by allowing herself to spend any time alone in the company of Lord Ravensmede. The trip to the seaside resort was the chance of a lifetime and she did not mean to spoil the opportunity with silly worrying. She would not shatter Lady Maybury's trust in her. And as for her own trust in herself, she knew that now, where Nicholas was concerned, that was something on which she could not completely depend. If she did not want to ruin her new life as the dowager's companion, then Kathryn had better have a care…especially here in Brighthelmstone.

'I trust you find the house to your liking?' Ravensmede sipped at his coffee the next morning and watched the ladies across the breakfast table.

Lady Maybury's ferocity of attack on a pile of carved ham mellowed slightly. 'I'm never anything but completely uncomfortable when anywhere but Landon Park, but…' she sniffed '…I suppose I will suffer to endure it.'

'Kathryn?' the Viscount asked politely.

'It's beautiful both inside and out, and our every comfort has been thought of. You spoke truthfully when you promised splendid views of the sea. I haven't seen the like for many a year.' She paused and looked at Lady Maybury. 'It was very kind of you to arrange that my bedchamber was seaward facing. It's a dream come true to wake up each morning and look out at the shoreline.'

'If you would be so good as to pass me that dish of eggs, Nick.' The dowager pointed to the silver heated dish on the serving table and waited expectantly. 'Had nothing to do with me, dear gel. It was Nicholas that took care of all the arrangements. Gave us the scenic chambers, took the one at the back for himself.' She helped herself to four large poached eggs and several slices of toast.

'Grandmama...' Ravensmede laughed '...I swear your appetite is expanding for a lady of such sylph-like proportions.' He did not want to discuss the sleeping arrangements, or the fact that there was a scant four feet of landing separating his chamber from Kathryn Marchant's. Such thoughts were dangerous and that was a direction in which he could not afford to wander if he did not want to disgrace them all. And anyway, hadn't his grandmother determined that Kathryn would be spoken for before the Season was out?

The old lady laughed. 'You'll not get round me with such flattery. Quite how these young females survive on fresh air and lemonade I shall never know. It's not natural. In my day we ate all we could and our stays did the rest. Wretchedly uncomfortable to wear, but a dashed necessity. Didn't pick at our food like sparrows then, I can tell you.'

'I fear you're embarrassing Kathryn.'

'Stuff and nonsense,' replied his grandparent. 'Kathryn's not some milk-and-water miss just out of the school room. Likes a good serving of food herself. No silly nonsense with this gel, is there, Kathryn?'

'I hope not, my lady.' Kathryn smiled at the dowager.

Ravensmede remembered Kathryn Marchant's collarbone outlined starkly against her bruised skin, and her gaunt cheeks when they had first brought her back to Ravensmede House. She had no need to starve herself; Anna Marchant had only been too willing to undertake that task, and her cruel treatment had had nothing to do with slender figures, of that he was quite sure. He brushed such disconcerting thoughts aside and forced his mind to more pleasant avenues. 'I've already paid my respects to the Master of Ceremonies and we are therefore welcome to attend all balls at both sets of assembly rooms. Those in the Castle Inn are on Mondays, and on Wednesdays the balls are in the Old Ship. Card parties are on Wednesdays and Fridays, and on Sundays there is a promenade and a public tea. There's also the theatre in North Street, and of course Brighthelmstone races. If you let me know which you prefer, I will make the necessary arrangements.'

His grandmother nodded. 'Yes, indeed. I think a shopping trip is first in order so that we may familiarise ourselves with the town. A walk along the pier, and a closer inspection of that monstrosity that the Prince Regent calls his Marine Pavilion would also be of benefit. I've a notion to view the new stables and riding house built in the Indian style. Thereafter, we'll see which cards arrive.'

'And the theatre?' her grandson prompted.

'I shall think about it,' the old lady pronounced.

And so their holiday by the sea began very well.

The Castle Inn suite of rooms were superbly adorned in the classical decorative style of Robert Adam. It seemed that the fine weather had brought out all of the town's polite society, for the rooms were filled despite the departure of many local families to London for the Season. It was a cosier affair than the grand London balls with less of those who called the tune that the rest of the *ton* were happy to dance to, nevertheless Kathryn hovered close to Lady Maybury. Despite arriving as a stranger, Lady Maybury soon discovered some old friends, through which numerous introductions were made. Thus, as had become usual, Kathryn's dance card was soon filled.

Nicholas chatted politely to the rather awestruck young men who flocked to meet the notorious Viscount of Ravensmede. He danced with the flustered giggling débutantes and made great efforts to ensure that his grandmother's friends' granddaughters were not ignored. And through it all he watched every move that Kathryn made, knew every man with whom she danced. It was a self-inflicted torture to which he readily ascribed. Indeed, he had taken great pains to ensure that they were not too much in each other's company that evening. He had brought her here to enjoy herself, to let her paint the sea scenes so dear to her heart. Damn it, but the girl deserved some little joy in her life. The last thing he intended doing was allowing some uncontrollable instinct spoil the whole set-up they had worked so hard to achieve. He'd damn well not risk both her and his grandmother's happiness, not to satisfy some selfish whim of his own. But he had to admit that his growing obsession with his grandparent's companion had never felt less like a whim.

'Your servant, Miss Linton.' Ravensmede delivered the simpering girl back to her mother, bowed and beat a hasty retreat. The chit's mama's eyes were positively ogling with speculation. 'Grandmama, you seem to be in high spirits.' Lady Maybury was fanning herself with an exuberance he'd rarely seen.

'Of course I am,' she crowed loudly. 'I haven't seen Jane Ballantyne for an age. All her granddaughters are married and she has twelve great-grandchildren to boot. I have only a paltry four to compete. What is that compared to twelve? And you show no signs of obliging me.'

'You begin to sound like my father, ma'am,' the Viscount replied. 'It is a favourite topic of his and has been for the last few years.'

The volume of her voice dropped somewhat. 'You cannot blame him, Nick, he does not wish all that he has worked for over the years to pass to the dreadful Herbert.'

Ravensmede thought of the selfish connivance of his cousin Herbert and was forced to agree. 'Neither do I. But I'll marry when I'm good and ready, and not because m'father wills it.'

The dowager raised one cynical white eyebrow. Any reply she might have made was forgotten when Lady Farrow, who was seated some six feet away, gestured at Lady Maybury and shouted, 'Is not the next dance the waltz?'

'I do believe you're correct, Hetty,' came the reply.

Just the mention of the dance was enough to have Ravensmede glancing around for Kathryn. He soon spotted her across the room partnering some fair-faced youth for a country dance. The final bars sounded and soon the couple were making their way back towards Lady Maybury. No sooner had Kathryn been deposited beside the dowager than a most insistent Mr Silverton appeared to spirit her away.

Her eyes turned to Ravensmede in question. The action was not lost on Lady Maybury, who seemed to positively encourage the young gentleman's interest in her companion. 'Off you go, Kathryn,' she said before turning to her grandson. 'He seems a delightful young man.'

Ravensmede could do nothing while the woman who had come to haunt his dreams was led out on to the floor and allowed herself to be held quite properly and at the allotted distance by Mr Silverton. She had never danced the waltz with anyone other than himself. And now she was in Silverton's arms. It was for the best, her best, or so he told himself.

'Nicholas,' Lady Maybury said, 'I have a need to seek the retiring room. Be so kind as to watch over Kathryn until I return. Do *not* let the gel come after me, and make sure that she dances with the next gentleman whose name is upon her card.' Lady Maybury drew him a fierce look and then disappeared across the room, leaving only the lingering scent of her lavender perfume.

Ravensmede was forced to watch Kathryn and Mr Silverton dance the whole of the waltz, before that young man returned her to him.

She smiled and a spasm of desire shot through him. 'Is all well with Lady Maybury? She is not here.'

'A visit to the retiring room. She'll rejoin us shortly.'

'Then I should assist her.' Without waiting for an answer she made to move towards the door.

His hand caught her arm. 'No, Kathryn. She has asked that you stay here. You know how she hates a fuss.' With a gentle tug he pulled her back towards him.

'Yes, you're right. I should wait for her to return.'

Sliding his fingers down to meet her hand, Ravensmede delivered a gentle squeeze. 'Did you enjoy your waltz?' The cream silk of her glove was smooth beneath his fingers. His hand encompassed hers possessively.

She glanced up at him, the hint of a blush just beginning on her cheeks, then peered around to check that no one was close enough to see what was happening between them.

'Nicholas,' she whispered, 'I—'

Whatever she intended to say was cut short by the return of Mr Silverton, followed closely by the dowager.

'Sir…' Lady Maybury tapped her fan in fake reproof against the young man's sleeve. 'I do believe you've already stood up with my companion not so very long ago.'

Mr Silverton smiled a charming smile. 'That is indeed the case, but with a lady as beautiful as Miss Marchant all others pale to insignificance. I would be honoured if she would stand up with me again.'

Lady Maybury smiled in her most agreeable manner. 'Well, as it's you,' she said indulgently.

'You have my undying gratitude, my lady,' replied Mr Silverton and moved to face Kathryn. 'I do believe you've granted me the honour of agreeing to partner me for the quadrille.'

'I…I…' Mr Silverton's name was indeed written upon her card against the quadrille. Kathryn shot a glance at Ravensmede. The expression on his face was unreadable.

'Don't dally, Kathryn,' urged the dowager.

She had little option but to place her hand in Mr Silverton's and allow him to lead her out on to the dance floor…again. 'Thank you, sir.' Kathryn's impression of Harry Silverton from their waltz was confirmed during the quadrille. He seemed a pleasant enough young man, even if he was prone to a rather overly dramatic turn of speech. It was all Kathryn could do to keep a straight face when he waxed lyrical on the extent of her beauty. She was sure that he lavished the gush of compliments upon every woman with whom he danced. She endured a eulogy on her fine eyes, but when he started to compare her hair to a cascade of rich autumn leaves she laughed and begged him to tell her something of the town of Brighthelmstone instead. When at last the dance was over Mr Silverton returned her, breathless and smiling, to Lady Maybury.

Mr Silverton bowed low to both the dowager and Kathryn. 'May I have your permission to call upon your companion, my lady?'

'*I* have no objection to your calling, sir,' said Lady Maybury, 'but you have yet to ask Miss Marchant her opinion on the matter.'

Three faces turned to Kathryn, who was looking both surprised and a little awkward.

'I…I think perhaps…'

'Thank you, my dear Miss Marchant, I shall count the minutes until we meet again,' said Mr Silverton.

It was then that Kathryn noticed the dangerous darkening of Lord Ravensmede's eyes and the glacial stare that he drew Mr Silverton. Harry Silverton saw it too. With a speedily executed bow the young gentleman was gone, leaving Kathryn to face Lord Ravensmede.

Chapter Eleven

The journey home was rather stilted. Lady Maybury seemed drained of energy, and lay back against the seat with her eyes closed. Lord Ravensmede's ill humour did not recede. His manner was distant and he seemed loath to converse. Only Kathryn, balanced precariously next to the dowager, was desperate for a chance to clear the air. She looked hopefully at Lady Maybury, but the old lady's eyes remained shut. And the Viscount had not yet glanced in her direction. Silence reined supreme. She cleared her throat in an attempt to draw his attention.

The dark profile did not turn from the window.

'Nicholas,' she said softly.

He looked at her then, but she could scarcely see his face through the darkness.

Where to begin? 'I…' It was clear that Mr Silverton's presumption had annoyed him. She was being paid as Lady Maybury's companion, not to court a suitor while the dowager sat alone and fatigued. She tried again. 'I did not encourage Mr Silverton's attentions.'

'Didn't you?' He sounded quite unlike his usual self. There was a distance in his voice, so different from anything that she had heard previously. And exactly what did he seem to be implying?

A gentle snoring sounded from the dowager.

'Of course not! We came to Brighthelmstone for the sake of Lady Maybury's health.'

Ravensmede did not correct her misconception.

'I'm her companion. It isn't right that gentlemen should call upon me here.'

'Then why did you not refuse your permission?'

She faltered. Why indeed? Shock, disbelief. She had fully intended to do so, but Mr Silverton had been too quick in his assumption. 'I didn't grant him my permission,' she insisted with a degree of stubbornness.

'I don't think that Mr Silverton understood that to be the case.'

He was taunting her! How could he change from the caring, passionate man she knew to the arrogant goading creature that sat before her now? Kathryn felt her temper rising. Not only had she to somehow contrive to get rid of Mr Silverton, but she now also had to explain herself to the Viscount. 'Then he's a fool,' she snapped.

'Kathryn, you must have given him some sign to encourage his attentions. Believe me, I know when a gentleman is intent upon securing a lady's interest. And you appeared to be enjoying his company immensely,' he said meaningfully.

'Indeed I did, sir, but with the exception of being civil, I assure you that I have given that gentleman no indication that his attentions would be welcomed.'

Silence.

She could just imagine the arrogant arch of his eyebrow at her reply, and it irked her, as did his ridiculous assumptions. 'How could you even think that I would encourage him?'

'How indeed?' Irony laid heavy on his words.

An exasperated sigh escaped her. 'You're being unfair, my lord.'

'And you're being completely fair, are you, Kathryn?'

A blush rose in her cheeks. 'I know my place,' she said quietly. 'Be assured that I have no intention of receiving Mr Silverton as a visitor.'

'Really? I think that my grandmother may have other ideas on that matter.'

'Then think what you will, Lord Ravensmede,' she said, 'your mind is clearly made up, far be it for me to try to change it.'

'Kathryn Marchant, you are the most infuriating of women.'

'Of that I'm most heartily glad!' she retorted.

The volume of Ravensmede's voice increased. 'God help me, you drive me to—'

'Nicholas?' Lady Maybury's croaked through the darkness.

'Grandmama,' the Viscount replied with forced serenity. It sounded as if his teeth had ground together.

'Why are you shouting at my companion?'

'I beg your pardon, ma'am.'

Kathryn felt the old lady raise herself up on the seat. 'It isn't my pardon you should be begging,' she said quietly. 'I haven't a mind to find myself a new companion quite yet.'

A slowing of the carriage. The crunch of footsteps outside the door.

'Forgive me, Miss Marchant.' Following his stiff words, the Viscount opened the door and jumped down from the carriage before the steps were in place. He waited until they were fitted before helping first Lady Maybury, and then her companion, out into the gloomily lit darkness. The glow of the street lanterns was not sufficient to safely light their path up the stone stairs to the front door of the house so Ravensmede took both ladies' arms in his to act as guide.

Kathryn felt the tension in the muscles beneath her fingers, though her touch was light as a dragonfly and knew the man beside her was angry beyond belief. What she did not yet fully understand was why. Assuredly she should not have answered him back, but his accusations were silly in the extreme. As if she would encourage any man's attentions! Her mind flitted back to the passions she had shared with Nicholas. Oh, heavens! She began to have an appreciation of his point. If she could respond so readily to him, then he had every reason to believe her a woman of loose moral fibre. Oh Lord, what a web she had spun herself into!

Mr Silverton waited only as long as the following afternoon to call upon Miss Marchant, and had the audacity to bring with him quite the most ridiculously outsized arrangement of flowers that had been seen for a long time.

'Ah, Mr Silverton.' Lady Maybury sounded encouraging.

'Lady Maybury, a pleasure to see you again, ma'am. Is Miss Marchant—'

The dowager smiled a smile of sweetness and light. 'She is almost ready. A young lady's *toilette* must never be rushed, sir. The result would be too disastrous to imagine.'

'Indeed, my lady. I didn't mean to hurry Miss Marchant. I'm happy to wait upon her leisure.'

'I'm sure you are.' The smile deepened.

Mr Silverton smoothed his neckcloth. 'Is Lord Ravensmede at home?'

'Why, did you wish for a word?' her ladyship asked.

'No, no,' Mr Silverton said with undue haste. 'I was merely being polite. No need to disturb his lordship.'

'Quite,' agreed Lady Maybury, and then confided, 'It is for the best. He can be prone to a cantankerous disposition when disturbed by unannounced visitors, although I'm sure that would not be the case with you.'

Mr Silverton appeared to have developed an irritation in his throat. He coughed loudly and shifted from one foot to the other.

The awkwardness of the moment was alleviated by the appearance of a maid who quietly informed her ladyship that Miss Marchant was feeling unwell and would not be able to receive Mr Silverton.

The dowager's brows knitted. 'What nonsense is this?' She peered at the unfortunate maid. 'She was as fit as a fiddle not half an hour ago. Tell Kathryn to come down this instant or I shall be forced to fetch her myself.'

Five minutes later Kathryn entered the drawing room to have the huge mass of flowers suddenly thrust upon her.

'How kind, Mr Silverton. Perhaps if I were to just put them down here until—'

The dowager interrupted. 'Of course, my dear. The maid shall see to them. What's all this about feeling unwell? Perhaps it would be better to postpone the drive until another day.'

A look of hope entered Kathryn's eyes.

'I shall ring for tea and cakes and leave you young things together.' She smiled again at Harry Silverton. 'And ensure that Lord Ravensmede knows not to disturb you.'

The young man coughed and glanced around nervously as if he thought Lord Ravensmede was about to appear..

With Nicholas's accusations still clear in Kathryn's mind, Lady Maybury's suggestion seemed unbearable. 'Thank you, my lady, but there's no need. I feel quite recovered.'

'Well, if you're sure,' said the dowager somewhat doubtfully.

'Absolutely positive,' said Kathryn.

'In that case, be sure to have a lovely time on your drive.'

Kathryn eyed Lady Maybury anxiously. 'I shall not be long, my lady.'

'Take as long as you like, dear gel.' The old lady's hand waved imperiously. 'No need to hurry back.'

Mr Silverton's nerves vanished in an instant. He beamed his gratitude at the dowager.

'Off you go, then,' said Lady Maybury from the other side of the drawing room.

The couple walked across the brightly decorated rug.

Just as Mr Silverton's hand touched to the door handle the elderly voice boomed, 'You will bring m'gel back safely, won't you, sir? I fear that I have a tendency to overprotectiveness when it comes to m'companion.'

The young man flushed an unbecoming shade of puce, and announced dramatically, 'Indeed, my lady. I shall guard Miss Marchant with my very life.'

Lord Ravensmede did not enter the drawing room until he had heard the bang of the front door. He strolled nonchalantly to the window and watched while Harry Silverton drove Kathryn away in a hideously over-decorated green-and-black painted phaeton.

'I fancy Mr Silverton is quite taken with her. If I'm not mistaken, an offer will be forthcoming before we leave for London,' said his grandmother from behind his shoulder.

'Unfortunately it appears that you may be right,' he said.

One white brow lifted. 'He's heir to a small fortune, I'll have you know.'

'True, though it's earned through trade.' Ravensmede's eyes were still trained upon the diminishing dot in the distance.

'What's wrong with that? He may not be an aristocrat, but he's wealthy enough to provide her with a life of comfort.'

'Harry Silverton's father owns a string of coffee houses across the country, as well as a sugar plantation in the West Indies. The family are from Bristol and are here only for a short break.' Despite the bright sunshine in the room a sombre aura clung to Lord Ravensmede. 'I've a notion that Kathryn wouldn't approve of the Silverton family's interest in slavery.'

His grandmother frowned. 'Good gad!'

'It's also rumoured that they have significant investments in the overseas slave trade, although if Lansdowne's bill goes through that won't last for much longer.'

'Blast! That means Silverton won't do at all. Can't have her marrying into a family like that.' She eyed him sharply. 'I suppose I should be thankful that you've been thorough in your enquiries, m'boy.' The old lady wandered across the room and sat herself neatly upon the sofa. 'Is there any gentleman either here or in London that you would recommend as a husband for Kathryn?'

'No.' The Viscount's reply was definite.

Lady Maybury's eyes were focused upon her grandson's face. 'But if you were to give the matter some thought, perhaps you would be able to come up with a suitable candidate.'

'I do not think so, ma'am.' Ravensmede's lips compressed into a hard line.

'It's unlike you to admit defeat with such ease,' his grandmother goaded.

An ache was growing in the Viscount's chest. 'I'm not normally asked to play matchmaker.'

She sighed. 'Does not Kathryn deserve this little happiness? A husband, children of her own?'

'She's happy as she is. There's no need for her to marry.'

'You wish her to stay a companion to me for ever? And what when I'm dead, what will happen to her then? Servant to another old woman? Or, worse still, mistress to some man? Believe me, Nick, when I tell you that it's no life for a girl like Kathryn. I know this is not easy for you, boy, but it's for the best. So, please, just give the matter a little thought.'

He sighed, running his fingers through his hair. 'Very well. I promise I'll give serious consideration to what you've asked.'

The faded green eyes held his with a sudden intensity. 'I sincerely hope so, Nick. I've come to care very much for Kathryn, and as an unmarried lady she's vulnerable...in all sorts of ways. I cannot rest easy until I know the gel is settled in marriage.'

'Grandmama, you've saved Kathryn from a life of misery, and offered her a home with you. What harm can come to her? She's safer now than she's ever been.'

'Is she?' she asked in a strange tone of voice. The old hand moved to clasp his, and she sighed. 'Life is never that simple.'

At last Kathryn saw the blessed emergence of the familiar front door. If the phaeton had not stood so high upon the ground, she would have leapt down herself without having to suffer the indignity of Harry Silverton's hands around her waist.

'Mr Silverton!' she chided when he seemed reluctant to relinquish his hold upon her person.

The gentleman's corn-gold hair glistened in the sunlight. His deep blue eyes held admiration. 'You're such a vision of loveliness as to make a gentleman forget himself.' But he released her nevertheless. 'Will you be attending Lady Richardson's ball tonight?'

'I don't know what Lady Maybury has planned. As her companion it's my duty to accompany her in whatever her wishes might be.' She struggled to remove her fingers from Mr Silverton's clasp and attempted to hurry up the stone stairs to the front door.

Mr Silverton matched her every step. 'May I be so bold as to suggest that I call again tomorrow? We could perhaps drive further out into the country.'

'No. I don't think so, sir.' Kathryn wished to spare Mr Silverton's pride; had seen the effects of her cousin's cruel words too many times not to feel some sympathy for the young man standing so hopefully beside her. 'I believe Lady Maybury has already made arrangements for tomorrow.'

'Then I shall call the following day.' They were standing beside the heavy wooden door.

Kathryn made to press the bell, but not before his fingers plucked her hand to his lips. 'No.' She surreptitiously tried to pull away, while taking care not to create a scene. 'I thank you for your kind invitation, and indeed I've enjoyed our pleasant drive today, but I cannot accompany you again any day this week.' Mr Silverton's grip was surprisingly strong.

'Why ever not, Miss Marchant?' The blue eyes held hers with rather too much intimacy than that with which she was comfortable. 'Without you I shall fade as a flower deprived of sunlight.' He pulled her closer.

'Because she'll be accompanying me,' a deep voice drawled as the door swung open.

Kathryn had never been so relieved to see Nicholas. 'Lord Ravensmede,' she uttered faintly, unsure of how much of the conversation he had overheard.

In one swift movement he had plucked Kathryn to stand

behind him in the hall, leaving the golden-haired young man upon the step. 'I bid you good day, Mr Silverton.'

Harry Silverton lingered only a moment longer, then, with a low and elaborate flourish of a bow, he was gone.

The door slammed in his wake.

'Oh, Nicholas, thank you!' Relief swamped Kathryn. She wrapped her arms around the Viscount's body in a bear hug and pressed her cheek to the broad expanse of his chest. 'I thought he would never go. He was so very insistent and I didn't wish to be unkind.' Freshly laundered linen, and soap, and bergamot tickled her nose. She relaxed against him. 'I can only pray that he doesn't mean to make me an offer!'

His hands touched to her back in a gentle gesture.

Her eyes were still closed, her body nestled into his.

Ravensmede stood very still. It seemed that even his breath had halted.

There was the sudden rattle of china and a footman carrying a heavily loaded tea tray appeared at the top of the staircase leading up from the kitchen.

Kathryn's eyes sprung open, her body tensed for flight.

The footman did not look in the entwined couple's direction once. He merely trotted across the hallway, tapped politely on the library door, and waited until a loud female voice bid him enter.

'Thank you, Toby,' said Lady Maybury. 'I thought I heard a carriage outside. If Miss Marchant has returned, have her come through for tea.'

By the time the footman had reappeared to impart this message Kathryn was standing innocently by Lord Ravensmede's side. Meekly she turned towards the library door.

'Ah, Nick as well,' said the dowager and raised an eyebrow. 'You had best come in before the tea grows cold.'

Only once three cups of steaming tea had been delivered in the finest of saucers did Lady Maybury continue between sips, 'Why, my dear gel, has Mr Silverton overtaxed you?' The faded green eyes peered sharply at her companion's face. 'I do declare that your colour appears unnaturally high and you seem to be a little out of breath.' The dowager appealed to her grandson. 'Am I not right, Nick? Pray do examine Kathryn's visage.'

It was true that Kathryn had indeed appeared a trifle flushed upon entering the library, her embarrassment due to the realisation that she had just thrown her arms around Lord Ravensmede and her wholly inappropriate action had been witnessed by a footman, who was now guaranteed to delight in informing the whole of Ravensmede's staff of what he had seen. Beneath the dowager's blatant scrutiny the faint rose bloom intensified to a scarlet flame of colour. Had the dowager heard her words to Nicholas? Did she have any inclination of exactly what her companion had just done? Kathryn forced herself to meet the faded green gaze. There was nothing of shock or anger there, only a little sadness.

'Grandmama, I'm sure Kathryn's cheeks are flushed only from the fresh air.'

'Perhaps,' said Lady Maybury. 'I'm all-agog to hear the news regarding her drive with Mr Silverton. Pray tell all, my dear.'

Kathryn took a fortifying gulp of tea. 'We travelled along the coastal road in order to enjoy the views. They are indeed quite spectacular.'

'How far along the coastal road?' said the Viscount.

'To a place named Rottingdean, whereupon we turned around and came back by the same route.'

Lady Maybury frowned. 'I had thought Mr Silverton's drive to be limited to the park.'

Kathryn did not want to cause trouble for the young man, but neither was she prepared to risk giving the impression that she liked him. 'He thought that I would prefer the scenery along the coast.'

'And did you agree to this change of plan?' asked the dowager.

A pause. 'No.'

'Shall Mr Silverton be calling again?' A white eyebrow raised in enquiry.

Ravensmede's gaze slid to Kathryn's.

'No,' she said, 'I hope that he will not.'

The old lady sighed. 'It is just as well.'

Kathryn's eyes widened. 'I thought—'

Lady Maybury leaned towards Kathryn. 'I had high hopes for you and him. He seemed such a personable young man too. But that was before I learned where his family's money comes from.' She sniffed disapprovingly. 'Slavery,' she said succinctly.

Kathryn's cup clanked back down against her saucer, and said quietly, 'Then it is for the best that he will not be coming back.'

A silence followed.

'You said the views along the coastal road are impressive,' said Ravensmede.

'Yes, they're wonderfully scenic.'

'In that case, why don't we travel the route ourselves? We could spend the day on the beach, Cook can pack us a basket of food…and you can take your paintbox. Would tomorrow suit?'

Kathryn's eyes lit up, and she smiled before waiting politely for Lady Maybury to deliver her verdict.

'It's certainly a splendid suggestion, but Kathryn and I will go alone. We've been monopolising you, Nicholas, and we should allow you to pursue your own interests for the day. You will grow bored with constantly escorting an old lady and her companion.' She faced her grandson. 'Is that not a better idea?'

Ravensmede returned his grandmother's look in full. Something unspoken flashed between them, something slightly dangerous that conflicted with the smiles upon their faces.

Sensing the underlying current, Kathryn felt unease prickle between her shoulder blades.

'A veritable genius.' replied Lord Ravensmede. 'Your concern for my welfare is admirable, Grandmama, but I am of a mind to enjoy the beach tomorrow too. You would not forbid my interest?'

Faded green eyes locked with bright green, in a battle of wills, and then the dowager inclined her head. 'Not this time,' she said.

Anna Marchant left the maid to close the gaping front door and hurried towards the parlour at the back of the house, pulling off her gloves and straw bonnet as she went. Just as she expected, she found her husband sitting comfortably spread out upon the sofa reading a newspaper. He glanced up briefly as she shut the door firmly behind her, then resumed his examination of the article in which he appeared engrossed.

'You're back sooner than I expected,' said Mr Marchant without taking his eyes from the paper. 'Did the visit not go well?'

'The place is empty. A serving girl told me that Lady Maybury and her companion have gone to Brighthelmstone.'

'So?' Mr Marchant could barely keep the boredom from his voice.

'With Lord Ravensmede.'

'So?' he said again.

'Oh, for heaven's sake!' snapped Mrs Marchant. 'Must I spell it out for you?'

Henry Marchant slowly lowered the newspaper from before his face and looked at his wife with an irritated expression. 'Madam, I'm sure that is what you intend, so hurry up and be done with it.'

'Lord Ravensmede has hired a house for them all in Brighthelmstone. He is living in the same premises as Kathryn!'

'And his grandmother,' pointed out Mr Marchant.

'It's all of a sham, I tell you. He's taken Kathryn as his mistress under the guise of her being Lady Maybury's companion.'

'Nonsense! Eleanor Maybury wouldn't risk her reputation with such a thing. And I doubt that even Ravensmede would drag his own grandmother into such a scheme. Besides, if Ravensmede wanted Kathryn as his mistress, he would have taken her by now, and as blatantly as he did all of the others.'

'Whatever you say, the rumours are already starting, Henry!' she snapped. 'Think what they'll do to Lottie. Where will her chances of a good match be then, when her cousin is publicly denounced as a slut?'

'I'm sure you're mistaken, Anna.'

'There's very much more danger than you realise.' She thought fleetingly of Amanda White's threat. 'I'm sure that a trip to Brighthelmstone is in order.'

Mr Marchant's eyes rolled up into his head. 'I think you're overreacting, my dear.'

'You'll see who is overreacting when your niece is the talk of the town and your own daughter's chance of marriage is ruined because of it. Hasn't Kathryn lived as part of this family for the past three years? Do you think I've learned nothing of the girl's nature? I've said all along that she is a sly and wanton miss, and now I'm proved right. Will you let her destroy Lottie's chance? Are you content to let your brother's daughter ruin everything for your own flesh and blood? Mark my words, if one hint of this comes out before Lottie has made a match, then she'll be on the shelf for ever!' Mrs Marchant pressed a small lace handkerchief to her eye and gave a sniff.

With the weary resignation of a man who knew full well that his wife would give him no peace, Henry Marchant closed the newspaper, folded it in two and sat it upon his lap. 'What do you wish to do?'

'Fetch Kathryn back from Brighthelmstone. Have her live here with us.'

'You dislike the girl immensely, Anna. Why do you want her back here?'

'If she's under our control, then we can limit any danger she might do. She's safer where we can keep an eye on her.' She made no mention of Mrs White and what the widow had insinuated. 'For the sake of my daughter's future I'm prepared to suffer Kathryn's presence.'

Mr Marchant digested his wife's words. 'Kathryn is now four and twenty. We cannot force her to come back with us. The last time I saw her she seemed determined in her role as Lady Maybury's companion. And I don't suppose she can have too fond a remembrance of this house.'

'Why should she should think of us with anything less than gratitude? Had it not been for this family Kathryn would have ended up in the gutter. However, I concede that she always was a selfish, addle-brained miss, and perhaps that has biased her memory,' said Mrs Marchant. 'That's why I have a plan.' For the first time since entering the parlour she smiled. 'You need not worry, Henry. A little family trip to partake of the sea air and Kathryn will return with us to Green Street.' Her smile broadened. 'And then she'll be sorry, very sorry indeed, for all the trouble that she's caused.'

The day was fine and warm with a pleasant sea breeze. They had encamped on the beach at a secluded spot not far removed from the town of Worthing, and enjoyed a tasty lunch from the depths of the hamper. Lady Maybury, having battled valiantly against the combined effects of fatigue, heat and a full stomach, lost the struggle and finally succumbed to sleep beneath the shade of her parasol.

Kathryn sat on a small stool placed upon the sand. The wooden drawing board was balanced on her thighs, and she stared completely entranced by the vast expanse of sea that stretched before her.

'Do you mind if I watch while you paint?' Ravensmede sat down beside the slight figure that seemed dwarfed beneath the drawing board. He could not see her face beneath that hideous monstrosity of a bonnet. Momentarily he wondered why she was still insistently wearing the mud-brown hat; he knew full well that his grandmother had been doggedly trying to add to her companion's wardrobe piece by piece.

She turned then and looked up. 'I don't mind, but I warn you that it shall not take long before you grow deeply and thoroughly bored.' The small pink mouth curved in a tantalising smile. An errant curl fluttered across her cheek.

She was teasing him! One dark eyebrow arched wryly. 'Perhaps. I've never watched an artist at work. This will be a new experience for me.'

'Then I hope it will be an enjoyable one.' She fixed her

paper into place and, after checking the sharpness of her pencil, began to sketch.

'I thought you meant to paint the scene.'

'Yes. But I'll draw it out first in pencil so that I may rectify any mistakes I make. Only when I'm happy that I have the proportions correct will I begin to paint.' All the while her hand moved swiftly, lightly against the paper, her gaze flickering constantly between the sea and the white patch of paper.

Ravensmede's gaze flitted from the view to the paper to the fine bones of the woman's face. She was clearly intent on her task, her gaze never wandering once. There was an openness about her expression, as if she had let fall the careful guard of politeness. This was the Kathryn that he'd witnessed humming behind the tree in St James's Park, who had gazed unseeing at a blackened fireplace in her aunt's house, and smiled when he touched his fingers to her cheek. It was the first time she'd knowingly let him witness her escape, to wherever it was she went when she looked so faraway. He could see the same look in her eye, as if she were present in body only and her mind somewhere else altogether. 'You must have had a very good drawing master!' The faint marks on the paper were beginning to take shape.

A laugh that caught on the wind was carried out to sea. 'I taught myself! Anyone can sketch if they practise enough, and believe me I practised!' Still her gaze moved methodically between the lapping water and the white page. Her eyes were narrowed and her face crinkled against the sun. 'Have you tried your hand at it?'

'As a child, never since. My mother said it was quite the most ugly picture she had ever seen. My talents lie elsewhere, or so I am told.'

Only then did she pause, and look up into his face. 'I'm

sure your mother was wrong.' Her voice was quietly serious and her eyes filled with compassion. Then she smiled and the moment was gone, as quickly as it had arrived. She resumed her scrutiny of the view. 'I can teach you if you like.' It was uttered lightly, as if it were of no importance. The pencil scraped against the page, making a vertical line here, a horizontal line there.

A blossoming of warmth erupted in Ravensmede's chest. He longed to lay his arm across her shoulders, to hold her to him. 'I would like that very much, Kathryn.' Since his dismissal of Harry Silverton he had felt extraordinarily happy. Knowing that she held the golden-haired youth in no regard and had sought his own protection gladdened his heart. It was better than winning a fortune night after night at the gaming tables. Better than an evening spent drinking with Caddie and the boys. And infinitely better than any time he had spent in any other woman's company. He watched while she covered the entirety of the page, excepting the odd patch here and there, in pale blue paint.

As if in answer to his unasked question she offered an explanation. 'It's a wash to unify the background. It should also stop the glare from the sun bouncing up from the page and dazzling my eyes. Conditions today are perfect and it should dry in no time. Would you like some paper and a pencil?'

'For now I'm content to watch you. But I'll hold you to your promise of sketching lessons.' The sun beat down with a relentless strength. 'Kathryn, would you mind if I removed my coat?'

She did not look up from mixing her paints. 'Of course not. You must be melting beneath all that wool.'

He peeled off the offending item and laid it down by his side. The cooling breeze fluttered through the fine lawn sleeves of his shirt, and he toyed with the idea of removing his waistcoat and neckcloth, but thought better of it. Daubs of paint were stroked on to the paper by her delicate hand. Just watching fascinated Ravensmede. The slow repetitive action, sometimes tentative, sometimes bold, held his attention so that he could not look away. A sheet of calm sparkling water, clear and deep, of quite the brightest turquoise coloration he had seen. Small waves lapping against the shoreline in the distance. Cloudless blue sky stretching out far to the horizon. She captured it all. And the air of peace that surrounded them. Nothing sounded except the soft rush of the sea on the sand and the cry of the gulls circling high overhead. It was enough just to sit by her, to be in her presence. No need for words. Soft sugary sand warm to the touch, all yellow and fawn, golden and white. On and on she painted, as if driven by the magic of the place to set down a record of what had existed for this one afternoon. And all the while Ravensmede sat by her side.

One last brush stroke and she cocked her head to the side. 'Mmm.' It was a gentle sigh of consideration. With deliberate care she set the board aside and clambered to her feet. 'Pins and needles in my legs.' She wiggled and stamped her feet to ease the numbness and, unmindful of her bonnet ribbons that were flapping around her chin, pressed the weighty drawing board into the Viscount's hands. 'Please can you hold this, just so that I may check that I haven't missed anything. I always find looking at it from a distance helps.' Without waiting for an answer she moved several paces away and turned to inspect the painting.

Ravensmede looked down at the drawing board. 'You've captured the view splendidly.'

'And you, sir, are looking at it upside down!' came the cheeky reply.

His mouth curved to a grin. 'I beg your pardon, but I can imagine how it will appear the right way round.'

'Here, let me hold it while you look.' Just as the board was halfway between them, a gust of wind lifted Kathryn's bonnet clear off her head. She loosed her grip on the board in order to catch it back, just as Ravensmede engaged in the same idea. The drawing board dropped to the sand, bouncing on its side before fortuitously landing on its back. The ties that had secured the painting dislodged in the fall, and, before either Kathryn or Nicholas could move, the sheets of paper were sent flapping and tumbling along the sand. 'Oh, no! That's all the paper I have left!' The bonnet forgotten, Kathryn scrabbled along the shore, and successfully captured the newly finished coastal painting along with four blank sheets. Another five blew ever further away.

Nicholas caught her elbow. 'You have the painting. Let the others go. We can buy some more.'

'No, paper is costly and all my money is accounted for. Please!'

With that look in her eyes and the long wind-blown hair tumbling in a cascade of curls reaching far past her shoulders, Ravensmede would have granted her anything. In a gallant gesture he chased the sheets until at last he had caught each and every one. His exertions had taken him quite some distance along the beach, but when he looked round the slight figure was running towards him. Her hair glinted a reddish golden brown in the sunlight and was billowing wantonly in every direction. A pair of finely shaped ankles and calves were visible each time the wind gusted around her skirts; moreover, the material was blown to cling revealingly against the shape of her thighs and hips. As he collected the papers into a tidy pile, one caught his eye. It was not blank, but contained a pencil drawing executed in great detail. The breath caught in Ravensmede's throat. His eyes raked the picture a moment longer before he bent low to the ground as if catching the papers up to him, and slipped the folded sheet into the secret inner pocket of his waistcoat.

'Nicholas!'

He glanced up and, with a smile upon his face, closed the empty distance between them.

She was breathless and pink-cheeked, wild and wind blown, and, judging from the look on her face, enormously glad to see him. Lord, but he could have taken her in his arms and tumbled her upon the sand there and then.

'Did you catch them?'

'Every last one!' He passed the sheets into her hands, and, unable to help himself, caught her to him and pressed a kiss to the top of her head.

She did not chastise him. Rather one small hand reached up and squeezed his arm. 'Thank you,' she said simply.

'Come on, we had best get you back to Grandmama. She won't be pleased when she wakens.'

The silver-grey eyes were lit with pearly hues. 'Perhaps she's still sleeping and has not seen this débâcle.'

The Viscount laughed and gently swept his thumb across the bridge of her nose. 'I was thinking more about your freckles. Although, personally, I find them quite delightful.' He cast her a wicked grin, held her hand in his and walked back towards his grandmother.

It was fortunate that the Viscount spotted Kathryn's hairpins in the sand close by her abandoned drawing board, and more fortunate still that the young lady had managed to secure her hair in some vestige of a respectable style before the dowager awakened. Alas, the mud-brown bonnet had been swept far out to sea, a mishap that caused his lordship much rejoicing. Indeed, Lord Ravensmede could not remember a more enjoyable day.

Chapter Twelve

It was one quiet afternoon close to the end of the second week of their holiday when Lady Maybury announced her intention to host a ball at her grandson's townhouse.

Lady Maybury continued, 'I haven't told him of m'idea yet, and I don't want you letting the cat out of the bag, young lady. It wouldn't do to pester him with all the details when we can sort those out ourselves.'

'But shouldn't we check that he's happy to host such an event first, before making any arrangements?'

'He shall not be hosting the ball. That's my job,' said the dowager. 'I assure you, Kathryn, he'll be most pleased with my efforts.'

'But…'

Lady Maybury raised an eyebrow. 'Are you questioning that I know what's best for m'own grandson?'

Kathryn saw all the warning signs and sought to pacify her employer. 'No, not at all, my lady. If you've made up your mind then—'

'My mind is made up,' came the adamant reply. 'Fetch paper, pen and ink and let us begin the list of guests. There's no time like the present. And remember that it's to remain, for the minute, a secret from Nicholas.'

'Of course.' Kathryn did as she was bid and waited.

Soon the dowager was reeling off names. 'Lord and Lady Radford, Lord and Lady Finlay, Lady Hadstone, Mrs Lee, Lady Farrow, oh, and Mr and Mrs Barchester and the Misses Barchester, but most certainly not Mr and Mrs Palmer—they're too vulgar for words.' She sighed and waited for Kathryn's neat script to stop. And then the pause stretched a little longer. 'Naturally, when Nicholas is married, his wife will take over such duties. This is likely to be the last time I'm able to play hostess for him.'

Something cold wrapped itself around Kathryn's chest and squeezed. She was quite unable to move. 'I didn't realise that the Viscount was betrothed.'

'Oh, he isn't…well, not officially.' Lady Maybury leaned forward and lowered her voice. 'If I'm not mistaken, that is something that will be remedied before the Season is at a close.' She gave a sage nod of the head. 'M'son Charles—that is, Nick's father, Earl Maybury—thinks it's more than time that the boy settled down and all that, what with him having sown more than his fair share of wild oats.' She sniffed.

A tinge of colour touched Kathryn's cheeks.

'Still, the least said about that side of things the better. Afraid us Mayburys are not a patient lot, as you may already have guessed, m'dear. But even Nick can't hold out much longer against his father. Charles's practically got it all arranged. Gel is from a decent family, good breeding and money too. Can't think why Nick's being so confoundedly stubborn. Wretched boy's got to marry at some time or other.'

Kathryn reeled as if she had suffered a hard blow to the stomach. 'May I…' she steeled herself to ask the question, knowing full well that she should not, that it was none of her business '…enquire as to the name of the lady that the Earl has in mind?'

The old lady's eyes washed bright with compassion. 'Her name is Miss Francesca Paton, my dear, and m'son is very determined that Nick weds her.' She stretched out one small hand and touched it consolingly to Kathryn's.

The slow terrible thud of Kathryn's heart intensified, and deep within the pit of her stomach she tasted the sourness of nausea. It seemed that there was a ligature tightening around her throat.

'There may very well be two weddings. Your future should be assured.' The dowager smiled a small smile. 'I'm very determined to catch *you* a good match.'

'No, my lady, that really isn't necessary,' Kathryn gasped. 'I'm here as your companion, not to find myself a husband.' In her distress she gripped the pen as if she would snap it clean in two, her fingers inadvertently touching too close to the nib and bleeding a large stain of ink across her skin.

'Tush! Don't you want a husband and children of your own?'

'I…' She struggled to keep the emotion from her voice. 'I'm happy here with you.'

'As I'm happy to have you here. But you deserve a life of your own, gel, and I mean to see that you get it.'

The flow of black letters upon the page began to swim. A strange dizziness was rolling up towards her head. She forced herself to inhale deeply, slowly, willed herself not to yield to it. Determination clamped her teeth hard together, and made her lips stiff and immobile. Surely she wasn't about to faint? She *never* fainted. Not Kathryn Marchant. But the dizzy sensation was expanding and black spots danced in the periphery of her vision. Sweat prickled down the length of her spine, and her chest felt so tight that she feared she could not draw the air into her lungs. She shut her eyelids tightly, struggling to regain control, doggedly telling herself that she would not faint, not here, not now, not when the dowager might guess the terrible truth.

'Kathryn.' The old lady's voice was soft. 'It is for the best.'

One breath, and then another. In. And out. She forced herself to breathe deeply, fingers clinging for dear life to the arms of the chair. Slowly the darkness receded, but the terrible weight upon her chest lay there still. It took great strength to hide the utter bleakness that swept over her. The constriction in her chest had spread to her throat, wherein the lump was making it difficult to swallow. But for that terrible tightness all else had grown numb, a creeping lack of sensation that rendered her trapped upon the Sheraton-style mahogany armchair. She could no longer see the words that she had penned so carefully on the neatly cut sheet, could scarcely see the paper itself. 'Please excuse me, Lady Maybury. I fear I'm feeling a little unwell,' she managed to say through lips that could barely move.

'Unwell?' A concerned old hand touched to Kathryn's arm. 'You have gone very pale of a sudden. And you feel so hot! Mary shall take you straight to bed. You'll feel better after a little rest.'

'I'll finish the guest list in the morning,' murmured Kathryn and laid the paper and pen down carefully beside the inkstand on the desk.

'Stop worrying over that. There's time enough yet.' The old lady tried to look severe and for the first time failed miserably. 'I'll brook no disobedience, gel, so off to bed with you.'

'Yes, thank you, my lady.' Kathryn kept her eyes averted, frightened of losing her last vestige of control, and quietly hurried from the room.

* * *

Not one last drop of blood lingered in Kathryn's face as she climbed the central staircase towards her bedchamber. Slowly, methodically her fingers worked at the material of her skirt, pleating and smoothing and pleating again, in a rhythmic repetitive motion. And all the while, with each and every step that she took, she wondered why it had taken such a revelation for her to realise the truth. Not that Lord Ravensmede was to marry. As Earl Maybury's heir that had always been a foregone conclusion. Perhaps she hadn't expected it to happen quite so soon, but that in itself was not the issue. No, the truth was much worse than that. In her time as Lady Maybury's companion, she, plain, penniless Kathryn Marchant, had fallen head over heels in love with Nicholas Maybury; a man who was not only an aristocrat and enormously wealthy, but also a rake. And the reward for such a foolish action could only be a broken heart.

At the same time as Kathryn was treading silently up the central staircase by the maid's side, Lord Ravensmede was sitting at the small reading table by the window of his bedchamber in the house in Brighthelmstone. Before him, spread out upon the fine polished cherry-wood, was a drawing. The piece had been executed with a fine attention to detail, capturing every nuance of the sitter, conveying, by the skilled use of line and shade, that person's precise character. Ravensmede studied every last pencil mark upon the paper until at last he sat back in the chair and smiled. It was clear that the artist viewed the model in a positive light. Indeed, he would go as far as to say that there was a distinct tenderness in the rendition. And that thought was a most appealing one to the Viscount, given that the artist was none other than Kathryn, and the model—himself.

Quite when she had secretly sketched his likeness he did not know. These last weeks in Brighthelmstone had only confirmed what he knew of her: that she was kind and compassionate and imbued with a freedom of imagination that allowed her to escape the mundane, the tiresome, and the downright painful. Whether it be through the pictures set down on paper or those that she wove in her head, Kathryn was an artist, and a passionate one at that.

Beneath that meek and mild exterior was hidden an ardour. But Ravensmede had seen beneath the mask, had known the essence of her from the very first night of their meeting, when he'd mistaken her for Amanda White—as if there could ever be any comparison. Mrs White was little better than a courtesan who sold herself to the highest bidder. Kathryn was quite simply the most amazing woman he had ever met. Lust or desire did not go near to explaining the compulsion he felt for her. Just to be near her, to make her laugh, to ensure her safety, to hear her voice, and hold her within his arms... It was far and beyond anything he had ever known.

A door opened across the corridor. Female voices. One that sounded to be the maid, the other so quiet as to almost hide its owner. But he didn't need to hear Kathryn's voice to know that she was near. Awareness coursed through him. And he knew that he could no longer ignore his need to see her, to watch her smile, to touch his lips to hers. Sandwiching the portrait between two blank sheets of paper, he hid it carefully under some papers within a drawer. Then, waiting until he heard the maid make her way along to the servants' stairwell, he quietly opened his door and stepped across the corridor to Kathryn's bedchamber.

Kathryn heard the light knock at her door and scrambled up from the top of the bed. 'I'm just coming,' she said in a small controlled voice. Before she had taken one step further Lord Ravensmede entered, closing the door noiselessly behind him. Her hand clasped at the bedside table. She could not speak.

'Kathryn!' Shock widened his eyes. Whatever he had been expecting to see, it wasn't the state of distress that he now witnessed. He reached her in two strides and without the slightest hesitation pulled her into his arms. Scanning her face, he took in the unnaturally white cheeks, and the haunted look in her eyes. 'What in Hades has happened?' His clasp was gentle, his hands firm and reassuring against her back.

'Nothing at all. You need not concern yourself with me, sir.' She struggled to release herself from his embrace, but he was having none of it. 'Lord Ravensmede, I must insist that you unhand me. It isn't fitting that you should be here in my bedchamber or that you have your arms around me.' The pale lips pressed tight together as she spoke the words quietly and with as much dignity as she could muster.

'What is this nonsense, Kathryn? I had thought us to have reached an understanding. Are we not friends?'

She lowered her face that he might not see her pain. 'Indeed we are, sir.'

'Then I would know what this about.'

'I made a mistake,' she said, choosing her words carefully. 'We cannot go on as before…even if we are friends. I'm your grandmother's companion…and I'm happy with that.'

'Have you had word from your aunt?' he asked suspiciously.

'No, of course not. She doesn't even know that I'm here.'

'Is it my grandmother?'

'No.' The word was determined and defiant.

'Then why are you so upset?'

'I'm not.'

A single dark eyebrow arched. With slow deliberation he traced a thumb down her cheek.

'No!' She twisted her face away. Then with more control, 'Please do not.'

His hand stilled in mid-air, then dropped back down to her arm. 'Tell me what's wrong, Kathryn.'

'I cannot.'

Silence hummed.

'Kathryn,' he said.

Slowly, unable to help herself, she looked round at him.

His eyes were dark as the depths of a forest where the light does not reach.

Beneath his gaze Kathryn felt her resolve waver. For there she could see concern and kindness…and something else, something for which hope flared…then died when rational thought intruded. It seemed that she had to drag the breath into her lungs, force it back out again. Pain burst anew into a thousand piercing shards at just how much she had come to love this man.

She could not tell him. Had to preserve some scrap of pride. He desired her…as she desired him, to touch, to kiss, to hold. He liked her, of that she was sure. But he did not love her; could not love her as she loved him. Before the summer was out he would be betrothed to another woman…married even. And Kathryn would be alone once more. She chided herself for the fool that she was. Even as he looked at her as if he could see into her very soul, she lowered her eyes.

She wanted to scream and cry and beat her hands upon the breadth of his chest. She wanted to condemn him for each kiss, for every caress of his hand, the very smile on his face, the tender light in his eyes. How dare he tempt her to love him knowing full well nothing decent could ever come of it!

The pain seared across her chest, tightening her throat. Through all the storm of emotions she held herself erect, clinging to her dignity, never once yielding to the sensations that battered her. 'Please leave now.' Those three small words so quietly, so politely spoken were more devastating than if she had roared at the top of her voice.

'No, not until you tell me what's going on.' One hand slid up the length of her arm to grip upon her shoulder.

She trembled beneath his touch. 'Please don't touch me.'

The green eyes widened, but her heart was so wounded she did not see his hurt.

His grip loosened until his fingers were nothing more than a featherlight touch. They lingered for a matter of seconds longer and then slowly, as if by an act of immense willpower, they were gone. And now, even though there was nothing holding her to him, she felt the warmth of his proximity, felt the urge to wrap her arms around him, bury her face against his chest. Her breath was uneven and shallow, coming in fits and starts, gasps and shudders. She forced herself to step back, to reject temptation before it caught her completely. One tiny step backwards, and then another.

He made to follow.

'Lord Ravensmede,' she said as coldly as she could.

Frustration boiled. 'Damnation, Kathryn, just tell me!'

For one tiny sliver of a moment she nearly did, and then common sense came to the fore once more and she shook her head.

She composed her face, unwilling to have him witness the full extent of her humiliation. 'I fear I have the headache, sir. If you would be so kind as to leave me to my rest.'

Nicholas's gaze did not falter. He made no move.

She swallowed hard. Her heart shuddered. 'Please,

Nicholas,' she whispered. 'Don't make this any harder than it already is. Just go.'

He looked at her for a moment longer, then turned and walked towards the door.

Ravensmede only suffered Kathryn's new cold formal treatment for two days before a visit from Harry Silverton forced a change in matters. The Viscount was staring moodily out of the library window, sipping his brandy when the footman arrived.

'Beggin' your pardon, m'lord, but her ladyship sent me. Mr Silverton has arrived and is refusing to leave until he's seen Miss Marchant.'

The ejection of Mr Silverton was to prove rather more problematic than Lord Ravensmede anticipated.

'Ravensmede, you dashed scoundrel!' Harry Silverton bellowed upon Ravensmede's entry to the drawing room.

'Mr Silverton, I must urge you to refrain from shouting when my grandmother is present.' Ravensmede looked meaningfully at the dowager perched uneasily on the edge of the sofa.

The younger man swayed a little unsteadily on his feet. 'Where have you hidden her?'

'If by *her* you're referring to Miss Marchant, then I regret to inform you that she is at present not in to any visitors, nor is she likely to be so in the near future.'

'You confounded cur!' The young gentleman's words had a distinctive slur to them. 'You mean to keep her for yourself. To have her as your mistress when a decent man like me would ask for nothing but her hand in marriage!' The stench of alcohol pervading the room intensified as Mr Silverton staggered closer.

Ravensmede's eyes narrowed at the insult, but he had no intention of bandying insults with a young man who was quite clearly well and truly foxed. 'I will ask you to leave, Mr Silverton, before you make even more of a fool of yourself than you have already.'

'Damn you, Ravensmede, but I love her, and I ain't leaving until I've seen her to tell her so.' He scrabbled about in his pocket and produced a sheet of folded paper. 'I've written a poem to her beauty. I mean for her to have it.' He tried to focus on the sheet for several minutes, but to no avail.

'I shall not ask you again, sir.' The Viscount's voice cut sharply through the room.

'I've heard all about you. Who hasn't? The infamous Viscount of Ravensmede and his affairs with the ladies, and the gaming tables.' The youngster sneered. 'A rake, a libertine and more! I've seen the way you look at Miss Marchant and I don't like it.' The dramatic effect of this little speech was somewhat ruined by the enormous belch that succeeded it. 'I do beg your pardon,' said Mr Silverton.

'You've said quite enough for one night, sir. And if you won't leave of your own accord, then I will throw you out, you insolent dog!' Lord Ravensmede moved to effect his threat.

'Stay where you are!' Silverton produced a pistol and waved it in the Viscount's direction. The poem fluttered unnoticed to the floor.

Lady Maybury, who had hitherto been silent throughout the two men's exchange, leapt to her feet. 'How dare you threaten m'grandson, you odious toad! Put that infernal thing away this instant!'

Mr Silverton looked momentarily at the barrel of his pistol as if he were surprised to find the object in his hand. 'I do beg your pardon, my lady. I was just trying to explain to Lord

Ravensmede that I...' he hiccuped and waved the pistol as he spoke '...am here to prevent him ruining Miss Marchant. I mean to have her as my wife, you see.'

'Yes, I see only too well, sir, that you are going about courting m'companion in quite the wrong manner. Not only are you rather the worse for drink, but I'm offended by your presence.' Lady Maybury sniffed and cast him the haughtiest of looks.

'I didn't mean to insult *you*, my lady. *You* are not a rake of the worst degree.' He gestured the muzzle in the dowager's direction as he stressed the word *you*. '*You* do not mean to keep her from me.' The pistol pointed directly at Lady Maybury, the young man's finger lingering unwittingly around the trigger.

Ravensmede had seen enough. He knew exactly how dangerous a weapon could be, particularly in the hands of a man who had clearly spent the best part of the day in the consumption of brandy if the reek was anything to go by. His grandmother was at risk and that was not something he was prepared to tolerate. Moving with a speed and agility that surprised them all, Ravensmede launched himself at the golden-haired visitor, placing his own body between the pistol and the old lady at whom it was levelled. The momentum of his flight carried both men to the floor, but not before an almighty roar reverberated around the drawing room. The stench of gunpowder arose, along with a plume of blue smoke.

Lady Maybury screamed.

Ravensmede clambered up from the prostrate body.

Harry Silverton's bright blue eyes stared up, round, unblinking.

The dowager scrabbled towards her grandson. 'Thank God you're safe!'

The door swung open. Pounding steps as the butler and two footmen clattered in.

'Escort this gentleman from the house. A carriage shall be required to send him on his way.' Ravensmede bent to retrieve the pistol from where it lay discarded upon the floor. 'He no longer has need of this.'

A soft gasp came from the doorway.

She was by his side, hands on his sleeve, eyes wide with fear. 'Nicholas?' No polite and distant 'Lord Ravensmede' this time.

He smiled a lazy smile, and pulled her against the right-hand side of his body. 'Mr Silverton was just leaving.'

Kathryn grabbed both of his arms and stared up into his face, all thoughts of propriety forgotten in her concern. 'What happened?'

An unmistakable wince, and an involuntary withdrawal.

'Nicholas?' With an escalating dread Kathryn let her gaze travel slowly to where her right hand clutched.

The material of his coat was warm and wet beneath her fingers. She drew them back, swallowed hard and looked down at the glistening red stain. The grey eyes swivelled to meet his. 'You're bleeding.'

'The smallest scratch, nothing more.'

Lady Maybury stepped closer, her bony fingers clutching to her throat. 'You're shot,' she whispered in disbelief.

Her words seemed to rouse Harry Silverton from his faint. The gentleman raised himself cautiously to his elbows, terror dawning upon his countenance. 'Was an accident.' And with that he groaned and gingerly replaced his head upon the polished wooden floorboards.

Time ceased. The moment stretched unending, until at last the dowager gave a frightened little mew. 'So much blood.'

'Grandmama.' Ravensmede stepped forward to reassure the elderly lady who was tottering rather unsteadily on her feet.

As if awakening from a stupor Kathryn sprang to life. She moved to gently, but firmly, place Lady Maybury in the closest armchair. 'My lady, please do not alarm yourself. It's as Nicholas says, a flesh wound that bleeds prolifically.' Even as she uttered the reassurance her own fears, her own darkest dread, were being thrust deep down, hidden far out of sight. But from across the years came an image of another man she had loved, of the faint lingering smell of gunpowder, and the raw stench of blood...and her father's lifeless fingers resting upon his desk, still wrapped around the handle of the pistol. Her eyes shuttered. Dear God, not Nicholas, never Nicholas. He could not die...she would not let him. Determination rose. She gritted her teeth hard, shock still kicking in her gut. Pushed away all memories, all thoughts of fear and panic. Allowed instinct to take over. Kathryn would do whatever she had to...for Nicholas's sake. So, having dealt with the dowager for the minute, she instructed the butler to send for a physician, the first footman to fetch boiled water and clean linen strips, and the remaining footman to collect four warm blankets from the press upstairs. Only then did she turn her attentions to Nicholas.

For all of the bemused expression that he presented to her, she could see the pallor in his face. It seemed that something grabbed hold of her heart and squeezed until it was tight and painful. She breathed deeply, squared her shoulders, and moved towards him. 'Nicholas, we must remove your coat.' Her voice was surprisingly calm and controlled. 'Here, let me assist you.'

'I assure you, Kathryn, there's no—' The deep voice got no further.

'Assure me only of your compliance, sir,' she said quietly.

A dark eyebrow arched, but before he could utter his protest she was peeling the fitted coat from his body.

She removed first the sleeve from his uninjured arm and then, without pausing, she caught him unawares and pushed him back on to the sofa.

'I think I might manage on my own,' he said wryly.

But her small bloodstained fingers were already on his arm, easing the cloth away from his wound. The coat was delivered close to the dowager's feet in a heap. His neckcloth and waistcoat received similar treatment and soon lay on top of the crumpled coat. Kathryn worked with a calm quiet efficiency that belied the frenzied beat of her heart.

She cleared her throat. 'Now for your shirt.'

'I beg your pardon?'

'Please remove your shirt, Nicholas.' Arms akimbo, smoky grey eyes that glistened with determination…and something else that she could not quite hide, Kathryn was unaware that she presented a most formidable sight, enough to make a man's pulse race, especially a man whom she'd been avoiding for the past two days.

The sensual mouth grinned wickedly. 'You're putting my grandmother to the blush, Kathryn.'

'I'm sure that Lady Maybury will forgive me this once,' she said with a great deal more confidence than she felt. 'Please, sir, for I don't mean to ask you again.'

His smile deepened and he deliberately lay back upon the cushions, and waited.

'Very well, my lord.' She swallowed hard, gathered her courage together in both hands, and, stepping forward, effected her action in one fell move. The tear of linen sounded loudly in the room. Shock showed upon his face.

And she knew that, whatever Nicholas had been expecting, it was not to have her quite literally rip the shirt from his body. Having disposed of the front and one arm of the garment, she lingered over the injured limb, gently easing the material away from the wounded area. The sight of the bloody mess of flesh was almost her undoing. *The smallest scratch* he had said, but Kathryn's heart turned over at what she saw once the last vestige of shirt had been removed. A few inches over and the ball would have lodged itself in his chest. A wave of dizziness swept through her at the thought.

'Kathryn!' Lady Maybury gave a weak protest.

Kathryn took a deep breath and pulled herself together. Such weakness would not help him. 'Don't worry, my lady. I know what I'm doing. All shall soon be ready for the physician's arrival.' Kathryn flung the words of reassurance over her shoulder, but there was no such assurance or confidence within. She forced herself not to think, just to act. 'Once we have this cleaned up, he shall be able to see the damage clearly.'

When the first footman eventually returned with two basins of boiled water that were still steaming and a small pile of linen strips, it was to a scene in which his master was lying semi-clothed upon the sofa with his grandmother's companion clasping his arm. It was the same footman that had witnessed Miss Marchant and the Viscount embracing by the front door not so very long ago. The man was wise enough to keep his thoughts to himself and made no sign as to having observed anything remotely untoward.

'Very good, Toby. Place the basins down here by me and the rags close by. Thank you.' She gave the footman a little nod and moved the bowls to exactly where she needed them. 'And Toby, send Mr Silverton home in the carriage as Lord

Ravensmede instructed.' A nod of her head indicated the young gentleman's prone body.

'Yes, miss.'

Then the second footman returned with the blankets and, having sat them upon the table, made to help carry the inebriated man from the room.

Kathryn washed her own red stained hands thoroughly in one basin before wetting the linen rag. For the first time since removing his clothes she sought Nicholas's gaze. Kathryn was unable to help herself; her hand fluttered to lightly cup his face. 'Although I'll be as gentle as I can, Nicholas, my cleansing of the wound is bound to cause you pain.' Her thumb stroked a gentle encouragement. 'I'll contrive to act as quickly as is possible.'

His eyes held hers. 'This isn't work for your hands, Kathryn.'

'Perhaps you're right,' she admitted softly. 'But I'll finish what I've started all the same.' She looked at him a moment longer, wanting to kiss the worry from his face. One last stroke of her thumb, a little smile, and then her hand left his face, and her gaze dropped once more to his injured arm.

'Dear Lord, but I'm too late!' a mumbled utterance escaped Mr Silverton's lips as the footmen manoeuvred him through the doorway. One pink-lined eye fixed itself on the woman bending low over the naked torso of Ravensmede. 'Miss Marchant!'

Kathryn did not divert her attention. Nothing else mattered save for Nicholas and his wound.

By the time Nicholas's arm had been cleansed and the deep furrow ploughed by the trajectory of the lead ball exposed, the Viscount lay back upon the sofa white-faced and with a grim line to his mouth. Perspiration beaded his forehead and upper lip, but he made no sound. There was a nausea in Kathryn's stomach at the pain her cleansing and probing had caused him. But the task was done now. The wound was tightly bound. And Kathryn could only be relieved. Taking his hand in hers, she guided it to lie across the top of the sofa back, allowing her fingers to linger when they should not have, desperate to give him some small comfort. There was nothing of embarrassment, no sense of impropriety at what she had done. Her thoughts were with Nicholas, and Nicholas alone.

His hand closed around hers. There was no strength in the light touch of his fingers, only the gentleness of a caress.

Green eyes met grey, and the smile they shared was both intimate and loving. It lasted only a moment, but it was enough. Kathryn tucked two warm blankets snugly around him, placed a cushion placed behind his head, and moved away. She had done what little she could; now there was Lady Maybury to attend to.

As she bent to hand the hot sweet tea to his grandmother, he could see that some of her hair had escaped her chignon, and was curling around her neck and shoulders. The long sleeves of her dress had been rolled back down into place, but the skirt and bodice were still marked with a liberal application of his blood. He knew that she had not been unaffected by what had just happened, had felt the slight tremble in her fingers, and admired her all the more for her courage. Her voice, quiet and clear, soothed, as did the slender scrubbed fingers carefully adjusting the mountain of blankets surrounding the old woman. He wondered that someone who had received so little care throughout her own life had so much to give. His grandmother looked pale and infinitely older than usual. A frown crinkled his brow.

'Kathryn,' he said.

She hurried across.

His gaze twitched to the dowager and back to the woman standing above him.

As if reading his mind, she bent her face lower to his.

'My grandmother should not have witnessed this. Her heart… She needs to rest. Help her up to her bedchamber.'

The grey eyes were filled with compassion. 'Nicholas, Lady Maybury has suffered a great shock. What she needs now is to know that her grandson is safe, that you've taken no great hurt and will recover,' she said quietly.

'I told you, it's nothing more than a scratch.'

'Maybe so. But you bled like a stuck pig. You must reassure her yourself by behaving as normal. It would be better if we did not retire until the physician arrives.' And with that she hurried back to attend to his grandmother.

He gave a slight nod in acquiescence, and smiled. Kathryn Marchant had courage and honour…and his love.

Kathryn stood alone by the window in her bedchamber and stared out at the expansive shimmering sea views. The water had a turquoise-green hue reminiscent of that captured in the many paintings of Mediterranean subjects that she'd seen over the years. The rhythmic sweep of the waves lulled and pacified her. White spray frothed where the waves broke upon the shoreline. Cool sea air flooded in through the open window, filling the room with its own peculiar scent: salt and seaweed and freshness. Curtains billowed in the stiff breeze and several strands of hair fluttered unnoticed across the pale skin of the woman's cheeks. Still, silent, outwardly serene, the image she presented was far removed from the turbulent emotions twisting within.

No matter that the physician had declared the Viscount to have been extremely lucky or that the damage to Lord Ravensmede's arm was minimal. Rest, clean dressings, and it would soon be healed, or so the doctor had said. The memory of Nicholas's blood smeared upon her palms would not leave her. So much blood that she could have cried her fears aloud on the spot. She had wanted to clutch him to her, to take his pain upon herself, anything but face the awful terror of that moment, when her mind was filled with the worst of imaginings.

Death. It had a starkness about it that pared everything else to insignificance. So she had done what she had to, in order to remedy the situation, with no consideration for propriety, without the slightest notion of how her actions might be construed. He was alive and well. Now she could think of nothing else except how close she'd come to losing him. And that cast quite a different light on all of her best-made resolutions. Her façade of coolness and politeness and distance had crumbled to dust. Nicholas might well marry Miss Paton, but that didn't change the fact that Kathryn loved him with a love so strong that it frightened her. She knew now that she couldn't just turn her back on him, and walk away as if their friendship had never been. Not for all of Lady Maybury's warnings, not even for the sake of her own good name. Kathryn Marchant was changed for ever.

Chapter Thirteen

Kathryn's hand trembled before she clenched it into a fist and knocked lightly against the mahogany wooden panels of the door. Her heart was thudding fast and loud, and she swallowed to alleviate the dryness in her throat.

'Come in.' His voice alone caused a fluttering within her stomach.

She smoothed her skirt down with nervous hands and, before her courage could desert her, opened the door and stepped into Lord Ravensmede's bedchamber.

His eyes widened momentarily at the sight of her standing there so awkwardly by the doorframe. 'Kathryn?' And then, as if catching himself, 'Please…come in.'

Her fingers betrayed her, plucking at the pale green of her afternoon dress, in small furtive movements. For a moment it seemed that she had not heard him, for she stood stock-still and cautious as a deer scenting the wind. Then, just when he would have spoken again, she did as he bade, shutting the door silently behind her.

'Nicholas.' There was a silver light in her eyes and the first hint of a rose blush in the apple of her cheeks. The rich russet brown of her curls had been arranged up behind her head tidily as if she had only just combed and pinned them. Already two curls had contrived to free themselves to dance enticingly against the creamy white skin of her neck. She stopped short of the bottom of the bed, her eyes flitting between him and the floor.

He could see her unease and the tension that ran through her slender body by the repetitive touch of her fingers to her skirt. Yet there was something in her gaze when it rose to meet his, something new, something that was both soft and generous yet, paradoxically, with the same determination he had witnessed the previous day in the drawing room when she had tended his wound with such calm competence. His senses tingled. She should not be here, in his bedchamber, while he sat beneath the bedcovers clad only in a nightshirt. He held his breath and waited for what she had come to say.

As if reading his mind she started, 'I know that I shouldn't be here, but I wanted to check that you…that your arm has not worsened.'

'It's the smallest scratch, nothing more. I'm only in bed today to satisfy my grandmother, and of course my own slothful nature.' He stretched out his injured arm, clenching and unclenching his fist as if to demonstrate the proof of his words. 'But thank you for your concern.'

The colour bloomed in her face. 'I should go.'

'No.'

The word hung between them.

'Kathryn,' he said a little more gently, 'come and sit here beside me. I would speak with you before you leave.'

She showed no sign of complying.

'I want to thank you for what you did yesterday. The physician said that your quick action saved me much blood loss from the wound.'

'Anyone would have done the same.'

'Even to the point of forcibly unclothing me? I do not think so,' he said with a roguish smile.

Kathryn's cheeks were now blazing a fiery hot red. 'Yes, well…' she muttered and stared down at her feet. 'That couldn't be helped. The wound needed my attention and you weren't proving to be of much assistance. I'm sorry if I embarrassed you.'

It was the same expression that she had used at Lady Finlay's ball, for the slip in her dance steps…and their shared kisses in the moonlit room. Ravensmede felt a warmth expand within his chest as the memories flowed. 'You could never embarrass me, Kathryn.'

The clear gaze slid up to meet his, and he felt a flood of desire and need and tenderness. A shy smile spread across her mouth.

'The other day when you sent me away, what had happened to upset you so much?' It was a question that had worried at him since walking in to find her in that state within her bedchamber. For all that she had endured he had never seen her so affected, not until that day. The sight of her pain and the sound of the formality in her voice had made him want to snatch her into his arms, to kiss her long and hard and passionately until she told him what was wrong. And that whispered plea, *Please, Nicholas, don't make this any harder than it already is*, had torn at his heart. For Ravensmede, a man used to taking what he wanted, when he wanted it, such impotence was frustrating. His grandmother knew what the matter was about, with her little looks of feigned innocence, and contrivance to keep him away from her companion. But the old lady had stubbornly refused to be forthcoming and doggedly changed the subject each time he had mentioned Kathryn's name.

He watched her fingers catch at the material again, grip it hard. 'It's of no consequence,' she said.

'Kathryn…' He raised one eyebrow and peered at her as if he would fathom the truth in that way.

But her head just shook a quick denial. 'It doesn't matter, not now.'

He heard the slight breathless catch in her voice, watched her take a single step closer. His right hand stretched towards her, reaching out for her, a gesture of conciliation and more.

It seemed that she hesitated, her gaze unmoving upon his hand, her face impassive. Then her eyes flickered up to his and he could see their colour had darkened to a soft smoky grey. The moment stretched. Time stilled. Awareness narrowed until there was only the two of them in existence. Thud of heart, flutter of pulse. Her small hand slid into his, his fingers closed around hers. From there he did not know quite how she came to be in his arms or his lips pressed against hers, possessing and yielding all at once.

She was warm and soft, an alluring mix of innocence and passion. His hands swept the length of her back, down to the curve of her hips, pulling her closer. Her mouth opened beneath his, inviting further exploration. The tip of his tongue slipped within, teasing, tantalising. Tongue touched tongue, lapped together, twisting, licking, sucking. All rational thought fled. She was his, to pleasure, to worship, to love. Even as he clutched her closer he heard the little mew sound in her throat, felt the nuzzle of her breasts against his chest. All of Lord Ravensmede's good intentions were lost.

His lips traced a pattern along the delicate line of her jaw to find the tender skin beneath her ear. She gave herself up to the sensations rippling through her. From the strange ache down deep and low in her pelvis to the pulsating heat in her thighs, Kathryn embraced what was happening to her. This was far beyond any dream. It was urgent and wicked and wild, but Kathryn wanted it never to stop. She needed to feel Nicholas's arms around her, wanted his mouth on hers. Her fingers caressed against his cheek, stroking down over the rough stubble of his chin. All the love that she felt welled up and flowed out to him, spilling over in every touch, in every kiss. And in her mind the silent words whispered again and again, *I love you, I love you,* until she knew not whether she gasped them aloud.

He plucked the pins from her hair, one by one, until the glorious mass of curls hung free. His fingers tangled within the heavy chestnut tresses, revelling in their glossy softness. Her hair smelled fresh and clean as if she'd rinsed it in a wash of lavender water. His hands followed her hair down to where it brushed against her breasts, cupped the two small mounds, massaging them through the material of her dress with gentle passion.

The soft white skin grew more sensitive with each caress, every stroke, until she thought that his heat would scorch her. And then when his fingers eventually found passage beneath the pale green bodice, to burrow under every layer of separating material to capture the bare skin of her breasts, she could not contain the sudden sharp inhalation of breath. Instinctively her back arched, thrusting her taut nipples hard against him, seeking more of something that she did not understand. Each and every touch sent sparks of pleasure writhing deep into her stomach. Rational thought had long since fled.

The groan growled low in his throat and his arms locked around her as he twisted and pushed her down so that she lay on the bed beside him. 'Kathryn,' he gasped her name as if it was air and he was a man suffocating for want of it. 'Kathryn,' he whispered again as he rolled his length on top of her.

'Oh, Nicholas,' she sighed and wrapped her arms around him.

A voice sounded from the direction of the stairs on the landing beyond the door of Ravensmede's bedchamber. 'What do you mean I can't go in there! I don't need you to announce me to m'own grandson,' bellowed Lady Maybury. 'If I want to see Lord Ravensmede I'll damn well see him!'

Kathryn and Nicholas froze as the full realisation of their situation hit them.

The dowager's small feet thumped noisily down the corridor, growing ever louder as she made her way to her grandson's bedchamber.

Kathryn's eyes widened in horror. She tried to scramble up, to repair the loosened bodice, the long curls that flowed wantonly over her shoulders. But Nicholas's hand stayed her frantic panic. He shook his head, touched a finger to her lips, and imprisoned her wrist with his other hand.

A sharp knock sounded at the door. 'Nicholas, are you decent?' Lady Maybury's words came clear through the mahogany.

''Fraid not, Grandmama,' said Ravensmede with a lazy drawl. 'I wouldn't want to shock your delicate constitution by the sight I present at this minute.' His eyes glowed wickedly as he looked down at Kathryn lying beneath him.

'Don't be absurd,' came the withering reply. 'I've seen it all before. Had you naked on m'knee before you were in breeches.'

Despite the predicament they found themselves in, Ravensmede smiled at his grandmother's words. 'Grant me ten minutes,' he said laughingly.

A surly-sounding grunt. 'I'll be back in five,' the dowager said, and the footsteps receded back along the landing.

Only then did a very white-faced Kathryn release the breath she had been holding. Realisation of her predicament screamed loud. And now that her ardour had disappeared without a trace, she was suddenly shamefully aware that she was on Lord Ravensmede's bed, with the man himself lying atop her. Nicholas had not the least look of embarrassment; indeed, he was smiling down at her in what could only be described as a positively dangerous manner. Her eyes widened with growing horror. 'N-Nicholas…' her tongue stumbled over his name, as she tried to free herself from her position.

The wickedness of Nicholas's smile intensified and slowly his face moved towards hers…to drop the smallest, innocent kiss on to the tip of her nose. 'Kathryn Marchant, you are quite the most beautiful, beguiling woman I've ever met.' Without another word he rolled off her and, leaning down, helped her up to her feet. In one fluid action he had reached around to the back of her dress and fastened the buttons he had undone not so very long ago. Everything about him was smooth, lazily efficient and supremely confident.

The same could not be said for Kathryn. Not only was she in a state of abject shock at the extent to which passion had pushed her, but her hands were shaking so much she could barely fashion her hair into some semblance of order.

'Here, let me,' he instructed, and simply turned her around, coiled her hair into a neat chignon and pinned it into place with much less fuss than any abigail would have caused.

'How do you—'

'Don't ask.' He spun her round, delivered a final kiss to her mouth, took her by the hand and guided her towards the door.

'And now you had better go before my grandmother decides to return.'

'Nicholas…' Kathryn bit at her bottom lip.

'We'll talk about this later, Kathryn.' Opening the door by the smallest crack, he scanned beyond, then, giving Kathryn's fingers one last reassuring squeeze, pushed her towards the door directly across the landing; the door that led into her own bedchamber.

It was exactly five minutes later that Lady Maybury made a reappearance, and an hour after that when she finally left him to his rest. And all the while Lord Ravensmede was forced to pretend that he had not just reached a decision of monumental proportions. Not until his grandmother left the room did he allow himself to think back on the woman who had come to him out of concern and whom he, in return, had practically seduced. Had not his grandmother come knocking at the door of his bedchamber he wondered if he would have had either the strength or the sense to stop what he was about.

Kathryn absorbed him, totally, completely. Just touching her, kissing her, made him forget all else. What chance had he then when she lay beneath him on his bed? It was enough to drive any man mad. For all these years Nicholas Maybury had called the tune when it came to women. And heaven knew he had practised it often enough, on rich women, powerful women; all of them widowed or well experienced at their profession, some of them even other men's wives.

Now one woman had changed all that. One woman alone could have called any tune she wanted, and he would have danced to it a thousand times over. One woman alone had the power to gladden his heart, to make him feel dizzy with desire, or to cast him into a doldrum of depression. She was neither wealthy nor titled, neither fashionable nor flirtatious. As Cadmount had so accurately observed, she was not even his type. None of it made any difference. Nicholas loved her. And he meant to marry her. The woman's name was Kathryn Marchant.

It was only later that same evening when he made enquiry of his butler as to the whereabouts of his grandmother and her companion that he discovered them to have departed for a dance in the local assembly rooms. First instinct told him to seek them out, check that Kathryn understood that his intentions were honourable—hadn't he given her every reason to think otherwise? Second thoughts suggested he wait where he was. Care must be taken to ensure that no contrary gossip linked Kathryn's name with his. As his wife she would be safe, but until then… Reputations were a fragile thing in the hands of the *ton*. He was sure that his grandmother already had her suspicions about his relationship with her companion, and was warning him off. Why else was she doing her damnedest to keep them apart? It was for the best that Kathryn be seen in Brighthelmstone without him. Soon they would be together. Ravensmede would have to content himself with that. But had he known what was unfolding in the assembly rooms, the Viscount would have decided very differently.

The air was unpleasantly stuffy and hot within the assembly rooms, and the fact that her dance card was full did not help matters. Lady Maybury was chatting with lively animation to a group of elderly ladies, and looking very pleased with the fact that Kathryn had not yet been off the dance floor. Parson John Andrew, who had a keen interest in lepidopterology, was describing to Kathryn in some detail the differences between the Red Admiral as compared to the Blue Butterfly, a feat to be much congratulated as they were engaged in dancing a robust Scottish reel at the time. The tempo of the music increased, urging the dancers to skip faster, twirl their partners with more force. Reverend Andrew's face grew redder, and his breathing more laboured. Sweat dribbled down his cheeks and chin. By the end of the dance both Kathryn and Reverend Andrew were much relieved. The gentleman mopped at his brow with a large white handkerchief before setting off to fetch two glasses of lemonade for the delightful Miss Marchant and himself.

'Kathryn?' The woman's voice inflected with surprise. 'Is that really you? What a surprise to find you here, my dear.'

The skin on the back of Kathryn's neck prickled. It was a voice she knew well, and one she had not thought to hear in this part of the country. She looked up to meet the cold blue eyes of Anna Marchant. 'Aunt Anna, the surprise is mutual.' Then, as Lottie stepped from behind her mother, 'And Cousin Lottie too. I had not thought to meet you both here in Brighthelmstone.'

The harshness in Mrs Marchant's eyes faded and she looked almost contrite. 'Our visit is not one of pleasure,' she said in a hushed tone. 'It is Mr Marchant…'

It seemed to Kathryn that her aunt was smaller than she remembered. 'What of Uncle Henry?'

Mrs Marchant swallowed, and compressed her lips as if trying to control some strong emotion assailing her. 'He…'

Guilt and concern pricked at Kathryn's conscience. She noticed the pallor of her aunt's face as she waited for what was to come.

'He has taken an inflammation of the lungs.' Mrs

Marchant clasped her perfectly manicured hands together and held them to her mouth. There was a suspicious sheen about her eyes. 'The doctor is not optimistic. He said…' Her eyes squeezed momentarily closed, and, when they opened again, there was in them a vulnerability Kathryn had never seen before. 'He said that clean sea air was our best hope. Hence I brought Mr Marchant here with all haste.'

Lottie clasped at her mother's hand and let out a little sob. 'Poor Papa.'

'It came on so suddenly,' said Mrs Marchant. 'One minute he was fine and well, and the next…' She glanced anxiously at Kathryn.

'I'm so sorry. I didn't know.'

'He insisted that I bring Lottie here tonight. Was so adamant that I dared not refuse him for fear of bringing on another coughing fit. We will not stay long and then we will get straight back to him.'

'Please send my uncle my best wishes that he recovers his good health as soon as possible.'

'Of course,' nodded Mrs Marchant, then paused before she added, 'Mr Marchant would benefit from your visit, Kathryn, that is, if you can find the time to see him. I believe it would make a difference to him.'

'I—I'm not sure—'

But before she could say what she would have, Anna Marchant interrupted, 'I haven't always treated you fairly, Kathryn, and for that I beg your forgiveness. Only now do I see things in a different light.'

The two women looked at one another, before Kathryn nodded and gave a small smile. 'If you tell me where you are staying, then I will visit my uncle.' So shocked was she by the news of her uncle's illness and the drastic change in her aunt that Kathryn failed to notice the gentleman until he stood directly by her side…rather closer than was seemly.

'Sorry to interrupt, Miss Marchant…' and he bowed '…but it's imperative that I speak with you on a matter of privacy.'

'Mr Silverton!' She could not keep the shock from her voice. The last time she had seen Harry Silverton he was being carried in a drunken stupor out of the drawing room of the rented house on The Steyne and into Lord Ravensmede's carriage. An image of a blood-soaked Nicholas flashed into her mind, and fear flickered. Both Aunt Anna and Lottie were looking at Mr Silverton with expressions of curiosity. Kathryn deliberately edged herself away from the young man's proximity, while making the necessary introductions. 'Aunt Anna, Lottie, this is Mr Silverton, whose family are enjoying the summer in Brighthelmstone. Mr Silverton, this is my aunt, Mrs Marchant, and my cousin, Miss Lottie Marchant.'

Mrs Marchant's devoirs went unnoticed as Lottie stepped forward into Harry Silverton's line of vision. 'Miss Lottie,' he said with awe, and stared at Lottie as if she was an apparition. 'Is this an angel I see before me?' And before the stunned Lottie could reply, he plucked her hand into his and placed upon it a reverential kiss.

Kathryn looked from Harry Silverton's stunned visage to her cousin's flushed excited one. Lottie was ogling right back at Mr Silverton.

Mrs Marchant cleared her throat. 'We must be going, Lottie, come along.'

'But I've only just arrived,' protested Mr Silverton, 'and not yet had the pleasure of dancing with the beautiful Miss Lottie.'

Lottie's lips moved to a pout. 'Mama, we are scarcely here.'

Kathryn had no wish to speak to Silverton, especially

knowing all that he had done to Nicholas, but she was wise enough to realise that the young man could be dangerous. It would be better to hear what he proposed to say over the matter. 'You wished to speak to me, Mr Silverton?'

Harry Silverton blinked like a man struggling to free himself from a drugged daze. 'Did I? It's of no matter, now.' He bestowed his most charming smile upon Lottie, and held out his hand for her dance card. 'May I hope to secure a dance with you, Miss Lottie?'

Kathryn could see quite clearly the way that things were progressing, especially after her aunt learned of the Silverton family's wealth. She was, therefore, considerably relieved when the Reverend Mr Andrews, carrying two glasses of lemonade, finally found his way back to her. And even more relieved when that same gentleman informed her that Lady Maybury had developed a headache and wanted to leave the assembly rooms.

During the journey home in the carriage Kathryn thought about her uncle's ill health, and the change in her aunt's manner. She thought about the sudden and rather overt attraction between Mr Silverton and Cousin Lottie. But most of all she thought about Nicholas Maybury, and of what had happened between them on his bed that very afternoon.

In the days following Nicholas and Kathryn's illicit tryst not one opportunity presented itself for them to speak together privately. Lady Maybury guarded her companion with all the tenacity of a terrier. Naps were forgotten. The independent old lady vanished. Her temper did not. She developed a need to have Kathryn with her at all times, from breakfast time to dinner. The very night of their return from the assembly rooms, she developed a nocturnal fear that necessitated Kathryn moving into Lady Maybury's bedchamber to keep her company. Matters grew even worse the next morning when Kathryn asked for leave to visit her uncle. The dowager embarked on what amounted to an inquisition over Uncle Henry's illness and Aunt Anna's invitation—and then claimed that she could not spare her companion even for half an hour. Every evening there were dances and trips to the theatre—all very public affairs—all with Ravensmede very much consigned to the background if her ladyship consented to his company at all.

In a way Kathryn was thankful to the old woman. She both desired and dreaded the time when she would be alone with Nicholas. She loved him, knew now that she could deny neither him nor herself. It was just a matter of time. Lady Maybury's tactics were only deferring the inevitable. Kathryn had her suspicions as to how much the dowager knew, loved the old lady all the more for trying to protect her poor companion.

Nausea rose at the thought of what becoming Nicholas's mistress would mean: a slap in the face to Lady Maybury for all that she had done to help Kathryn, and the loss of her own good name. No matter how hard they tried to keep the affair hidden, it would come out—such secrets always did. And what about when he tired of her, when he found some other woman to fill her place? The thought churned cold in her stomach. She was a fool a hundred times over, a fool caught between the devil and a high place...with little idea of how to solve her quandary.

Within the drawing room of the rented townhouse in Brighthelmstone Mrs Marchant was pacing with a great deal of excitement. 'You're certain, Henry, that Mr Silverton means to ask her?'

'Yes, he asked my permission to pay suit to Lottie. The boy is clearly besotted with her and wants to marry her.'

'Very good. Lottie will be married before either of us thought,' purred his wife. Her blue eyes narrowed and her slash of a smile broadened. 'I like Mr Silverton immensely. He has such very interesting tales to tell…particularly concerning our niece and Lord Ravensmede.'

Mr Marchant worried at his chins. 'There is an indecent haste about the affair. Mr Silverton is talking as if he means to marry Lottie tomorrow. They have only known each other a matter of days!'

His wife delivered him a withering look. 'What's to know? Harry Silverton is an only son; he has two sisters, and his parents are elderly. He stands to inherit his father's chain of coffee houses and sugar plantation in the West Indies. Not only that, but he's currently worth fifteen thousand a year, and will receive a large and fashionable new townhouse in Bristol as part of his wedding gift from the old man.'

'But he's trade, and I thought you wanted better for Lottie; a baronet at least, you said.'

'Bah, half the aristocracy have pockets to let. Fifteen thousand. And think what he stands to inherit.'

Mr Marchant nodded in agreement. 'I concede it to be a fortune.'

'Although I should prefer Lottie's wedding to be a grand affair, I would not want to stand in the way of true love.'

Her husband rolled his eyes.

'And there would be other advantages to them marrying sooner rather than later.'

'I see none,' said Mr Marchant somewhat sourly, 'other than the cost to my pocket.'

'There is the little matter of Kathryn. Have you forgotten about her?'

'The chance would be a fine thing,' he muttered beneath his breath, then spoke out loud, 'What difference can Lottie's marriage make to Kathryn?'

Mrs Marchant cheeks grew rather red from excitement. 'Why, if Lottie has already caught herself a husband, and we distance ourselves from Kathryn, then any damage that attaches itself to her reputation will not affect us.'

'She is still our niece.'

'We will publicly disown her. And with Lottie safely wed and sent to Bristol, then what harm can Kathryn do us?'

'Then I can cease this pathetic charade of illness in an attempt to lure the girl here?'

'Yes.' Anna Marchant beamed. 'We no longer need coax the little trollop back to London with us.' That had only been to please Amanda White and that woman had just been rendered powerless. She laughed aloud at the good fortune Harry Silverton had brought them.

'Hallelujah,' said Mr Marchant with sarcasm.

'You must concentrate on persuading Mr Silverton to London. He needs to visit Doctors' Commons as soon as possible—and come to Green Street with a special licence in his pocket. If we play our cards right, we should have Lottie married by next week. And then I can turn my attentions to Kathryn. I'll send her a note today telling of your unexpected recovery and that we have to leave Brighthelmstone. Do you know that I actually had to apologise to the little bitch the other day? How I'm longing to make her suffer for that. She's made her bed, and now I mean to make sure that she damn well lies in it. By the time I've finished, Kathryn Marchant will wish that she'd never been born.'

* * *

Less than a fortnight later and Lady Maybury was proving to be as demanding as ever. The two women sat at the breakfast table, the dowager consuming a second helping of ham and eggs, Kathryn sipping her coffee and reading aloud from the notices in *The Times*. Of Ravensmede there was no sign. Kathryn was trying hard to keep her thoughts from his possible whereabouts when one particular marriage announcement caught her attention. Her words faltered. The coffee cup stilled its motion halfway to her mouth.

Lady Maybury glanced up from her plate. 'Pray continue with the next one. I want to see if Mrs Pearsall's granddaughter's marriage to young Fox is in there.'

With exaggerated care Kathryn set the coffee cup down upon the table. There was the tiniest of pauses, and then she started to read again. 'On Friday June 25, at her father's house in Green Street, by the Reverend J. Blundell, Charlotte, only daughter of Mr and Mrs Henry Marchant of London, to Mr Harold Silverton, only son of Mr and Mrs James Silverton of Bristol.' Lottie had married Harry Silverton!

'Good gad!' exclaimed Lady Maybury. 'I thought they only met at that wretched dance the other week.'

'They did, but it was immediately apparent that their interests were captured.'

'Well, never you mind, Kathryn. He's a nincompoop. Showed his true colours when he came round here, brandishing that pistol in m'face. You'll catch better than him. Mark my words.'

'I don't understand.' Kathryn's brow rumpled in perplexity. 'Aunt Anna was different the last time we spoke. She seemed changed: softer, kinder somehow. She wanted to put the past behind us, to start anew. And then when she sent that letter telling of my uncle's sudden recovery and their intended return to London, she made no mention of Mr Silverton. I thought…' She shook her head. 'It doesn't make sense.'

'You thought what? That your aunt would at least inform you of your cousin's wedding?'

'I should know her better than that,' said Kathryn.

'So you should. A leopard doesn't change its spots,' replied the dowager, giving Kathryn a strange little look. 'What a surprise that your aunt was up to organising a wedding so soon after Mr Marchant's recent illness. But then the speed of your poor dear uncle's recovery was truly miraculous. Such a shame I couldn't spare you to visit him…' She raised her eyebrows with just the faintest suggestion of cynicism, before turning her attention once more to her breakfast plate. 'Now read the rest of the announcements before m'eggs grow cold.'

The first leg of the journey back to London was, as Kathryn expected, both slow and tedious. There was little conversation between the ladies as Lady Maybury managed to sleep almost continuously with no regard for the jolting of the carriage. Despite his recent injury Lord Ravensmede accompanied the carriage on horseback, the thud of his horse's hooves never far away.

He watched her pale face at the carriage window.

She studied the dark figure that rode so close by.

Green eyes met grey, again and again, binding the man and his woman together, promising what was to come.

She worried as to his arm, and that he should be riding.

He worried as to why she should look so anxious when he meant to claim her for his own.

Mile after mile. So close as to almost touch, so near as to

almost whisper. Yet they could do nothing. By the time the coach entered into the yard of the King's Arms at Horley Common, the tension between them was unbearable. The party was shown to their bedchambers, given some little time to refresh their travel-stained selves, then the landlord showed them to a private parlour and dinner was served.

At the first opportunity Ravensmede addressed himself to Kathryn, 'How did you find the first part of your journey?'

'Comfortable, thank you, my lord.'

'Don't lie,' interrupted the dowager between mouthfuls of salmon and boiled potatoes. 'It was damnably uncomfortable. It was all I could do to manage the briefest of naps. You really must have that carriage seen to, Nick.'

'I will do so upon our arrival in town,' he replied.

A silence descended upon the little group.

Kathryn poked at the small mound of potatoes on her plate, and tried not to look at Nicholas. She could feel the burn of his gaze upon her, could feel her face colour beneath his scrutiny. Surely the dowager would notice if he continued to stare so? She sought to distract her employer. 'My lady, how do you find the fish? Is it to your taste?'

Lady Maybury shovelled a large portion of the salmon steak into her mouth before replying. 'I'm afraid to say that it's barely edible. When one's appetite is as fragile as mine, it's important that only the best quality of food be consumed.' A large swig of wine passed her lips. 'The potatoes are hard, the pie is lacking in flavour and the soup is too poor to comment upon. I'm forced to nibble upon a meagre portion to sustain my strength.' The shrewd pale eyes swept over Kathryn's barely touched food. 'You would be wise to do the same, my dear, for our journey tomorrow will be as long as today and you heard what the landlord said of the weather.'

'It's going to rain,' supplied her companion quietly, and ate a little more of the pie.

Ravensmede drew a mocking smile at his grandmother. 'Perhaps then you will agree to let me travel awhile inside the carriage, instead of banishing me to the road.'

'The fresh air is good for you, boy,' she said. 'Besides, I thought you enjoyed riding.'

He raised an eyebrow and glanced across at Kathryn, before refilling all three glasses with claret.

Kathryn concentrated on watching the pale red liquid slosh against the glass. Within her chest her heart had kicked up to a canter. She ignored it, along with the peculiar battle of wills that seemed to be going on between Ravensmede and his grandmother. 'May I suggest an early night, my lady. You must be very tired and tomorrow will be more fatiguing than today.'

For once the dowager appeared to be in agreement. With a shrewd expression she patted Kathryn's hand. 'Go on ahead, gel. I shall not be long. Just want to finish m'wine, then I'll be up.'

Kathryn nodded and began to rise, but Nicholas was there before her. 'I'll escort Miss Marchant to her room.'

The blush in Kathryn's cheeks intensified. The flurry of her heart hastened. One glance up into those green eyes that glowed so bright beneath the flickering flame of the candles and she froze, for there was everything of intimacy and possession in Nicholas's gaze. It was as if a hand reached in and squeezed Kathryn's heart. 'Really, there is no need, my lord.' She felt his fingers brush her arm, felt too the instinctive sway of her body towards his. 'I—'

The dowager interrupted. 'Kathryn is right, Nick. Besides, I want a word with you.' She fixed a belligerent eye upon her grandson.

Kathryn's eyes shuttered for the briefest moment. Every nerve in her body was vibrating and taut. What she had feared was about to pass. For Kathryn could not shake the unassailable conviction that Lady Maybury knew. As surely as they were sitting here within the little parlour, as surely as the attraction that flowed between Nicholas and herself, the dowager knew. Why else was the tension wound so tight between the three of them? Dread weighed heavy on her chest. She rose swiftly to her feet, unwilling for either Lady Maybury or Lord Ravensmede to witness her fear. 'Thank you, my lady.' With every last scrap of dignity that Kathryn possessed she turned and, without a backward glance, walked quietly from the room.

'Well?' said the dowager.

'Well?' said her grandson.

'Enough is enough, Nicholas. Don't think to fob me off this time with some tale of "there's nothing going on". I'm not in m'dotage yet, and I'd have to be deaf, blind and stupid not to see what's right in front of m'very nose.'

'I have not compromised her, nor do I intend to,' said Ravensmede.

'You came damn near to doing so. If it ever gets out that she visited you alone in your bedchamber, then I can assure you that she'll be well and truly ruined...and even I won't be able to save her.'

Ravensmede was genuinely shocked. 'You knew?'

'Of course I knew. What do you take me for, some kind of gibbering idiot? You've been looking at her like you're going to eat her. Why else do you think I've had to resort to guarding the gel night and day? Shouldn't have to do it from m'own grandson.'

His fingers raked through his hair. 'It's not what you think.'

'It's everything that I think and more. Hell's teeth, Nick, I thought you had some semblance of care for her. Couldn't you have just kept your breeches on for once?'

'They've never been off,' he protested, and then he remembered that he had been wearing his nightshirt the day that Kathryn had come to his bedchamber.

A snowy white eyebrow raised and a faded green eye stared hard.

'You're much mistaken, Grandmama.'

'Faugh! I know a seduction when I see one.'

'Grandmama,' He pushed the glass away.

'You might not have a care for the gel, Nick, but I'll be damned if I just sit back and let you ruin her in a public inn of all places, and make a fool of me in the process.' The faded eyes flashed their angry determination.

He lounged back in his chair. 'Contrary to what you think, I care very much for Kathryn,' he said quietly. 'Do you honestly think I would seek to ruin the lady whom I mean to make my wife?'

Lady Maybury's jaw gaped. 'Did you say *wife*?'

'Most certainly so.'

'I had no idea.'

'Evidently not.'

'But…' The dowager shook her head in disbelief, unable to finish what she had started. A silence grew between them, and then, at last, Lady Maybury asked, 'Does Kathryn know of your intentions?'

Ravensmede's mouth crooked. 'For some strange reason I have been unable to find Miss Marchant alone these past weeks to ask her.'

'Well, I wasn't to know. I thought you were planning on bedding her!' said his grandmother indignantly.

'So you won't be insisting on my riding tomorrow?'

'Only if you behave yourself,' said the dowager. 'You aren't home and dry yet. Better have a care until the ring's on her finger.'

'You're taking the news remarkably well.'

'I find myself resolved to the situation. She might be m'companion and without a penny to her name, but she's got breeding; anyone with an eye in their head can see that. Besides, I like the gel. She's good for you.'

Ravensmede set his napkin down on the table. 'I'm glad we agree.'

'However, there is Miss Paton to consider.'

'Any possibility of an alliance between Miss Paton and me existed only in m'father's head.'

'Your father won't agree.'

'So much the better.' He paused. 'My father might protest, but he'll be relieved that I've chosen to marry at all.'

'If you say so, Nick. But the sooner you tell him about Kathryn the better.'

Ravensmede smiled, but gave no reply.

'You know, of course, there's bound to be gossip. It's not every day one's grandson marries one's companion.'

'There's always gossip.'

'Not about my family there isn't!' The dowager peered haughtily at him.

Ravensmede laughed. 'The tabbies wouldn't dare discuss my misdemeanours in your presence, Grandmama. They're really rather afraid of you.'

'I don't know why!' she snorted, but the glimmer of a smile touched to her lips. Then the smile faded. 'If you marry her, you'll find yourself related to Henry and Anna Marchant. You cannot alter the fact that they are her uncle and aunt.'

'The Marchants have no part in Kathryn's life now, nor will they do so in the future. I mean to see to that.'

'Then, your mind's made up.'

'Yes, Grandmama, my mind's made up.'

They looked at one another in silence for a moment.

'To Kathryn, the future Viscountess of Ravensmede.'

Clink of glasses in a toast, and then the wine was drained, and the small private parlour stood empty.

Chapter Fourteen

The next morning, when it came time to depart, Ravensmede was in the process of escorting Kathryn and his grandmother out to the waiting carriage when they came face to face with a lady and gentleman known to them from London.

'Mr and Mrs Parker.' Ravensmede bowed politely.

Ernest Parker's chubby cheeks took on a ruddy hue. 'Lord Ravensmede, Lady Maybury. Arrived last night from town, travelling down for a brief sojourn in Brighthelmstone. Emily has a notion to try one of those bathing contraptions.' His wife's head nodded in the most peculiar manner and she seemed to be having difficulty in meeting the Viscount's gaze.

'We too have been enjoying the delights of Brighthelmstone.' The dowager smiled. 'May I introduce my companion, Miss Marchant.' An elderly hand of surprising strength thrust Kathryn forward.

Emily Parker's expression froze into one of horror. For one awkward minute there was silence. Then, without even so much as a glance in Kathryn's direction, Mrs Parker grabbed her husband's arm in a lock that would have crushed a smaller man, and announced, 'Dear Lady Maybury, I'm afraid we really must leave. Please do excuse us.' And with that she practically ran across the courtyard, dragging her husband in her wake.

Ernest Parker cast a silent appeal at Lord Ravensmede. 'Your servant, sir,' came the gruff utterance as he disappeared into the carriage.

'Well, of all the most ninny-headed females, Emily Parker must take the biscuit!' said Lady Maybury with a scowl. 'Such an appalling lack of manners, I'm not surprised she's not invited anywhere of consequence.'

Ravensmede cast a curious look at the Parkers' carriage, but the door had been shut and the curtain closed across the window.

The dowager's breast puffed dangerously towards high dudgeon. 'How dare she slight m'companion. Kathryn's got more breeding in her little toe than that creature shall ever have!'

'My lady,' cajoled Kathryn from the lady's side, 'I'm not in the least offended. No doubt it is still too early in the morning for Mrs Parker.'

Lady Maybury seemed marginally calmed by Kathryn's words and allowed herself to be steered across the yard to the waiting carriage.

The landlord's predictions concerning the weather proved to be true. The day was quite the foulest that the summer had seen. Blustery cold winds and one heavy rain shower after the other slowed their journey considerably. The roads were muddied and filled with expanding puddles, the sky grey and forbidding with rain.

In contrast to her behaviour of the past fortnight, Lady Maybury showed not the slightest objection to her grandson sitting within the carriage beside her and her companion. Indeed, she positively encouraged Lord Ravensmede's presence, something of which Kathryn could only be glad on seeing the deterioration in the weather conditions. And rather than keeping a close scrutiny upon his person as she had taken to doing of late, the dowager was not five minutes into the journey when she fell asleep beneath her mound of travelling rugs. The snuffle of her snore competed with the rumble of the wheels and the pounding of the horses' hooves.

Kathryn looked at Nicholas.

Nicholas looked at Kathryn sitting at Lady Maybury's side.

He seeming to fill the whole of the carriage with his presence just by sitting on the seat opposite.

'At last,' he said.

Kathryn's gaze flickered towards the dowager.

'My grandmother is an extremely heavy sleeper.'

A tremor of panic fluttered through her.

Something of her feelings must have shown on her face, for Lord Ravensmede moved back to lounge against the squabs. 'I only wish to speak to you.' The smouldering intensity in his green eyes sent a shiver of anticipation from the top of her head down to the very tips of her toes. He did not look like he wanted to talk to her. Everything about his long lean body seemed poised to pull her into his arms and ravage her mouth with his. A lazy lop-sided smile spread across his face and he stretched out his legs so that his booted shins brushed against her skirt.

She waited.

'When you came to my bedchamber in Brighthelmstone—'

'Nicholas…' Her throat was dry and his name little more than a whisper. Her eyes flicked nervously towards the sleeping form of the dowager. 'We do not need to discuss this.'

'I think that we do,' he said.

She gave a little shake of her head, and a curl escaped down to drizzle against her cheek. 'Things need not change.'

'They already have.'

'We could be friends just as we were before,' she said, grasping at straws.

He sat upright and leaned forward, oblivious to the shake and heave of the carriage. 'We both know that there is much more than friendship between us, Kathryn.'

The breaths came small and fast and shallow in her chest. Her gaze dropped to the floor. 'There should not be.'

'*Should* does not enter into it. There is, and it's clear that you cannot remain as my grandmother's companion for much longer.'

She raised startled eyes to his. 'I would not hurt Lady Maybury.'

'Neither would I.'

'Then why…'

'You know why,' he said and, reaching across, laid his hand over hers.

His touch was light yet possessive. He was right. Kathryn knew very well the answer to her question. He could not take his grandmother's companion as his mistress.

The noise of hooves and wheels and rain and snores filled the minutes.

'There is something that I want to ask you.'

Her heart lurched. She withdrew her hand from his, her fingers stumbling to the skirt of her travelling dress and gripping for dear life at the material. She knew what he was going to ask, had known it for quite some time. Now that the moment had come she feared that her courage had deserted her. It was one thing to be drawn into it while in the throes of passion; it was quite another to agree to it in the cold light of day. An arrangement. To suit them both. He desired her. She loved him. And for the sake of that love she would bear the shame that being his mistress would bring. But this wasn't how it was supposed to be. For all that had passed between them, for all that she had tried to convince herself, she knew that if he asked her here, sitting in his travelling coach, with his grandmother asleep by her side, she would refuse him.

'No,' she whispered. 'Do not say it.'

A curious expression flitted across his face. 'But you don't yet know yet what I mean to ask.'

She swallowed hard. 'Even so, I would not have you ask it here, in front of Lady Maybury. That…that would not be right.'

A dark eyebrow arched in the familiar gesture that she had come to know and love, and he subjected her to a long knowing scrutiny. When at last he spoke there was a gentleness to his words. 'I'll warrant my question is not the one you expect it to be, Kathryn. But…' he captured her hand again in his and stroked his thumb against her skin '…if you would prefer I took a more conventional route with my proposal then so be it. I will wait until we reach London.'

She blushed and stared down at where their hands joined. 'Thank you.'

The coach rumbled on. The rain continued to pour. The dowager's snoring grew louder. Nicholas watched Kathryn. Kathryn watched the passing countryside…until they reached London.

The next morning was fine and warm, with no sign of the unseasonable weather of the previous day. Kathryn sat alone in the carriage, content with what she had found during her visit to young Maggie. The visit had distracted her thoughts from Nicholas and had been most enjoyable. The little girl's pleasure at the doll made the selling of the last of Kathryn's papa's books worthwhile, and the tasty biscuits and cakes from the dowager had doubled both the child and her brothers' pleasure. Beneath the warm golden sunlight Kathryn recalled the small hands pressed to hers and the laughter in those large pansy eyes. Maggie was a joyful delight for all her squeals and clambering.

A slender hand pressed to her cheek as she remembered how the child's mother had thanked her for the food parcels that had seemingly arrived with conscientious punctuality every week since Maggie's return home, and for the job in which her husband was now employed. Nicholas. There could be no one else responsible, after all. The knowledge made her smile. Beneath that devil-may-care attitude was a man who cared about a poor child's welfare, a man who doted upon his elderly grandmother…and a man who was going to ask her to become his mistress… just as he had before. Only this time she would give him a very different answer.

A barouche passed close by, travelling only marginally faster than that belonging to Lady Maybury. Miss Dawson's face looked out.

Kathryn raised her hand in salutation through the open window and smiled.

Miss Dawson's cheeks reddened and she turned her head away with a startling abruptness.

She must not have seen me, thought Kathryn, and returned to her musings without the slightest hint of rancour.

It was only later that same day that she had cause to remember the incident and place quite a different interpretation upon it.

* * *

It was late that evening when Ravensmede made himself comfortable in the wing chair within the library of his own house in Berkeley Square and accepted the brandy glass from his friend.

Cadmount's white fingers drummed upon the chair arm. 'How is the delightful dowager?'

'In fine mettle.'

'And li'l Miss Marchant?' asked Cadmount a trifle too innocently.

'She's well. I'm meeting them both at the King's later this evening, if you want to come.'

Cadmount coughed discreetly. 'You encountered no problems in Brighthelmstone?'

'No. Should I have?'

The fair-haired man cleared his throat and avoided Ravensmede's eye. 'You did bed her.'

Ravensmede carefully set the brandy glass down upon the table. 'Question or statement? Before you start down that line, Caddie, there's something you should know: I mean to marry Kathryn.'

Cadmount sighed, reached for the decanter and refilled Ravensmede's glass. 'In that case, best drink it down, old man,' he instructed. 'There have been some developments while you were away, and you ain't going to like them, not one little bit.'

The atmosphere within the King's Theatre was stuffy and oppressive, too many bodies crammed into too small a space, and all for Mr Kelly's benefit night. Those in the gallery were in jovial form and were already shouting and laughing even before the play had begun. When the curtain finally rose on the comedy *Road to Ruin* their crude comments grew louder, thus creating a raucous atmosphere in which the actors struggled in vain to portray their parts with some level of decorum. The dowager's face showed all too well exactly what she thought of such a coarse display.

'No sign of Nicholas yet?' Lady Maybury fanned herself with vigour.

'No, my lady.'

'Not like him to be late, but then he does have other things on his mind at the minute,' she said, resting her faded green gaze knowingly upon her companion.

Kathryn glanced uneasily at her employer. Surely the dowager did not know what her grandson was planning? 'Does he?' she asked, trying not to sound guilty.

'Most certainly,' said Lady Maybury with a twinkle in her eye.

A smile, then Kathryn decided to steer the conversation to safer ground. 'Are you enjoying the performance, my lady?'

'Blasted nonsense with those louts crowing in the background. Damnable waste of time,' she pronounced with venom. 'And it's so uncomfortably hot in this wretched place.'

'Would you like me to fetch you a lemonade before the curtain goes up again?'

'Would you, dear gel?'

'Of course.' And so saying Kathryn exited the box, brushing against the scarlet curtains as she did so. She had barely walked more than a few paces when she became aware of the libidinous stares of several gentlemen who were loitering close by the marble pillars. With an averted gaze and a determined thrust of the chin she headed to the stairwell, only to be intercepted by Lord Stanfield.

'Miss Marchant,' he said. 'Enchanted to see you again. I hope that you enjoyed your stay in Brighthelmstone.'

'Indeed, sir. It was most enjoyable.' Something in the man's manner made her uncomfortable, not that his words could be faulted. He was politeness itself, but beneath the polished veneer... It hardly seemed possible that this was the same man she had danced with so many times in the weeks preceding Brighthelmstone. There was a subtle change, something that she could not quite define.

He lingered a trifle too long over her hand, pressed his lips that bit too ardently to her fingers.

She retrieved her hand and saw his focus drop to her bosom where it remained in undisguised and leisurely pleasure. 'Please excuse me, Lord Stanfield,' she said coldly and moved swiftly past. The thump in her chest and heat in her cheeks persuaded her she had not misinterpreted his behaviour. Thrusting the thought from her mind, she made her way down the stairs and started to traverse the crowded hallway to the queue at the refreshments table. A hush descended, marred only by whisperings and snide laughter. On either side men and women slowly, deliberately, turned their backs to her. There could be no mistaking that clear signal, a cut to her face.

With a hammering heart and trembling legs Kathryn held her head up and walked with quiet dignity towards the table. The crowd parted before her, contempt upon the faces of the fine ladies before they turned them away, and something worse upon the gentlemen's. And then straight ahead, barely a few feet away, she saw Mr and Mrs Marchant. Her eyes met those of her aunt, and for a moment she thought that the woman meant to help her, to rescue her from the nightmare in which she suddenly found herself. Anna Marchant smiled, and her eyes were cold, hard chips of ice. There was nothing of kindness and everything of malice contained in her look. Vulnerability had long fled, as had any vestige of all other pretence. With slow deliberation Mrs Marchant turned to present her back. Uncle Henry followed suit. Voices buzzed in the background. Kathryn swallowed down the aridity in her throat and refused to be beaten. She walked on through the cleared route hedged by a line of smartly presented backs. With her eyes fixed ahead she purchased two lemonades and turned to retrace her steps, running the gauntlet once more. Quite how she did so with such cool reserve she would never know, not when the very ground seemed to loom up towards her.

Halfway up the stairwell she encountered Mr Roodley on his way down. Although he did not address her, his knowing brown eyes swept brazenly over her body as he passed.

The safety of the box was in sight when she felt the firm touch of a hand upon her bottom. Lecherous sniggers sounded from a small group of gentlemen lounging against a wall. Kathryn stopped, and drawing herself up to her full height, turned with icy fury. She would never know the image she presented at that moment, with her ashen skin and stormy grey eyes, her small nose flared and full lips parted in readiness for battle, the steady rise and fall of her breasts and the rigid stance of her body. Indignation personified. Deathly silence. The pulse thrummed in her throat, as one by one she fixed her chill gaze upon them, until their leers and smiles vanished and they looked away. Then she turned and walked to the box, white knuckles gripping the glasses for dear life.

'Oh there you are, my dear. Thank you.' Lady Maybury gratefully sipped at the lemonade. 'So refreshing.' The faded green eyes raked her companion's countenance. 'Kathryn?'

She could not speak, sat frozen in a state of shock, the lemonade untouched before her.

The dowager's hand gripped to hers. 'What is it? What has happened? You look as if you've seen a ghost...and you're shaking.'

'I'm feeling a little unwell. I'm sure it will shortly pass,' she whispered. 'Please do not concern yourself, my lady.'

Lady Maybury frowned, 'But I am concerned, gel, and do not give me that old flannel of feeling unwell. You left here fine enough ten minutes ago and return looking like death warmed up. Am I not entitled to some explanation?'

Her hand pressed to her brow. Where to begin? What to say? Blasted, pulverised, unable to think straight. Kathryn squeezed her eyes shut and swallowed hard at the memory of what had just occurred. But what *had* just happened? And why? Her fingers trembled as they pulled at the silk of her skirt. Why? The question sounded again and again in her mind. The reason did not matter, not once Lady Maybury witnessed the sorry state of affairs upon their exit. It was perhaps fortuitous that they had arrived at the theatre early to beat the crowds, thus stalling the inevitability of what was to come.

'Kathryn—' the elderly voice sounded close to her ear '—come, we'd better get you home, my dear.'

'But Lord Ravensmede—'

'Will know where to find us,' finished Lady Maybury. 'There's nothing to worry about.'

At the sound of such genuine concern Kathryn could bear her shame no longer. 'I'm sorry, my lady, so very sorry. You've been so kind, like my own grandmother instead of an employer. I would do anything to save you from... Please forgive me.' Her voice ruptured into hoarseness and she spoke no more, just touched the frail old hand to her cheek in a gesture of affection.

'Come on,' came the imperious command.

'The play is not yet finished.'

'A bigger load of tripe I've yet to see. I'll not waste any more of my time on it. Hurry along now.' Lady Maybury rose from her seat.

'My lady, there's something you should know before you…before you leave this box.' Kathryn's fingers plucked nervously at one another.

A white eyebrow raised in a gesture similar to that so favoured by the lady's grandson.

The smoky grey gaze dropped to the floor. 'It seems that I have…incurred the condemnation of…that is to say, I have invoked the displeasure of…'

'You may explain it to me in detail once we're home. I've no mind to stay here any longer.' Lady Maybury swept from the box with regal elegance, seemingly oblivious to the whisperings and raising of viewing glasses all around.

They passed few people of any significance on their way from the theatre to the carriage, but the manner of those in their path soon enlightened Lady Maybury as to the cause of her companion's distress.

'Of all the most idiotic, petty and malicious behaviours!' The dowager was working herself into a lofty dudgeon. 'How dare they cut m'companion!'

'Their treatment of me is inconsequential, but I'm dismayed to see that Lady Collins was so frosty to you, my lady. I'm sorry that you should be so affected. I will, of course, leave at once to save you further embarrassment.'

'Don't be ridiculous,' the lady snapped fiercely. 'You were quite the toast of the town when we left only a few weeks ago. And while in Brighthelmstone you barely strayed from the view of my beady eye.'

Kathryn thought of the hungry kisses from Nicholas's mouth. She remembered the warmth of his body lying on top of hers and the press of his bed against her back. The memories brought a guilty heat to her cheeks. Mercifully the carriage interior was dim.

'This abominable treatment is without the slightest merit.'

Kathryn said nothing.

The remainder of the journey continued in silence with the dowager brooding and Kathryn in a state of numb disbelief.

The ladies did not have to wait long before Ravensmede arrived at Upper Grosvenor Street.

'Grandmama, Kathryn.' The green gaze saw in an instant the tension etched upon the girl's face. 'I went to the theatre first. My apologies for being late.'

'Well, you're here now, thank goodness. Kathryn and I have encountered something of a problem.' The dowager threw off her cashmere shawl in a flurry, ordered that the brandy decanter be brought to the library and ushered both her companion and her grandson into that small cosy room.

'If I may be so bold as to comment, ma'am, you appear a trifle put out,' said Ravensmede, trying to gauge just how far the gossip had spread. 'Was the play not to your satisfaction?'

She waved the butler away, shut the door with a decisive thud and poured three glasses of brandy. Kathryn was then pushed unceremoniously down into a chair and a glass pressed firmly in her hand. 'Drink!' commanded the dowager.

It seemed the gossip-mongers had been busy. Ravensmede could see the tremor in the girl's fingers.

A minute's pause and the glass raised to those lips that were so unnaturally pale. She sipped on the spirit, made a face at the strength of its taste, and swallowed it down.

His grandmother wasted no time in emptying the contents of her glass and soon had it refilled.

'Grandmama.' Ravensmede made to take his grandparent's arm. 'Perhaps you should sit down and tell me what has happened.'

'Polite society,' said Lady Maybury acidly, 'has decided that m'companion is no longer acceptable. Kathryn has received the cut direct.'

'I see,' replied Ravensmede without the least surprise.

'And we have no notion as to the cause of this sudden outlandish behaviour,' said the old lady.

His eyes skimmed to Kathryn once more, but she had not moved one inch, just sat with the brandy glass gripped within her fingers, the amber liquid almost untouched. 'Ah,' he said softly, 'I think I may be able to help you with that.'

Two pairs of eyes swivelled to his.

There was no easy way to say what must be said. A dagger twisted in his gut at the very thought, but he rose nevertheless, without a shadow of the anger and pain that troubled him. He leaned back against the small wooden desk and stretched out his legs before him.

Time slowed within the library. No one spoke. No one moved. They sat as statues and waited.

He could defer no longer. 'It seems that there's a malicious rumour circulating regarding Kathryn's relationship with a certain gentleman. The couple are believed to have behaved without propriety.'

The fire crackled in the grate. The soft wheeze of Lady Maybury's breathing.

He looked up at Kathryn's white face, her eyes huge and dark, overwhelmed by the blackness of her pupils.

'With whom am I purported to have established such a…relationship?' The words forced from her bloodless lips.

Ravensmede calmed the leap of his pulse. The merest twitch of the muscle in his jaw.

She was watching him still, a mask of calmness across her face.

'With myself,' came the dry reply.

Silence echoed.

'They think you're keeping m'companion as your mistress?' Lady Maybury questioned with alarming candour.

A sharp intake of air from the slender figure opposite, and the stormy grey eyes with all their hurt, all their fury, all their incredulity, dropped to the floor.

'It would appear so, ma'am,' Ravensmede conceded.

She turned to face her grandson. 'Then you had better speak to Kathryn,' said the dowager, and walked out of the room.

The latch clicked into place. The grandfather clock ticked its slow steady rhythm.

'Tell me the whole of it,' Kathryn said in a small, tightly controlled voice.

'It's better that I don't.'

Her shoulders squared back, her chin thrust out in defiance. 'I need to know.'

He gave a curt nod. 'Harry Silverton has been busy informing anyone who will listen that I was responsible for the ruination of a young lady acting in the capacity of my grandmother's companion. He's adamant that he witnessed you within my arms while I was in state of some undress upon the sofa in the drawing room of our rented accommodation.'

Kathryn's temper flared, 'What nonsense! He's misinterpreting the whole thing. Where is the mention of his drunken state, or the fact that he shot his pistol at you?' Her eyes flashed and colour burned in her previously pale cheeks. 'Can we not discredit his lies?'

'Even if we could, I'm afraid that Silverton's tale is not all.'

'There's more?' An incredulous frown wrinkled her brow. He reached for her.

Adamant, she shook her head. 'No. Just tell me.' If he touched her, the last of her brittle control would shatter.

In a calm mellow voice the Viscount proceeded to apprise Kathryn of the worst of their problem.

'And you have seen this printed leaflet yourself?'

'Yes,' he said grimly. 'Cadmount kept one copy and destroyed all the others he could find. Unfortunately, it seems that the damage was already done.'

She held out her hand. 'May I see it, please?'

'I'm afraid it is a crude and vulgar piece, not fit for the eyes of any lady.'

'Not even the subject of its story? Have I not a right to know?'

His eyes did not leave her face. 'It is where it belongs, Kathryn, burned to a cinder.'

She swallowed hard, determination and anger and devastation glinting in her eyes. 'What exactly did it say?'

An uncompromising expression slipped across Ravensmede's face.

'Tell me.'

His jaw set firm.

'Would you have me alone ignorant of what all of London is saying?' She saw the flicker in his focus, knew he was weakening. 'Please, Nicholas.'

He sighed. 'It is a tale in which the Viscount of R. and the widowed Mrs W. arrange an illicit liaison in a back room at Lady Finlay's ball. The widow arrives, only to interrupt a scene of impropriety between Lord R. and a certain Miss M., whom he later installed as his mistress under the guise of his grandmother's companion.' He did not tell her that every tawdry detail of the encounter had been obscenely exaggerated.

Kathryn's face paled. 'Only Mrs White knew,' she whispered.

'Mrs White is hardly portrayed in a flattering light within the article. Had Amanda White been responsible, I'd warrant it would have read a tad more in her favour.'

'Who would do such a thing? Pay from their own pocket to print and distribute such a spiteful piece of work? No one else knew.'

The bright green eyes narrowed of a sudden. He indicated Kathryn's barely touched glass of brandy. 'It might be a good idea to take another sip…a big one.'

Kathryn gripped her hands together tightly to stop them from shaking. 'You know, don't you?'

His gaze faltered. 'It is not pleasant,' he said.

'None of it is.' A terrible coldness was spreading through her body, tensing each and every muscle. And the dread of foreboding writhed in her gut. She waited, watching his anger vie with compassion, his rage with tenderness.

There was nothing but the moment and the waiting.

'I've spoken to the printer and the boy who delivered the article and instruction to him.'

'Already?'

His shoulders shrugged. 'I was still late for the theatre, and I would not have had you face that alone for all the world, Kathryn.' Their eyes locked. 'The boy took me to the house from where the letter was sent…'

She wetted the dryness of her lips. Suddenly knew the name that would pass his lips. The blood roared in her ears, so loud she feared she would not hear him.

'It was in Green Street. The woman who paid for the article was your aunt.'

Even as he confirmed what she feared she sat still as a statue in the chair, unmoving, lifeless, her expression frozen, her eyes wide and unblinking. And then her eyelids shuttered.

She did not hear him move, was not aware that anything had changed around her until she felt him kneel before her and pull her into his arms. His warmth thawed her, his strength anchored her. All around her a storm was breaking, and he was her only haven. She felt the wetness upon her cheeks, tasted the salt upon her lips, and did not know that she was weeping. A sobbing escaped her throat before she could catch it back. She laid her face against his chest, felt his hands upon her back, reassuring, protective. They did not speak; they did not have to.

A dam had broken, and all the misery, all the suffering, everything that Kathryn had so carefully stoppered through the past years rushed out. Fear and frustration and fury. Hurt and betrayal and grief. In three long years she had not wept, not once. Now that the tears had started it seemed that they would never cease. She wept until there were no more tears to weep. When finally she stopped there was nothing. Just an emptiness, and the throb of her head and the gritty nip of her eyes.

She noticed then the damp wool of Nicholas's coat lapels against her cheek, the warmth of his arms wrapped around her. Noticed too that she was standing, her body pressed into his, although quite how or when she rose from the chair she could not say. Neither of them moved. Both seemed content just to be, unmoving in the calm hush of peace. Steady thud of heartbeats, gentle rise and fall of breath. It was a place in which she could rest for ever. Seconds stretched to minutes, minutes dragged to hours, until at last his fingers found her chin, tilted her face up towards his, and Kathryn knew she could hide no longer.

'I never meant for this to happen,' he said.

'I know.'

A little pause.

'You know too that you'll have to marry me.'

A rapid inhalation of air. She should have known it was coming. He was too honourable a man to do anything else, despite all that society thought him. A proposal of marriage from Nicholas Maybury, the man that she loved, the man of whom she had dreamed. She should have been ecstatic with happiness. But she wasn't. He was a viscount, heir to an earldom, wealthier than she could imagine. She was untitled, poor, with neither dowry nor connections. Moreover, he was expected to marry Miss Francesca Paton, if the scandal had not already jeopardised that arrangement. Kathryn could not hope to wed…not as a fallen woman. She was alone, and would stay alone.

There was also the small matter of love. She felt it. He did not. Her eyes closed. She thought of Nicholas's father and the Earl's expectations. She thought of Lady Maybury and of all that the dowager had done for her. She thought of Miss Paton waiting patiently for Nicholas's offer of marriage. But most of all she thought of Nicholas and how much she loved him. Her pulse steadied. When her eyes opened Kathryn knew what she must do. 'No,' she said quietly. 'I know no such thing.'

Nicholas gave a crooked smile. 'You do now.'

'No, Nicholas.' She captured his fingers within her hand.

'I thank you for your kind offer, but I'm afraid I cannot be your wife.'

'Kathryn, you're ruined. You've no other choice but to marry me.'

Slowly she shook her head. 'It's my reputation that's ruined, not myself.'

'You'll exist as a pariah, not received in any decent house. If you think your treatment harsh so far, it will only get worse.' His gaze razed her. 'Men will think you an easy target for their attentions. You'll be subjected to the worst of their lechery.'

Still she did not speak.

'You must know that you cannot possibly continue as my grandmother's companion.'

Her head bowed. She swallowed hard. 'I understand.'

The green eyes narrowed as if he understood for the first time the absolute certainty of her resolve. 'Don't be ridiculous, Kathryn. You've no other option.'

'I can think of one,' she said, and her cheeks burned pink at the audacity of what she was about to suggest.

A tiny frown creased between his eyebrows. 'Pray enlighten me,' he said in a quietly dangerous voice.

Her fingers still touched lightly against his. She could not look him in the eye. Drawing all of her courage together, she forced the words out quickly before she could catch them back. 'Once before, in St James's Park, you made me…a different offer. Yesterday, in the coach on the way back from Brighthelmstone, you would have asked me the same thing. If the offer is still open…I accept.' She felt his fingers stiffen beneath hers. Saw the incredulity in his eyes.

He gave a spurt of ironic laughter. 'Let me check that I understand you correctly, Kathryn. You'll consent to become my mistress, but not my wife?'

It sounded so brazen that she felt the heat spread from her cheeks to burn the very tips of her ears. 'Yes,' a hoarse whisper of agreement.

'May I ask why?'

She loosed his hand. Stepped back. Met his gaze. 'I would not force you to a *mésalliance*.'

He said nothing, just waited expectantly.

The explanation came tripping out of her mouth unbidden. 'I am not titled or wealthy. Indeed, I cannot bring you either a dowry or connections.'

No reply.

'And this is not the first scandal to attach itself to my family name.'

Still he did not speak.

She found herself rambling on. 'It would not be fair to either Lady Maybury or your father.' Her eyes darted away. 'And then there is Miss Paton.'

'What of Miss Paton?' he asked, and his face was leaner and harder than ever she had seen it.

'You have long been promised to marry her.'

'Have I?' His focus pulled her back, never wavering for a moment. 'And what if I say that it is not true? That I have no need of more money. That each and every one of the reasons you list is nothing more than an excuse. And that the proposal I would have made you yesterday was one of marriage.'

She shook her head, knowing that his honour forced him to deny the truth.

'Yet you still offer yourself as my mistress?'

The breath felt trapped within her lungs. Her fingers gripped against her skirt. She could feel his tension as clearly as if it were her own.

'Why would you do that, Kathryn?' he said silkily, and moved closer.

She could not tell him. Would not speak of love. That small last vestige of pride held strong. She stepped back, striving to maintain a distance between them.

'You think that is what you want, do you?' Without any further warning he pulled her to him, crushing her in a brutal embrace. His lips raked hers, punishing, hard, taking what they would. This time there was no tenderness, no teasing affection. It was a kiss to brand her, a kiss of possession.

She was powerless to resist such an assault.

At last he raised his face from hers and the determination in his eyes took her breath away. 'I disagree. Besides, the offer I made you in the park no longer stands, Kathryn.' He released her and stepped away, watching while she stumbled back into the chair. And then he was gone, leaving Kathryn more confused than she had ever thought possible.

Chapter Fifteen

It was early the next morning when a commotion sounded in the hallway of Ravensmede House.

'I don't give a damn what he's doing. I want to see him, and I want to see him now!' A man's face contorted with fury as he strode uninvited into the drawing room. The volume of his voice carried throughout the house.

Within the breakfast room Ravensmede set down his coffee cup. He waved away the footman and without further dalliance moved swiftly and sleekly along the corridor to meet his father.

They faced each other across the drawing room.

The Earl was almost as tall as his son; his silver locks glistened in the sunlight that streamed into the room through the four large-paned windows. 'So it has come to this,' he said, 'as ever I knew it would.' His hand slipped into the pocket of his immaculately tailored coat and withdrew a folded piece of paper. With a deft flick of his wrist he unfolded the paper and, turning it round so that his son might see the printed side, dangled it between the tips of two fingers as if he thought to contaminate himself from its touch.

One glance at the sheet told Ravensmede all he needed to know. It was Anna Marchant's leaflet.

'You've gone too far this time, boy. What the hell do you think you're playing at, dragging your family into your schemes? I didn't think that even you would stoop so low as to attach such scandal to your own grandmother's name.'

Not one glimmer of emotion showed upon Ravensmede's face. Only the slight tension around his jaw betrayed the mask for what it was. 'For that I beg her forgiveness. It was never my intention.'

'God knows I've tried my best to warn you, but you always were intent on going your own way.'

'So it would seem, sir,' said Ravensmede coolly.

'And what of this Miss Marchant?'

'Surely your sources will have told you of her? It seems they have not omitted aught else,' came the gritted reply.

The Earl's eyes narrowed. 'I've heard something of Mr and Mrs Henry Marchant. If that family's character is any estimation of their niece, you are well caught by your own folly.'

'Kathryn has the misfortune to share her name with those people, nothing more.'

A silver brow arched in an arrogant gesture Ravensmede himself so frequently used. 'It matters little,' he said. 'It's one thing to waste your time and your money with widows and harlots, it's quite another to seduce unmarried young *ladies*, especially those that must make their own way in the world.'

Their gazes met and locked. 'For once we are in agreement, sir. Nevertheless, I would have you know that the leaflet is nothing but a piece of malicious spite. Miss Marchant is a lady of unimpeachable virtue.' In his mind he heard again the whisper of her soft voice. *Once before, in St James's Park, you made me a...different offer. If the offer is still open...I accept*. The thought of what it must have cost her to say those words wrenched at his heart. She was an innocent…in every aspect of the word. He would not have his father think otherwise. There could only be one real reason why Kathryn had declined marriage in favour of a more illicit relationship. And Nicholas had a very shrewd idea just what that might be. 'You may say what you will, sir, but I mean to marry Miss Marchant all the same.'

Lord Maybury sauntered to the brandy decanter and poured two large glasses. He lifted one himself and left the other for his son to retrieve. 'I'm relieved to hear that for once you're prepared to do the honourable thing. Whether you laid a finger on the girl or not is irrelevant. To all intents and purposes she's well and truly ruined.'

Ravensmede did not move from his stance next to the blackened grate. 'I assure you that the leaflet does not figure the slightest in my plans, sir. I have intended making Kathryn my wife for some time.' The expression on Nicholas's face was one that the Earl had never before seen.

Maybury grunted. 'And what of Miss Paton?' A swig of brandy disappeared down his throat.

A dry laugh erupted into the silence. 'There was never the remotest possibility that Francesca and I would marry. We would not suit, no matter how much you and her father will it otherwise.'

Silence hissed around them, and from both faces the same green eyes looked out.

The glass banged against the mahogany of the table as Maybury set it down hard. 'I think that I should meet Miss Marchant.'

'We may see her in half an hour's time at Grandmama's house.'

'It's a trifle early to call upon ladies,' the Earl protested.

'The visit has already been arranged: there is someone else whom I want Kathryn to meet.'

Kathryn lay awake all the night through, worrying over what to do. Sunlight was infiltrating the blinds and the birds chirping a lively racket by the time she finally reached a decision. Only then did she succumb to the oblivion of sleep. It seemed only minutes later when there was a knock at the door to her bedchamber, the pad of feet, and the rustle of skirt material. The aroma of freshly brewed coffee and bread still warm from the oven drifted to her nose. Kathryn groaned, pulled the bedcover over her head and rolled on to her stomach.

'Beggin' you pardon, miss, but her ladyship said as how I was to bring you a little breakfast.' The maid set the tray down on the bedside table and moved across to the other side of the room.

'Thank you, Betsy. How very kind.' One bleary eye peeped out from beneath the covers, just as Betsy raised the blind, and bright white sunlight flooded across the room. Another groan escaped Kathryn.

Betsy cast a curious look in the direction of the bed. Lying late in bed was out of character for Miss Marchant, who was normally up and about with the larks. But then again, if the gossip below stairs was anything to go by, the situation that the dowager's companion now found herself in was far removed from normal. The maid wondered if the rumours were true. Lord Ravensmede was a fine-looking gent, and as the old saying went, there was no smoke without fire. Certainly Toby knew more than he was letting on; no doubt his lordship had greased the footman's palm to keep him quiet. 'Are you ill, miss? Shall I fetch Lady Maybury?'

Kathryn pushed herself upright, and sat back against her pillows. 'No, I'm quite well, thank you, just tired. The coffee shall revive me admirably.'

Not by the look of the dark shadows beneath Miss Marchant's eyes it wouldn't, thought Betsy, and then remembered the other message that she had been instructed to impart. 'Oh, I nearly forgot miss, her ladyship would like to see you in the drawing room at ten o'clock.'

Kathryn glanced at the clock on the mantel. 'It's half past nine now!'

'Yes, miss.'

'Heavens! How on earth could I have slept so late?' Kathryn swung her legs out of the bed.

'I'll fetch you some warm water, miss.' And Betsy disappeared.

Kathryn drank the coffee down and ate two bread rolls smeared with honey. There would be no room for weakness in today's dealings. She was under no illusion as to what the dowager wanted to say. The old lady could hardly be expected to keep on a companion whose name had been linked so scandalously with the lady's own grandson. Even Nicholas had said as much.

Nicholas. The mere thought of him made her feel uncomfortably warm. The uncomfortable feeling expanded at the memory of what had passed between them yesterday. Kathryn's cheeks flamed. It was bad enough to offer herself like a common trollop. His rejection was a thousand times worse. She blew out air from between her lips, feeling the sting of shame yet again. He had offered her marriage. Marriage, for goodness' sake! Better than all of her dreams put together. To spend the rest of her life as his wife… How very easy it would have been to say that one tiny word, yes. Yes.

Yes! She should have shouted it from the boughs of the trees. But she had thought better, and now the offer was gone. As was his desire. He had said she was ruined, and so she was. With little money and nowhere to go, Kathryn knew her options were limited. She could only pray that the gossip would not reach Hampshire. Her mother's relatives were her last hope. With a heavy heart she moved to fetch the old trunk she had brought with her from Green Street.

It was only a little after ten when Kathryn was washed, dressed and ready. She had turned a deaf ear to Betsy's protestations and worn her old blue muslin dress. The trunk sitting ominously by the door was as empty as when it had arrived. Madame Dupont's skilfully fashioned dresses, for which Kathryn had not yet fully reimbursed Lady Maybury, were left hanging in the clothes-press. The pearl necklace and earrings gifted by her ladyship sat neatly in the jewellery box on the dressing table. Kathryn was unadorned. Her fingers carefully skimmed her hair just to check that none of her neatly pinned curls had escaped. A deep breath, a squaring of her shoulders, one final smoothing of her skirt, and then she opened the door and walked towards the drawing room…and Lady Maybury's dismissal.

The scene within the drawing room was not what Kathryn expected. She stood for a moment, unnoticed, staring, drinking in the sight before her. The dowager sat in her usual chair by the unlit fireplace, chatting ten to the dozen. Her expression was warm and lively, her manner familiar as if she knew the young woman who was seated demurely upon the nearby sofa very well indeed. In a glance Kathryn could see that the girl was tall and willowy, with silky dark brown hair worn in an elaborate coiffure. Two tiny white pearls dangled from her ears. Her white-and-pastel-blue dress was well cut and fashionably stylish. Everything about her bespoke money and breeding, and she wore it all with an air of effortless relaxation. Kathryn's fingers strayed self-consciously to her own shabby gown. By the window stood two men, both tall, both with the same green eyes, both wearing the same defiant arrogance, one with hair as dark as night, the other whose head had silvered with age. Kathryn's heart skipped a beat as it did whenever she saw Nicholas. It was not hard to guess the identity of the older man standing by his side.

The little group looked comfortable, at ease, like they belonged together. There was only one outsider. For a minute she felt the urge to turn and run, and then the moment was gone. Before she could think any further as to what was going on, she heard Nicholas's voice.

'Miss Marchant,' he said, and made his way to her side. 'Come in.'

She ignored the hammering of her heart and held her head high. 'Lord Ravensmede,' she replied politely, and gave a small curtsy. And then turning to his grandmother, 'Lady Maybury.'

Although she was careful to keep her gaze averted from his, she could feel his scrutiny. Just his voice was enough to set her insides aquiver. She set her face determinedly and prayed that her cheeks did not appear as scalded as the rest of her felt.

He wasted no time in the introductions. 'This is my father, Earl Maybury.'

The man by his side bowed. 'I'm pleased to welcome you to our family, Miss Marchant.' Pleased did not describe the expression on his face. Appraising came closer.

Kathryn froze at the implication of his words. It was clear

that Lord Maybury misunderstood the situation. She glanced at Nicholas, waiting for his reaction.

Ravensmede made no notice of having heard anything untoward. He met her gaze with a strange look, as if he was poised, as if he was waiting. There was a pause that was slightly too long for comfort, and then he said, 'Kathryn, this is Miss Francesca Paton.'

Kathryn stifled the gasp, blinked back the black dots swimming before her eyes and breathed deeply. The dizziness diminished. A warm hand pressed against the small of her back. Without looking she knew it to belong to Nicholas. She forced herself to step towards Miss Paton, away from the support that Nicholas offered. 'Miss Paton,' she said, and was relieved to hear that her voice sounded a deal calmer than she felt.

Miss Paton made her reply.

An awkwardness followed.

Then the dowager rose to her feet, and smiled. 'There's something to which I must attend. Please do excuse me.' And she tottered out of the door.

Nicholas stepped closer. 'My father and I must also take our leave of you…for now.' Then they too were gone.

A pair of fine hazel eyes turned upon her. 'Miss Marchant, please do come and sit beside me.' She patted a hand to the cushion to her left. 'Nicholas has told me all about you.'

Not *all*, Kathryn sincerely prayed. 'Thank you, Miss Paton,' she said with as much dignity as she could muster, and seated herself on the sofa.

Miss Paton leaned forward and smiled. 'Please call me Francesca.' Her expression was open and honest and sincere. 'You must be wondering as to the reason for my visit at such an early hour.' Without waiting for an answer she continued. 'Firstly, I came to wish you happy.'

Every muscle in Kathryn's body stiffened. She wetted her lips, unsure of what to say.

'And, secondly, I wished to meet for myself the lady that has finely succeeded in capturing Nicholas's heart.' Her smile broadened and there was a definite twinkle in her eyes.

Kathryn tried to smile, but her mouth seemed unwilling to respond. Something akin to a grimace stretched across her face. 'I fear that you may have misunderstood the—'

Miss Paton let her get no further. Her hand touched to Kathryn's in a gesture of friendship. 'Miss Marchant,' she started, and then said as an aside, 'Or may I call you Kathryn?'

'Of course,' murmured Kathryn.

'Kathryn, let me tell you how heartily relieved I am that Nicholas has at last decided to marry. You know my father and Lord Maybury are great friends, and have for years been trying to force a match between Nicholas and myself.' She laughed. 'Have you ever heard anything more ridiculous?'

It did not sound in the least ridiculous to Kathryn. Miss Paton was heiress to a considerable fortune. Lord Ravensmede was heir to an earldom. There was no disputing that the two were well matched. Kathryn held her tongue.

'Why, my dear Kathryn, Nicholas and I would not suit at all. He's a dear man, and a very great friend of the family, but that is all.'

'I thought...' Kathryn found her voice at last. 'I thought that there was an informal betrothal between you both, an understanding that you would marry.'

'Oh, no, not at all!' Miss Paton exclaimed. 'Besides, my interest lies elsewhere.'

Kathryn watched as two pink patches suddenly appeared on Miss Paton's cheeks. 'You have a *tendre* for someone else?'

Miss Paton's cheeks dimpled, and her face lit up. 'There is a certain curate. He's kind and diligent and of quite the most admirable character. But he's a little shy of approaching my father. Little wonder, for although Papa is the best of fathers, he can appear a tiny bit intimidating in his manner to those with whom he is unfamiliar.' Worry washed across Miss Paton's face. 'I beg you will not speak of it, Kathryn. We have told no one, though now that you've taken care of Nicholas for me, the way is clear for Thomas to speak to my papa.'

A weight lifted from Kathryn's shoulders. 'Your secret is safe with me. And I sincerely hope that you and Thomas find happiness.'

'Thank you,' said Miss Paton.

'No, thank *you,* Francesca,' Kathryn said, and meant it.

They moved to talk of the weather, and then discussed the Duke of Wellington's recent victory against Napoleon. Miss Paton told Kathryn all about the magnificent firework display at Vauxhall Gardens to celebrate the event. From there talk led on to the latest fashions, and then the birth of Lady Harrington's twins. Never once did she make the slightest mention of the most scandalous rumours sweeping every drawing room in London, especially those concerning Lord Ravensmede and his grandmother's companion.

Indeed, when Nicholas returned, alone, it was to find the two women chatting as if they were the best of friends.

Within a few minutes of the Viscount entering the drawing room, Miss Paton took her leave.

Nicholas leaned against the mantel above the fireplace.

Kathryn stayed where she was upon the sofa.

He was careful to keep his face expressionless. 'Did you and Miss Paton find anything interesting to discuss?'

Her face raised to his and he could see that much of the

earlier tension had vanished. The silver eyes held a glimmer of mischief. 'Perhaps.'

He moved from the fireplace to take up the seat that Miss Paton had so recently vacated. Kathryn edged closer to the opposite arm of the sofa. He arched an eyebrow. 'Scared?'

'No. Should I be?'

A nearly smile pulled at his mouth. 'Most definitely so. I've just neatly disposed of two of your objections to marrying me. Two more to go and then you're mine, Kathryn Marchant.'

Shock rippled across her face. 'You still wish to wed me?' There was a definite breathy catch to her voice. 'Even after...'

'*Especially* after your proposition.' His eyebrow twitched.

Colour flooded her cheeks. 'It was not a proposition,' she said stubbornly.

He gave her a knowing look. 'If you say so.'

Her gaze fluttered away, and her fingers picked at the skirt of her dress.

He couldn't afford to let himself touch her...not yet. He produced a letter from his pocket and threw it on to the sofa between them. It was addressed to Miss Kathryn Marchant. No other direction had been added.

She peered at it suspiciously.

'Open it.'

A moment's hesitation, and then she did. The wafer broke beneath her fingers and the paper unfolded to reveal the lines of black flowing script. Disbelief creased her forehead. Slowly, concentrating on each word, she read the letter's contents again. 'It's from my uncle. He has enclosed a banker's draft for five hundred pounds...as a dowry.' The paper fluttered to her lap. She stared at him. 'I don't understand.'

'You're his brother's daughter. It is only to be expected that he would supply you with a dowry.'

'But…the scandal…my uncle and aunt have disowned me.'

'It would appear that they have changed their minds.'

Her eyelids shuttered momentarily. She pressed her fingers to her lips, as if to stopper any flow of emotion.

'So it seems, Kathryn, that you now have a dowry…if you should choose to use it as such.'

'I…' He could see her confusion.

His voice gentled. 'Which leaves only your last excuse… your family.'

'You cannot change that, nor would I wish you to,' she said softly.

'Why would I want to, when you have such good connections?' A wry smile curved. 'I have it upon the best of authorities that your mother was a Thornley of Overton.'

She wiped the emotion from her face, fixed her expression to one of blandness. Several heartbeats passed. 'Before you say any more, Nicholas, there is something I should tell you.' Not one movement. Not one betraying flicker of her eyes. 'This is not the first scandal to be attached to my family name. My father…' An image of her papa lying slumped upon his desk, a spent pistol in his hand. She stopped. Cleared her throat. The blink of her eyes lasted just fractionally too long. 'My father…' Again it seemed she could not bring herself to say the words.

'I know, Kathryn,' he said, wishing to spare her the worst of it.

Her gaze clung to his. 'How did you find out?'

'Does it matter?'

She shook her head, inadvertently dislodging a few curls. 'No. I suppose not. It's just that I've never spoken of it.

Never. But not one day has passed without its memory. So much blood…and the pistol still in his hand…and his face…' She caught at her lower lip with her teeth.

He moved then. Closed the space between them, until their legs touched together on the sofa. Took her hands in his. Gripped them firm. 'I did not mean to remind you.'

'I cannot forget,' she said. 'But with time it grows easier, and there are other things that help me not to think of it.' Such as daydreaming and the man who sat so closely by her side, but she would never say so.

Her fingers were small and cool beneath his. His thumb stroked at the back of her hand. 'Your father's death was a tragedy, but the blame is not yours. It has no bearing on our marriage.' He leaned back against the sofa, keeping her within his gaze, watching the emotion cloud the brilliance of her eyes. 'So,' he said, 'Kathryn Marchant, will you do me the honour of becoming my wife?' Blood pulsed through the pulse point at the side of his neck. Thud. Thud. Thud. His hand still covered hers. Everything was still. Motionless. Breath caught and held, waiting to exhale.

She looked at him, really looked at him, as if seeing him for the first time.

His grip unwittingly tightened.

'Yes,' she said, in a whisper. And a small sigh escaped her.

Whether it was a sigh of sadness or resignation or relief, Nicholas did not know. He pulled her into his arms and dropped a kiss to the top of her hair.

It was Kathryn who pulled back. Kathryn, whose free hand touched to his cheek, her thumb brushing against his lips, tracing down to his chin. He saw her eyes drop to his lips, sensed her need. And then her mouth touched to his, her lips moving in sweet tentative enquiry.

The green eyes sparked. His lips answered her call, sliding and teasing, caressing and tickling.

Her mouth opened in sensual invitation.

The hot moisture of his tongue penetrated. She met his probing with her own. Tongue lapped against tongue.

He groaned and pulled her fully into his arms. 'Kathryn!' The rawness of emotion rendered his voice hoarse. His hands moved upon her back weaving patterns of age-old magic that she could not ignore.

Her fingers threaded through the burnt umber of his hair. Deep within her was an ache of longing. The hardness of his chest grazed her breasts, and she thrust against him and felt the thrum of his heart beneath that warm solid wall of muscle.

His hand moved to claim first one breast and then the other. Much more of this and he would be lost. The last vestige of reason pulled him back from temptation. Gently he eased himself away, looking her full in eyes that smouldered with passion and emotion. 'Sweetheart,' he said, 'it's a good thing I already have the special licence. I don't think my restraint will last much longer.'

With only two days to go before the wedding Lady Maybury decided a mammoth shopping expedition was in order. 'It's such a shame that there's not time to have a new gown made for you. We'll have to make do with a new bonnet and gloves. Oh, and a bandeau perhaps, and stockings…and a matching reticule.' The dowager was warming to her theme. 'And most definitely a new and rather exciting nightdress.' She slid a mischievous look at the young woman by her side.

Kathryn ignored the heat rising in her cheeks. 'It's very kind of you to offer such luxuries, but I already have more than enough.'

'Nonsense,' replied Lady Maybury. 'I can't have my granddaughter dressing in rags. We shall start with Miss Walters, move to Madame Devy, and Mills, then work our way along to Mrs Shabner, not forgetting Millards.'

A sigh was stifled as Kathryn allowed herself to be led into first one shop, then many more.

The day was warm in the extreme. Lady Maybury did not appear to notice. She was busily immersed in yards of ribbons and lace, and had just dispatched their footman to empty his arms of the multitude of parcels into the carriage.

'How dashed inconvenient!' Lady Maybury's nose wrinkled with irritation.

The woman serving behind the counter looked up, shock displayed across her face.

'James has taken the turquoise turban and I need it in order to select the best matching feathers.'

'I'm sure we can make a very good guess at which colours will suit,' Kathryn said.

The dowager raised an imperious white brow. 'Indeed we will not. When he returns, I'll send him back for it.'

Kathryn thought of the rising heat of the day. She thought of the footman's warm woollen coat, and the long walk he would have to reach their carriage. 'He's only just left and cannot have gone far. Perhaps I could stop him in time.'

'My dear gel—'

But the slender figure was already disappearing through the doorway.

The shop assistant sniffed, but said nothing.

Kathryn scanned the street and there in the distance was the retreating footman struggling under his load. Without a further thought she hurried towards him. Her breath became laboured and she felt the sweat bead upon her brow. 'James!' she said in a loud voice.

The footman disappeared around the corner.

Kathryn walked faster still. From out of nowhere an arm snaked around her waist, pulled her into an alleyway and slammed her hard against a wall. Her scream was rendered useless by the hand clamped across her mouth.

'Out walking alone, Kathryn, without even the accompaniment of a maid? What will people say? But then I'm forgetting that your reputation is already in tatters.'

She stared up into the face of Anna Marchant. Kathryn ceased her struggles, the blood draining from her cheeks until, beneath the heat of the day, a cold tremor pricked upon her skin.

The kid-clad hand dropped from her lips, but the grip remained around her wrist.

'Aunt Anna!' she exclaimed, unable to believe who it was that stood before her.

The older woman's lips smirked. 'Why so pale, niece? Did you think to play me for the fool quite so easily?'

'I don't know what you mean,' she whispered, feeling the stirrings of fear.

'Oh, but I think that you do, Kathryn. Sending Ravensmede to blackmail your uncle into paying a dowry.'

'Blackmail? I thought…' The words trailed off.

'You thought what?' sneered her aunt. 'That your uncle paid the money out of some sense of obligation? Affection, even? So sorry to disappoint you, my dear, but only Ravensmede's threats forced Mr Marchant's pen to paper. You could rot in hell for all we care.'

Realisation hit Kathryn between the eyes. 'He used the leaflet.'

'Very good. Did you like it? Really most effective, even if I do say so myself. Because of it, Amanda White dare not show her face. Did you know that she's left the country? Ran away to Italy, so they say. And you and Ravensmede are the scandal of London. All according to plan. Such a shame that he discovered my part in the affair.'

'Nicholas threatened to reveal the truth if Uncle Henry did not supply a dowry?'

'Of course. What choice did we have?'

It made sense. Kathryn looked directly into her aunt's eyes and saw the depths of the other woman's hatred. 'Why did you do it, Aunt Anna? Why should you want to destroy me so much as to publish such a thing?'

A smile stretched across Anna Marchant's face. 'Why do you think? I loathe you. I've always loathed you since the minute you crossed the threshold into my house. Trying to make claims upon your uncle's affection, thinking you were due our hospitality. I saw what you intended from the start. Trying to cast my own daughter into the shade, thinking yourself superior, and always with that look upon your face as if nothing we did could ever touch you.'

Kathryn stared as if she could not believe the words tumbling from her aunt's mouth. 'You are mistaken, Aunt, much more than you could ever know.'

The thing that passed for a smile upon Anna Marchant's face faded. 'No, Kathryn. I know full well what you are.' The ribbons of her bonnet danced in the breeze. 'I never wanted to take you into my home. You may thank Henry and his sense of duty for that. But why should my family and I suffer? It was not our fault that your slut of a mother died, or that your pathetic sot of a father killed himself.'

Instinct took over. Kathryn drew her hand back, and an almighty crack reverberated through the alley.

The imprint of Kathryn's hand, stark and red, appeared upon her aunt's cheek.

For a moment the two women just stared at each other, and then Anna Marchant's voice dropped to a snarl. 'You're going to regret that,' she said, and tightened her grip around her niece's wrist. 'You think to thwart me, but I won't let it happen. Ruined before all of London, and somehow you end up forcing Ravensmede into marriage in an effort to outdo your cousin. Lottie catches herself a decent gentleman for a husband, but you have to go one better with a viscount, and a rich one at that. Do you think after all that has happened that I shall just sit back and let you marry Ravensmede, and worm you way back into society's favour?'

'Take your hand off me.' Inside Kathryn was shaking, but her voice was clear and calm.

'Gladly,' said her aunt, and released her grip on her niece's wrist. She stepped back.

Kathryn made to leave.

'Not so fast.' Anna Marchant drew the small pistol from her reticule and aimed it at Kathryn's forehead. 'I'll see you dead first.'

Kathryn's heart hammered hard enough to escape her chest and her legs wobbled. 'You'll never get away with it. Lady Maybury is in the shop just a few yards along the street. I was merely trying to catch her footman. If I don't return soon, she'll come looking for me.'

'I know exactly where the old woman is. Did you think that I just chanced to be here? I was following you, awaiting my opportunity… which you have very obligingly just handed me.' A low hollow laugh sounded. 'I'll be long gone by the time the footman returns and the dowager realises that you're not with him.'

The pistol poked closer. Kathryn determined not to flinch.

'Just think, dear niece, a lead ball in the head, the same as your papa.' Scrape of metal, and the pistol was cocked.

A thousand thoughts flashed through Kathryn's head in that single moment. Images of her father, her mother, her sister, scenes from throughout the years of her life. But one picture dominated all others: Nicholas Maybury. And her one regret was that she would die without telling him of her love. Her eyes closed of their own volition. Her heart was beating in a frenzy, blood pumping so hard that it sounded like the rush of wind in her ears. Yet somewhere in the middle of the storm of emotion was an unexpected calmness, a silent place, a peaceful place.

'Kathryn!' The deep masculine voice echoed, and all at once she knew she was safe.

Somehow, by some sliver of chance, he was here. 'Nicholas!' she gasped.

'Ravensmede?' Anna Marchant swung to face the tall athletic figure. She paled, gulped and stumbled back in the opposite direction.

Kathryn had never seen such a look upon Nicholas's face. The green eyes glowered dark and menacing, the deep brown of his eyebrows drawn low and angled warned of a mood as black as the devil's. His hair rippled around a face that was the antithesis of colour. Even his lips, pressed firmly together, glowed with an unearthly pallor. Everything about him was still, tense, controlled. Dressed entirely in the deepest darkest black, he loomed a huge stark silhouette against the skyline. A chill stole through the air, the sky dimmed as a cloud obliterated the sun. 'Mrs Marchant,' he said in a voice filled with menace.

Kathryn shivered.

Anna Marchant's eyes widened and with fumbling fingers she swung the pistol towards Ravensmede.

'No!' Kathryn grabbed for her aunt's arm, deflecting the pistol's aim.

A loud bang. Smell of gunpowder. The drift of wispy plumes of blue smoke.

And when the smoke cleared Anna Marchant was lying on her back amidst the filth of the alley, bonnet askew, eyes bulging in terror. The dark figure stood above her, a large pistol trained on her sweating forehead. He crouched lower to look directly into the woman's eyes and when he spoke it was with that same terrible quiet control. 'Death can be mercifully quick, Mrs Marchant.' He touched the pistol muzzle between her eyes. 'And then again, there are ways to make it slow and painful.' The muzzle slid down to rest against her collarbone.

'Please,' came the high pitched whimper. 'Please.'

'Please what?' he asked. 'Do it quickly? I don't believe that the choice is yours to make.'

'No, don't kill me. Please don't kill me.' A sob sounded.

Ravensmede pressed the pistol a little harder. 'Crying for yourself, Mrs Marchant? Do you think that your tears of self-pity will stay my hand? After everything that you have done to make Kathryn's life miserable, to hurt her, even trying to kill her, there is nothing that can do that…'

Anna Marchant began to weep in earnest.

'Save to spare Kathryn the distress of witnessing such an act. She's suffered enough because of you. For her sake, and her sake alone, I'm prepared to offer you an alternative. England would fare better for your absence, madam. Therefore, you should remove yourself, your husband, your daughter, and the slanderous Mr Silverton to a place overseas with immediate effect. I'm sure that Silverton can make arrangements with his contacts in the West Indies. So, what is it to be?'

Mrs Marchant whimpered.

'Speak up, Mrs Marchant. Let us hear your decision.'

'We'll leave the country.'

'Never to return,' pressed Ravensmede.

'Never to return,' repeated a shaken Anna Marchant.

'I'm glad that we both understand the situation. Make no mistake, if you renege on this agreement I'll see you hanged for your attempt on Kathryn's life,' said Ravensmede, and removed the pistol to his pocket. He rose and walked slowly over to Kathryn.

His eyes scanned her face. 'Are you all right?'

Words would not come. Her head nodded, never for a minute breaking their gaze.

And then his arms were around her, strong, and safe. He pulled her to him and held her like he would never let her go.

The sun shone from a glorious cloudless sky as Kathryn made her way down the sweeping staircase of the house in Upper Grosvenor Street on Earl Maybury's arm. She was dressed in a simple gown of cream silk that, with its fashionable high-waist, flattered her petite stature. The décolletage swept low, revealing the gentle swell of her breasts. Tiny shimmering beads adorned the bodice and the edge of the short puff sleeves. Her hair was worn high with the soft curls allowed to drape teasingly down to her neck. Threaded throughout the chestnut locks piled upon her crown were narrow bead-studded ribbons of the palest cream, highlighting the rich red undertone of her hair.

'It's not too late to change your mind. Are you sure you can wed such a scoundrel, even if he is my son?' teased Lord Maybury.

She inclined her head as if deep in thought. 'To wed Nicholas,' she said softly, 'is something of which I thought only to dream.' Then the strange intensity of the moment was lost. She laughed and her curls danced. 'Does he know that you're inciting me to such rebellion?'

His shoulders shrugged. 'Most probably—he would expect nothing less.' The sunlight burnished the silver of his hair. 'I may be Nicholas's father, but for today I also take the role that your own dear papa should have had.' He tucked her hand into the crook of his arm.

'Yes.' A sad little smile stole across her face.

'I'm sure that he would have approved of your marriage.' He patted her small hand. 'That is, once he got to know Nick, of course.'

They laughed and stepped from the staircase on to the cool marble floor of the hallway.

Kathryn stopped and glanced at the door ahead of them, the last barrier that remained between her and Nicholas Maybury. Once she stepped beyond it there would be no going back.

'You plan to keep him on his toes, then?' The green eyes twinkled mischievously. 'Even though you are but fashionably late, he should have started to worry by now. I never thought to see him so tamed.'

Taking a deep breath, she stepped forward and allowed Lord Maybury to open the door.

He was standing facing the priest, with Cadmount by his side. A tall, imposing figure at the best of times, Kathryn thought she had never seen him look so magnificent as he did today. The ebony coat looked to have been sculpted upon his body and highlighted the snow-white sheen of his neckcloth, shirt and waistcoat. Long muscular legs were wrapped in white breeches. Even his deep dark brown locks had been shaped to perfection. Her heart turned over and she felt strangely shy.

Lord Maybury deposited her by Nicholas's side and moved back to sit beside the dowager and Miss Paton.

The palms of Kathryn's hands grew suddenly clammy and her throat dry.

Then the tall figure by her side smiled down at her, and there was such warmth and tenderness in his eyes that she quite forgot her nervousness and relaxed in his protective gaze. And when the priest asked her what she knew he would, she was able to answer in a clear voice without the slightest hint of a tremor. The ring slid smoothly on to her finger as if it had always been destined to fit there.

It seemed that the ceremony had barely started when she heard the priest pronounce them man and wife.

Nicholas's hands moved to take her arms.

She raised her face to receive the chaste kiss that would seal their union.

His lips slid intimately over hers with a prolonged passion that raised the colour to her cheeks.

'Nicholas!' she whispered in scandalised tones and made to pull away.

He held her tight. 'It's quite all right, sweetheart, we're married now.' He smiled a wicked smile and shot her a smouldering glance. And throughout the day when he looked at her she could see the promise in his eyes.

When he entered her bedchamber she was standing by the window as if mesmerised by the luminous glow of the full moon. Curls of chestnut hair cascaded over her shoulders, leading his eye down to the sheer cream gossamer of her nightdress and the barely concealed skin beneath. Small bare feet peeped out from under the hem of the nightdress and the slender hands were held loosely by her side. Although he had not spoken, she must have heard him and glanced round over her shoulder. A shy smile flashed at him, 'Nicholas.' But she did not change her stance, turning her face once more towards the moon.

Ravensmede felt his loins harden at the very sight of her. He had longed for this night for so long and now it was here, finally, at last. Kathryn was his, his wife, to have and to hold, to love and to cherish, for ever. With determined effort he schooled his passion and moved slowly towards her, until he stood so close behind her that the cream gossamer brushed the black satin of his dressing gown.

She shivered.

'Are you cold?' He touched his hands to her shoulders, sliding them down to capture her fingers.

'Just a little. It's this nightdress, it's just so…' She blushed and looked back at the moon.

'So very becoming,' he supplied, and slipped his arms around her so that her back was pressed full against him. The clean scent of her hair drifted up. Unlike most of the women that he had known, she wore no perfume, but her own sweet smell was intoxicating enough. He lowered his face to the red-brown curls and inhaled. By their own accord his hands crept up to cup her breasts. The soft thunder of her heart raced beneath the small firm mounds and he thought he detected a slight tremble in her body. 'Don't be afraid, sweetheart, there's nothing to fear.' A kiss dropped to the top of her head.

'I know,' she said and, twisting round in his arms, buried

her head against his chest. 'It's just that there's something I need to tell you, something I should have told you a long time ago, had it not been for fear and for pride.' She laid her palms flat against his chest, and gave her bottom lip a little nibble. 'But when I stood in that alley with Aunt Anna's pistol in my face, I realised that I had been a coward not to tell you the truth: I love you, Nicholas.'

'I know,' he said. 'I've known since you turned down my offer of marriage in favour of a more scandalous proposition.'

'Oh.' Embarrassment warmed her cheeks. Her eyes held level with his chest. 'From all that you've done for me, I know that you must feel some measure of affection, and… and desire…and I want to tell you that it is enough. It doesn't matter that you don't love me in return.'

His thumb and forefinger captured her chin and tilted her face up to his. 'Some measure of affection and desire,' he said and moved his lips to hover above hers, 'goes nowhere near it, Kathryn.'

It seemed that her heart shuddered to a stop.

'I want you…' his head lowered to hers '…I need you…' until their lips almost touched '…I love you…' and they shared the same breath. 'Why else did you think that I went to so much trouble to make you my wife?'

She caught her breath.

'I love you, sweetheart,' he said again in a voice that was low and seductive. 'Completely. Utterly.'

The clear grey eyes darkened to a deep smoky charcoal. A gasp escaped her and his mouth closed over hers.

It was a kiss of longing and of love. A kiss to prove the words he had spoken. A kiss of passion and of need.

The last barrier crumbled. Nicholas loved her. Loved her,

just as she loved him. He was her husband, and she was his wife. Kathryn gave herself up to the sweetness of the moment.

Nicholas teased. He tantalised. His hot breath seared the path his mouth had taken, slowly, enticingly, determined to prolong her pleasure.

Beneath the slick caress of his tongue, her lips parted in invitation, offering herself to his touch, his taste. Her palms flattened and crept up and across the broad strength of his back, her fingers sliding on the cool satin of his robe.

His hands skimmed down to her buttocks, the sensual massage a prelude to the grip that pressed her to the hard core of his arousal.

A soft moan escaped her lips.

With shaking fingers he untied the ribbons of her thin filmy gown so that it fell from her shoulders, exposing the pearl lustre of her skin.

Her eyes flickered open and she watched his gaze travel over every inch of her bare body.

'My love,' he said and fluttered soft kisses to her eyelids, her cheeks, across her passion-swollen lips down to the pale column of her neck and further. She arched against him as his mouth moved over the softness of her breast, his tongue washing its rosy peak with erotic precision.

Slender fingers threaded through his dark locks, pulling him to her, guiding him to her other breast. Shallow reedy breaths. Her hardened nipples ached with desire. Something fluttered and contracted deep within her. 'Nicholas.' She whispered his name, not fully understanding the escalating need. A liquid warmth melted between her thighs as he suckled her taut peaks. Then his mouth was gone.

A tiny sound of frustration, and her hands attempted to guide his head back to where it had lain. But Nicholas had other plans. Slowly, deliberately, he traced a line of tiny butterfly kisses beneath each breast then dipped lower, getting down on to his knees to follow the central line of her stomach, down across the soft plain of her abdomen.

'Nicholas!' Her eyes opened wide and round.

The green gaze found hers, and lingered with ardent intensity while his lips slid lower over the smooth silk of her skin towards that most secret of places.

Her legs trembled as his tongue tasted her sweetness and his hands, which had been steering her hips so expertly, gently lifted her and lowered her on to the bed.

He raised his head to hers, their eyes never leaving each other's for a moment, even when their lips met in honeyed reunion. His long, toned body covered hers, the tight muscles rippling beneath the sheen of sweat that drenched his skin.

Naked and hot, their bodies entwined beneath the silver glow of the moonlight. There was no need for covers, the heat of their passion scorched all that it touched. His low murmurs of encouragement caused her breath to come in short pants. She rose against him, unwittingly rubbing the tip of his heated desire. His fingers caressed her hidden moistness, sliding in sensual circles while his kisses played upon the soft whiteness of her inner thighs. Beneath the laboured breaths he felt the urgency of her need.

'Nicholas.' Her arms pulled him closer, until their skin slid together with the moisture of passion. Her lips trembled beneath his, heavy lids shuttered over eyes in which the pupils were huge and dilated.

He moved to take her then, thrusting once into the heat of her molten core.

A sharp intake of air. The grey eyes opened, stared up into his, searching.

He held still. And then his mouth found hers and indulged in slow deep sensual passion. Between those sweet swollen lips his tongue lingered, then lunged in a steady rhythm until he felt her tension loosen. He felt the first tentative wriggle of her hips, and a deep sensuous smile curved to his mouth. When those slender fingers wove a pattern of delight upon the firm muscle of his buttocks he could wait no longer. His muscles tensed to spiral them both into an ecstasy of oblivion for the first of many times that night.

Sunlight flooded the breakfast room. The Viscountess of Ravensmede smiled up at the tall handsome man by her side.

'You should not have risen so early,' he chided. 'I would not have you tired for tonight.' His eyes darkened with simmering desire, as he stared down into the face that he loved so well.

She laughed and, for Nicholas, it lit up the room brighter than any sunshine ever could. 'I promise that I shall not be tired, but what of you, dear heart? I would not want to wear you out,' and her voice held a husky teasing edge. The blush rose in her cheeks at the boldness of her words.

'Minx!' he chuckled. 'At this rate it won't be long before we're able to fulfil young Maggie's expectation of us becoming the *ma* and the *pa*!'

'A child of our own,' she said wondrously.

'Children,' he corrected. 'I don't mean to let you off that easily.' Drawing her to him, he placed a tender kiss upon her lips. His dark glossy hair mixed with the rich red-brown ringlets dancing temptingly at the sides of her beautiful face. He moved back to stare into her eyes, eyes that were of a serene silver coloration. 'I love you, Kathryn Marchant!' he declared with passion and kissed her again, mindful not to spoil the arrangement of her new and highly fashionable lemon silk dress. What was once a dream was now reality.

* * * * *

ANN ELIZABETH CREE

The Venetian's Mistress

> DID YOU PURCHASE THIS BOOK WITHOUT A COVER?
> If you did, you should be aware it is **stolen property** as it was reported 'unsold and destroyed' by a retailer.
> Neither the author nor the publisher has received any payment for this book.

First Published 2005
First Australian Paperback Edition 2006
ISBN 0 733 57276 6

THE VENETIAN'S MISTRESS © 2005 by Annmarie Hasnain
Philippine Copyright 2005
Australian Copyright 2005
New Zealand Copyright 2005
Except for use in any review, the reproduction or utilisation of this work in whole or in part in any form by any electronic, mechanical or other means, now known or hereafter invented, including xerography, photocopying and recording, or in any information storage or retrieval system, is forbidden without the permission of the publisher, Harlequin Mills & Boon, Locked Bag 7002, Chatswood D.C. N.S.W., Australia 2067.

All the characters in this book have no existence outside the imagination of the author, and have no relation whatsoever to anyone bearing the same name or names. They are not even distantly inspired by any individual known or unknown to the author, and all the incidents are pure invention.

This book is sold subject to the condition that it shall not, by way of trade or otherwise, be lent, resold, hired out or otherwise circulated without the prior consent of the publisher in any form of binding or cover other than that in which it is published and without a similar condition including this condition being imposed on the subsequent purchaser.

All rights reserved including the right of reproduction in whole or in part in any form. This edition is published by arrangement with Harlequin Books S.A.

Published by
Harlequin Mills & Boon
3 Gibbes Street
CHATSWOOD NSW 2067
AUSTRALIA

HARLEQUIN MILLS & BOON and the Rose Device are trademarks used under license and registered in Australia, New Zealand, Philippines, United States Patent & Trademark Office and in other countries.

Printed and bound in Australia by
McPherson's Printing Group

To Linda Kruger, whose encouragement and faith has helped me grow both as a writer and a person. You've been a special friend as well as a wonderful agent.

Chapter One

Lady Thais Margate's long-lashed blue eyes were filled with concern. 'I did not mean to overset you. Perhaps I should not have said anything.'

Cecily Renato took a deep breath and willed herself to remain calm. 'Oh, no, you were quite right to tell me. It is just I am rather surprised.' Actually she was quite shocked, but hardly wanted to tell her companion that. 'I will speak to Mariana straight away.'

'You must not be too hard on them for it was not a very…very improper kiss, but I know you would not want such a thing to happen again. If the wrong persons should come upon them…one would hate for there to be gossip.'

'No. Of course not.'

Lady Margate rose in a rustle of fashionable blue silk. 'I must go for I have an appointment very soon, but I wished to see you the very first thing today. You may be assured that none of this will pass my lips.'

Cecily stood as well. 'I know you will not say anything.' At least she hoped she would not as Cecily hardly knew Lady Margate, who had leased a house in Avezza just over a month ago. But the lovely young widow had already impressed Avezza's residents, both Italian and English, by donating to several charitable causes as well as by heading up a committee to repair the damage done to the church of Santa Sofia during the French occupation.

Lady Margate took Cecily's hand. Although Cecily was not particularly tall, Lady Margate's fine-boned features and delicate build made Cecily feel ungainly next to her. Lady Margate smiled kindly. 'You are such a devoted mother. I have no doubt you will do the right thing, although you must not be too harsh with your stepdaughter or Lord Ballister. The very first time I saw them together I could sense a special sympathy between them. It is most unfortunate that the Duke of Severin is unlikely to allow them to marry. I have heard from Severin himself that he wishes to procure an heiress for his cousin, preferably the daughter of a peer. There is a certain earl's daughter that I have heard…but that is only a rumour.' She regarded Cecily with sympathetic eyes. 'It would not be easy for your stepdaughter to live in England. The society is so very different, as you know.'

'Yes, it is different.' Cecily attempted to suppress the twinge of resentment she felt at Lady Margate's implication that Severin would not consider Mariana suitable for his cousin. 'I will see you out.'

'That will not be necessary. You must give your lovely daughter my regards. And Signora Zanetti.' She pressed Cecily's hand before releasing it, her grip surprisingly strong. Cecily accompanied her across the small salon to the staircase, which led to the ground floor.

She watched Lady Margate depart, her thoughts in turmoil. Mariana and Lord Ballister? How had this happened when she had made certain they never met except in company? Why had she not watched Mariana more closely last night at Lady Margate's *conversazione*?

Because she had been certain that Mariana's *tendre* for Lord Ballister had faded just as she was certain Lord Ballister's initial interest in her stepdaughter had died away. So when Mariana had gone to the garden with her friend, Teresa Carasco, and Teresa's brother, Cecily had not been concerned. Nor had she worried very much when Mariana had been unusually quiet and preoccupied on the carriage ride back home.

'Why was she here? That woman?'

Cecily jumped when her sister-in-law spoke from behind her. Barbarina had the disconcerting habit of suddenly appearing and startling her.

She turned. 'Lady Margate was here to pay a visit, that is all.'

'She is not good. She brings nothing but trouble.'

'Surely not.' When Barbarina merely stared at her, she tried again. 'At least not today. I must speak to Mariana now.'

'She came to tell you that the English lord has kissed Mariana, no? You must hope that she does not tell anyone else. Such as his cousin, the Duke. Or Rafaele.'

'I have no idea why she would want to do so.' Cecily said. 'Please, Barbarina, do not eavesdrop.'

'What can I do when you hold your conversations in the salon where everyone can hear?' She shrugged and fixed her dark gaze on Cecily. 'You must send Mariana away before Rafaele learns of this. It will not please him to discover that you have allowed the cousin of the Duke to kiss Mariana.'

'Rafaele is in Verona so it is unlikely he will hear of this. At any rate, nothing more will happen.'

'You must hope not. For if Rafaele does, he will come and challenge the Lord Ballister to a duel. If that happens, the Duke will come and there will be another fight. In the end, Rafaele will send Mariana to the convent. Where you should have sent her as her mother, Caterina, had wished. Then there would be no need to worry about kisses.'

Cecily quelled the sharp pang of hurt she still felt when Barbarina compared Cecily to her husband Marco's first wife and Mariana's mother. 'I would hope that everyone would behave in a more civilised manner than that. Why do you think that they will fight if they meet? Is it because of something that happened in the past? When the Duke was here?' This was not the first time since Lord Ballister's arrival in Avezza that Barbarina had hinted at some sort of quarrel between Mariana's trustee, Rafaele Vianoli, and the Duke of Severin, who was Lord Ballister's guardian.

'It would be better if you do not ask more questions.'

Cecily bit back her frustration. Barbarina always lapsed into odd, cryptic pronouncements when she no longer wished to answer any questions. 'Very well. I won't. For now, I am going to speak to Mariana.' She walked away before she said something she would later regret. She tried to be patient with Barbarina for, before he died, Marco had asked her to watch over his older widowed half-sister. She reminded herself as well that Barbarina had never really recovered from the discovery that her beloved husband had died while running off with another woman. But sometimes it was all she could do to keep her temper. Particularly at times like this.

***

Mariana was in her bedchamber. She sat on a chair near the window and when Cecily entered she looked up from the book on her lap. Cecily crossed the room and pulled the small stool near the bed to the chair and sat down. 'I must talk to you.'

'Is something wrong, Mama?' From the anxious look on her daughter's lovely face, she suspected Mariana had a very good idea of why Cecily was there.

'Lady Margate came to tell me that she found you and Lord Ballister in an embrace last night. That he kissed you. Is this true?'

Mariana looked away for an instant before she answered. 'He kissed me and I kissed him back.'

Oh, dear. 'I do not need to remind you that it is most improper for young unmarried girls to be alone with a man. And very improper to exchange a kiss with any man except a fiancé or a husband. Lord Ballister should know this. He also must know that he risked your reputation by such behaviour. You are fortunate that Lady Margate discovered you and not one of the other guests.'

'It is not Si— Lord Ballister's fault. I asked him to meet me in the garden.'

'Why would you do that?'

'I…I wished to talk to him.'

'Have you met him alone like this before?'

'Only a…a few times.'

Cecily tried to hide her shock. 'Has he ever done anything besides kiss you?'

'No. We only talk. He has not kissed me before last night.'

Thank God. 'Then I must forbid you to see Lord

Ballister again, except in the presence of others. I will not allow him to ruin your reputation.'

'He wants to marry me,' Mariana said flatly.

Cecily's heart stopped for a fraction. 'Did he tell you that?' she asked carefully.

'Yes. But he said he would not ask me until I am seventeen and then he will speak to you.'

Cecily drew in a breath. 'I see.' She felt as if she'd been hit in the stomach. Did Lord Ballister hope to seduce Mariana by promising marriage? He did not seem the sort of young man to do so, but then she had not thought Mariana would ever arrange a rendezvous with a young man in a dark garden.

'You will approve, will you not?' Mariana asked. A note of anxiety had crept into her voice.

'You are still young, too young to think of marriage,' she began.

'Mama was seventeen when she married Papa.'

'Yes, but they had known each other since childhood. You have known Lord Ballister scarcely a month.' She hesitated. 'It hardly matters whether I approve or not, for it is unlikely the Duke of Severin will. Or Rafaele.'

'But why not? Because Cousin Raf and the Duke have quarrelled?'

Cecily started. 'How do you know that?'

'Zia told me. But she would not tell me what the quarrel was about.'

A surge of anger shot through Cecily. Barbarina had no business telling Mariana such a thing. 'I am not even certain they did quarrel. There are other reasons, however, why a marriage between you and Lord Ballister is impossible.'

Mariana stared at her, her expression stricken. Cecily took her hands. 'I am sorry, but you are scarcely more than a child. Some day you will meet a man whom you can love, someone more suited to you.'

'There will be no one else.' Mariana rose and Cecily could see she was fighting back tears. She walked to the door and stopped her hand on the handle. 'You are wrong. I am not a child.' She left, her pale quietness more alarming than if she had burst into tears and run from the room as she had in the past when angry or upset.

Cecily quelled her impulse to go after Mariana, suspecting she would only make matters worse. Mixed in with her anger and worry was fear. Fear that Lord Ballister was more to her stepdaughter than a young girl's first love; fear that if Mariana was capable of meeting him alone, she was capable of something even more rash.

Surely Lord Ballister must realise he could not marry Mariana without his cousin's consent. He must have some idea that his cousin wished him to marry an heiress; although Mariana was not penniless, she was far from wealthy.

He must know, as well, that Mariana could not marry without Raf's and Cecily's permission. Although Raf was Mariana's trustee, Marco had left Mariana in Cecily's care and had made it clear that both Raf and Cecily were to approve any potential husband for Mariana.

If Raf and the Duke had indeed quarrelled, it was even more unlikely either man would approve, thank goodness.

Then she felt guilty for even thinking such a thing when Mariana was so unhappy. For her own selfish reasons, Cecily did not want Mariana to marry an Englishman. She could not bear to have Mariana go away and live in a country that Cecily could never return to.

Lord Ballister had told Mariana he would wait until she was seventeen before speaking to Cecily. She assumed he would wait until then to speak to his cousin as well. She only hoped that, by that time, Lord Ballister would be long gone and that Mariana would have recovered from her infatuation. What if they did not? What if they decided to run off together? She knew only too well how easy it was to take such a course.

She could not entertain that possibility. She must speak to Lord Ballister today and tell him in no uncertain terms that he was not to see Mariana alone and he was not to speak of marriage again.

Nico stood in front of the window of the small villa Simon had leased. It stood on one of the hills that gently sloped up from the town providing a clear view of the red tile roofs and green trees against the blue background of the distant Dolomites. To the right he could see the brownish-red roof of the Villa Guiliani, the villa that had once belonged to Angelina's family. He turned away, as an unexpected surge of regret and longing shot through him.

He was not in Avezza to relive the past, but to deal with the present in the form of his cousin and ward, Simon, Viscount Ballister. If Simon's friend, Philip Ashton, was correct and Simon was indeed flirting with Mariana Renato, then Simon needed to be removed from her vicinity as quickly as possible. Before Rafaele Vianoli got wind of this and decided to call Simon out. For according to Ashton, Vianoli was Mariana Renato's guardian, although

Ashton had also told him Vianoli had not set foot in Avezza for months.

Vianoli would return quickly enough if he thought Simon was trifling with his ward. It was unlikely he wanted an alliance between the two families any more than Nico did.

He could not fathom why the girl's stepmother did not put a stop to this, although it was possible she did not know of the quarrel between himself and Vianoli. Perhaps she did not care and hoped to attach herself to a duke's family through her stepdaughter. At any rate, he intended to put a quick halt to any such plans. His first order of business was to call on Signora Renato and make it clear she was to keep her daughter away from Simon. He would deal with Simon after that.

For now, he needed to find the housekeeper and have his trunk taken to his room so he could change out of his dusty travelling clothes. He crossed the room and as he did heard a woman's, *'Buongiorno?'*

He strode into the hall and saw a woman standing near his trunk. The missing housekeeper, undoubtedly. 'I will use the blue bedchamber. Tell Giovanni to take my luggage there directly. I wish to change.'

'I suggest you tell Giovanni yourself, *signor*.'

Her cool voice startled him as much as her words. He looked hard at her. She was much younger than he'd expect for a housekeeper and much too pretty with a pair of large eyes set in a delicate oval face. 'I beg your pardon, *signora*?' he said coldly.

'I said you should tell Giovanni yourself.'

'And who are you, *signora*?' She was not Simon's housekeeper; she carried herself too well and her gown, although worn and unfashionable, was made of good material. Her dark eyes met his despite the flush that stole over her cheeks. He had an impression of quiet dignity.

'I was looking for Lord Ballister. Is he at home?'

'Not at the moment. Perhaps I might help you.' Perhaps it was not Mariana Renato he needed to worry about, but this woman who seemed to be running free in his cousin's home.

'I…I doubt that. My business is with Lord Ballister.'

'Is it? Then I suspect it might be with me as well since I am Lord Ballister's guardian. First you will tell me your name.'

Her eyes widened. 'You are the Duke?'

He allowed a smile to touch his mouth. '*Sì*, and you, *signora*?'

'But why are you not in Venice?'

'Because I am here. Your name, please,

'I am Signora Renato.'

This time he started. Ashton had not mentioned that Signora Renato looked to be a scarce dozen years older than her stepdaughter. He recovered quickly. 'Signora Renato? How convenient. I believe your business is with me after all.'

'I have no idea what you are talking about.' Her slightly apprehensive expression belied her words.

'But I think you do. You have a daughter, I believe.'

'Oh, drat.'

He'd hardly expected that. 'Such a very English expression.'

'But I am English.'

Ashton had said nothing about that either. 'Are you?' He switched to English. 'Then allow me to compliment you on your command of Italian. I would have thought you spoke the language from birth.'

'I might say the same thing for you, your Grace.'

'But I have. My mother is Italian. You may come to the library with me. I do not wish to continue this discussion here.'

'I do not wish to continue this discussion at all. My business is with Lord Ballister and since he is not here, then I will take my leave.' She turned and started towards the door.

He caught her arm. 'Any business you have with my cousin is with me. And since I came to Avezza particularly to see you, then I've no intention of allowing you to leave before I accomplish the task.'

She turned and looked up, her expressive eyes meeting his. Her soft mouth was parted slightly and he felt the faint stirrings of desire.

She swallowed before she spoke, 'Please let go of my arm. It is not necessary to take me prisoner.' Her voice was calm.

His hand fell away. 'Then you will come with me to the library.'

She eyed him for a moment. 'Very well,' she said coolly.

'Good.'

A short dark, woman bustled into the hall. Her face broke into a smile when she saw Signora Renato. *'Buongiorno, signora.'* Her smile faltered a little when she glanced at Nico. She fidgeted as he gave her brief instructions, then she curtsied and bustled away in obvious relief.

He led Signora Renato to the library, a small room off the grand salon, a pleasant room that faced south towards the green fields beyond. He indicated one of the upholstered chairs. 'You may sit here, *signora.*'

Instead of sitting, he leaned against the marble-topped table near her. Signora Renato sat on the edge of the chair, her hands locked around her reticule. She looked like a young girl herself, although he guessed her to be in her late twenties. 'I assume from the enthusiastic manner in which the housekeeper greeted you that you must be a frequent visitor here.'

'I have never been here before. Flavia's sister is my housekeeper.' She looked insulted that he would even suggest such a thing.

'Is she? Then I will get to the point of this conversation. It has come to my attention that you have been encouraging a match between your daughter and my cousin.'

She stared at him as if he'd run mad. 'I have been encouraging a match? I assure you I have done no such thing!'

Her outraged seemed genuine. Or she was a consummate actress. 'Are you denying that my cousin has an interest in your daughter?'

'I really have no idea whether he does or not. You will have to ask him.'

'I will. But first I wish to ask you.'

'You may ask as much as you wish, but I will still give you the same answer,' she snapped. From the stubborn look on her face, he doubted she'd tell him much more.

'As you wish, *signora*.' He felt his own temper rising. 'However, I will suggest that you curtail any sort of plans you have made that include my cousin.'

She stood, her hand trembling around her reticule. 'I have no idea who told you such things but your…your informant was quite wrong. Lord Ballister is the last person I would want my daughter to marry. Good day, your Grace.' She stalked to the door. This time he made no move to stop her. At the door, she turned, her eyes blazing. 'There is one more thing. If you do anything to hurt my daughter, I will cheerfully tear you limb from limb.'

He was too taken aback to speak. She left the room, her head high, and he stared after her with the sense he'd lost the round. Tear him limb from limb? He'd hardly expected that from such a mild-looking creature. But then, nothing about the encounter had gone as planned. Certainly he had not expected her to declare in such disdainful tones that Simon was the last man she would want for her daughter.

He frowned. Was it possible Ashton was wrong and there was nothing between Simon and Signorina Renato? If that was the case, why had Signora Renato told him to ask Simon instead of telling him she did not know? He had failed as well to ask her why she had called on Simon today. Not that she would have told him. She would probably look at him with her large disdainful eyes and tell him it was none of his affair.

He was hardly finished with her. Not until he discovered if Simon indeed harboured feelings for Mariana Renato. Particularly if it turned out that Signora Renato knew about it all along.

Cecily did not slow her pace until she had passed through the pillared gates of the Villa. Anger, coupled with the irrational fear that the Duke of Severin might try and stop her from leaving, had driven her steps. Now that she was safe, she realised her legs were shaking. She started down the narrow road that led towards the village, her thoughts in turmoil.

Whoever had told Severin that she was promoting a match between Lord Ballister and Mariana? And how dare he come here and accuse her before he even knew the facts? Just thinking of the cool, arrogant way he had looked at her made her angry all over again. He was not at all what she had expected—if she thought of him at all, she had pictured him as much older, which did not make sense for he must be Raf's age and Raf was two years her senior. Nor had she expected to find him as darkly attractive. If one liked that sort of cool, male look.

Which she did not. In fact, there had been nothing about him she liked. She would never allow Mariana to marry into a family with that man in it. He would ride roughshod over her just as he had attempted to do with Cecily.

She could only hope that, in time, Mariana's infatuation with Lord Ballister would fade. Perhaps she should send Mariana to stay with her mother's cousins in Padua. Vittoria and Serefina were strict but kind, and doted on Mariana. She would send a letter off to Padua tomorrow.

If only she had someone to turn to for advice. Someone to reassure her that she need not worry about Mariana—that her feelings for Lord Ballister were the normal ones any young girl felt for her first *tendre*.

Barbarina was no help. Even if she knew exactly where Raf was, she could hardly write to him if there was any possibility at all he would quarrel with Lord Ballister or his cousin.

Perhaps she should have returned to England a year ago when her grandmother had summoned her, but the bitterness over Lady Telford's rejection of Marco and Mariana still hurt. And, despite her grandmother's adding that, of course, 'the child must come', Cecily could not put aside her pride.

Well, it was too late now. She had dashed off a chilly response, making it quite clear she neither wanted nor needed her grandmother's help and she was doing very well on her own. She was already regretting her rash words before the letter had left Italy, but she had no way of retrieving it.

She was on her own.

Chapter Two

'Nic? What are you doing here? I thought you were in Venice.'

Nico looked up and for a moment was startled to see his cousin in the doorway. Simon moved into the room, a handsome youth with a pair of startling blue eyes, and a charming smile. He was dressed in a riding coat and boots, and carried a crop.

'As you can see, I am not.' His gaze raked over Simon. 'You look well. Italy must agree with you.' In the time Simon had been away from England, he had grown. His shoulders were broader and his face had lost some of its boyishness.

'It does. I cannot imagine returning to another English winter after this. So why are you here?'

'To see you safely to Venice,' Nico said carelessly. 'Since we have not set eyes on you for the past five months, my mother and Eleanora are understandably anxious to see for themselves that you are well. They are in Milan, but will be in Venice by the end of the week.'

Simon hesitated a fraction. 'Then there's no rush. I can stay for a few more days.'

'You are not bored yet? If I recall, Avezza is not exactly filled with the sort of entertainments that you favour. And it is a two-day journey to Venice. I would have expected you would prefer to be closer.'

Simon shrugged. 'Oh, 'tis not so bad. I find I rather like the quiet. I've learned to speak a tolerable Italian and there have been enough *conversaziones*—they are rather like our routs—and the like to keep us entertained. There's going to be some sort of fête at the end of the week—rather like a miniature Vauxhall, I am told. In fact, there is to be a *musicale* tonight I had planned to attend, but since you are here... I know you detest that sort of thing.'

'You do not need to change your plans on my account. I will accompany you, of course. If you wish me to.'

'That would be splendid.' He grinned at Nico. 'You will cause a stir. I must change. Do you have everything you need?'

'Yes. I am quite comfortable. By the way, you had a visitor today. A Signora Renato.'

Simon, who had started towards the door, stopped. 'Signora Renato? Are you certain?'

'Quite. She gave me her name herself. You seem surprised that she would call.'

'I am. I have always had the impression she does not like me above half. Did she say what she wanted?'

'No, she left no message.'

'I see. Most likely nothing of importance.'

Nico thought his voice was a little too casual, but decided not to pursue the matter, at least for now. 'Will you dine here tonight?'

'Yes.' He started to leave the room and then paused. He flashed Nico a boyish grin. 'I am glad you are here.'

Nico watched him go. He'd said nothing about Signorina Renato, but then he had hardly expected him to. So Signora Renato did not like him? He wondered why, for most people liked Simon. He hoped Signora Renato and her daughter would attend the *musicale* tonight—he was now very curious to find out exactly what was going on between his cousin and the Renatos.

Cecily glanced down the dinner table, grateful the tense meal was nearly finished. Barbarina ate in her usual silence, speaking only to complain about the food. A thin woman, dressed from head to foot in black, she resembled an underfed crow although her appetite was certainly not lacking. Mariana sat next to Cecily, her eyes slightly swollen, her manner subdued. She answered Cecily politely, but refused to look her in the eye or contribute anything more than necessary to Cecily's efforts at conversation.

'There is something I must tell both of you,' Cecily said finally.

Barbarina continued to pick at her fish without looking up. Mariana said nothing.

'The Duke of Severin, Lord Ballister's cousin, is in Avezza.'

Barbarina paused, her fork in mid-air. Mariana raised her head. 'Why?'

'He should not have come,' Barbarina said before Cecily

could answer. 'He brings nothing but trouble.' She forked the bite of fish into her mouth.

'I pray you will not say such things.' Cecily was in no mood to put up with Barbarina's vague, dire predictions.

Mariana's sulks had vanished. She propped her chin upon her hand, her eyes sparkling with interest. 'Because of cousin Raf? Do you suppose if Raf returns they will fight?'

'There will be no fights. I am certain the Duke means to leave very soon.' At least she hoped he would once Mariana was gone.

'If he has any sense, he will leave right away. Before there is more tragedy,' Barbarina said.

It was clearly time for dinner to end before Barbarina said something about Raf and Lord Ballister, which would only serve to upset Mariana. Cecily rose. 'I do not want to hear any more talk of fights and tragedy. We must get ready for Signora Bartolini's salon. Are you certain you do not wish to go, Barbarina? I can order the carriage be brought around.' Barbarina never went to such events, but Cecily always felt obligated to ask her.

Barbarina frowned at her. 'I never go out in the evenings.'

'Do you suppose the Duke will be at Signora Bartolini's tonight?' Mariana asked. She now looked worried.

'He might be, which is why I wished to tell you.' Cecily hesitated. Should she hint to Mariana that the Duke's purpose for coming to Avezza was to quell any romance between her and Simon?

Looking at Mariana's pretty face, she decided it would not be wise. 'Perhaps you should go and make certain the gown I had laid out for you is the one you wish to wear.'

As soon as Mariana left the room, Cecily approached

Barbarina. 'Please do not say such things in Mariana's presence. I do not want to worry her.' She tried to keep her voice as reasonable as possible.

Barbarina fixed her small black eyes on Cecily. 'It is a bad sign that they both are in Avezza. That woman and the Duke.'

'You are speaking of Lady Margate?'

'Yes.'

Barbarina's conversation was proving to be more confusing than usual. 'But what does she have to do with the Duke? Why do you say he will bring more tragedy? Are you referring to his quarrel with Raf?'

'Perhaps.'

'But what did they quarrel about? Why has no one ever said a thing about it until now? Not even Marco told me.'

'Why should he? It happened before you came and has nothing to do with you. Why is it your business?'

Because she cared about Mariana and Raf, but she had given up telling Barbarina that. It made no difference that Cecily had been Marco's wife for two years and his widow for the past seven—Barbarina still considered Cecily an outsider. 'Perhaps it is not,' she said quietly, 'but I do not want Mariana upset. I must go and change. You should let me know if you need anything before I go.'

She waited a moment, but Barbarina merely grunted. Cecily left the room. She wished it were possible to plead a headache and stay home, but she had promised Signora Bartolini she would attend. She feared it would be a very long evening.

Cecily glanced around Signora Bartolini's crowded salon and was relieved that neither Lord Ballister nor his disturbing cousin seemed to be present. She spotted her friend, Viola Carasco, and her daughter Teresa sitting nearby. Viola smiled and motioned and Cecily saw two empty chairs next to her.

Viola moved over a chair so that Mariana and Teresa could sit together. She was a plump, pretty woman with a pair of sparkling, dark eyes. She leaned towards Cecily. 'I have heard the most interesting rumour. It is said that Lord Ballister's cousin has arrived in Avezza. Perhaps you have heard that also?'

'Yes.' Cecily hesitated and then decided against telling Viola about her encounter with him since she had not told Mariana or Barbarina. 'You met him, did you not?' She recalled Viola had mentioned that shortly after Lord Ballister arrived in Avezza.

'Once or twice, but the Conte's family did not spend as much time at the Villa Guiliani as they did at their villa near Treviso. They were here so much that summer because of the damage done to their primary villa when the French occupied it.'

Cecily wanted to ask more, but just then the pianist played the opening measures of an aria and soon the high clear notes of the soprano filled the salon.

The applause had just died down when two latecomers entered. Cecily paid little attention until Viola craned her head around to look. She turned back to Cecily. 'He is here,' she whispered.

She did not need to ask whom Viola referred to. Unable to resist, Cecily looked towards the door. To her chagrin, Severin's eyes fell on her and a cool smile touched his mouth. She quickly looked away. Mariana touched her arm. 'Is that the Duke?'

'Yes, but please do not stare.'

Mariana sniffed and looked indignant. 'I was not.'

Cecily found Viola staring at her. 'He seems to know you.'

Her cheeks heated. 'I did meet him. Quite by accident.' She was grateful when the next piece started. Not that she paid the least heed to it, for she was planning how to convince Mariana to leave during the interval. She certainly did not want Severin and Mariana to meet.

Her plans were thwarted by Lady Margate who appeared almost as soon as Signora Bartolini announced there were refreshments in the adjoining salon. She was charmingly dressed in her favourite shade of pale blue, her fashionable gown overshadowing the made-over and outdated gowns worn by most of the other women in the room, including Cecily. Napoleon was now gone, but nearly a decade and a half of French rule had left many of the residents of Avezza impoverished.

Lady Margate greeted Viola and then turned to Cecily. 'I must speak with you for a moment if Signora Carasco does not mind.'

'Of course not,' Viola said.

Lady Margate waited until they were out of earshot. 'I do not know if you saw the man with Lord Ballister, but that is his cousin, the Duke of Severin. Because of our conversation today, I felt I must warn you.'

'Thank you.' She did not think it prudent to tell Lady Margate her warning was much too late.

'We are old acquaintances so you must tell me if there is any difficulty.'

Out of the corner of her eye, Cecily saw Teresa and Mariana heading towards the refreshment room. She prayed Mariana would stay away from Lord Ballister. And that Lord Ballister would stay away from her.

She smiled politely at Lady Margate. 'I am certain there will be none. You are most kind to offer. I must beg your pardon—I need to speak to Mariana for a moment.'

'I do understand.'

Cecily paused in the doorway of the salon. The table in the centre of the room was filled with trays of cakes. She did not see Mariana or Teresa among the guests, but finally spotted Lord Ballister talking to Paolo Carasco, Viola's son. Thank goodness he was not with Mariana.

'*Buonasera*, Signora Renato.'

She spun around, her relief vanishing. 'What are you doing here?' Severin stood next to her, tall and far too attractive in a well-fitting coat of dark blue over black pantaloons. A small diamond gleamed in the folds of his snowy cravat. Despite his elegant attire, he looked equally as dangerous as he had this afternoon.

'As in this particular spot? Or in the house?' A slight smile touched his mouth. 'Not that it matters at any rate— my sole purpose for coming tonight was to see you. As well as meet Signorina Renato.'

'I cannot think why you would wish to do either.' Heat stole into her cheeks despite her effort to remain cool. 'Nor do I want you to meet my daughter. I will not allow you to frighten her.'

'I would not dare. Not unless I wished to be torn limb from limb. Cheerfully, I believe you said.'

'I still mean it.'

'I have no doubt that you do.'

'Severin! How naughty of you to come to Avezza without

telling me!' Lady Margate glided up to them. She glanced at Cecily and arched a brow. 'Signora Renato, you have been naughty as well, for you did not tell me you knew Severin.'

'I do not know him. I met him quite by accident.' Lady Margate's tone was quite playful, but Cecily suspected matters would only be complicated further if Lady Margate discovered they had met earlier.

'Just now? You seemed to be engaged in such serious conversation for meeting so very recently.' She turned to Severin.

'We have not been formally introduced,' he said coolly.

'Then I must set that to rights. Signora Renato, may I present his Grace, the Duke of Severin? Severin, Signora Renato. She is one of the nicest persons in all of Avezza.'

Cecily found herself giving her hand to Severin. He took it, the warm strength of his fingers closing around hers. 'Then you must be if Lady Margate says so. Signora Renato, I am more than delighted to meet you.' His expression was all that was polite.

'As I am to meet you.' She kept her voice equally polite.

He released her hand. Lady Margate smiled. 'Signora Renato has the most lovely daughter. You met her when she was very young, I believe.'

Cecily stared at her, dismayed. Why would she say such a thing?

'Then I hope to become reacquainted with her very soon.' Severin's voice was bland.

'Perhaps.' Cecily gave him a vague smile. 'I am certain you and Lady Margate have much to discuss, so I will leave you. Goodnight, Lady Margate, your Grace.'

'You are not staying for the rest of the concert?' Lady Margate asked.

'No, I promised Barbarina we would return early. She has one of her headaches.'

'The poor thing. Of course you must go.'

'Yes.' Cecily made her escape before something else happened, such as Severin suggesting to Lady Margate that they meet Mariana.

Mariana was neither near the refreshment table nor anywhere else in the room. Cecily left through the door that led to the next small room, intending to return to the salon through it so she wouldn't have to pass Severin. A number of people had drifted to this room. To her consternation, Mariana and Simon stood in one corner, engaged in conversation. Neither Teresa nor Paolo was anywhere in sight.

She crossed the room. 'Good evening, Lord Ballister,' she said. 'Mariana, I have been looking for you.'

Mariana looked decidedly guilty. 'Oh, have you?'

'I fear I detained her,' Simon said in his easy way. His face sobered. 'My cousin said you had wished to speak to me when you called this afternoon.'

Mariana swung around to face Cecily, who managed a smile. 'It was nothing of importance. However, Mariana and I must leave so we will bid you goodnight.'

'But, Mama—' Mariana began.

'We must go.' She gave Mariana a sharp look. Mariana stared back at her, her expression a mixture of defiance and misery.

'Don't,' Lord Ballister said softly. 'Everything will be fine.' The tender look he bestowed upon Mariana made Cecily feel odd and, when Mariana nodded, her heart suddenly felt like lead.

Someone appeared beside her and the skin on her neck prickled. She did not need Lord Ballister's surprised, 'Nic,' to tell her who it was. How had he managed to extract himself from Lady Margate so quickly? She felt rather ill—if he saw the expression on Lord Ballister's face he would never believe the young couple were mere acquaintances.

Mariana looked up and the faint apprehension on her face made Cecily move closer to her. 'We must go. Goodnight, Lord Ballister.' She glanced at Severin. 'Your Grace.'

'But not before you introduce me to your daughter.' The slight smile at his mouth did not quite reach his eyes.

She could not evade him unless she wanted to be insufferably rude and she knew she was coming close to it. 'Very well.' She looked up; a smile of her own on her lips although she knew it was equally as false as his. She performed the introduction, her eyes never leaving his face.

He took Mariana's hand. 'It is unlikely that you remember, but I met you when you were very young, perhaps only three.' He spoke in Italian, his voice polite, his expression surprisingly kind.

Mariana gave him a tentative smile. 'I am pleased to meet you, your...your Grace.' She glanced at Lord Ballister.

'That is correct.' Lord Ballister looked at his cousin. 'Signorina Renato was not quite certain how one addressed an English duke.'

'You did very well.' Severin released her hand and Mariana flushed, her face shyly pleased. She looked pretty and charming and vulnerable and Cecily wanted nothing more than to protect her.

She took Mariana's arm. She could see the other guests

were starting to drift towards the salon. The second half of the concert was about to start. 'Come, we must take our leave of Signora Bartolini.'

'Did you walk?' Lord Ballister asked.

'Yes.'

'Then you will allow us to escort you home,' Severin said.

That was the last thing Cecily desired. 'That is hardly necessary. It is not far and we prefer to walk. Besides, I have no doubt you wish to hear the rest of the concert.'

Lord Ballister laughed. 'You do not know my cousin well. He almost always leaves in the middle of any sort of performance. Claims he does not like to sit for long.'

'Quite true. In addition, I have what I came for tonight so I have no incentive to stay.' He met her gaze, challenging her.

'Indeed. But we would still prefer to walk. I should not want to inconvenience you.'

'It will be no inconvenience.'

'No use arguing with him, Signora Renato,' Lord Ballister interjected. 'He always has his way.'

'I imagine that must be rather annoying at times.' She spoke more tartly than she intended to. Lord Ballister looked rather startled and Mariana now had the expression she always wore when she feared Cecily was about to argue with a shopkeeper and embarrass her.

Severin appeared unaffected. 'Very annoying, I have been told. My cousin will send for the carriage while we bid our hostess farewell.'

Cecily opened her mouth to protest, but Mariana tugged on her arm. 'Mama, please do not say anything more,' she whispered.

'But...' She caught a glimpse of faint amusement in

Severin's eyes and suspected he had overheard Mariana's plea.

'Very well,' she said.

Signora Bartolini was quite sympathetic, although she only half-listened to Cecily's explanation. 'Ah, the headache, of course you must go. How kind of the Duke and Lord Ballister to see you home so you do not risk making it worse.' She turned to the Duke before Cecily could correct her impression. 'You have been away from here far too long. How are your dear mama and your sister? They are not with you?'

'They are in Milan visiting cousins. They are both well.'

'Very good. How long will you stay with us?'

'I have not decided.'

She glanced at Cecily and Mariana with a little smile. 'I quite understand.'

What did she understand? Oh, lord, at this rate, he would never be convinced she had not plotted to bring his cousin and Mariana together.

She could hardly wait to escape, but after leaving the salon they were forced to remain in the hall while the footman fetched their shawls. 'I did not realise you had a headache as well,' Severin said, with what she considered false concern.

'I did not earlier, but I most certainly have one now.'

'I wonder why,' he murmured. For the first time she saw genuine amusement in his face. It was quite unnerving. She pulled her gaze away just as the footman returned with their shawls. Severin took them. 'Allow me,' he said. He draped Mariana's around her shoulders with a gentle touch and then turned to Cecily. 'Signora Renato?'

'I prefer to carry my shawl.' She held out her hand.

'As you wish.' He gave it to her, his hand brushing hers. She nearly jumped at the contact and prayed he had not noticed anything amiss.

'The carriage is here,' he said. He was looking at her rather than the door.

She felt rather breathless. 'How do you know? You have not looked.'

'Are you always this argumentative?'

'Goodness, the poor soprano will have no audience if anyone else leaves!'

Lady Margate stood in the hall behind them, her gaze going from one to the other. 'I had no idea you wished to leave as well, Severin. But then I should not be too surprised, for you never do like these things!' She descended the last few steps and smiled at Cecily. 'I hope he is not being too difficult.' She tossed a quick glance in Mariana's direction. Mariana had now drifted towards the door.

'No, he is not.' It was quite apparent to Cecily that Lady Margate and Severin were much more than acquaintances. She suddenly did not want to reveal anything more about Mariana in front of the other woman.

'Then you have no more objections to accepting my offer to take you and Signorina Renato home in my carriage,' Severin said smoothly.

'He is to escort you home?' Lady Margate said. Her look of arch surprise made Cecily cringe. 'I had come out for the sole purpose of offering the very same thing after Signora Bartolini told me you had the headache. You must allow me to do so since there would only be three of us instead of four and you would be much more comfortable.'

'You are very kind—' Cecily began, only to be cut off.

'I have no doubt Signora Renato appreciates your offer, but my carriage has already been brought around. She will be more comfortable if she does not have to wait any longer.'

Brief discomfiture flitted across Lady Margate's face and then she was smiling again. 'You are always so logical—it is quite appalling. You must not bully Signora Renato too much then, particularly if she has the headache.'

'I have no intention of doing so,' he said coolly. 'Goodnight, Thais.'

'Goodnight. And, dear Signora Renato, I will call on you tomorrow, if I may, to see how you have fared.'

'Thank you. Goodnight, Lady Margate.'

Although Severin's touch was light as he took her arm and then guided her across the hall, Cecily still felt like a prisoner. Worse, Mariana had disappeared outside; when they stepped out, Cecily could see her and Lord Ballister talking together on the steps. They quickly drew apart when Severin and Cecily appeared. She dared not look at Severin's face as he helped her into the carriage after assisting Mariana.

No one said much on the short distance down the hill to her house. Severin escorted Mariana and Cecily to the door. 'Goodnight, Signorina,' he said to Mariana. 'I trust you will not object if I detain Signora Renato for a minute.'

'No, your Grace.' She cast Cecily a hesitant look before going inside.

He waited until Mariana had gone. 'I will call on you tomorrow,' he said to Cecily.

'I cannot imagine why.'

'No? After tonight I think we have a great deal to discuss.' He braced one arm on the wall and looked down at her.

'I believe we agree that neither one of us wants a match between them.'

'Perhaps I have another reason as well.'

'And what would that be?'

'To further our acquaintance.'

Her heart slammed against her ribs. 'I…it is quite unlikely I will be at home.'

'I think you will be. Goodnight, *signora*.' The slight smile at his mouth panicked her more than anything else he'd yet said. He turned and strode towards the carriage before she could answer.

Cecily dashed inside her house and leaned against the door. Of course, he meant nothing by that last enigmatic remark. He undoubtedly wished to intimidate her by implying he had an…an interest in her. She very much feared, however, if that had been his intention, he had quite succeeded.

Reluctant to go inside, Nico leaned against one of the pillars on the portico. The night was pleasant—the sort of night he remembered. He could not fault Simon for flirting with Mariana Renato, for she had grown from a charming small child with a pair of large dark eyes and a sweet smile into a beautiful young girl with large dark eyes and an equally sweet smile. Very much like her mother, Caterina. She had died after he left Italy and he had been sorry to hear of her death for she had been kind as well as lovely. He idly wondered how Marco Renato had come to marry a young Englishwoman. Had they met in England, Italy or elsewhere?

He reluctantly decided he could not blame Marco Renato for choosing her as a second wife, for Cecily Renato was certainly as lovely as Caterina had been although in a quieter way. She was intelligent, and, from the protective, anxious way she regarded her stepdaughter, he did not doubt her devotion to Mariana was genuine.

'What do you think of Signora Renato and her daughter?' Simon asked as he joined Nico. 'But then you knew Signorina Renato when she was very young.'

'I found her a very pleasing child then and I still do. I know very little about her stepmother, however.'

'Her maternal grandmother is the Countess of Telford.'

'The stiff-necked old woman who went to school with Grandmama?'

Simon grinned. 'The very same.'

He was surprised. Not only did Cecily Renato seem an unlikely granddaughter for the cool, aristocratic Countess, he would not have expected the Countess to allow her granddaughter to marry a man such as Marco Renato. Although he was from an old Venetian family, he had not been particularly wealthy and he was not English. 'When did she marry Marco Renato?'

'She has been Mari…Signorina Renato's stepmother since Signorina Renato was seven years of age.'

Nine years if Mariana was now sixteen. Cecily Renato had indeed been young when she married Marco Renato. 'You seem well versed in their affairs. Is Signorina Renato a particular friend of yours?'

'What do you mean by a particular friend?'

'I noticed that you spent a good deal of time with her. I will own I was surprised. She does not seem the sort of girl who usually attracts you,' he said carelessly.

'No, which is why—' Simon stopped. 'Is this why you

are here? Because you were informed that I have a *tendre* for Mariana?'

'Do you?'

Simon's eyes narrowed. 'No. I do not have a *tendre* for her. I am in love with her. I plan to marry her. As soon as she reaches her seventeenth birthday.'

'You are too young. So is she.'

'That does not matter.'

'You have a reputation for flirtation, so why is Signorina Renato more than one of your other flirts?'

'She has a kind heart,' he said quietly. 'I can talk to her, tell her anything and she listens. And...' he paused '...the first time I saw her I felt as if I had been waiting for her all of my life.'

'Does Signorina Renato feel the same way?'

'Yes.'

He looked at his cousin's quiet, determined face and wanted to curse. This was much more than an idle flirtation. His cousin was in love. He should know—he had felt exactly the same way when he first laid eyes on Angelina.

Chapter Three

Cecily tugged the sole weed from the damp dirt and then leaned back on her heels and pushed an escaped tendril of hair from her face. Now she probably had a smear of mud on her cheek. Not that she cared—in light of everything else it was hardly important.

She rose and stood for a moment, looking down at the now tidy patch of flowers. The only thing that seemed tidy about her life at the moment. After seeing Mariana and Simon together last night, she knew she could not expect Severin to believe they were mere acquaintances. She certainly did not. Which was why Mariana could not remain in Avezza. Not as long as Lord Ballister was here.

Or his cousin.

What if Raf heard the same sort of rumour that Severin had and thought Cecily was promoting a match between Lord Ballister and Mariana? And what if Barbarina was right—that Raf and Severin would fight if they met?

She could only surmise that their quarrel had something to do with Angelina Guiliani. Marco had told her very little; only that Angelina had been the daughter of his uncle, the Conte Guiliani. The cousins, Angelina and Marco and Raf, had been playmates since childhood. When she was sixteen she had become engaged to the son of an English duke. Less than a week before the wedding, Angelina had died in a tragic fall. Her mother, heartbroken over the death of her remaining child, had fallen ill and, less than a year later, died. The Conte had sold the lovely old villa shortly after that and had never returned to Avezza.

Until Lord Ballister had come to Avezza a month ago, almost nothing had been said about the young Englishman whom Angelina was to marry. Cecily had been shocked when Viola mentioned Lord Ballister's guardian had been betrothed to Angelina. When Cecily confronted Barbarina, she had merely shrugged and replied it was not Cecily's business. It was only recently that Barbarina had begun hinting at quarrels and fights.

She wished Marco was here. At times like this she missed him terribly. He had not loved her the way she had loved him, but he had always been unfailingly kind and gentle. She missed his strength and the certainty that he would always know the right thing to do, whereas she often felt so much at sea, most particularly when it came to Mariana.

A bee buzzing around her head brought her back to the garden. She bent down to retrieve her basket of cut flowers when she heard footsteps on the path. She looked up and froze. The Duke of Severin stood behind her, regarding her with his dark, slightly sardonic expression. 'Whatever are you doing here?'

'I told you I planned to call on you.'

'And I said I would not be home.' His mere presence made her feel uncomfortable, and, in a faded gown and dirt-smeared apron with her hair escaping beneath an old bonnet, she felt even more at a disadvantage.

'Apparently you did not make that clear to your housekeeper. Signora Zanetti did her best, however, to convince me that not only were you not home, but that my presence in Avezza was likely to prove disastrous.'

'Oh, dear.' She had never even considered the possibility that Severin and Barbarina would meet. 'I am sorry. She sometimes entertains the oddest notions—you must not heed anything she says. She seems to be becoming more and more eccentric.'

'A fearsome thought, for she was eccentric enough thirteen years ago.' He looked down at her, a little frown on his brow. 'How did Barbarina Zanetti end up living with you rather than with the Conte Guiliani? Or Rafaele Vianoli?'

'She came to live with Marco and Mariana after Caterina died. After Marco's death she stayed on. The Conte offered her a home, but she refused. Raf is gone too much, but I am certain she would not go to him anyway. She fears I cannot bring Mariana up properly without her.'

'It is apparent your stepdaughter has been brought up very well and I suspect Signora Zanetti deserves little credit for it.'

His unexpected compliment filled her with pleasure and pride in Mariana. She smiled. 'It is really to Mariana's credit—she has been the sweetest, most loving child imaginable. She means everything to me.'

'She is very fortunate.'

'No, I am.' Her smile faded. 'But you did not come here so that I can praise Mariana.'

'No. We can sit on the bench under the arbour and talk.'

'I was going back to the house.' She bent to retrieve her basket, only to have him reach it first. His hand brushed hers, sending a warm tingle through her gloved hand. She jerked her hand back and straightened. 'It is really not necessary. I can carry it very well on my own.'

'I've no doubt of that, but I wish to do so.'

'It is rather dirty. You might soil your coat.'

He actually looked amused. 'Then you may brush off any stray dirt with your handkerchief.'

'I do not have a handkerchief.'

She felt even more stupid when his mouth quirked. 'Then I will loan you mine.'

She suspected he was teasing her, but instead of coming back with a witty rejoinder she could only make the same sort of silly remarks as a schoolgirl.

'What is it you want, your Grace?' she asked as they started along the path.

The amusement left his face. 'Last night my cousin informed me that he planned to marry your stepdaughter when she turned seventeen.'

'Oh, no.' Mariana had spoken the truth; and if Simon had gone so far as to tell his cousin, he was indeed serious. 'This is impossible.'

'What is impossible? That he told me?'

'No, that he would even think of such a thing. That they would…. Of course they cannot marry. They are too young and you would never approve and I would never approve and…'

He stopped. 'My cousin is in love with Signorina Renato.'

'He cannot be. She is too young. Both of them are and they have known each other for scarcely a month.'

'Neither of which precludes falling in love. Have you not heard of love at first sight?' His voice was laced with irony. He began walking again.

'I have always considered it ridiculous.'

'You are not a romantic, *signora*?'

'Not at all.' She looked straight ahead. 'I have written to Mariana's cousins in Padua. I will send her there as soon as possible.'

'Have you told her that?'

'No. I wish to put it off until I receive a reply, for I suspect Mariana will not be pleased. Until then I will make certain that she and Lord Ballister have no opportunity to meet.'

'Is she in love with Simon?'

Again, he startled her. 'He is very charming and attentive and I can see why a young girl might develop a *tendre* for him, particularly if she is very sheltered.'

'I am asking about your stepdaughter, not young girls in general.'

'I am certain she considers herself to be.'

By now they had reached the edge of the garden next to the narrow strip of lawn near the steps to the house. He stopped. 'I wonder if one can distinguish between considering oneself to be and the actual thing?' he asked drily. 'I suggest neither one of us makes it too obvious that we wish to separate them, for I would not wish to drive them into each other's arms.'

'No.' She had not expected a man with his cool arrogant demeanour to be quite so understanding. As if he had once been in love. Had what she'd heard been true? Had he loved Angelina? She realised she knew nothing about him at all. 'No, that would never do.'

'Where is Vianoli, by the way?'

She looked quickly up at him, but saw nothing more in his expression than polite curiosity. 'He is in Verona, or at least I think he is. He has undertaken a commission to oversee the restoration of a church.'

'He is not often in Avezza?'

'No, not often.' She held out her hand. 'Thank you for carrying my basket. I…I can take it.'

'There is one more thing.'

'Is there?'

'You have a smudge of dirt on your cheek.'

'Oh!' Her hand flew to her face and then just as quickly fell away as she remembered her gloves were dirtier than her face.

'Now you have dirt on both sides. We will need a handkerchief after all.' He set her basket down on the top step and then reached into his waistcoat pocket and produced a snowy handkerchief. Before she could protest he had tilted her chin. 'Let me do this.'

She froze as he dabbed at her cheeks. His touch was surprisingly gentle, but her entire body prickled with awareness. 'Better,' he murmured. He still cupped her chin. 'Do you always do your own gardening?'

'It is very conducive to mulling over one's concerns.' She felt rather dizzy.

He dropped his hand. 'I did not see many weeds left. You must have a number of concerns.'

'I…yes.' Over his shoulder she saw Lady Margate standing near the corner of the house, watching them. 'Oh, drat.' She backed away from him.

Severin's brow rose but before he could speak, Lady Margate crossed the lawn towards them.

'Dear Severin,' she said with a smile. 'Must I warn Signora Renato about you already?'

'It depends on what you wish to warn her about.'

'That you are quite dangerous. For women. They are far too susceptible to your charm. I would not want Signora Renato to become a victim.'

He glanced at Cecily. 'You need not worry about Signora Renato. She seems quite immune,' he said drily.

'Then she is a rare exception.' Lady Margate smiled at Cecily.

Cecily wished she could disappear. Not only did the conversation make her uncomfortable, but she also felt even more clumsy and untidy next to Lady Margate's petite grace. She was relieved when Severin said he must depart. Lady Margate waited until he disappeared around the corner of the house before speaking.

'He really can be quite charming, but he is also quite ruthless when he wants something. You must not let him turn your head.'

'He was not trying to. You are quite mistaken if you think that.'

'My dear, you must not be so serious! I was only teasing you a little, although I must own I was rather startled to see him touching you in such a way. And on such short acquaintance!' She was smiling, but Cecily sensed she was not completely teasing.

'I had mud on my cheeks and foolishly forgot my handkerchief. He removed the mud for me. I have no doubt he would have done the same for anyone.'

'Well, not quite anyone! Do not worry, he meant nothing by it. If he does anything to distress you, then you must tell me. I have known him for a very long time so I can speak freely with him.'

'Thank you, but I am certain that will not be necessary.'

'You are no doubt right. Goodbye, dear *signora*.'

Cecily slowly walked up the steps to the house. Her cheek still burned from Severin's touch. Since her husband's death, no man had caressed her face as intimately. Not that she thought he meant anything by it, as Lady Margate had pointed out.

All of this was ridiculous. She was ridiculous. A widow of eight and twenty should not be making such a fuss over a mere touch of a hand. Nor should she allow Lady Margate's words to affect her. She needed to think of Mariana.

She realised she had no idea why Lady Margate had even called.

'Severin!' Nico, who had just passed through Signora Renato's gate, halted. Thais Margate was hurrying down the path towards him. She reached his side, her usually pale cheeks becomingly pink with the exertion. 'I was not certain whether I would catch up with you or not!'

'Your visit with Signora Renato was not very long.'

She looked up at him, her rosebud lips parted in a charming smile. 'I merely called to see how she was getting on. I will own I hardly expected to find you there!'

'No?' He felt rather bored. 'Did you walk? Or do you have a carriage lurking about?'

'I walked, of course. And now I expect you to escort me home.' She took his arm. 'Do not seem so surprised. Since coming to Avezza, I have discovered the benefits of exercise. The weather is so much nicer than at home.'

'Why are you in Italy? And why Avezza?' Nico asked as they began walking down the hill that led to the centre of the town.

'Because you are here, of course.' She flashed another smile at him. 'Do not flatter yourself. After dear George died, I realised I needed to go away. So many memories, of course, and then his family was never very kind to me. They accused me of keeping them away from George when he was ill, but I was only following Dr Johnson's orders. I have bought a little palazzo in Venice for not very much. The poor family—they had lived there for three hundred years, but now they cannot afford it. But Venice was rather tedious so I decided to come here—I remember it as such a peaceful place. But I am certain you do not wish to hear about that! I should really ask—why are you here?'

'For various reasons.'

'You are being elusive as usual! Shall I guess? You worry that Lord Ballister is becoming too fond of a certain young lady and you wish to put a stop to it, which of course you must. I cannot imagine what Rafaele would do if he discovered your cousin wished to marry his cousin. He is her trustee, you know, although she is in Signora Renato's care. What an odd coincidence that your cousin and Rafaele's should meet and fall in love.' She spoke in a guileless manner that made him wonder what she was up to.

'Are you not presuming too much?'

She gave an amused little laugh. 'I do not think so. Everyone can quite see that Lord Ballister and Signorina Renato are rather too fond of one another. Why else would you call on Signora Renato if not to warn her not to pin her hopes on attracting a viscount for her daughter?'

She had always possessed the shrewd ability to sum up a situation, but her assumption that because of that she had the right to make it her business both amused and irked him. As did her certainty that she knew the motives of the parties involved. He could not help toying with her a little.

'There are perhaps other reasons I wished to call on Signora Renato,' he said deliberately.

'Really? What might those be?' She looked up at him, still laughing. 'Do not tell me you find her attractive?'

'Then I won't.'

She stopped in front of a house that sat slightly back from the cobbled street and was surrounded by a wrought-iron fence. She looked up at him with her large blue eyes. 'Why, Severin, I believe you actually do! I would not have thought she was at all your style. However, I must warn you that it will not do for you to become too attached.' Her smile was now gone. 'I have heard from several sources—several very reliable sources—that Signora Renato already has an admirer. A man who has been in love with her for an age, although it is not possible for them to marry—at least, not quite yet.' She paused as if waiting for him to ask. 'Rafaele Vianoli. Unless you want history to repeat itself, you must stay away from her.'

'Why were they here?' Barbarina spoke from her chair near the window overlooking the lane, and nearly caused Cecily, who had just entered the salon, to drop her basket.

'Goodness! You frightened me.' Cecily set the flowers on the table and went to Barbarina's side.

'What did he want, the Duke? He does not like it that his

cousin wishes to court Mariana, no? Now we have only to wait for Rafaele to come and fight the Duke.'

'I will send Mariana to Vittoria and Serefina as soon as possible. So no one needs to worry about fights. I have brought you a rose. There was only one blooming.' She realised Barbarina was staring at her with a peculiar expression. 'What is it?'

'You must leave Avezza as well.'

'I will accompany Mariana to Padua, of course. Then I will return.'

'You must stay away from the English Duke. You must not return to Avezza until he is gone.'

Cecily stared at her, a peculiar chill creeping down her spine. 'I assure you I have no desire to be anywhere near the Duke. I do not particularly like him.'

'That does not matter.' She kept her gaze on Cecily. 'For I saw the way he looked at you just now in the garden. You will be in danger as long as he is here.'

'Why would I possibly be in danger from him?'

'Not from him. Because of him.'

'That does not make any sense. What do you mean?'

'He will bring danger to you. Just as he did to Angelina.'

Chapter Four

Cecily received a reply from Vittoria a few days later. Yes, they would be delighted to have Mariana. She should come for a month, perhaps two. Cecily, of course, must stay for as long as she wished as well. Although Caterina's relations, rather than Marco's, they had always been quite kind to Cecily and their warm response made her feel guilty that she did not visit them more often.

Perhaps she should consider staying with them for an extended visit. Since the day in the garden, Barbarina's words hung heavily over her. *He will bring danger to you. Just as he did to Angelina.* Not that Cecily really thought she was in any sort of peril; she was more disturbed by Barbarina's implication that Angelina had been in danger and that Severin was somehow responsible. Did she think that Angelina's death was not an accident, but something more sinister? But Barbarina would not answer Cecily's questions and Cecily could only hope it was another one of her peculiar notions.

She wished she knew what had happened between Severin and Raf, but Barbarina was unlikely to tell her.

Perhaps none of it would matter once Mariana was safely away from Avezza. She wondered if Viola would know. She had not spoken to her since the night at Signora Bartolini's. She decided she would call on her today.

Viola lived in one of the narrow streets on the other side of Avezza's small piazza. The day was fine; a dog slept in the sun near the butcher shop and across the square two Austrian soldiers lingered near the café. No one was sorry to see the French leave Venice and its former territories, but whether her new Austrian masters were an improvement was yet to be determined.

She passed the old church, now undergoing repairs, which made her think of Thais Margate and her peculiar idea that Severin might be interested in Cecily. In many ways, she was as odd as Barbarina in regard to Severin.

If only he had never come to Avezza—since his arrival, everyone and everything seemed overset.

Viola leased the top floor of one of the tall narrow houses that lined either side of the street. A maid let Cecily in and Cecily followed her up the steep stairway to the upper floor. Viola greeted Cecily with a hug. Like Cecily, Viola was now a widow, her husband killed at the Battle of Borodino while fighting under Napoleon. Along with many other men in the towns that were once part of the Venetian Republic, he had been conscripted into the French army against his will, which only made his death more tragic.

As soon as they were seated on the small sofa, Viola turned to Cecily. 'So, my dear Cecily, I have heard the handsome Duke was seen leaving your house yesterday. This following the *musicale*, when he insisted on escorting you home.'

'It was not a social call. He wishes to make sure I am not encouraging a match between Lord Ballister and Mariana.'

'Are you certain that is all? A little flirtation with you might soften his heart towards Mariana and her young suitor.'

'Even if I wished to do so, I would never think of flirting with him. At any rate, we are in agreement; neither of us wants a match between them. They are far too young.' She did not want to discuss Mariana and Lord Ballister any further, for she suspected Viola sympathised with the couple's predicament, although she had never exactly said so. 'Not only that, but Barbarina has told me if Raf finds out about any of this he will fight not only Lord Ballister but the Duke as well. She speaks of some sort of quarrel between the Duke and Raf, but will not tell me why. Have you ever heard about any sort of quarrel?'

Viola frowned. 'No, but I do remember that some people were surprised when the Conte announced that Angelina was to marry Lord St Gervase, as he was then, for everyone had always thought she would marry Rafaele Vianoli.'

'Angelina and Raf?' Cecily was truly shocked. 'Why would anyone think that?'

'Because he was the Conte's heir and it seemed only natural that they would marry.'

'Was Raf in love with Angelina?'

'I do not know. No one doubted, however, that Lord St Gervase was in love with Angelina and that she was equally in love with him. Everyone could see how happy they were together, as if fate decreed it to be. I only saw him once after she died and he looked as if his heart had died with her.'

'I did not know that,' Cecily said slowly. So Severin had loved her. 'No one has really said much about Angelina except Barbarina. She seems to be one person Barbarina truly cared about.'

'Angelina was beautiful. She reminded me of the Madonna in one of Bellini's paintings. No one said a word against her because she was always laughing and teasing and had a smile for everyone. I do not think there was anyone she disliked, even the Lady Margate.'

'She knew Lady Margate?' For the second time in the past hour Cecily was stunned.

'She was not Lady Margate, of course, but Miss...' Viola frowned a little, 'Miss Winters, I think. Yes, it was Miss Winters. She also stayed with the Conte's family that summer. Her father was a friend of the Conte's.'

'Lady Margate has said nothing of that, nor has anyone else.'

'I do not think anyone has recognised her. She was only there that one summer and she was the sort of pale, thin girl that no one ever notices. She is quite different now. It is very odd, but I did not recognise her until I saw her with the Duke at the *musicale*. There was a certain way she tilted her head when she looked at him and suddenly I remembered her doing the same all those years ago. As was every other girl that summer, she was a little in love with him. Not that he noticed, for he saw only Angelina.'

'I wonder why she has said nothing.'

'Perhaps she does not want to be remembered as she was.'

'Perhaps not.'

It was all so peculiar. Did Barbarina recognise her? Perhaps that would explain why Barbarina had regarded her with such animosity from the very beginning, but not what she had done to incur it. Why had Barbarina not told her she knew Lady Margate? So many secrets and for what purpose?

'I do not know if any of this explains why Rafaele and the Duke quarrelled unless it was over Angelina,' Viola said.

'That is possible, but if the Conte announced the betrothal it seems *he* must have approved. If he really wished Raf to marry Angelina, he surely would have tried to stop a marriage between the Duke and his daughter.'

'Perhaps you should ask Rafaele. Or the Duke.' A hint of mischief appeared in her eyes.

'Raf is not here and the Duke would send me scurrying away with a cool set-down.'

Viola laughed. 'You are not such a coward. Is Raf still in Verona? He has not been to Avezza for a long time, but should we be expecting him now that the Duke is here?'

'I certainly hope not. Yes, he is still in Verona. We have not seen him for nearly three months. Mariana misses him; we both do.' During Marco's prolonged illness and after his death, he had been like a brother to her; helping her with legal matters, holding Mariana when she cried and then making her laugh, teasing Cecily into smiles when she became too serious.

'At least he will not starve,' Viola said, always practical. 'And he still has the palazzo, no? He has not been forced to sell that?'

'I hope he will never need to. He would be devastated.' It was all that was left of his family's holdings for the French policies had impoverished a good portion of the Venetian nobility, including his family as well as the Guiliani family. After the Conte's death, he had been forced to sell many of the holdings of both families.

'Perhaps he will fall in love with a wealthy woman and then his troubles will be gone.'

'Perhaps, although there does not seem to be an abundance of such women around.' Cecily could not imagine Raf marrying for such reasons, for she suspected that his laughing eyes and cool intelligence hid a romantic heart.

Their talk turned to other matters, such as the fête at the end of the week in the gardens of Signor Palmero's villa. They agreed to share a supper box, then Cecily rose to leave.

She stepped out into the narrow street and started for home, so occupied in thought she barely noticed her surroundings. She had come away from Viola with more questions than before. Questions about Angelina and Raf, Raf and the Duke, and, to add to the confusion, Lady Margate. The only thing she knew for certain was that Severin and Angelina had been in love and were to marry, she had died, and in the thirteen years since her death he had never married.

Cecily had decided she would wait until after the fête before telling Mariana they were to leave for Padua. She knew Mariana looked forward to this affair each year and Cecily hated to spoil it for her. Mariana had been compliant and almost too subdued over the past few days. Except for a visit from Teresa, she had spent most of her time reading or sitting in the garden and Cecily was now troubled by visions of a decline.

On the night of the fête, Mariana appeared to have recovered some of her usual spirits. She wore a muslin gown in a soft rose colour. The gown itself was several years old, but, newly trimmed with ribbon and lace and set off with a new sash in a darker shade of rose, it looked quite presentable. Her black curls were gathered in a knot at the top of her head and fell in a cascade of ringlets to her shoulders and her eyes held some of their old sparkle. To Cecily's eyes, she was beautiful and she could hardly blame Lord Ballister for falling in love with her.

Cecily herself was dressed in pale peach muslin. It was a trifle outdated—the skirt was not quite as full as the current fashion, but at least it was not very worn. She was stunned, however, when Barbarina suddenly appeared in the salon and announced she planned to attend the fête with them. Cecily was equally taken aback by her appearance. Over her black dress she wore a black mantle, instead of her plain black veil she wore one of black lace, and, if Cecily was not mistaken, she had even applied a touch of rouge.

'How pretty you look!' Cecily exclaimed and then prayed she had not offended Barbarina. Barbarina merely gave a 'hmph' but Cecily thought she looked a little pleased. She did not protest when Mariana fingered her lacy veil and told her she must wear such things more often.

Shades of purple, pink and orange tinted the sky by the time Cecily, Mariana and Barbarina arrived at the Palermos' villa. A long line of carriages already stood in the villa's drive so they were forced to dismount a small distance away. A number of other guests were doing the same. Cecily worried that the distance would be too much for Barbarina, but she managed the walk to the garden entrance without complaint, albeit slowly.

They joined the crowd drifting between the stone pillars to the garden. As they entered the grounds, Cecily wondered if Severin and Lord Ballister would be here, for this was the villa that had once belonged to Angelina's family. Would Severin find it too difficult to visit this place with its surely painful memories?

She had found herself thinking far too much about him and Angelina since her visit to Viola. Tonight, she must make an effort to put them from her thoughts or she feared she would see their ghosts everywhere, which would make for a most melancholy evening.

The gardens were behind the house itself. Signor Palermo been quite taken with a visit to Vauxhall a number of years ago and had attempted to recreate the English pleasure garden. He added a pavilion for musicians and a number of supper boxes. Although lacking a Thames river, the garden could boast of a small artificial lake with a fountain in the middle. He had left the old maze that proved to be one of the most popular attractions.

A footman showed their party to the supper box. Viola and Teresa were already there; Viola arched a brow in astonishment when she saw Barbarina. After Barbarina had been seated near the front of the box so that she could observe the crowd, and Mariana and Teresa were deep in conversation, Viola turned to Cecily. 'How did you persuade Signora Zanetti to come?' she asked in a low voice.

'I did not. She decided on her own.'

'How very strange. Has she ever been here before? At a fête, that is, for I know she stayed here quite often with the Guiliani family.'

'I do not think so. I have no idea why she wanted to come.'

'Mama,' Teresa said, 'Paolo and Frederico wish to take Mariana and me to the maze. May we go?'

Cecily saw that Paolo, Teresa's brother, and their cousin,

Frederico, a pleasant-looking, plump youth, were standing just outside their supper box.

Viola glanced at Cecily. 'If Signora Renato does not object.'

Cecily hesitated. What if Lord Ballister were here and joined them? On the other hand, Severin had said they must not make it too obvious they wished to separate them. And Mariana scarcely mentioned Lord Ballister this week.

'Please, Mama,' Mariana said, regarding Cecily with large pleading eyes.

'You may go, but please stay together.'

'Thank you.' Mariana gave her a radiant smile and, after planting a brief kiss on Barbarina's cheek, left with the others. By now the evening shadows had fallen and the servants had begun lighting various lanterns and torches scattered throughout the garden, giving the garden a festive air.

Barbarina seemed disinclined to talk and spoke only to ask for a glass of lemonade from one of the waiters. The strains of a Vivaldi concerto reached them from somewhere in the garden. Viola suddenly touched Cecily's hand. 'He is coming.'

'Who?'

'Your duke. He is very certainly most handsome.'

'He is not my duke!' Cecily half-turned her face to the back of the box and pretended very hard to be studying the painting of cherubs dancing around a fountain. He most likely would walk by.

The skin at the back of her neck prickled and she knew he had come to stand next to them.

'*Buonasera*, Signora Zanetti, Signora Carasco. And Signora Renato.' He switched to English. 'A fascinating work, Signora Renato. What is it that has caught your attention? The cherubs dancing in drunken abandon around a fountain or the cupid peering from beneath the leaves?'

'There is a cupid? Where?' Then she coloured and forced herself to turn around. 'Good evening, your Grace.'

'It must be the cherubs, then, since you did not notice the cupid.'

'I was admiring the use of colour.'

'Can you even tell in this fading light?' He was openly amused, which only served to fluster Cecily more.

Viola was watching with rapt interest. 'You must join us, your Grace.'

'If Signora Zanetti does not object.'

Barbarina was staring at him with something like consternation. 'You must stay away from Signora Renato. She is not safe with you.'

Viola's mouth fell open and Cecily wanted to sink through the floor of the box. She could not look at Severin.

'What precisely do you mean by that?' he asked. His voice was level, but there was a hardness to it.

'She will not be safe with you,' Barbarina repeated.

'Have you visited the maze, your Grace?' Viola asked brightly.

'Not yet.' He glanced down at Cecily. 'Where is Signorina Renato?'

'She has gone to visit the maze. With Signorina Carasco and her brother and cousin.'

His eyes narrowed. 'Has she? An interesting coincidence. My brother has gone there as well.'

She did not like his implication. She spoke in English, hoping Barbarina would not understand very much. 'I hope you are not suggesting what I think you are. If you are so worried about that, then you should keep a tighter rein on him.'

'Just as you should keep a tighter rein on your daughter, madam. I believe I will visit the maze after all. Good evening, ladies.' He walked briskly away.

Cecily was not about to let him confront Mariana without her. She started to rise, only to find Barbarina's hand clasped around her wrist. 'Where are you going?'

'To the maze. To find Mariana.'

'You must not go with him.'

'I am not going with him. I am going by myself.'

'Then I will come with you.'

'No, you must stay here with Viola.' She gently removed Barbarina's hand. 'I will return shortly,' she said to Viola.

'Of course.' Viola looked as if she wanted to laugh.

Cecily hurried after Severin, whose progress had been slowed by a trio of jugglers. He started to move around them when he caught sight of Cecily. He stopped. 'I doubt there will be much benefit in both of us showing up.'

She gave him a tight smile. 'Then you may go elsewhere while I find them. I am going to find my daughter because I do not want her subjected to one of your intimidating stares.'

'I've no intention of intimidating her. You are wasting time by arguing. You may do as you please.'

He stalked off. She followed him, although she grew a trifle breathless as she was forced to trot in order to keep up with his long strides. The crowds had grown and she had a hard time weaving around them. Despite the number of lanterns the gardens were not particularly well lit and some of the paths were dark.

Most of the crowd seemed to be heading towards the

grotto where the musicians played. By the time Cecily reached the maze she had lost Severin because of a crowd of people who had got in her way. She felt more than a little trepidation when she entered the first path with its tall, shadowy shrubs. It suddenly seemed very dark and foreboding despite the voices and laugher coming from within. She stopped, uncertain which way to proceed.

'What happened to you? I turned around and you were gone.'

Severin's voice made her jump. He was standing near the entrance.

'I thought that was what you wanted.'

He made an impatient sound. 'I wanted you to stay with Signora Carasco, not get lost in the dark. Despite Signora Zanetti's dire predictions, you are better off with me.'

'I am sorry that she said such stupid things to you. At any rate, I have been here any number of times. I can manage quite well on my own.' Although the maze did look quite different in the dark.

'Not unless you wish to be the object of some man's attentions.' He caught her arm. 'You are wasting time again.'

'Me?' But he was already leading her into the first winding passage between two tall rows of yews.

There were not as many people as she had expected. Once they entered the second passage she knew why. Without the benefit of sunlight or a full moon, it was nearly impossible to see much. She could still hear laughter and voices from somewhere in the maze and she froze when she heard Mariana's breathless laugh and then Simon's deeper voice.

'Oh, dear.'

'Yes.' The grimness of Severin's tone made her shiver.

He glanced down at her face. 'There is no need to look so frightened. I'm not planning to beat either of them. Just lock Simon up until your daughter is safely away from Avezza. You might consider doing the same thing for your daughter.'

'I am beginning to agree.' How could Mariana do this? Did she not know, did neither of them realise, that they were both risking their reputations? Or perhaps that is what they meant to do so they would be forced to marry. The thought made her blood run cold.

They rounded another corner and found themselves nearly careening into a couple locked in a passionate embrace. For a horrid moment, Cecily feared it was Mariana and Simon, but realised the man was much too stocky. Embarrassed, she backed up and stepped on Severin's foot. 'I beg your pardon.'

The man lifted his head and saw them. 'You will need to find your own corner, *signora*.' His lady made a breathless little protest as her swain pulled her harder against him.

Severin steered her back around the corner. 'We've taken a wrong turn. We will have to retrace our steps.'

She nodded and followed him. By now, the clouds had covered the moon and the maze was even more dark and shadowy. The music and voices seemed far away and Cecily no longer heard anything from inside the maze. It was if they were the only ones here except for the couple they had just left behind.

Severin suddenly stopped. 'We've hit another dead end.' He ran a hand through his hair. 'You said you've been here a number of times. Do you have the faintest idea how we make our way out of here?'

He was asking for her help? Astounded, she stared at him

before speaking. 'I have only been here during the day.' He was not going to like what she had to say next. She forced herself to meet his eyes. 'And I have lost my way every single time. Mariana has always had to rescue me.'

She braced herself for the derision in his voice. To her astonishment, he laughed. 'Of course. And you had hoped to find them yourself?'

'I had planned on following you.'

His mouth curved in genuine amusement. 'Next time you should think twice before you decide to follow me.'

'I doubt there will be a next time.' She rubbed her arms as a cool breeze brushed her bare arms. 'If we can find the centre of the maze, there is one path that leads directly to the back entrance near the lake.'

'If I recall, the centre of the maze is to the left.'

'How do you know that?'

He slanted a look at her. 'I have been here as well, although it has grown considerably since I was last here. The paths seemed to have been rearranged, which is why I made the wrong turn.'

'Signor Palermo changes the paths each year. He digs up some of the shrubs and then replants them so the paths are never the same.'

'Very clever. But one should be able to find the old path by observing where the shrubs have been replanted.'

'I suppose,' she said doubtfully.

'Come. We will test my theory.' He took her hand, his hand warm and strong around hers, and began to walk. She glanced at his face and then looked away, her breath catching. She was suddenly aware it was too dark, too quiet, too alone. Too intimate.

A peculiar pit formed in her stomach and she felt almost panicked. Of course they would find their way out. He had been the perfect gentleman. She could not fault him for that at all. She would be safe with him.

'This way, I think.' He tugged her around a corner. She realised she had been paying no attention at all to where they were going. In a moment they were in the centre of the maze. He dropped her hand and looked around. 'I do not recall a statue last time I was here.' He spoke almost to himself.

He had been here with Angelina. She was certain of that. 'Signor Palermo added them only recently.' Her words seemed an intrusion on his memories so she moved away.

It was then she heard the faintest rustling in the bushes surrounding the small garden. She jumped and looked around, but there was nothing. She rubbed her arms, suddenly cold, her light shawl not at all adequate.

She heard the small sound again almost as if someone was in the bushes. Her sense of uneasiness increased and, when Severin appeared behind her, she jumped. 'You have the most damnable habit of disappearing,' he said.

'I did not want to interrupt you.'

'Interrupt me in doing what?'

'Thinking.'

'Thinking?' The edge of his mouth lifted. 'I can do that any time. Shall we go?'

'Yes, we should. In fact, we should leave now.' She realised her teeth were chattering.

'Why didn't you tell me you were cold? I can give you my coat.' He started to shrug out of the garment.

'It is not that. I...I don't like it here. I wish to go back. The way we came.'

'And get lost again?' He looked at her more closely. 'You are frightened. Do not worry, I won't let anything happen to you.' He removed his coat and draped it over her shoulders. 'Come, we'd best leave before you start to imagine ghosts or other such unnatural beings.'

She managed a smile. 'I suppose I have been reading too many of Mariana's novels lately. There always seems to be some sort of spectre or headless monk.' Coupled with Barbarina's odd predictions, it was no wonder she was imagining things.

A smile tugged at his mouth. 'You should find different literature in the future. Come.'

They passed through the arch and entered the straight, dark walk that led to the artificial lake on the other side of the maze. The yews were tall and forbidding and, despite her attempts to reassure herself she had only imagined hearing footsteps earlier, she found she was increasing her pace. Severin glanced down at her once, but said nothing.

She nearly collapsed with relief when the walk opened on to a small grassy lawn with the lake beyond. A number of people strolled near the water and she even saw a few daring souls had taken out the rowboats. The normality of the scene filled her with the same relief she felt after waking up from a disturbing dream.

'You really were frightened. Why?'

She looked up at him and found his gaze fixed on her face. 'I...I had the oddest sense that someone was watching us. I was being ridiculous, of course.'

'Perhaps.' His eyes were still on her.

'I suppose we should go and find Mariana and Simon.'

'We should.' He took a step towards her. 'But first there is something else I want to do.'

'What?'

'This.' He took another step towards her. His hands slipped under his coat and caught her shoulders and slowly drew her towards him. Mesmerised, she made no protest as his lips descended on hers in a surprisingly gentle kiss.

Perhaps her nerves were still on edge, but a faint movement caught her attention just as her eyes started to drift shut. The prickle of danger she'd felt in the maze struck her with renewed force. She pulled away from him and jerked her eyes open in time to see a shadowy figure drifting towards them, the glint of metal in the raised hand exactly like one of Mariana's gothic spectres. The cry broke from her throat just as the hand plunged towards Severin's back.

He half-turned and the stiletto caught his arm. 'What the hell?' he exclaimed. The assailant fled into the shadowy maze.

He stared at Cecily, his hand going to his arm for a moment. He pulled it away and her stomach lurched when she saw the blood on his hand. 'You are hurt,' she said stupidly.

'A mere scratch. Are you all right?' he asked quickly.

'Yes.'

'Stay here. I am going after him.'

She caught his other arm. 'No, you are not. Unless you want to bleed to death in Signor Palermo's maze.'

His eyes glinted down at her. 'That is unlikely.' And then he swayed.

She managed to steady him. 'Sit down. Please.'

He did not argue. He sat down on the grass, still holding his arm. She dropped his coat from her shoulders and knelt beside him. 'Let me see your arm.'

'It is fine.'

'It is not.' She gently removed his hand and suppressed a shiver when she saw the jagged slash. 'I think it will need to be stitched. First we must stop the bleeding.'

'Use my cravat.' His voice was thick.

'Good God! What has happened?'

Cecily looked up and with some astonishment saw two men and a woman standing over them. She had nearly forgotten they were at a fête. 'He has been stabbed. I must stop the bleeding and he needs a doctor.'

'Of course.' One of the men began to shout and the other dropped down beside Cecily. 'Allow me, *signora*. I have seen such wounds when I was with the army. Your sash, if you please, *signora*. I am Signor Canelli.' He produced a handkerchief and Cecily, with trembling fingers, untied the pale green sash encircling her bodice and handed it to Signor Canelli. He formed the handkerchief into a pad and pressed it to the wound, then began winding the sash about the pad.

'Severin!' Lady Margate's voice broke through the crowd that now surrounded them. 'What has happened?' In a moment, she had dropped to her knees next to Cecily. 'Oh, dear God! Who did this to you?'

'A robber of some sort.' He glanced at Cecily as if challenging her to deny it.

'Dear God!' Lady Margate stared at him, her expression horrified.

Signor Canelli finished his task just as Signor Palermo appeared. He took charge; two burly men were assigned to assist Severin to the house; another man was sent for Signor Palermo's physician. In the midst of all this, Cecily caught sight of Simon leaving the maze, followed by Paolo. She ran to them.

'What has happened?' Simon exclaimed when he saw her face.

'Your cousin…he was stabbed, just as we were coming from the maze.' She caught his hand when she saw his face. 'His arm was injured, but nothing vital. The bleeding has been stopped and Signor Palermo has sent for a physician. He is to be taken to the house.'

'And you? You are not hurt?' he asked quickly.

'No, I am fine.'

He nodded and dashed towards the small crowd around his cousin. Paolo looked shaken. 'He was stabbed? Who would do such a thing?'

'We do not know. Mariana, where is she?'

'With Mama and Teresa. Frederico has gone to look for Signora Zanetti. When we returned to the box, not only had you disappeared, but Signora Zanetti as well. Mama said she and Signora Zanetti had gone to view the fountain and became separated.'

Barbarina was missing? She recalled the black-clad figure and a frightening thought crossed her mind. 'How long has Signora Zanetti been gone?'

'I do not know. Only that she was not there and Mama was worried because both you and Signora Zanetti had not returned. She sent Lord Ballister and me to find you.'

'I see.' No, it was not possible, Barbarina would not have attempted to harm anyone. Despite her odd ways she had never shown any signs of violence. The assailant had been much too tall, or had he?

'Signora Renato? Are you unwell?' Paolo asked.

'No, I am quite well.'

'We should perhaps return to the box.'

She glanced towards the others and saw that Severin now stood supported by the two men. Lady Margate hovered nearby and, as Cecily watched, Simon took her arm as if to comfort her. Cecily turned away, a pang darting through her. 'Yes, we should. We can do nothing more here.'

Barbarina had been found by the time she and Paolo returned. The others were horrified by the news. Even Barbarina looked stricken. Cecily tried to tell herself that surely she would not look so if she had committed such a terrible act.

Later, in her bed, she was not so certain. She went over and over the assault in her mind, but somehow the shadowy figure turned into Barbarina, no matter how hard she tried to think otherwise.

When she finally fell into a restless sleep, however, she did not dream of assailants and daggers, but of being kissed by a tall, dark stranger who bore a disturbing resemblance to the Duke of Severin.

Chapter Five

Nico sat on the edge of his bed and waited for his head to clear. He'd slept a good part of the day away if the light peeping through the curtains was any indication. His arm hurt like the devil, but at least he had only a mild headache from the brandy he had drunk last night to dull the pain while the doctor stitched his arm.

As much as he would like to, he could not afford to lie in bed. His first business was to call on Barbarina Zanetti. For a stomach-wrenching moment last night, he thought the assailant would stab Signora Renato as well. The thought continued to trouble him. What if Cecily Renato had indeed been the intended victim? The attack seemed too much of a coincidence after Barbarina's warning.

He had no idea if she actually possessed some sort of ability to predict the future. Her odd black clothes and strange way of looking at one, combined with her dire pronouncements, had prompted Raf to laughingly call her *una strega*, a witch.

Did she know something? Or had she been the assailant? The person had fled and he could not imagine Barbarina moving that quickly. It was possible her shuffling walk was merely an act.

Why would she want to hurt Cecily? It would make more sense if she tried to hurt him, for she had never wanted Angelina to marry him. But if she intended to stab him, why had she said that Cecily would be in danger?

Or was the attack completely unrelated and the assailant had some other purpose in mind, such as robbery? Or had they been mistaken for someone else?

He did not like it at all. After he spoke with Signora Zanetti, he would see Cecily. For until he found out who was behind the assault, he did not want Cecily Renato anywhere near Avezza.

'Why? Why must I go? They are old and fat and I might as well be locked up!' Mariana clutched the sheet covering her with white-knuckled hands and regarded Cecily, who sat on the edge of her bed, with an accusing, angry stare.

Cecily forced herself to remain calm. She had slept very little last night and was in no mood to argue. 'You must not speak of Vittoria and Serefina in such a disrespectful way. They love you very much and quite look forward to your visit. We will leave tomorrow.'

'It is because of Simon that you wish me to go, is it not?'

'I think it best if you are away from Avezza for a while.'

'Because you do not want me to marry Simon,' Mariana said flatly.

Cecily hesitated. 'It is not possible for you to marry Lord Ballister,' she finally said. 'I am truly sorry.' The stricken look on Mariana's face nearly broke her heart, but she could not allow Mariana to nourish any false hopes.

Mariana bowed her head and said nothing. Cecily rose from the bed. 'We must begin packing today. I hope you will collect yourself enough to decide if you wish to take any books or your sketching implements.'

Mariana lifted a tear-stained face. 'If...if my mama were here, my real mama, I know she would understand! She would not make me go away. She would let me marry Simon.'

A knife tore through Cecily's heart. Never in the seven years Cecily had been her stepmother had Mariana ever said such a thing. She silently closed the door behind her and realised her hands were trembling. Of course, Mariana was hurt and angry and wanted to lash out at Cecily any way she could. Still, her words stung.

And then there was Barbarina. When Cecily questioned her this morning, Barbarina had been no more forthcoming about her disappearance than she had been last night. She had become separated from Signora Carasco in the crowd and then lost her way. Finally Cecily had asked her if she knew anything about Severin's attack.

Barbarina stared at her for so long that Cecily wondered if she had gone into a trance. She finally spoke. 'I wanted to find you because you were with him.'

'Do you know who did this?'

Barbarina shook her head. 'I know nothing else.' She suddenly looked very tired.

Cecily was beginning to wonder if Barbarina was possibly mad. She sometimes suspected Barbarina's dire warnings and predictions were a way of making herself important, but never before had anything much come of them. Certainly nothing like this.

She slowly went downstairs. Her housekeeper met her at

the bottom. 'The Duke of Severin is here, *signora*. He is in the salon.'

Severin? Whatever was he doing here? She could not imagine that after the wound she saw last night he would wish to leave his bed, let alone pay a call.

'*Signora?* Do you wish to see him?'

'Yes. Yes, I will.'

The first thing she noticed was his arm in a sling, his coat draped across his shoulders. His white shirt was tucked into his breeches and he wore no cravat.

He noticed her gaze. 'I apologise for my attire.'

She crossed the room. 'You should not even be dressed at all. I cannot imagine what you are doing out of bed.'

'I needed to see you.'

'Surely it could have waited. Or you should have sent for me.'

'No.'

His pallor alarmed her. 'You must sit down.'

'After you, *signora*.'

She took the nearest chair. To her relief he took the chair across from her. He winced a little as his arm brushed the back. The scowl on his face kept her from expressing any sort of sympathy. 'How are you feeling?'

His eyes flickered over her and, for some idiotic reason, she suddenly recalled last night's dream. Heat crept into her cheeks and she hoped he did not notice.

'Well enough.' His gaze was still on her. 'I came to see Signora Zanetti, but your housekeeper informed me she has gone out.'

'She went to the market. Is there something in particular you wished to see her about? Perhaps I can help you?'

He looked at her for a moment. 'Tell me why you knew someone was in the bushes last night,' he said abruptly.

'I heard something…a rustling. At first I thought it was perhaps the breeze or an animal, but I saw nothing. Then I had the most odd feeling that something was not right. That we were being watched. It was so dark and no one seemed to be around and I knew we needed to leave as soon as possible.'

'That was all? Just a premonition of sorts? You did not see anyone?'

'Not until you were…we were occupied.'

'Apparently you were not so well occupied that you failed to notice a person with a dagger behind us,' he said drily.

She flushed. 'I was still very uneasy, so I could not really think of anything else.'

A glint appeared in his eye. 'Next time I will make certain there is nothing to distract you when I decide to kiss you. Not that I am complaining this time—if you had not been distracted, one of us might have been gravely wounded. Do you have any idea of who it was?'

'No, I thought…' She pulled her gaze away from his mouth and tried to concentrate on the matter at hand rather than on the idea he might kiss her again. 'No.'

He looked at her hard. 'But you do suspect someone? Barbarina Zanetti, perhaps?'

'She was missing last night. Paolo told me that when he and Simon came to find us, but by the time we returned to the box Mariana and Viola had found her. I asked her this morning where she had been, but she would only say that she had gone to look for me because I was with you.' She swallowed. 'Do you think it was Barbarina?'

'I think it unlikely. Regardless of who was behind the

attacks, you need to leave Avezza. Go to Padua with your daughter.'

'You will leave Avezza as well, will you not?'

'Not right away. I have business here.'

'What sort of business do you have here once Mariana is gone? You cannot stay here after last night. For if you do, then I will as well.'

'For what purpose? To protect me?'

'If I need to.'

Surprise crossed his face. 'My dear, I am touched, but I am in no need of your protection. If you recall, Signora Zanetti said you would not be safe with me. She proved to be correct. If you had any sense, you would stay as far away from me as possible.'

'But you were the one who was injured, not I.'

He rose, although she could see it was an effort. 'Have you considered that perhaps you were the intended victim?'

She stood as well. Frustration and fear washed over her. 'I cannot imagine why anyone would wish to hurt me. But then I do not know why anyone would wish to hurt you either. Why? What has happened? Barbarina will tell me nothing! Only that you and Raf quarrelled, but I do not even know why!' She realised her voice had risen alarmingly and she made an effort to collect herself. 'I should not shout at you. You are not well…and…' To her horror, her voice broke.

He took a step towards her, the cool arrogance gone. '*Cara*, don't.'

'I think you should…should go.'

'*Maldezione,*' he muttered. The next thing she knew he had pulled her against him. 'Don't,' he said roughly. He released her, but only to tilt her chin towards him. His lips came down on hers and her mouth parted under his as reality and dream merged into one.

He finally released her; for a moment, she had no idea where she was. Her eyes shot open and she stared at him, the blood pounding in her head. He looked equally dazed and then his expression closed. 'As you can see, I pose another danger to you as well. For, if you stay, I have every intention of seducing you.'

Nothing came to her mind for a moment. 'I...I do not think I would be that easy to seduce.'

He laughed, but it held no amusement. 'That very fact would present a challenge I could not possibly resist. I've no doubt I would have you in my bed within a fortnight.'

'I think you are impossibly conceited.'

'Perhaps.' He moved towards her, standing so close his body was a hair's breath away. 'Shall we find out? I would start by kissing you again.'

'If it was like your last kiss, then I doubt I would be in any danger at all. I do not like such...such assaults. Besides, I think you only want to frighten me into doing what you want.'

'Oh, it wouldn't be like that at all. It would be like this.' This time his mouth was gentle and firm, his lips moving over hers in a slow burning caress. His body was pressed into hers, his knee gently parting her legs, then he shifted and she could feel his arousal through her thin skirts. She melted into his embrace, her lips parting beneath his.

It wasn't until he finally lifted his head that cold sanity returned. A great pounding wave of shock and embarrassment washed over her.

'Cecily?'

The use of her first name startled her. She jerked her eyes open. 'I suppose you are quite right. I am so stupid that I would allow a man I scarcely know to seduce me.' She did not look at him.

'You are not stupid,' he said quietly. 'Merely a passionate, desirable woman, which is why you had best leave Avezza.'

'Very well. I will travel to Padua with Mariana,' she said.

'Good.' He looked at her and then hesitated. 'Goodbye, then.'

'Please be careful. I...I should not want anything to happen to you.'

A sardonic smile touched his mouth. 'If you continue to say such things, then I will be sorely tempted to take you here and now. I do not think that would be wise for either of us.' He was gone.

Nico stepped into his carriage and sank back against the cushions. Why the devil had he kissed her? Because she had looked so damned distressed that he'd wanted to comfort her. Once she was in his arms, it had been only natural to kiss her.

She was right—he had intended to scare her for, despite her sweet response to his kiss, he had guessed she would be appalled if he told her he planned to seduce her. He hoped that would be enough to drive her away from Avezza. Until he had a chance to determine what was going on.

There was another reason as well. He could not allow his attraction to Cecily Renato to get any further out of hand. Not if there were the slightest chance that Rafaele Vianoli was in love with her.

Chapter Six

Cecily rose early the following morning. She had slept poorly again and, as she had the night before, spent the night in restless dreams. Most disturbing of all was the dream in which she was trying desperately to save Severin's life from a faceless murderer while she attempted to persuade him to leave Avezza.

She had woken suddenly in the night with the realisation that he had never said he would leave Avezza. What he did was none of her affair. Not even if his kisses did make her long for something she could not have.

During one of her lengthy periods of restless tossing she had convinced herself that he had only meant to scare her into leaving Avezza. She was not the sort of woman that would interest a man such as the arrogant Duke of Severin.

Her head was beginning to hurt again from all the questions to which she had no answers. It was no use lying abed any longer. She threw on her dressing gown and went downstairs. Most of their luggage was piled in the hall. Perhaps if she ate she would feel better. She went into the small breakfast room and forced a few pieces of buttered toast and a cup of steaming chocolate down her throat.

She finally stood. She must wake Mariana for their journey.

Her soft rap on the door brought no response. She pushed the door open. The bedcovers were rumpled. 'Mariana?' She approached the bed and her heart stopped when she saw that it was empty.

'Oh, dear lord,' she whispered. Then she saw the note. She unfolded it with trembling fingers.

I cannot bear being parted from Simon. Do not worry, I will be quite safe. Your loving daughter, Mariana.

Not worry? Her daughter had decided to elope and she was not to worry? Where would they even go? And how was she to find them?

She could think of only one person who could help her.

Nico had just poured himself a second cup of strong coffee when he heard rapid footsteps and an agitated feminine voice. He rose just as Signora Renato burst into the dining room.

Her hair, tied back in a loose knot, trailed down her back. Astonished, he realised she wore a night rail underneath her pelisse. 'She is gone!' she said.

'Who is gone?'

'Mariana! She…she has run away with your cousin!'

He set his cup down and took her arm. 'Sit down.'

'No! I…I cannot. Where is Lord Ballister?'

'Sit.' This time she took the chair. 'Now tell me what has happened. Calmly, if you please.'

She took a deep breath and stared up at him. 'We…we are to leave today. I rose early for I could not sleep and went downstairs to eat—I thought I might feel better—but when

I went upstairs to wake Mariana, she was not there. She left this…this note.' She held out a crumpled piece of paper.

He took it and perused the contents. 'Why do you think she eloped with my cousin?'

'Because she said she could not bear to be parted from him. Why else would she write such a thing?' She stood, obviously too agitated to sit. 'Please, you must see if Simon is here. If she did not run away with him, perhaps he has some idea where she has gone!'

'Stay here. I'll find my cousin.' He strode out of the room and saw the housekeeper hovering outside the door. Undoubtedly high drama. 'Is Lord Ballister still abed?' he asked.

'I do not know, milord.'

'Can you find out?'

'*Sì*, milord.' She scurried off.

He returned to the dining room where Cecily was pacing. She turned. 'Is he here?'

'I've sent my housekeeper to find out.' He took her arm. Deep circles surrounded her eyes. 'You need to sit. You did not even take the time to dress properly.'

Colour stained her pale cheeks. 'I needed to see you straight away. I did not want to waste time dressing.'

Hell. She looked as if she had just tumbled out of bed. Her pelisse had parted slightly and he could see the nipple of one rounded breast through the thin fabric of her night rail. His body responded with a lust that was completely inappropriate at the moment. He dropped her arm just as Flavia bustled into the room. 'He is gone. His bed has not been slept in. Oh, milord, do you think it is the same person who attacked you at the gardens?'

'No. I am quite certain Lord Ballister has gone of his own accord. Did he leave a note?' Not that he expected Simon to leave a message on his pillow.

'A note?'

'Allow me to see for myself. Send Enrico to the study. I want to speak with him.' He strode out of the room, only to find Cecily on his heels.

'Wait for me in the dining room. There is coffee and I've no doubt Flavia can make you tea if you'd prefer.'

Her face closed. 'Very well, your Grace.'

Flavia was correct: Simon's bed was untouched. He saw no note, but his cousin did indeed seem to have deliberately disappeared. His small valise was gone and, although most of his clothing remained, his favourite pair of boots was missing and several shirts and waistcoats were flung over the chair as if he'd pulled them out and rejected them.

Enrico waited for him in the salon. He answered Nico's questions in his rather vague way. No, Lord Ballister did not return home last night. No, Lord Ballister said nothing about a journey. Nico dismissed him, but just as Enrico reached the door he turned. 'Ah, but the young lord did wish me to give you this.' He pulled a folded paper from his pocket and held it out to Nico. The paper was now grubby with dirt and sweat. He opened it. The ink had smeared but he was able to make out part of the message.

Gone to V... Tell Signora Renato not to worry. Mariana...

'When did he give this to you?'

Enrico shrugged. 'Last night. He said to give it to you today.'

Nico cursed and returned to the breakfast salon. Cecily stood by the window. She whirled around.

'It appears they are together,' he said.

'Oh, dear lord! How do you know?'

'He also left a note. I cannot read all of it, but he does mention your daughter's name and that you are not to worry.'

'Mariana wrote exactly the same. They must be mad if they think we will not worry!' She looked shaken, but to her credit she made an effort to collect herself. 'If they plan to marry, where would they go?'

'There is an English vicar in Vicenza who, for the right fee, is said to be amenable to conducting marriages under rather clandestine circumstances. It is possible they have gone there. He might refuse to marry them if he thought Mariana was not of age, but if they convince him that Mariana is old enough then he might. At any rate, the legality of the marriage would be in question. Not that it makes a whit of difference if this gets out. Go home, I'll find them.'

'You cannot go. Your arm!'

'My arm is fine.'

'I am going with you.'

'You are not. You've no need to ruin your reputation as well by leaving with me. At any rate, I will go by horseback. There is a shortcut I know.'

'That is quite insane. I am going with you.'

'Then you will need to make your own way,' he said carelessly. 'I doubt if you want to leave in your current dishabille, so by the time you dress and are ready to go, I will be far down the road.' He hoped to God that would discourage her.

She stared at him, her expression a mix of worry and anger. 'Very well, your Grace.' She turned without another word and left.

***

Cecily stood outside the villa gates for a moment. His words rang in her head. *Then you will need to make your own way.*

Very well. She would dash off a note for Vittoria and Serefina with some excuse why Mariana was suddenly unable to make the journey. Her things and Mariana's were packed, so there would be no worries there. There was Barbarina… Perhaps she could tell her that Mariana was too distraught to say goodbye.

And then, she would do exactly as he told her.

Cecily brushed a strand of hair from her forehead and then glanced up at the darkening sky. She should climb back into her carriage, but she had become restless as she sat in its musty interior waiting for the bridge to be cleared. Shortly before she arrived at the bridge, a horse pulling a loaded wagon had shied. A wheel had caught in the groove where the road and bridge met and the wagon had tipped, spilling cabbages everywhere.

Now her carriage was stuck along with a number of other carts and wagons. There had been a great deal of loud talking and shouting while everyone argued about what should be done and how best to move the wagon. The wheel had broken and someone had gone to fetch a blacksmith. She suspected it would be another hour before the bridge would be passable.

She was so close to Vicenza. Only another few miles. She had briefly considered walking except she would still be faced with the problem of crossing the stream. Now it looked as if it were about to rain. She had no idea if she wanted to cry. Or throw something. What were Simon and

Mariana doing? Had they already been married? Or were they turned away and forced to go elsewhere? But where would that be? Had Severin discovered anything?

Her mind kept spinning in circles and this idleness had not helped.

She walked down the grassy slope towards the stream, hoping to see progress of some sort. No one seemed to be doing much; several men were standing in a small cluster and talking with much waving of arms. Her coachman, Figaro, was leaning against the carriage, his eyes closed.

A drop of rain fell on the brim of her bonnet and hit her on the nose. 'Drat!'

'Somehow this does not surprise me.'

She whirled around, her heart thudding. Severin sat astride a large bay horse, a sardonic expression on his face.

She lifted her skirts and climbed towards him. 'Did you find them? Were they in Vicenza?'

'No. There was no sign of them.'

Disappointment coursed through her. She stared at him and then looked away, praying she would not cry. 'I see.'

'She will be safe with Simon.' His voice was surprisingly gentle.

She looked back at him. 'I...I suppose. That is, yes, I...I know.'

Another drop of rain hit her on the nose. He frowned. 'It is too late to return to Avezza. I doubt the bridge will be repaired any time in the next few hours. There is an inn, not far from here. Your coachman will need to turn the carriage around, however. Where is your maid? In the carriage? She had best dismount.'

'I did not bring my maid. She becomes exceedingly carriage-sick.' His expression told her what he thought of that. 'I will speak with Figaro now.'

'I will do so,' Severin said. He urged his horse before she could say a thing.

She eyed the narrow road, really not much more than a lane, with some misgiving and wondered how they could possibly turn the huge lumbering coach around without becoming stuck in the soft dirt next to the road.

She walked around the back of the coach and was astonished to see that Severin had dismounted and was involved in an animated discussion with several of her fellow travellers who were pointing at the coach. One of the young boys ran forward to hold Severin's horse. But when Figaro helped him slide his good arm from his coat, her amazement turned to dismay. Surely he did not intend to help.

At first he gave directions, but when one of the heavy wheels temporarily stuck in the mud, she was alarmed to see him set his good shoulder to the coach. She bit her lip to keep from calling out to him—she doubted he would welcome her concern.

Another quarter of an hour passed before her carriage was finally facing the right direction.

Severin returned to her side. A circle of dirt stained his white shirt and a smear of mud was on his cheek. 'It is safe for you to ride inside now.' He eyed the heavy old coach. 'There are lighter vehicles, you know. Ones that do not look as if they are about to lose a wheel at any moment.'

'Since I rarely use a carriage, I cannot see much sense in purchasing a new one. This suits me very well. It has proved to be very reliable.' She certainly did not intend to spend her small portion on such a thing. She frowned at him. 'Whatever possessed you to help move the carriage? What if you have injured your arm again?'

'I haven't,' he said briefly. 'Get into the carriage. I will ride alongside you to the inn.'

She searched his face, suddenly noticing he looked rather tired. 'Are you not going to stay there? I do not think you should travel any further.'

'I am fine,' he said curtly.

She turned and mounted the carriage before he could notice her flushed cheeks. She did not look at him as he closed the door. She stared out of the window at the sky, which was darkening. She hoped it would not rain on him. But, of course, what did it matter to her? He did not want her concern.

They had gone perhaps a mile, before the wind whipped up and rain spattered on the carriage roof. She saw a flash of lightning towards the distant hills. When the thunder came, she jumped, clutching her reticule. Then the storm began in earnest as hail pelted the roof of the carriage. The vehicle ground to a halt and she saw Figaro had stopped under a clump of trees. The pelting of the hail and rain lessened. In a moment, the door opened and Severin appeared. Water dripped from his hat down his face. 'We must halt until the hail stops.'

'You and Figaro must come inside.'

He shook his head. 'We cannot. We must stay with the horses.'

'Is there anything I can do?' She did not like the idea of remaining inside while they were out in the elements.

'Stay here.'

He closed the door. She cringed at the next crash of thunder. What if they were hit by lightning? Her worries turned to Mariana, who had always been afraid of such storms. Would Simon be able to comfort her? What if they, too, were on some road, seeking shelter from the storm instead of somewhere dry and warm?

She could feel the horses' nervousness for, when they moved, the carriage rocked. She peered out the window and saw Severin standing with his horse under another clump of trees. He was speaking to the animal, stroking its neck as water dripped down their necks. A lump rose to her throat. Not only because they both looked rather forlorn, but because she had not expected him to show such tenderness.

The thunder rumbled again, but this time further away and the rain suddenly let up as quickly as it had come.

Severin gathered the reins of his horse and led him to the carriage. Cecily opened the door. 'Are you all right?'

'Yes. And you?'

'I was not out in the rain. You must ride the rest of the way inside. Could we not tie your horse to the back of the carriage?'

'I could, but he is limping a little and I don't want to risk further injury. We are not far from the inn. I'll lead him the rest of the way.'

'But what if you catch a chill?'

'You are fussing again,' he said, his expression cool. 'Don't.'

Feeling rebuffed, Cecily sat back against the cushions, as the carriage started forward. He had made it clear he did not welcome her concern, so why she persisted was beyond her.

The sudden rain had left great puddles on the road. The

carriage lumbered into the inn yard only a little ahead of Severin. By the time she had dismounted, he had arrived. His horse was indeed limping. She caught up to Figaro and spoke to him in a low voice so Severin would not hear. 'Please see to the Duke's horse. Even if he refuses to allow you, you must do so when he is not present.'

Figaro nodded. '*Sì*. I will not allow him to refuse.'

'*Grazie.*' To her great relief, Severin handed over the reins without argument. She hesitated for a moment and then decided Severin would most likely favour her with one of his sarcastic remarks if she appeared to be waiting for him.

The inn was old and dark and smelled of dampness and onions. From somewhere down a hall drifted the low murmur of conversation punctuated with laughter. No one appeared behind the heavy wooden counter, so she rang the bell. A man came through the door, wiping his hands on the dirty apron covering his large stomach. 'May I help you, *signora*?'

'I wish to procure a room for the night. No, two rooms.'

'Alas, I have only one, which another gentleman has requested. But since he has not yet paid and you are here, I will allow you to have it. But only if you pay now.' He named a sum that nearly sent her reeling.

Only one? Severin would need it. He could not possibly travel any further. She would think of something. Perhaps there was another inn nearby. 'I will take it.' She started to open her reticule.

'I would at least demand to see the room before handing over such a sum.' Severin spoke from behind her. He turned to the proprietor and spoke to him in rapid Italian. 'I require two rooms for the night. With a private salon. At a reasonable price.' His cool manner brooked no argument.

The proprietor, whose name was Signor Bernelli, now appeared apologetic. His prices were always reasonable; perhaps the *signora* had misunderstood. Certainly there was a second room, although it was small and, since it was over the common rooms, noisy as well, but he would charge next to nothing for it. But a private salon…! After much haggling, Severin managed to procure a private parlour for an exorbitant price. He paid no heed to Cecily's protest that it was not necessary. 'I've no doubt I could purchase the inn several times over if I desired,' he said after they were shown to the small, musty room.

'Sit down. I've requested tea to be brought to you and a fire lit.' He started towards the door.

She remained standing. 'Where are you going?'

'To the stables. I need to see to my horse.'

'I asked Figaro to do that. You must sit.'

'I have been sitting all day.'

'Sitting on a horse is hardly the same thing. Perhaps you do not recall that two nights ago you were badly injured.'

His half-smile was sardonic. 'Oh, I recall it all right.'

'Then I forbid you to go out.'

'You are beginning to sound like my sister.'

'I am beginning to think a sister is exactly what you need.'

'I do not quite envision you in that role. Don't fuss. I don't like it.' He left.

Cecily plopped down into the chair. She felt a great deal of pity for his sister. Reasoning with him was impossible, which perhaps came from him being a duke, though she strongly suspected he would be just as intractable if he were a peasant. Not that it was her affair if he chose to injure himself further except that he would be useless in looking for Mariana and Simon. She would look for them herself.

None the less, she found herself on edge until she heard his footsteps. A rather sullen maid had come in and lit the fire so the room had lost some of its chill. He entered, water dripping from the brim of his hat.

She jumped up. 'Now you are soaked as well!'

'Yes.' He removed his hat and shrugged his good arm out of his coat. 'I forbid you to say any more about my condition.' He draped his coat over a chair in front of the fire and set his hat on the seat. He stood there for a moment and then turned just as the maid returned with a tray.

Severin directed her to place it on the table. This time she smiled in quite a flirtatious fashion, and lingered to inquire if milord needed anything further.

Cecily sat back down in her chair and waited as the girl removed the covers. Severin took the chair across from her. The maid left and the room suddenly seemed too quiet despite the sounds coming from elsewhere in the inn. She glanced over at Severin. His face was drawn and his eyes had a peculiar glassiness about them she had come to associate with a fever. She had no doubt that, if she said anything, he would snap at her. His eyes locked with hers for a moment so she looked away and picked up her fork.

The food was remarkably good and she found she was actually hungry. She had eaten a good quarter of her meal when she glanced up and found Severin watching her, his plate untouched. She put down her fork. 'Are you not going to eat?'

'I am not hungry.'

'You should at least eat a few bites.'

'I prefer not to.'

'Then at least drink some of your wine.'

'You are beginning to sound like my old nanny. Or a wife,' he said deliberately.

If he hoped to quiet her, he succeeded. 'I certainly have no desire for those roles either.' She rose, her appetite suddenly gone. 'I am finished as well. In fact, I am extremely fatigued. If you do not object, I believe I will retire.'

He stood. 'Of course.'

'Are you retiring as well?'

'Yes.'

He looked terrible, but she doubted he would listen if she said anything. 'Goodnight then, your Grace.'

'I will escort you to your chamber.'

'I am certain I can find my way.'

'Not tonight.'

She bit back the sharp retort that sprang to her lips. 'If you wish.'

The room was at the end of a long passage. He waited until she stepped inside. *'Buonanotte, signora.'* He leaned heavily against the doorpost, his breathing laboured. It was then that she noticed the bright red stain on his sling.

'Your arm. It is bleeding.'

He glanced down. 'So it appears. I will bid you—'

'I need to look at your arm.'

'I assure you there is no need.' His face had that haughty duke look that made her want to hit him.

'You look as if you are about to swoon as well. You must come in and let me look at your arm. If you do not do it willingly, then I vow I will force you!'

'I rather think I might like that,' he drawled.

'Stop it! Must you say such idiotic things now? You are

bleeding; if you dare tell me to stop fussing over you, I will hit you!'

'I wouldn't dream of it.' He pushed away from the doorpost and then swayed. She caught his good arm. 'Please come with me.'

'If you insist.' He followed her into the room and sprawled down on one of the chairs. 'Now what?'

'I must remove your sling.'

'I can do it.'

'Let me do it.'

He did not protest as she knelt next to him and untied the cloth from his shoulder. He wore no waistcoat under his coat, only a loose linen shirt, and her stomach knotted when she saw how much blood had seeped on to his sleeve. His shirt was soaked with sweat and, from the heat radiating from his body, she feared he was feverish as well.

'You are not about to faint, I trust.'

She looked up and found his eyes on her face. 'Of course not. I am going to remove your shirt.' She reached for the first button, only to find his hand on hers.

'I think not.'

'There is no need for modesty. I was married, you know.'

'The only women who undress me are those I plan to make love to.'

She willed herself to meet his eyes, despite the heat in her cheeks. 'Then you must make an exception this time. I am not planning to completely undress you.'

'A pity—I suspect I would quite enjoy that.'

'I am beginning to think you are delirious.'

'Only with your presence.'

Her cheeks must be as flushed as his by now. She shook

off his hand. 'I am going to remove your shirt because I must look at your wound. I pray you will cease teasing me.'

'But I am not teasing you. I told you in Avezza that I would very much like to seduce you.'

She finally looked at him. 'I am about to lose my temper regardless of whether you are hurt or not. So I suggest you allow me to continue before I do something you will not like.'

'Then I had best allow you to have your way with me,' he said softly. His hand fell away.

'Yes.' She undid the remaining two buttons, pleased her fingers did not tremble despite her proximity to him and her tingling awareness. She finally rose. 'Can you raise your good arm? I can then slip the shirt over your head on one side and slip it down your injured arm without your having to raise it.'

'Very well.'

She managed to get his shirt off, although he tensed as she gently pried it from around the wound. Some of the blood had dried and, as gentle as she tried to be, she had no doubt it pulled on his skin. 'I am sorry if I hurt you.'

'On the contrary, you seem remarkably skilled at this sort of thing.'

'I often helped my husband when he was ill.' She brought the candle closer and suppressed a shiver. The wound was an angry red and the flesh around it was swollen. Although much of the blood was dried, she could see fresh blood seeping from one side of the jagged wound. 'How long have you been bleeding like this?'

'I've no idea. Hardly enough to concern yourself over.'

'I think some of the stitches have come loose, but I will have to clean the wound before I can tell.' She rose. 'I will ask Signor Bernelli for clean cloths, brandy and water. And to send for a physician. First you need to get into bed.'

'Then you will need to help me into my clothes. I've no intention of walking the halls half-naked.'

'I meant you must get into this bed.'

'Any other time I would be delighted, but I fear I cannot oblige you tonight.'

She gave him an exasperated look. 'Don't be difficult.' She picked up his shirt. 'I will see if these can be washed. By the time I return I expect to find you in bed.' She did not wait to hear his reply.

She suspected he was attempting to fob her off by his improper remarks, but she had no intention of allowing him to do so. She very much feared he had developed an infection and the thought terrified her.

She found Signor Bernelli in the taproom. She hesitated in the doorway of the crowded room but then the man spotted her and bustled forward. He listened to her, a little frown on his brow, and then his face cleared. 'You are more than fortunate tonight for at this very inn a most distinguished physician is staying. Doctor Pascali is doctor to the most prominent of personages many of them your fellow countrymen. I will inform him that his services are needed at once.'

Cecily was rather alarmed to see Signor Bernelli approaching one of the more boisterous tables and speaking to one of the men. The last thing she wanted was a man in his cups examining Severin. To her relief, the tall man with a pair of intelligent eyes in a thin face that followed Signor Bernelli, appeared sober enough. She was even more reassured after he followed her into the hall and inquired what he could do for her in a pleasant, cultivated voice and questioned the symptoms.

'Allow me to fetch my bag and then I will join you in your chamber immediately. I will have Signor Bernelli send up a basin of water and cloths.'

She returned to the room. Severin sprawled halfway on the bed, his eyes closed. She thought he was sleeping until he opened his eyes. 'I've taken your bed. My apologies, but I don't think I can leave it any time soon.'

'I would not allow it.' She resisted the urge to brush the dark locks away from his forehead. 'A physician will be here shortly.' Someone rapped on the door. 'In fact, he may be here now.'

'You constantly surprise me,' he murmured.

Cecily opened the door and found Dr Pascali, accompanied by one of the innkeeper's pink-cheeked daughters carrying a basin of water and some cloths.

Cecily stayed back while Dr Pascali examined Severin. He finally straightened. 'Your wound has developed a slight infection and the *signora* is quite correct in suspecting that you have torn several of the stitches. We must clean your wound and put in new stitches. And then you are not to move until your fever has gone unless you wish serious consequences.' He turned to the girl. 'Kindly fetch some brandy. You, Signora Renato, will assist me in cleaning and restitching his wound.'

'Of course.'

'I would prefer she leave the room,' Severin said.'

'I will need an assistant and I have no doubt Signora Renato is quite capable.'

Severin made no more protests. He refused the laudanum, but was finally persuaded to take a small glass of brandy. From his clenched fists and gritted teeth, she could tell he was fighting pain as they cleaned and then closed his wound. By the time the doctor finished, his forehead was dripping with sweat and he was breathing heavily. He fell back against the pillow.

Dr Pascali instructed her to bathe his forehead with water to bring down his fever. She could send for him if his condition worsened. Then he departed, leaving Cecily alone with Severin.

She dipped the cloth in the basin of water and wrung as much of the excess from it as possible. She turned to the bed and, as she leaned over him, he opened his eyes. 'My apologies, *cara*.' Then he promptly closed his eyes again.

Cecily finally collapsed into the chair next to the bed. Severin had fallen into a fitful sleep, the strong features of his face unexpectedly vulnerable. She realised with shock that she had not even thought of Mariana and Simon.

Chapter Seven

'*Signora, signora.*' The soft, urgent voice jerked Cecily awake. She opened her eyes, disorientated for a moment to find Signora Bernelli, the innkeeper's wife, standing next to her chair. Her mind cleared. She was in the parlour of the inn and she must have fallen asleep while reading.

'*Signora*, the Duke has awakened and asks for you.'

She bolted up. 'Is something wrong?'

'No, no. He wishes to see you.'

'I will be up directly.' She stood and winced. If she continued to sleep in chairs, she would barely be able to move.

She followed Signora Bernelli to Severin's room, the book clutched in her hand. He was sitting up in bed. He wore a loose white shirt, which she suspected belonged to Signor Bernelli since it appeared far too big. A scowl crossed his face when he saw her. 'Where were you?' he demanded.

Any worry she had entertained vanished. 'In the parlour. I suppose you had some reason for summoning me other than ascertaining my whereabouts.'

'I did not know where you were.'

'Did you ask Signora Bernelli?'

His scowl deepened. 'I wanted to see you.'

'Did you need something?'

'What were you doing?'

'Reading, and then I fell asleep. Is there something you wanted?'

His gaze raked over her. 'No. Nothing. I apologise for disturbing you.' Now his voice was stiff.

She bit back a sigh and advanced towards the bed. 'Is your arm giving you much pain?'

'Nothing to signify. Go back to your book.'

Something was obviously amiss. 'What is it you wanted? I thought by going to the parlour I might give you a chance to rest quietly. I did not intend to abandon you.'

'I've no doubt you find sitting with me damnably tedious.'

'Do you wish me to sit with you?' It had never occurred to her he might actually want her company.

'I do not wish to bore you.'

So he did want her company. At least that is what she read into his cryptic conversation. She took the wooden chair next to the bed, vaguely noting that Signora Bernelli had left the room. 'That is quite understandable when one is ill. Marc...my husband complained of the same thing.' Until the end when he was too weak to do much of anything. 'I would read to him or we would play cards or sometimes just converse if he wished to.'

Something flickered in his eyes. 'So I do not suppose you would care to do any of those things with me,' he asked carelessly.

'If you want me to. Which do you wish? I would not recommend having me read to you unless you have a taste for Gothic romances.'

A little smile touched his mouth. 'Ah, yes. I recall you mentioned reading about headless spectres when we were in the maze.'

'It is not my romance, but one left behind by another English traveller. Signora Bernelli loaned the volume to me.'

'But you intend to read it?'

She flushed. 'I did not wish to offend Signora Bernelli by refusing it.'

His eyes held a wicked gleam. 'Of course not. Then you may read it to me. I should not want you to insult the good *signora*.'

She stared at him. 'You wish to hear a romance?'

'I suspect it will be quite entertaining.' He settled more comfortably against the pillows. 'You may begin whenever you wish.'

She eyed him, attempting to determine whether he meant to annoy her or really wished her to read to him. She could tell nothing by his expression. When she did not begin, he raised an expectant brow.

Very well. She would read *The Count of Bleakwood Forest* to him. It would undoubtedly serve him right if he was completely bored by the end of the first chapter. She opened the book.

Ten minutes later she glanced over at him. His eyes were closed, which reminded her of how sleepy she felt herself. Now that he was asleep she could attempt to wake herself by walking down to the parlour and back. She closed the volume.

'What does Amelia do now that her father has gone mad?'

Cecily jumped. 'I thought you were sleeping!'

'How could I when the fair heroine is about to be

evicted from her picturesque cottage?' he murmured. His eyes were now open.

'You were actually paying attention?'

'I would not insult you by falling asleep in the middle of such a riveting tale.'

She suspected he was amusing himself. 'I would hardly be insulted. Do you wish me to continue?'

'A few more pages.'

'Very well.' She reopened the book and began to read. She stifled a yawn after the first paragraph and forced herself to go on. Her voice trailed off and she refocused her eyes with an effort.

Cecily's voice had grown so soft Nico could scarcely hear her. Her head was nodding as if she were about to fall asleep at any moment. He was not faring much better. Her sweet, soothing voice had nearly put him into a pleasurable sleep and it was all he could do to keep from fading away himself. He was tired, but she must be equally so. Forcing her to read to him because he was bored was hardly gentlemanly. 'Signora Renato. Cecily.'

When she did not respond, he realised she had indeed read herself to sleep. Her head drooped to one side. He should have realised how tired she was. She had been up with him most of the night. His gaze roved over her flushed cheeks, her lips slightly parted. His groin tightened. He could almost taste her mouth under his; imagine carrying her half-asleep to the bed. She would lie beneath him, her hair tousled around her face, her eyes opening in sleepy invitation as he bent over her. He would…

He jerked his lustful thoughts back to reality. What the

devil was he thinking of? No matter how desirable he found Cecily Renato, he could not afford to involve himself with her. He could not make her his mistress even if he knew she would agree, which he very much doubted. She would be too complicated and not only because of Simon and Mariana.

She turned a little and made a small sound. She must be uncomfortable. He scowled and threw back the covers. He sat on the edge of the bed for a moment, pleased his head did not spin quite so much this time. He stood and looked down at her. He doubted she weighed much. If he was careful, he was unlikely to re-injure his arm. He slipped his good arm under her arms and his injured arm under her legs. Making certain his uninjured arm supported most of her weight, he lifted her from the chair. She murmured something, but did not wake as he gently laid her on the bed. He drew the sheet up over her shoulders and then sat on the bed next to her, annoyed to find he was slightly dizzy from the exertion. He gazed down at her for a moment and he found himself wanting to plant a tender, intimate kiss on her forehead.

He rose abruptly, ignoring his spinning head. He could not afford any tender feelings towards this woman.

Cecily awoke with a start to the sound of rain pounding on the window. She had no idea where she was and could not fathom why she was in a bed, fully clothed. She vaguely remembered reading to Severin and she must have fallen asleep. She sat up abruptly and saw she was in Severin's bed. Her gaze fell on the chair next to the bed and she saw he was sprawled in it, eyes closed, his head lolling against the back.

Her confusion increased. Why was he in the chair and

she in the bed? And how long had they both been sleeping? She glimpsed the sky through the window and thought it was still early evening despite the dark sky.

She swung her legs over the side of the bed. Severin did not move. He must be terribly uncomfortable. She had been cramped, but he must be doubly so with his long, muscular frame. It was a wonder he had been able to fall asleep. It occurred to her, then, that he must have carried her to the bed, for she could not remember stirring enough to make her way on her own.

Her cheeks heated just thinking about it. At the same time she wondered what had possessed him to do so in the first place. What if he had opened his wound?

Worried, she slid from the bed so that she could look more closely at him. Thank goodness, she saw no telltale red staining the rough linen of his shirt. She should wake him and insist he return to the bed. He stirred a little. Her gaze fell to his mouth and her knees felt almost weak as she suddenly remembered how his mouth had felt on hers. What would it be like to kiss him again? But this time she would want to tangle her hands in his thick dark hair and then...

She drew away, horrified at the direction of her thoughts. Whatever was she thinking of? She could not possibly be lusting after the Duke of Severin. Respectable women did not do such things. At least she did not do such things. She had enjoyed the intimacy of the marriage bed, as brief as it had been before Marco became ill, but had not thought about such things at all since his death.

He stirred again and she stiffened. He slowly opened his eyes and she jumped. 'You are awake,' he said.

'So…so are you.' She prayed he would not guess the direction of her thoughts.

'Yes.' He raised his head and winced.

'Your neck must be very stiff. I…I have no idea why you are not in bed.'

A faint smile touched his lips. 'Because you were there. I was not certain you would appreciate my joining you.'

'I should not have been there in the first place. I am not the one who is wounded.'

'You needed to sleep. In a bed. I've no intention of allowing you to collapse because you've worn yourself out by nursing me and sleeping in chairs.'

His kindness touched her. 'You should have wakened me.'

'And deny myself the pleasure of holding you in my arms?'

She flushed and decided to ignore his ridiculous comment. 'You might have reopened your wound.'

'But I did not.' He rose. 'This argument is pointless since the deed has already been done. You will be glad to know, however, that Signor Bernelli has informed me that the room next to this one is available for your use.'

'Yes. That will be nice.'

He watched her with his impenetrable expression. 'You do not seem over-enthused at the prospect.'

'Of course I am. As long as you are certain you will not need anything in the night.'

'Any needs I might have are ones I am certain you would not wish to fulfil.'

She managed to keep her voice calm. 'Then I had best move my possessions next door. Are you well enough to come to down for dinner? Or do you wish a tray in your room?'

'A tray in my room.'

'Very well.' She inched towards the door. 'I will inform Signora Bernelli, your Grace.'

She turned, but not before she saw his swift frown.

By the next day, the rain had let up and the sky was blue and cloudless. Cecily ate breakfast and then made her way out to the stables. She was forced to skirt around several large puddles, one of which seemed to be the size of a small pond. She was relieved to see the horses were in good condition, although the fetlock of Severin's bay was still a little swollen. Figaro did not seem very hopeful about the condition of the road, however, and thought it would be another day before they dried enough to make a journey at all possible.

She picked her way back to the inn, disappointed by the news. Now that Severin did not seem to be in imminent danger, she was anxious to resume the search for Mariana. She would not worry that, if she left him, he would have no one to look after him. Not that he seemed to want her anyway. He had avoided her since she had moved to the adjoining room and they had barely spoken, which was just as well—she had made every attempt to avoid him as well. He would not mind if she went on without him.

At least, she hoped he would not.

She wiped her now muddy half-boots on the old rug in the inn's hall and then wandered into the parlour. Whatever was she to do for the day? Her room, although neat, was small and cramped. She could take a short walk, but she would probably ruin her half-boots. Or she could—

'Good morning.'

She gasped when Severin suddenly rose from a chair on

the other side of the room. He was dressed in one of Signor Bernelli's loose white shirts, with his injured arm in a sling, and a pair of borrowed breeches that were both too short and too loose. The ill-fitting clothes did nothing to detract from his dangerous masculine appeal and her heart thudded much too hard. 'What are you doing up?'

'Looking for you. I had almost begun to think you had deserted me.'

'Of course not.' At least not for a while. 'Why ever would you think that?'

'I have not seen you since yesterday when you woke up in my bed.'

He did not need to make it sound so…so provocative. 'It was my bed to begin with, might I remind you.'

'You are correct. Your bed, then. I have not seen you since you woke up in your bed.'

'I rather thought you did not wish to be disturbed.'

'It depends on who is disturbing me.'

'I see.' He was going to be difficult again. When was he not? 'Are you certain you should be up?'

'Quite certain. I need to check on the horses.'

'I have already done so. They are in good health, although the swelling on your bay is not completely gone. Figaro does not seem to think the roads are yet passable.'

He looked faintly surprised. 'You have gone to the stables?'

'I wished to see if it was possible to leave today.'

'I trust you intended to discuss these plans with me.' He finally moved into the room.

'Well, yes. I thought, if you were still not very well, that I could perhaps go on to search for Mariana.'

'Sit down.'

She frowned at him and then realised he still appeared rather pale. He would not sit if she did not. She took the chair near the small table and he seated himself in one across from her. 'I doubt if one more day will make much difference,' he said coolly. 'Simon will see that Mariana is safe. It is possible they are already married. If they are not, they will be. He will not ruin her, if that is what worries you.'

'I never thought he meant to ruin her. But they are so young…what can they possibly know about marriage? I know how much you object to a marriage between them and I would not want her to be unhappy because you…his family does not approve. Nor do I want your family to be unhappy because they do not approve of Mariana. One does not marry just a person; one marries their entire family. I could not bear for Mariana or Simon to be miserable because they have married like this.'

'You do not need to worry about how Mariana will be received. I suspect my mother will be more than delighted to have someone in the family who is from her own country. Her family knew Mariana's uncle's family very well.'

She had forgotten that. 'Dear Lord, what will I tell Raf?'

His expression hardened a trifle. 'I will deal with Vianoli.'

She took a deep breath. 'Is it true that you and Raf have quarrelled?' For a moment, she did not think he would answer.

'Yes,' he finally said.

'Will you tell me why? Barbarina will only talk of duels and fights, but will tell me nothing more. Raf has never said anything. I would not ask if it were not for Mariana and Simon.'

'You know nothing about it?'

'No.'

'Very well, I will tell you.' His eyes did not leave her face. 'We quarrelled, if one can call it that, after Angelina, my fiancée, died. He said that, if he ever discovered I had anything to do with her death, he would kill me. I blackened his eye.' His voice was cold, emotionless.

She stared at him, a sick feeling in her stomach. 'Why? Why would he say such a thing? Marco told me her death was an accident.'

He rose. 'She asked to meet me that day. She was agitated, upset when she left the house. Raf also knew that Angelina and I had argued the day before.' His hand gripped the back of the chair in front of him. 'Her death was ruled an accident, but there were bruises on her arm as if someone had grabbed her. The physician said they were a result of her fall.'

Dear God. Beneath his cool recital she sensed his deep anguish. She had felt a sort of general sorrow that Angelina's young life had ended so tragically, but until now had not really experienced the full impact of her death on those around her. She wanted to go to him, put her arms around him as she would Mariana, but he would reject her. Instead she said, 'It is hardly unnatural that you and Angelina argued, for people do. And unless one knew why Angelina was upset, one cannot assume it had to do with you. It does not make any sense at all for Raf to even think of blaming you.'

'Oh, but it does.' His gaze was fixed on her face, his eyes bleak. 'For Angelina had begun to have doubts about our marriage. I fully expected her to end our betrothal that day. Raf knew about her misgivings. There is one more thing, something I did not believe to be true until I saw his face that day. He was my friend; I should have known. Known that Raf, too, was in love with Angelina.'

She stood then and went to him and placed her hand on the sleeve of his coat. 'I am so sorry,' she whispered.

He stared down at her for a moment. 'Don't be.' He pulled away from her. 'I must make my apologies. I am going to the stables and then for a walk. We will leave for my villa tomorrow. It is possible Mariana and Simon are there. If not, we will continue on to Venice. You will stay with my mother until we discover Mariana and Simon's whereabouts.'

She could not manage any sort of reply. He sketched a brief bow and walked away while a little part of her heart seemed to die within her.

Chapter Eight

Nico finished tucking his shirt into the top of his freshly washed breeches and then leaned back against the dresser for a moment, biting back a curse. He was still weaker than he cared to admit, but he was determined they would leave this place today.

As well as apologise to Cecily for walking out on her in such a boorish fashion. He still saw the stricken look on her face when he pulled away from her.

He'd never told anyone why he and Raf had argued. He had never spoken the words he'd carried in his heart and mind: Raf was in love with Angelina. The compassion in Cecily's eyes only increased his guilt and, in some strange sense, made him angry. He wanted neither her kindness nor her pity—he did not want her concern stirring up the feelings he'd long buried.

Which did not excuse his rudeness. They could not afford to be on poor terms, particularly since they were most likely to soon be related—which would pose a new set of damnable complications.

'*Signora.*' Cecily started out of her reverie and looked over at Severin who sat in the opposite corner of the carriage. He had decided to stable his horse at the inn and ride in the carriage with her. He'd said little as they readied for the journey and she had been in no mood to attempt conversation. Not after yesterday. Not when he made it clear he wanted nothing from her.

'Yes, your Grace?'

'I wish to speak to you for a moment.'

'If you wish.'

'I wish to apologise to you for my rudeness yesterday when I walked away from you.' His voice was cool, but the hint of stiffness in his tone told her that the apology did not come easily.

'You do not need to apologise. I quite understand that you were—'

'I do not want your understanding. I am apologising to you, not asking you to justify my behaviour.'

'Very well. I accept your apology.' She knew her voice was equally icy, but she did not want him to guess how much his coldness hurt. She turned her gaze to the window, telling herself it did not matter. His affairs were none of her concern. He was none of her concern. Once they found Simon and Mariana they would part company and she would never need to lay eyes on him again. Except if Mariana and Simon were married, then they would be related by marriage and she would be forced to see him. She would treat him coolly and quite put aside—

'Hell. Cecily.'

'Yes?' she said, her gaze now on a passing vineyard.

'Will you at least look at me?'

She finally turned to him. 'Why?'

'Because I'd at least like to see your face when I offer you another apology.'

'I have no idea why you would wish to do so.' She was being quite childish. In fact, she was behaving very much like Mariana did when she was hurt.

'For—' He stopped. 'For being so damnably difficult.'

'I do not suppose you can help it.'

He stared at her and then laughed shortly. 'You never fail to surprise me. Do you not wish to take me to task over this?'

'I doubt that would change anything. We would probably quarrel and then the rest of the journey would be exceeding uncomfortable.'

'You are undoubtedly right.' His eyes were still on her. 'Do you think we could possibly declare a truce? I'll promise to be less difficult and you…' he paused '…you will promise to converse with me.'

'How can I tell when you are fulfilling your terms?'

'You mean to say I am always difficult?'

'Yes.'

'You are wrong, I can be very agreeable at times.'

'Most likely when you are getting your own way.'

This time his laugh held genuine amusement. 'Of course. So, if you converse with me, I can demonstrate how very agreeable I can be.'

Her hurt was fading and she found she was starting to enjoy herself. 'I imagine the topics must be ones of your own choosing as well?'

'Yes, although I might be generous and allow you to choose one.'

'Only one?'

'It depends. Perhaps another if you meet certain terms.'

'What terms?'

'First you must call me Nico.'

'That is hardly proper.'

'But since I have been improper enough to address you by your given name, it is only fair that you do so in return. Say it.'

'Nico.'

His gaze fell to her mouth. 'Very nice,' he said softly.

She felt as if she had stumbled into dangerous waters. 'Which topic should we start with?' Her voice was too bright. Too breathless.

He leaned back against the squabs. 'Tell me how you came to marry Marco Renato.'

For a moment, she was taken aback. 'I met him when he came to London to visit a cousin. We were married shortly after that.'

'That hardly tells me anything.'

'What is it you want to know?'

'Were you in love with him?'

She stared at him and then looked away for a moment. 'Yes, I loved him.' But not at first. No, at first jovial Marco, with his ready laugh and twinkling, intelligent eyes, was only an escape from another marriage she knew would break her heart. She did not know then that her marriage to Marco would break her heart as well.

'And your family? I cannot imagine they were pleased to have you so far away.'

'My parents died when I was fourteen. I had only my grandmother. She was not pleased when I married Marco.' She tried to smile. 'Perhaps we could choose another topic.'

'Why?' he asked quietly. 'Why was your grandmother displeased?'

'Because I was to marry someone else. I...I broke the betrothal and then I met Marco. We were married in Scotland.' She waited for his condemnation, but there was none. 'I fear my past is quite disreputable.'

'Why did you break the betrothal?' His voice was impersonally curious.

'Because the man I was to marry kept a mistress. I know I should not have been shocked and accepted it—it is not at all unusual—but he made no secret of his relationship. Once I saw them together. It was at a ball... I did not mean to see them and they never saw me.' Her cheeks heated and she stared down at her folded hands. 'After that I could not bear the thought of marrying him.' Or having him touch her. She had thought herself in love with Charles Winstead and had treasured the thought that his attentive behaviour and charming manners meant he had begun to care for her. Stumbling upon him locked in an embrace with his mistress shattered her illusions.

'He was a damnable idiot.'

She looked up, taken aback to see the anger in his face. 'He was only doing what most men do, I suppose.' That is what her grandmother had told her.

'You are wrong. Not all men would behave so despicably. Any man who would keep a mistress when betrothed to you is a fool. And wholly undeserving of you.'

She shook her head, not believing his words. 'His mistress was very beautiful and sophisticated. All the things I was not. Sometimes I could scarcely utter a sentence when I was around him. I have no doubt he found me very dull.'

'You are anything but dull. As for the other, you are quite lovely.'

'I really am not. I am very ordinary—'

'Quite lovely, as I have told you before. And very desirable.'

Something in his cool tone told her he was not paying her an idle compliment. She glanced away, feeling oddly vulnerable and a little afraid. Of what, she did not know. He had flirted with her and kissed her and she had not been half as shaken as she was now with him sitting across from her in the close confines of her carriage.

Thank goodness he said nothing more, although conversation would have been difficult for, as they continued on, the road became increasingly uneven and the carriage bumped and jolted along. She hung on to the strap and prayed the carriage would not fall apart.

The carriage suddenly shuddered and jerked to an abrupt, rocking halt.

'What is it?' she asked.

'I don't know. Wait and I'll find out.' He opened the door and stepped out. A moment later he returned. 'The back wheel is loose. We are fortunate Figaro noticed something was amiss and halted before it came completely off.' He held out his hand. 'I will help you down. You should not remain in the carriage much longer.'

'No.' She took his hand and cautiously stepped from the carriage. The road was deserted and nothing but vineyards stretched in either direction. The fresh air was welcome, but the sight of the back wheel was worrisome.

'Can you manage the horses while Figaro and I examine the wheel?' Nico asked.

'Yes.'

He gave her a brief smile. 'Good.'

She went to the horses' heads. They appeared unconcerned about the matter, the bay gelding merely blowing on Cecily's cheek while his companion stretched his neck towards an enticing patch of weeds. She heard Severin and Figaro speaking in rapid Italian, but could not quite make out the words. The late morning sun was warm on her cheeks, the sky a peaceful cerulean blue. She took a deep breath, willing her headache to go away.

Nico returned. 'The wheel is about to come off. The inn is perhaps a mile from here. We can walk while Figaro stays with the carriage or remain here while Figaro goes for help.'

'I would prefer to walk. Will Figaro be safe?'

'I doubt there are any *banditti* about now. I will leave him one of my pistols.' He looked down at her. 'Are you certain you want to walk?'

'I will be fine.' Anything was better than remaining idle along the road.

He did not look completely convinced, but said nothing more.

She waited while he gave Figaro instructions. She was beginning to wonder if they would ever find Mariana and Simon. She could only pray they were safe and trust Nico when he said Simon would not let anything happen to Mariana.

He returned to her side and then set off towards the village. The road ran along a river, which Nico said was the Brenta. A passage-boat passed them, towed by horses and across the river, through the trees, she could see the stucco roof of a villa.

The inn was located just outside the village. A grey cat sunned itself on a bench and opened one lazy eye as they approached. Inside, the stone hall was cool. Sounds of conversation and laughter came from one of the rooms. Nico turned to her. 'Sit down while I find the proprietor. I will procure rooms as I've no idea how long it will take to have the wheel repaired.'

Cecily took one of the benches just as a short, stocky man entered the hall. He came forward. *'Signor, signora.* I am Benvenuto Salvidori. How might I assist you?'

Nico told him, but when he requested two rooms the proprietor frowned. 'Two?' A slight frown crossed the man's face. 'I fear we only have one. There is a party of the English staying here a number of days. Perhaps as husband and wife you would not object to sharing a room. It is quite large and I am certain your lady would be most comfortable.'

Husband and wife? Her startled gaze flew to Nico's face. Wholly expecting him to deny it, she nearly fell off the bench when he said, 'Very well, we will take the room.'

The proprietor beamed. 'Good. Good. The room is prepared, so if the *signor* wishes to discuss the arrangements, my wife will be delighted to show the *signora* to the room.' He turned towards the door. 'Sophia!' he boomed out.

Almost instantly, a well-endowed woman who stood several inches taller than her husband burst through the door. He spoke to her in rapid Italian and she turned to Cecily. 'Of course, you must go immediately to the room and rest while the *signor* sees to the carriage.'

Cecily rose and cast an uncertain glance at Nico, but Signora Salvidori was already walking away. Cecily had no choice but to follow her.

The room was indeed large, much larger than those at the previous inn. Sunlight flooded the room with cheerful warmth. The bed was high and old.

Signora Salvidori was speaking. 'You did not bring your maid? Then I will send my Portia to you. And then you will sleep. You must remove your pelisse and boots and I will find Portia.'

Signora Salvidori bustled away before Cecily could tell her she really did not need to rest. She unbuttoned her pelisse and removed it and then sat on a chair to remove her half-boots. She rose. The bed really did look quite inviting. Perhaps she could lie down for a very short time. A plump girl who must be about Mariana's age entered the room. 'Mama wishes me to assist you,' she announced.

She did not really look much like Mariana, but Cecily felt a tug at her heart and a surge of longing for her daughter. She smiled. '*Grazie*, but I do not intend to rest for very long. I can sleep in my gown.'

The girl's face fell and Cecily relented. 'Very well. Just my gown, then.'

Portia helped her from her muslin gown and her stays with surprising alacrity. Cecily thanked her and, as soon as Portia departed, climbed into the bed. She closed her eyes, images of the carriage and Severin's face swimming before her eyes as he told her she was lovely. And desirable. Soon the images blurred together and then she faded away.

Cecily opened her eyes and for a moment, had no idea where she was and why she was in bed in the middle of the day. Then she remembered; she had gone to bed intending to take only a short nap. It appeared, however, she had been asleep for a very long time.

She sat up abruptly and nearly gasped when she saw Nico's long frame sprawled in a wing chair near the window. His head lolled against the high back and from his deep even breathing she knew he was asleep.

Heat stained her cheeks when she realised her shift had slipped off one shoulder, exposing far too much flesh. No matter that he was hardly in a state to notice, she still felt self-conscious. How was she to dress if he were still in the room?

She spotted her gown draped over the back of a chair. He seemed to be sleeping soundly; she could quietly retrieve her gown and at least put it on over her shift. She could probably manage to tie the tapes of her gown and, after Nico left the room, summon Portia to help her into her stays.

She threw back the covers and slipped from the bed as silently as possible. Fortunately, the gown was on the opposite side of the bed from Severin. She slipped it on but her attempts to tie the tapes proved futile.

She reached around and found she could not quite close the back 'Drat!'

'What are you doing?'

She gasped and her head jerked up. Horrified, she froze and the gown slid from her shoulder. Cecily tugged it up and crossed her arms over her chest to keep it from falling any more. She forced herself to meet his gaze. 'Putting on my gown.'

'The procedure does not seem to be going well. You appear to need help.' To her mortification, he stood and she backed up as he came towards her.

'I assure you I do not.'

He stopped in front of her. 'But I think you do.' He held out his hand. 'Allow me.'

'I couldn't possibly.' She took another step back.

'I only wish to return the favour.' A slight smile touched his mouth. 'I believe you helped me numerous times with my, er…personal needs over the past few days.'

'You were ill, so there was a difference. This would not be at all proper.'

'We seem to be far beyond the proprieties at this point. Turn around. I merely wish to help you into your gown, not out of it.' His voice was rather impatient.

She had no doubt he would persist. Complying now would save further argument. Besides, his voice was too impatient to imagine he had seduction in mind. She turned.

As soon as she felt his fingers at her back, she knew this was a mistake. A shiver ran down her spine and languidness crept over her as he tied the tapes. When he lifted the hair away from her neck, she thought her knees might crumble. She closed her eyes and willed her body to stay still as he did the tape at the neck of her bodice. She prayed he would step away quickly.

He did not. He stood so close behind her she could almost hear his heart beat. She nearly stopped breathing and then his hand again brushed the hair from the nape of her neck. His arm came about her, pulling her back against his chest. His mouth moved across her nape and a little moan escaped her.

His mouth travelled to her ear and to her shoulder where he pushed down the left sleeve of her gown and rained kisses upon the exposed shoulder. When his hand cupped her breast through the layers of shift and gown, she thought she would explode. Her body was on fire, the warm throbbing growing between her legs and, for the first time since Marco, she felt a pure, hot desire that shocked her.

Panicked, she forced her eyes open, her hand going to the hand that covered her breast. He lifted his head almost right away and released her. He waited a moment before speaking. 'I was wrong. I do want to help you from your gown after all. But not against your will.'

'No.' She forced herself to turn although she could not quite make herself look at him. 'Th…thank you for fastening my gown.'

A surprised laugh escaped him. 'Ah, my sweet Cecily, I have just declared my desire to seduce you and you respond by merely thanking me.'

'I cannot think of what else to say. I imagine you merely wish to…to…' Words trailed off. Last time she had suspected that he meant to scare her from following him; this time, she sensed his purpose was far different.

'Make love to you, take you to my bed, be your lover,' he said bluntly. His eyes were on her face.

'I…' Her knees trembled and she thought her cheeks must be on fire. 'I…I fear I have not been offered *carte blanche* very often. I have no idea what one is supposed to say.'

'No, in most cases.'

'And this time?' The words sprang out of their own accord.

His eyes darkened, but his words were deliberate. 'I think you would be wise to say "no" this time as well.'

'Do you?'

'It would complicate matters damnably.'

'I suppose it might.'

'It would. Believe me, sweetheart.' He moved away from her. 'I will leave you to finish dressing.' He stalked to the door. Once there he turned. 'I had hoped to reach my villa tonight, but it appears the wheel will not be fixed in time so we will put up here. You do not need to worry about tonight's sleeping arrangements. I'll sleep in the stables if necessary.'

Cecily sank down on the chair, with the sensation of having been run over by a team of horses. Had the Duke of Severin really just declared he wanted to be her lover? He was undoubtedly mad, but then so was she.

Or else completely wanton…because the idea did not shock her half as much as it should.

Chapter Nine

Cecily watched as Nico's strong lean fingers curled around his wine glass. She forced her gaze to her nearly untouched plate. It was not the first time during dinner she'd found herself covertly watching him instead of eating. What would he do if she were to tell him she wished to accept his offer—well, not quite an offer, for he only said that was what he wished to do before he then proceeded to discourage her. What would he do if she told him she actually wanted to…to lie with him?

She closed her own eyes, an embarrassing stab of desire shooting through her. No doubt dozens of women had thrown themselves at him. She would be only one of many. He probably desired many women and, due to the unfortunate circumstances of finding themselves together, he had developed some sort of strange attraction to her, which would vanish as soon as they returned to society. Thank goodness, they would reach Venice in another day.

'Are you unwell?'

She jerked her head up and found him staring at her with a slight frown. 'I beg your pardon?'

'Are you not well? Your eyes were shut and you've hardly touched your dinner.'

'I am not very hungry. But I am perfectly well. Just rather tired. In fact, I will go to my room as soon as we finish the meal.'

'I am done.'

'Are you? You have not eaten much either.'

'It appears we share a common affliction, then.' He finished off his wine and rose. 'I will escort you to your room.'

She hesitated to ask him where he planned to spend the night. She doubted from his cool, polite manner he would tell her. She had just reached the door when it opened. She jumped back and found herself face to face with a man who stood on the other side. She saw his face and gasped. 'Raf?'

Rafaele Vianoli looked equally startled. 'Cecily? So it is your carriage. I...' He caught sight of Nico. His mouth fell open. 'Domenico?'

'Good evening, Vianoli.'

Raf stared at him and then back at Cecily, his expression incredulous. 'You are with him?'

'Well, yes.'

Raf's gaze returned to Nico and his eyes narrowed. 'I trust you have a reasonable explanation for your presence.'

'I've no idea whether you'll consider it reasonable or not. Nor do I particularly care.' Nico met Raf's eyes, his own hard. 'At this moment, I am taking Signora Renato to her room. She is tired.'

'She is coming with me.'

'She is under my protection. She stays with me.'

'I must contradict you. She is under my protection.'

'The hell she is.' Nico's hand closed over Cecily's arm. 'Step aside, Vianoli.'

'Release her.'

Horrified, Cecily saw Raf point a small pistol at Nico. 'Raf? What are you doing?'

Raf paid no attention. 'Let her go or I will shoot you.'

Nico dropped her arm. 'Go ahead.'

Furious, Cecily placed herself directly in front of the pistol. 'You will have to shoot me before you shoot him. But if you so much as touch him, I will spend the rest of my life making you pay.'

'Cecily, stay out of this,' Nico said.

Raf stared at her and lowered the pistol. He looked back at Nico, his expression cold. 'So you have seduced her. Why? Revenge? Because of Angelina?'

'You bastard,' Nico said softly. 'Put down the pistol. I want an equal chance to kill you for insulting Cecily and suggesting I would dishonour her in such a despicable way. I'll send you to hell before I let you near her.'

Raf dumped the pistol on the table near the door. 'You are accusing me of insulting her?'

'Yes, damn you.'

Raf lunged at Nico. They both went down, crashing into the table, sending it and its contents to the floor.

'Stop! Stop!'

They were oblivious to Cecily's shouts as they tumbled over each other like a pair of deadly, snarling dogs. She was terrified Nico's wound would open and equally terrified they would succeed in killing each other. They rolled into an elegant wing chair, Rafaele hitting his head, and then he had his hands around Nico's throat. Then Nico's hands were around his.

'No!' She snatched the pistol from the floor and pointed it at them. 'Stop! Or I will shoot you!'

They paid her no heed. She looked around and her eyes lit upon a vase filled with flowers. She snatched it up and dumped the contents over the nearest man. Raf reared back in shock as water and flowers poured down his neck.

'*Maledizione!* What are you doing?'

'Stopping you from killing each other.' With a shaking hand, she pointed the pistol at them. 'If either of you moves, I will shoot you.'

Nico had managed to sit and was now slumped against the wall. Water dripped from his head and he was breathing heavily. None the less, a corner of his mouth twitched. 'Do you even know how to use that thing?' he managed to ask.

'I can swear she does not. She refused to allow my cousin to instruct her.' To her astonishment, Raf looked amused. 'You had best give me the pistol before you do shoot one of us.'

'No, for I think you have both gone mad. How dare you accuse him of seducing me? He was ill most of the time!'

'Cecily, I did not mean…' Raf held out his hand. 'You are upset. At least give me the pistol.'

'No!' She backed up and stepped on something soft and slick. Her foot slid and she was falling. She attempted to regain her balance and then was pitching forward on to the floor. A sharp pain shot through the side of her head and for a moment the world spun around her. She closed her eyes.

Someone knelt next to her. 'Cecily. Damn it! Can you hear me?'

Nico. He touched her cheek.

'Swearing at her less might help.' Now Raf was next to her.

She forced her eyes open and attempted to roll to her side. She could not allow Raf to hurt Nico. 'No. Stop.'

Nico's face hovered over hers, his eyes dark with worry. 'Don't talk, sweetheart.' He slipped one arm under her head and the other under her legs and rose with her in his arms. The movement made her head hurt and she moaned.

'I am taking her to her room. Tell Signor Salvidori to send for a physician. Send Signora Salvidori to her as soon as possible.'

'Yes.' Raf's voice sounded equally grim. 'I will go now.'

'You cannot carry me. Your arm.'

'My arm is fine. Don't argue.' He strode from the room and she could do nothing but close her eyes while he carried her up the stairs and down the passage to the room. Somehow he managed to unlock and open the door and set her gently on the bed. She winced when her head touched the pillow. To her surprise he sat on the bed next to her. 'Where does your head hurt?'

'Only on the right side.'

'Let me see.' Despite his gentle touch, she jumped when his hand brushed over the spot.

'There is a small cut and you will undoubtedly have a nasty lump.' He drew back and she saw the bruise across his cheekbone.

'You are hurt.'

'Not as badly as Vianoli, however.' He took her hand. 'Do not do such a foolish thing again. Give me your word you will never step in front of a pistol again.'

'I did not want him to kill you,' she said softly.

'Cecily,' he said hoarsely. He lifted her hand to his lips.

'Perhaps I should call you out after all.' Raf had entered the room.

Nico jerked back and dropped her hand. 'As you wish.'

Cecily shot up and her head spun for a moment. 'No! I will...will strangle both of you if you even say such a thing again!'

Raf's expression was hard to interpret, perhaps due to his swollen lip. He, too, sported a bruise across one cheekbone. 'I was only teasing, *cara*. I assure you I have no wish to have another vase of flowers thrown at me.'

Nico scowled at him. 'I suggest you do nothing more to distress her. Unless you want a bullet through you.'

'Nico, please.'

He looked back down at her, his expression softening. 'I am sorry. I promise no more fights.' Nico stood just as Signora Salvidori bustled in, carrying a basin of water with several cloths draped over one arm.

She went directly to Cecily. 'Ah, the poor *signora*! What have you done?' She set the basin on a table and looked at accusingly at Rafaele and Nico. 'Go, I will attend to the *signora*, for she needs a dry gown. Doctor Tartelli will be here soon and after he sees the *signora* I will have him see you.'

Raf glanced at Nico. 'We both need to change and then we will talk.'

'Yes.' Nico's expression had hardened.

'Raf!' Cecily said desperately.

He moved to the side of the bed. 'What is it?'

'Promise me you will not fight him again.'

He observed her for a moment. 'I promise I will not.'

He bent and brushed a kiss across her forehead. When he

straightened, she caught a glimpse of Nico's face. His bleak expression made her shiver. He met her eyes and looked away.

Doctor Tartelli came shortly after that. He cleaned and dressed her cut and said it was not very deep, but she must rest for a few days. He closed his bag and announced he would see to the *signori*. He promised Cecily he would examine the Englishman's arm. She could only hope Nico would allow that.

Signora Salvidori had just left the room when she remembered Raf did not know about Mariana and Simon. She sat up, dizziness overtaking her. She would probably faint if she attempted to get out of bed to look for him. She could only pray Raf would not find out until she had a chance to talk to him. For she dreaded to think of what Raf would do when he learned they had run off together.

Doctor Tartelli finished applying a plaster to the cut on Nico's forehead and straightened. 'There is one more thing. The *signora* asked me to look at a wound on your arm.'

Nico rose from the hard-backed chair. 'It is not necessary.'

'She was quite adamant, *signor*.'

'Then I suggest you allow him to do so,' Raf said. 'Unless you wish to distress Cecily further.'

The slight amusement in Raf's eyes hardly helped Nico's temper. 'There is no need for you to stay.'

'Except to ensure you comply.'

'I will, damn you. Go.'

Raf merely raised a brow. Nico slid his coat off one shoulder and then winced as it brushed against his injury. He nearly cursed when he glanced down and saw the small red stain on the sleeve of his linen shirt.

'We will need to remove your waistcoat and shirt, *signor*.'

The waistcoat came off easily enough, but raising his arm to allow the physician to help ease his shirt over his head made his arm hurt. He sat back down and then scowled when Raf crossed the room to his side and watched in silence while Dr Tartelli examined the wound.

'A stitch has come out, but I do not think it will be necessary to restitch it. The bleeding has stopped and there are no signs of infection. You would do well to restrain yourself from doing battle until the wound is properly healed.' He put his implements away, shut his bag and, after saying he would find someone to help Nico dress, left.

Nico saw Raf staring at his arm, his expression grim. 'When did that happen?'

'At the Villa Guiliani,' Nico said shortly. 'During the local fête. Cecily was with me. The attack occurred just outside the maze. She came very close to taking the knife instead of me.'

Raf's eyes hardened. 'What was she doing with you?'

'We were looking for my cousin and Signorina Renato. We thought they were in the maze together.'

'And were they?'

'Yes.'

'Do you have any idea where they are now?'

Nico eyed him, his eyes narrowing. 'No. Do you?'

'Yes. They are in Venice. At the Ca' Cappelletti.'

'Damn you,' he said shortly. He rose and reached for his shirt. 'Have they wed?'

'Not yet. They will as soon as you and Cecily reach Venice.'

Nico tugged the shirt over his head and winced. 'Contrary to your suspicions, I have not run off with Cecily for nefarious purposes. We hoped to stop them.'

'In Cecily's carriage? I am surprised you made it this far.'

'Her carriage has been the least of our problems.' He eyed Raf. 'What are you doing here?'

'I have just returned from Avezza, looking for you and for Cecily. No one seemed to know where either of you had gone. However, I did not expect to find you together.'

'I have not seduced her.'

'I apologise for that.' Raf hesitated. 'I must apologise to you for other words as well. The ones I spoke thirteen years ago. I know you had nothing to do with Angelina's death.'

Nico looked at the man who had once been his best friend. He had changed; his face was still handsome, despite the bruises, but more chiselled, and there was a hardness that had not been there before. At this moment, Nico had no idea whether he hated him or not.

'Perhaps you will tell me what has led you to this conclusion?' Nico could not keep the bitterness from his voice.

'You loved her.'

'So did you.'

'Yes. I loved her.'

'I did not realise that until after her death. I never intended to take her from you,' Nico said.

'But she was not mine. She loved you. Just as you loved her.' Raf glanced away for a moment. 'I understand if you do not wish to accept my apology. It seems very little in comparison to what we have lost.' He started towards the door, then paused. 'You are much in Cecily's debt. She would not threaten me if she did not believe in you. I promised her I would not hurt you. But if I find out that you have hurt her in any way, I will change my mind.'

'We are in agreement. For I would have no hesitation in

calling out any man who even thinks of hurting her. Including you.'

'I believe you would.' Raf left the room, closing the door quietly behind him.

Chapter Ten

Cecily rose from the edge of the bed. She held on to the bedpost for a moment while the room spun and then righted itself. She released it and took a few steps, pleased to find she could walk without swaying.

Through the open shutters she could see the brilliant blue of the sky. Although Signora Salvidori had informed her that the *signori* wished her to remain in bed for the day, Cecily had insisted on dressing. She was not about to stay in bed while there was any possibility that Raf and Nico might kill each other. Particularly after Raf learned of Mariana and Simon.

She left her room and entered the passageway outside her room. The staircase was to her left. She descended it and halted in the hall below. If she recalled, the room where she and Nico had dined was to her right. She skirted around a mound of luggage and started down the short hall. She found the room easily enough and the door was slightly ajar. She peered in and saw Raf and Nico standing together at the other end of the room. To her great relief, she saw no signs of impending violence.

Nico saw her first. A swift frown crossed his brow. He

broke away from Raf and strode towards her. She saw he was wearing a clean shirt and breeches and a coat she did not recognise. He was shaved. 'What the devil are you doing out of bed?' he demanded as he reached her side.

'I needed to speak to Raf.' She looked up into his face, now so familiar that she thought she had memorised every feature. The bruise across his cheekbone was now a dark purple. She resisted the urge to touch his face. 'Are you all right?'

'Yes,' he said shortly.

'You should be in bed as well.'

'Cecily.' His voice held a warning.

'I know. You don't like me to fuss and I remind you of your old nanny.'

A reluctant grin tugged at his lips. 'I apologise for that. You are nothing like my old nanny.' The look in his eyes suddenly made her feel shy.

She looked quickly away, only to find Raf's interested gaze upon them. For some reason, she felt even more flustered. To cover it, she said quickly, 'Raf, I must talk to you. I do not know what Ni…Severin has told you but—'

'What he did not tell me I have guessed. Nico is right, however. You should not be up.'

'But I am, so it is no use telling me I should go back to bed.'

Raf glanced at Nico over her head. 'Then come and sit down. We have things to discuss.'

She took the sofa he indicated and looked up at him. His lip was still swollen and he wore a dressing over the cut across his brow. 'You look horrid,' she said. 'In fact, both of you do.'

His smile was lopsided. 'I hope you will remember that

when you hear what we have to tell you.' He glanced at Nico, who now stood next to him.

'What is it?' A knot started to form in her stomach.

Nico spoke. 'Mariana and Simon are in Venice with my mother and sister.'

'Thank God!' Relief washed over her. 'Thank you. Oh, thank you.' Her daughter was safe. Then a thought struck her. She glanced from one to the other. 'Did you know that last night?'

'Yes.' Raf spoke this time. 'I told Nico after you were in your room. I was on my way back from Avezza and saw your carriage in the road, which is how I found you here.'

She stared at him. 'And you said nothing about it last night?'

He spread out his hands. 'I apologise. I fear that seeing you with Nico drove all other thoughts from my mind.'

'If you saw them, you must know that they ran away together! And that I would be frantic with worry! Instead you must fight after hurling the most stupid accusations at him! Could you not have guessed that we were travelling together because of them? I should strangle you! Both of you, actually!' she added when she saw the faint amusement in Nico's face. 'You knew last night as well!'

The amusement fled. 'By the time I knew, you were in bed.'

'You should have wakened me. But it does not matter now.' She took a deep breath, almost dreading the answer to her next question 'Did they…they marry?'

'They started out intending to do so, but changed their minds. By then it was too late to turn back to Avezza,' Raf said. 'They spent the night at an inn and the next day travelled to Venice. Lord Ballister brought her to the Ca'

Cappelletti. The Duchess knew I was in Venice and sent for me. Lord Ballister assured us his behaviour towards Mariana was honourable. I have no reason to doubt his word.'

'Is it possible, then, that they may not need to marry?'

'No, it is not possible,' Raf said gently. 'They spent the night at an inn without a proper chaperon. We could not insist they marry until you and Severin gave your consent.'

She looked at Nico, her heart sinking. He met her gaze. 'I have given my consent. We only need yours.'

She stared down at her lap and felt as if her heart was breaking. The reality she had tried to push away broke over her. Mariana would be gone, starting a new life in a faraway place where Cecily would never be welcomed. Her daughter's lovely face swam before her eyes and she already felt the pangs of missing her.

'Cecily?' Raf asked.

She looked up. 'Of course you have my consent.' She rose, her head spinning from the sudden movement. She waited until the world righted itself. 'I must beg your pardon. I believe I will take a walk.' She brushed past them before they could see how devastated she felt.

'Cecily. Wait,' Nico said.

'No.'

'Cecily. At least return to your room.' Raf had followed her across the room.

She shook her head and left them both staring after her.

'Are you going to let her walk away like that?' Nico demanded. 'She's hardly well—she looked as if she was about to swoon a moment ago.'

'I have found that it is impossible to force Cecily to do

anything she does not want to do. Or stop her from doing something she has set her mind to. You did not discover that in the time you spent with her?'

Nico scowled. 'I would expect you to exert more control over her. Particularly when it comes to her health.'

Raf's brow raised a fraction. 'What would you suggest? I carry her back to bed and lock her in her room?'

'If necessary, yes.' He wanted to wipe the crooked grin from Raf's face. 'What?'

The grin on Raf's swollen lips only widened. 'I suspect your journey together was most interesting.'

'Hardly,' Nico snapped. 'I was in bed a good part of the time with an infection and she was forced to nurse me.'

'Poor Cecily. I trust you were not too difficult.'

'I was damnably difficult. Are you going to find her or not?'

'I will leave it to you to do so,' Raf said blandly. 'I do not relish the prospect of informing Cecily I plan to lock her in her room after I carry her into the house.'

'Damn you,' Nico said and stalked out of the room before he broke his promise to Cecily and strangled Raf.

He found her sitting on a bench in the small overgrown garden on one side of the inn. He stopped and watched her for a moment. She sat on a bench in the shade of a tree. In her cream-coloured gown, her head bare and her hands clasped lightly in her lap, she looked like some sort of lovely, vulnerable creature in need of protection. His protection.

She was no longer his concern. Not with Raf here. Only a fool would fail to notice the affection and tenderness between them, the easy way they spoke to one another. He could imagine that once Mariana was gone, she would turn to Raf for comfort. Raf would—

He jerked his thoughts away, angry with himself for caring about her. Angry that once again he was in danger of wanting a woman already claimed by Raf.

He entered the garden. 'Cecily.'

She looked up at him and sniffed. He wanted to gather her into his arms and kiss away her tears. He frowned at her in an attempt to hide his traitorous thoughts. 'You should not be out here. You are far from well.'

'I am fine.' The little tremble of her lip betrayed her true state. She looked away from him as if she wanted him to leave.

'You are not. You are clearly distressed. Why? Because of Mariana and Simon?'

'I…I will be quite fine. As soon as I have composed myself I will return to the inn. Please go.' Her face was still averted.

'I meant what I told you before. Mariana will be welcomed into our family. You do not need to worry that she will not be accepted.'

'I…I know.' She half-looked at him now, her lips slightly parted.

'Then what is it? Simon? He will be a good husband and he loves her.' He was finding her soft vulnerable mouth distracting. 'You will miss her,' he finally came up with.

'Y…yes.'

'They will return to Italy probably quite often since Napoleon is gone. You can always come to England. And stay as long as you want.' He would do his best to stay away from her.

He was shocked when her mouth suddenly trembled. 'No, I…I can never return to England.' She stood. 'I…I must go to the house.'

'No.' He stood as well and caught her shoulders. 'Why can you not return to England?'

She held his gaze. 'Because I...I left in disgrace. My grandmother will not speak to me...and....'

'And?'

'There...there was a scandal when I ran away with Marco. I...I cannot let that hurt Mariana or Simon.'

'I will see to it that it will not.'

'You are very kind, but—'

'I am not kind,' he said roughly. 'But I vow I won't let anything or anyone hurt you.'

'You are kind,' she whispered. Her eyes, wide and vulnerable, and her slightly parted lips threatened his control.

'Cecily,' he said hoarsely. He bent his head towards her, but before he could possess her mouth some instinct made him look up. It was as if a fist slammed into his stomach when he saw Raf standing there. He dropped his hands from her shoulders as if he'd been burned. 'I beg your pardon.'

'Why?' Nothing in Raf's demeanour indicated he found anything amiss.

'Because—' He stopped. Confessing he was about to kiss Cecily would only make matters worse. 'We were about to return to the inn.' He sounded like a nodcock.

'Is that it? I hardly think you need beg my pardon for that. Or was it Cecily's pardon you wished to beg?'

'I've no idea.' What the devil was wrong with Raf? He was an idiot if he hadn't noticed anything amiss and damnably casual about Cecily if he had. Last night he'd been ready to kill Nico over Cecily but today he acted as if nothing had happened. 'We need to talk,' he told Raf.

'First you should greet your mother?'

'My mother?'

'The Duchess. She has just now arrived.'

He nearly reeled. 'What is my mother doing here?'

'She was at the Villa Cappelletti. I sent for her.'

'You sent for her?'

'Yes. She is understandably anxious to see you and Cecily.'

'She knows that I am here?' Cecily looked stricken.

Raf's lip twitched. 'I could hardly keep your presence a secret.'

'No, of course you could not.' She managed a wobbly smile, which made Nico want to gather her into his arms and reassure her all would be well.

Raf, damn him, should be doing exactly that. Nico intended to make certain that Raf understand exactly what his responsibilities were regarding Cecily. And that if Raf did not fulfil them, he would answer to Nico.

Chapter Eleven

The petite, dark-haired woman who caught Nico's hands looked nothing like the formidable Duchess of Cecily's imagination. She looked up into her son's face, half-smiling, half-crying. 'I should scold you terribly, only I was so worried when you disappeared and no one knew anything! Then we discovered Signora Renato was also gone, so Rafaele brought me to the villa and I was to wait there until he returned from Avezza. You cannot know how I felt when I received his message telling me that both you and Signora Renato are safe. Except now I see that you and Rafaele have fought and I will scold both of you for that.'

Nico lifted her hand and brushed a kiss over the back. 'We have called a truce, so you do not need to worry. I must apologise as well for not sending a message to you, but I expected to reach Venice long before this.'

'Next time you will do so.' She stepped back and her gaze fell on Cecily, who stood a little behind Nico and next to Raf. 'You are Signora Renato? But no one told me that you are so very young!' She went to Cecily and took her hands.

'Before I say anything, I must reassure you that Mariana is quite well for I know you must be anxious about her.'

'Thank you.' For she had not expected the Duchess to greet her with such generous warmth. 'I do not know how to thank you for caring for her, particularly under the circumstances. You are more than kind.'

'You do not need to thank me. I am only grateful that Simon thought to bring her to Venice and to us.' Her large dark eyes searched Cecily's face. 'Are you well, my dear? Your face is quite pale.'

'I am fine, only a little tired.'

'She is hardly fine,' Nico said. 'She fell and hit her head last night.'

'Then why have you allowed her out of bed?' The Duchess shot a reproving look at her son. She took Cecily's hand. 'You must sit down and after that Domenico and Rafaele will explain to me why they permitted you to hurt yourself in such a way.' Her hand on Cecily's arm, she guided her to the sofa. After Cecily sat, she turned a cool eye on the two men.

Nico glanced at Raf before he spoke. 'Cecily threw the contents of a pitcher over us. She slipped in the puddle.'

The Duchess started. 'And why did you do that, my dear?' she asked Cecily.

'They were fighting and I wanted to stop them. I feared they would kill each other.'

'I have heard it is very effective in stopping a dogfight. Did they come to their senses after that?'

'Only after Cecily threatened us with a pistol,' Raf interjected. 'She slipped when I attempted to take it from her because she thought I intended to shoot Nico. I consider myself responsible for her fall.'

The Duchess stared at them. 'I consider both of you at fault for behaving in such an ungentlemanly and unseemly manner.' She pressed Cecily's hand. 'I think, my dear, that you have had too many things to worry you in the past few days. For now you must go to your room and rest and after that I will take you back to Ca' Cappelletti so that I can properly look after you for a few days. We will leave for Venice after that. I am certain both Domenico and Rafaele will agree.'

'Of course,' Nico said politely. He did not quite look at her, nor was his manner any more warm when she left with the Duchess to go up to her room.

Cecily sat on the bed after the Duchess left her inn room, too restless to sleep. It was as if Nico had withdrawn from her ever since Raf had come upon them in the garden. For an instant she thought he intended to kiss her, but when Raf appeared he looked stricken as if he'd been caught committing a crime. Perhaps he thought Raf would call him out, but Raf had not seemed to notice anything amiss.

She sensed it was more than that—that it had something to do with her. It was possible that he regretted his earlier words when he had said he would not let anything or anyone hurt her, that he really did not want anything to do with her. Which was for the best, for she feared that he might have the power to hurt her most of all.

They had arrived at the Villa Cappelletti in the late afternoon. The house, situated on the Brenta River, in the midst of a large park, was built in the classical style with wide shallow steps leading to the entrance with its row of columns. The Duchess had insisted that Cecily be shown straight to her room and that for tonight, she would have her dinner on a tray. Cecily had just sent the tray away when the Duchess entered her room. 'I came to see if you would object to a visitor.'

'No, of course not.' She looked up and then fought down a stab of disappointment when she saw Raf. The Duchess quietly left them as he came to her side. He pulled a chair to the bed and sat down. 'We have not had a chance to talk. How are you feeling?'

'Better. And you? Your face still looks horrible.'

He flashed her a crooked grin. 'Thank you.' He took her hand. 'But it is you that I worry about.'

'I am fine.' She hesitated. 'I am sorry about Mariana. I should have guessed that matters were more serious between them. I never thought that she…that they would run away together. I would hardly fault you if you were very angry with me.'

'I am not. Mariana and Lord Ballister both assured me that you did everything you could to stop them. In fact, Mariana seemed to worry I would hold you to blame. However, it is not Mariana's affairs I wish to discuss, but yours.'

'Mine? I have none worth discussing.'

'Not even Nico?'

'Nico? He is not one of my affairs!' She flushed. 'Not that I have any affairs…that is, not those sort of affairs.' Under Raf's interested gaze, her words seemed even more tangled.

'You mean affairs of the heart? But why not? You are still young. Now that Mariana is to be married it is time that you consider your own heart. Marco never intended that you spend the rest of your life alone and without love.'

'I am not without love,' she said, stung. 'I have Mariana and you, and Vittoria and Serefina are very fond of me. I will have Barbarina, so I will hardly be alone.'

'Barbarina is not quite what Marco intended. Or what I meant. I am speaking of a husband or perhaps a lover.'

She flushed. 'I do not want to remarry and I have always thought that a lover would be most inconvenient!'

'Even Nico?'

'Why would you say such a thing?'

'I have seen the way he looks at you,' he said gently. 'If I had not come upon you today, he would have kissed you. Nor would you have objected, I think.'

'We were together on the journey and I…I suppose it was not unnatural for some sort of bond to develop. There is nothing more.'

'Are you certain?'

'Yes, of course.' Even as she spoke, the day at the inn flashed through her mind when Nico had told her he wanted her. Heat flooded her cheeks. 'Please, Raf, I pray you will say no more about this.'

'As you wish.'

'I do wish! Can we not speak of something else?'

'Then we will. I do not wish to distress you, but there is one more thing I must ask. Nico told me you were with him the night he was stabbed. He said the man wore a cloak and mask. Can you tell me anything more?'

'Only that I felt someone was watching us when we were in the maze.'

'But you saw no one?'

'No, no one. I thought perhaps I heard something in the bushes, but I was not certain. It was so dark and quiet.' She hesitated and decided she must tell Raf the whole of it. 'Barbarina had been saying such odd things that I wondered if I was being fanciful.'

'What sort of odd things?'

'Earlier that night, when we were in the supper booth, she told Ni...the Duke that he must stay away from me because I would not be safe with him. But he was the one who was hurt.' The sudden change in his expression alarmed her. 'Raf? What is it? Do you know why she would say such peculiar things?'

The dark look disappeared. 'No, I can think of no reason. I can only think she is becoming increasingly eccentric. I am only sorry she has frightened you.'

'You think, then, that Nico's attack had nothing to do with...with Barbarina?'

He took her hand. 'What I think is that you must not worry.' He released her and stood. 'I will leave you for now. I wish to tell you, however, that I am leaving tomorrow for Vicenza. I will return to Venice in time for Mariana's wedding.'

'Must you go?'

'Yes. It is possible I will have another commission. Do not look so worried. Everything will turn out as it should.' He bent and kissed her cheek. 'Be kind to Nico.' He left.

Be kind to Nico. The words echoed in her head. How could Raf suggest that she consider Nico for a lover? But then, two days ago she had been tempted to tell Nico that was exactly what she wanted.

This was madness. She meant to keep a safe distance between herself and Nico. She could not allow herself to think of him as anything other than Simon's guardian. In time, they would undoubtedly come to regard each other in the polite manner of those distantly related by marriage. Their journey together would fade away like a half-remembered dream.

Nico glanced at the clock. What the devil was Raf doing with Cecily? He'd gone into her bedchamber over a half an hour ago. Visions of Raf leaning forward to kiss her soft, desirable mouth, her sweet shy response, assailed him. Would she be surprised? Did she suspect Raf cared about her?

Did Raf suspect how much he desired her?

'Nico.'

He whirled around. Raf stood behind him. 'How is Cecily?' he asked.

'Better. It is good she will be under your care here.'

'She is under my mother's care.'

'But of course,' Raf said in the bland way that filled Nico with the all-too-familiar desire to mow him down. He did not seem to notice, however. 'I need to talk to you.' All traces of amusement left his face.

'What about?' Nico tensed, half-expecting Raf to tell him that he and Cecily were now betrothed.

'You did not tell me that before you were attacked that night, Barbarina told you that Cecily would not be safe with you.'

'I beg your pardon?'

'Shortly before you were attacked, Cecily said that Barbarina told you Cecily would not be safe with you.'

'She did. As it turned out, she was right.'

'Barbarina said much the same thing to me before Angelina died.'

Nico stared at him, a chill creeping up his spine. 'What exactly did she say?'

'She said that because of you Angelina was in danger.'

'When did she say that?'

'Perhaps a week before Angelina died.'

'Why did you not tell me?'

'Barbarina had always assumed that I would wed Angelina, which was one reason she did not approve of you. I thought she hoped that, if she could convince me that you were a danger to Angelina, I would stop the marriage. Afterwards, I thought that...'

'That perhaps you had been right,' Nico said grimly.

'Yes. But I was wrong.'

'You were wrong about me, but Angelina is still dead. It is possible Cecily was the intended victim, not me. If so, then it seems too much of a coincidence.'

'You are suggesting that Barbarina is responsible?'

'I did not think so at first, but now...' Nico looked away for a moment, and then back at Raf. 'Yes, I am beginning to think it is possible. But why?'

'She has always been rather mad,' Raf said slowly. 'But I have never thought her capable of violence. Until we know, we must consider the possibility that Cecily is in danger. I told Cecily that I am leaving tomorrow for Vicenza. I wished to ask you to watch over Cecily while I am away.'

'I would hope that under the circumstances you would remain here.'

'What circumstances?'

'Cecily is here. She has been injured; she is worried about Mariana, and now this. After yesterday, I would think you would realise that I am the last person you should ask to watch over Cecily.'

'After yesterday, I am convinced you are exactly the right person to keep her safe.'

'Perhaps you failed to notice that I nearly kissed her.'

'It was quite obvious.'

'I came damnably close to seducing her when we were together.'

'I suspected that as well.'

'I would expect that, instead of standing there with that devilish calm expression, you would be threatening to put a bullet through me.'

'And risk Cecily's wrath for the rest of my life? I think not.'

Nico resisted the urge to throttle him. 'Are you or are you not in love with Cecily?' he demanded. 'Because if you are, I've half a mind to put a bullet through you for allowing another man to touch her.'

Raf blinked. 'In love with Cecily?' He looked truly astounded. 'Where did you get that idea?'

'From Thais Margate.'

'Thais Margate? I had heard she was in Venice, but I did not know she had met Cecily.'

'She leased a house in Avezza.'

'Has she? Then perhaps she still hopes to become a duchess, so she would naturally try to dissuade you away from Cecily. She did the same with Angelina, did she not?'

'Last time she was right. Do you love Cecily?'

'I love Cecily, but I regard her as my sister just as she regards me as her brother. So you thought I was in love with her. That explains much.'

Nico's relief only made him surlier. 'Then as her brother I would hope you would tell me to stay away from her. If you recall, I just told you I wanted to seduce her.'

'But you did not.' He regarded Nico thoughtfully. 'I think it is perhaps best that Cecily visits England until we are assured she is safe. You will watch out for her in my place. Although she is at an age where she can decide whether she wishes to remarry or take a lover, I would be most grateful if you would see to it that any man who interests her is acceptable.'

The nonchalant tone of this pronouncement made Nico curl his fists. 'I suppose you will next ask me to interview suitable candidates,' he said through gritted teeth.

Raf's expression was bland. 'If you wish.'

'You know damn well I don't wish,' Nico snapped. 'If you continue on in this vein, I might decide to call you out after all.'

Raf eyed Nico's face, a smile tugging at his lips. 'Precisely why I know Cecily will be quite safe with you. I will retire now, for I wish to leave early tomorrow. I will see you in Venice in a week at Mariana and Simon's wedding. I have no objections if you are tempted to kiss Cecily again.' He was gone before Nico could gather his wits together to form a reply.

Why the devil had he worried about coming between Raf and Cecily when it turned out Raf had done everything but thrust Cecily into his arms?

He would laugh at the irony, only the matter was too serious. Now he no longer had Raf to use as an excuse to prevent him from giving in to his desire for Cecily. To make matters worse, he knew she was not indifferent to him. He could not ask her to become his mistress—she would be too complicated and not only because of Simon and Mariana.

Hell. He was known for his cool control. There was no reason he could not keep his head around Cecily. None at all.

Chapter Twelve

The following evening Cecily stood in front of the looking glass and smoothed down the skirt of her peach gown with nervous fingers. The Duchess had invited a cousin and her family to dinner and in a few minutes Cecily would go downstairs to join them. She had been to many a dinner party so she had no reason to feel so apprehensive. Perhaps it was that ever since she had left her house that fateful morning she'd had the sense of living in a different existence. A dinner party seemed so normal that she feared she would hardly know how to go on. Which was ridiculous, of course, she still remembered the conventions of polite society.

The knock at her door startled her. She opened it. Nico stood on the other side. Her pulse quickened at his appearance. Dressed in a bottle-green coat, and snowy starched cravat, his dark hair trimmed and fashionably arranged, he looked every bit the cool, arrogant English peer. The sort of man she would never dare approach in a London drawing room.

Her cheeks coloured when she saw he was staring at her

with similar appraisal. 'I am to escort you to the salon,' he finally said. 'If you are ready.'

'Yes. Yes, I am.' She started to step from the room when she realised she had forgotten her fan. 'I must get my fan first.'

She turned and went to her dressing table and found her fan. She took a deep breath. He was still the polite distant host. Raf had been quite mistaken—it was apparent Nico wanted to keep their relationship on a strictly impersonal basis. She would do the same.

He said nothing as they walked down the stairs to the next floor, the *piano nobile*, and entered the salon. The other guests were already there, a pretty, plump woman in a purple gown, a man with greying hair and a young man and woman.

The Duchess spotted them and broke away from the others. She took Cecily's hand. 'How charming you look! Do you not think, Domenico?'

'Signora Renato always looks charming,' he said.

The Duchess's eyes twinkled. 'But of course.' She took Cecily's arm. 'Come and meet Signor and Signora Parvatti and their younger daughter. Domenico once attempted to frighten Octavia away with a large toad, for she used to follow him and Rafaele about like a small puppy.'

'How gentlemanly,' was all Cecily could come up with. She glanced at Nico.

His mouth twitched. 'I was eleven and thought most females excessively annoying.'

She smiled at him and for a moment they were in perfect accord. The accord vanished as soon as she met Signor and Signora Parvatti and their daughter. Octavia was no longer an annoying young girl but an alluring young woman with great dark eyes and a curvaceous figure and, from the way Nico returned her smile, Cecily suspected he would no longer mind so much if she trailed him around.

Their son, Bernardo, was a handsome young man who proclaimed himself most delighted to make her acquaintance. He then attached himself to her until dinner was announced.

Cecily, seated between Signor Parvatti and Bernardo, was determined she would not glance in Nico's direction. Signor Parvatti was a quiet, polite man whom Cecily liked very much. Bernardo, who must be at least five years her junior, persisted in flirting with her. Despite those distractions, she could not completely ignore that Octavia was flirting with Nico almost as persistently as Bernardo was with her. A few covert glances in his direction revealed he did not seem to object at all.

Well, that should not matter to her. She turned to Bernardo and smiled at his latest ridiculous compliment.

She was glad, however, that the guests did not linger too long into the evening. Her head had begun to hurt and she felt fatigued from the effort to make conversation. As soon as the Parvattis departed, she rose. 'If you do not mind, I should like to retire.'

'But of course. I can see that the evening has tired you.' The Duchess smiled kindly at her. 'We will see you in the morning.'

Cecily turned to Nico, who had stood as well. She forced a smile to her lips. 'Goodnight, your Grace.'

'Goodnight, Signora Renato,' he said coolly.

She looked away before he saw the stab of hurt that shot through her. She walked from the room. Even with the door closed safely behind her, she refused to allow more than a tear or two to fall.

Nico unwound his cravat and tossed it on a chair in his dressing room. Instead of summoning Hobbes, he threw himself down in a chair and stretched his legs out before him. He needed to think.

He had scarcely seen Cecily at all today. He had been busy, that was true, but he had been careful to avoid being alone with her. At dinner he attempted to treat her with the polite civility he would show any guest of his mother's.

Not that she showed any particular inclination to seek his company. In fact, he suspected she wished to avoid him as well. He had told himself a cool relationship with her was for the best. Until tonight, when pure hot jealousy seared him as he watched her respond to Bernardo's blatant flirtation. Not even Octavia's smouldering glances and *double entendres* distracted him.

He realised, as he watched Cecily smile at something Bernardo said, that he did not want to let her go. He did not want Bernardo or any other man flirting with her, much less touching her. In the short time he'd spent with her, he had come to think of her as his.

He could marry her.

He needed a wife. He'd made up his mind that he would choose a wife once returned to England. None of the possible candidates held any strong appeal. He had not expected love; merely a mutual understanding of the duties of marriage and some measure of affection.

With Cecily he would have much more.

He did not know if he loved her. He had loved Angelina

with all of his being and he doubted he would ever care for a woman in that way again. But until Cecily, he had not expected to find a woman he would consider marriage to more than a mere duty.

His attraction to her was far more complex than mere lust, although her very presence made him think of nothing but taking her to his bed. He liked her, even the little things such as the way she walked, the way she tilted her head a little when she was listening, the quick flush that sprang to her cheeks when she was flustered. He needed her in some way he could not quite define.

She was not indifferent to him. He did not know if she was in love with him, but he thought she might be.

He would not allow her to refuse him.

The Duchess added more sugar to her coffee before looking across the table at Cecily. They were at breakfast the following day.

'I am glad we have had this time together before we leave for Venice, for I feel I would not have had a chance to know you so well if we had first met there. I hope that after the wedding you will consider staying with us. I know you and Eleanora will have much in common.'

'I look forward to meeting Lady Eleanora.' She was not quite so certain about staying with them, especially if it meant she would see Nico very often.

'I would also like you to consider returning to England with us. You have not been back for a number of years, I think.'

Cecily nearly dropped the cup of coffee she held. She set it down, spilling a few drops on the white table linen. 'I cannot return to England.'

'Of course you can. You need not worry about how Lady Telford will receive you, for I believe she very much wishes to see you again.'

'You know my grandmother?'

'A little. She and my husband's mother went to school together, so she knows of our connection to Avezza. When she learned we were to travel to Venice, she asked me to inquire after you. She is worried about you and I can see the breach between you distresses her.'

'I refused her invitation last year. I told her I would never return to England. It was not a very kind letter. She never accepted my marriage to Marco, nor Mariana as my stepdaughter, and although she invited me to come to England and to bring Mariana, I was still angry.' She felt ashamed thinking about it. 'I was sorry almost as soon as I sent it off.'

'Perhaps it is time for you to forgive your grandmother,' the Duchess said gently. 'Although she does not suffer from any serious malady, her health is not quite what it should be. One does not want to wait too long to forgive.' Sadness crossed her face. 'I did and it is one of the sorrows I still carry.' She glanced away and then looked back at Cecily. 'So you must promise you will consider returning with us, not only for Mariana, but for yourself and your grandmother.'

Cecily stared down at her coffee cup. She had been away so long, England had taken on an almost dream-like quality. 'I will consider it,' she finally said, looking up at the Duchess.

'I am glad.' The Duchess smiled and then her expression sobered. 'There is one more thing I wish to speak of now. I have not yet thanked you for taking such good care of my son. I have no doubt he would be much more seriously ill if you had not looked after him so well. Not only that, you saved him and Rafaele from much foolishness. He told me that it was because of you that he and Rafaele finally reached a truce.'

The sincere gratitude in her eyes made Cecily uncomfortable. 'I did nothing more than anyone else would do.'

'But there is a difference—I think you care for my son, do you not?'

Cecily's startled gaze met that of the Duchess. Hot colour rose to her cheeks. 'I...I cannot imagine why anyone...any woman would not.'

'Not all women see past his title and his appearance. Or into his soul.'

Cecily felt as if her own soul had been stripped naked. She could only stare at the Duchess, who regarded her with kindly understanding. 'I do not wish to distress you, but I felt I must speak of this. For the first time since Angelina's death, he has lost a little of the hardness. He has a tenderness and a protectiveness towards you that I have not seen for a very long time.' She smiled a little. 'I can see he has tried to hide it, particularly in the past few days, for he has been too polite with you, which has made me wish to scold him. He is always like this, even as a young boy, when he does not wish to reveal his feelings. I hope you will not allow that to send you away from him.'

'I...I fear you are mistaken. We are friends, but there is nothing else between us. We have never...I do not want...' She stopped, stricken.

The Duchess reached across the table and took Cecily's hand. 'He needs you. As I suspect you need him. I only ask that you do not run away from him too quickly.'

'No.' Cecily rose. 'I...I should see to my packing. You

are much too kind.' She fled the room, cheeks burning. She went to her bedchamber, where the maid had already started folding her clothes in neat piles. The walls seemed to close in on her and she knew she needed to move, walk, do anything to calm her churning emotions. She grabbed a bonnet from the bed and left the room.

Cecily tugged another weed from the stubborn ground. She had walked down a wooded path before coming upon a small building in the shape of a small temple hidden in the trees. Behind it she could see the roses and lavender and rosemary and her hands had almost itched with the need to clear the weeds around them, freeing them from the vines that entwined them like a sorcerer's spell.

First Raf, and now the Duchess. Why did they both think that she and Nico had some sort of special regard for each other? More puzzling, why were they both encouraging it? They seemed to think that Nico actually needed her, which was ridiculous. If ever a man did not need another person, it was the stubborn, self-sufficient, Duke of Severin. He certainly did not need her if his behaviour for the past two days was any indication. He had confessed to wanting her, but she could only think that had been because of the odd circumstances that had forced them together. In the ordinary world, he never would have noticed her. She would have found him impossibly arrogant.

Cecily pulled out another weed.

'We do have a gardener.'

She gasped and looked up. Nico stood on the path behind her, his expression quizzical.

'Good day, your Grace.' She rose.

'Your Grace? I thought we agreed that you would call me by my given name.'

'Under the circumstances, I do not think that would be wise.'

'What circumstances are those?'

'We are now in society, so it would be most improper for us to address each other with such familiarity. It is best if we keep a certain distance between us.'

He took a step towards her. 'I do not agree. I would prefer that there is no distance between us at all.'

The arrogant Duke had fallen away, but the intense expression in his eyes made her feel vulnerable. 'I had best return to the house. My gloves are quite dirty and I must see to my packing since we are leaving tomorrow.'

He took another step towards her. 'Don't run away.'

His mother had said almost the same thing. She looked up at him and the uncertainty in his face made her pause. 'Why shouldn't I?'

'Because I want you. Need you.'

'Nico?'

He caught her to him. His dark face hovered over hers for an instant before he lowered his head and possessed her mouth in a fierce, seeking kiss. Her knees trembled and she clung to him, returning his kisses, meeting his growing need with her own need.

But when his lips left her mouth and trailed down her neck to the top of her breast, her desire to give dissolved into an even greater need for completion. She arched into him, feeling his hardness through her skirts. She hardly noticed when they sank down on the ground and he was above her, his weight pressing her into the grass and herbs. He lifted his head, his eyes glazed with passion. 'Cecily, *cara*...'

'Don't talk. Please not now.' She threw her arms around his neck, pulling his head towards her. With a groan, his mouth sought hers in brief possession before moving down her neck in a series of fiery, mind-numbing kisses. With one hand he pushed down her bodice and shift and she felt his fingers fumble with the drawstring of her stays. He shoved the confining garment away and briefly caressed her breast before he took the erect nipple into his mouth, licking and teasing the swollen bud. Liquid heat spilled through her and when his hand stroked the silky soft flesh of her thighs, her legs parted of their own accord.

When he finally touched her intimately, she bit her lip to keep from whimpering with need. She pressed down on his hand as he stroked and caressed and when he suddenly withdrew, a little moan of protest escaped her.

'In a moment, *cara*.' He dropped a hard kiss on her lips and rose to his knees, his legs braced on either side of her. She waited, eyes closed, afraid that if she moved the spell would break. The scent of lavender and rosemary enveloped her while she waited. She finally felt his welcome weight on her and then he cupped either side of her face. 'Look at me,' he commanded.

She opened her eyes and found his face hovered over hers. The hint of gentleness mixed in with passion amazed her. 'Do you want this?' he asked roughly. 'Because if you do not...'

'I want this. I want you.' She touched his cheek.

He stiffened and then his eyes darkened. He pushed her skirts up around her knees, his gaze never leaving her face and then his weight pressed into her. He parted her thighs and lowered himself between her legs. Her body arched in response but he paused, his gaze holding hers. Then he kissed her, a kiss that was surprisingly gentle. She moaned, her body aching and swollen with desire, and when she thought she could bear no more, he entered her.

She closed her eyes and clung to him, biting her lip at the slight discomfort and then he was moving inside her and her own body was finding a rhythm to match, her need for release relentlessly growing with every stroke. When it came, she cried out as wave after wave of throbbing pleasure washed over her and an instant later Nico spilled his seed into her, and then collapsed on top of her.

They lay in silence, his heartbeat melding with hers. After a little while, he brushed the hair from her face. '*Cara*, sweetheart,' he murmured.

She opened her eyes. His face hovered over hers, his eyes still heavy with passion, but with something else as well. 'Marry me,' he said.

Her heart nearly stopped. 'Please, please do not say anything more. It is not necessary to offer me marriage because of this. I am not a young girl but a…a widow and I am—'

'I am not giving you a choice. You will marry me.'

'I will not. I…I cannot.'

He rolled off her and sat. 'I suggest we both make ourselves presentable and then we will talk.' He reached over and gently pulled down her tangled skirts. She sat up and averted her eyes as he pulled up his breeches and then fastened them.

'There is a bench we can sit on.'

He now stood and held out his hand to help her up. He led her to a stone bench near the wall. 'Sit,' he said.

'Only if you will.' She did not intend to have him hover over her while he demanded that she marry him.

He complied and pulled her down next to him. 'Why can't you marry me?' His eyes narrowed. 'Is there someone else?'

'That is ridiculous! Of course there is not!'

'Then why? From your response just now, I hardly think you are indifferent to me. Unless I forced you.'

'No! No, you did not force me. I...I am not indifferent to you but I...I do not wish to be married.' She knotted her hands together to keep them from trembling. 'I would not make you a suitable wife.'

'Why not?'

'I would make a deplorable duchess. I am not very organised and have been away from English society for so long that I would have no idea how to go on.'

'You will have my mother to guide you.' His gaze raked her face. 'I am not asking you only because of what happened today. I need a wife. I want to marry you. I made up my mind last night to ask you.'

'But why me?' she blurted out. 'You must have dozens of women falling over themselves to marry you.'

He almost smiled. 'Not quite. However, I am flattered by your perception.' He held her gaze. 'After this, you can have no doubt that I find you desirable—very desirable. But over the time we have spent together, I have come to hold you in higher esteem than any of the dozens of women you seemed to think wish to marry me. Not since Angelina have I been able to envision another woman as my wife. I can envision you.'

'I see.' Coldness crept over her—Marco had said much the same thing. *Since the death of my beloved Caterina, I had not thought I would marry again until I met you.* She forced herself to look at him. 'I am sorry, but I cannot accept your offer.'

'So, despite your passionate acceptance of my lovemaking, you cannot bring yourself to marry me. Precisely why did you give yourself to me? Out of pity? Another one of the many services you have performed for me?'

The slight sneer in his voice filled her with cold fury and propelled her to her feet. 'You do not need to insult me. Or yourself. If you think that, then you are beyond despicable. I would never lie with a man I did not care about!'

'You are saying you care about me?' He sounded almost stunned.

'Yes, if you must know!'

'Despite that, you do not want to marry me,' he said flatly.

'No, I…I cannot. I do not want to marry again.' She made an awkward gesture. 'I am sorry,' she repeated when he said nothing.

She was taken aback by the fleeting bleakness in his face. 'There is no need to be. You have made it clear enough that you find the thought of marriage to me repugnant.'

'Not repugnant. I…I do not wish to be married. To anyone.'

'I see. However, there is one thing I wish to make clear. If you find yourself with child because of today, you will marry me. If necessary, I will force you to the altar. Do you understand?'

'A child is most unlikely. I was married to Marco for two years and there…there was no child.'

'You told me he became ill shortly after you married. How often did you lie together as husband and wife after that?'

'That is none of your concern!'

'Just because you did not conceive with Marco does not mean you are immune from such a possibility now.'

She looked away so he would not see he had guessed the truth. After the first few months of marriage, Marco had rarely come to her bed and eventually he did not come at all.

'If you are with child, you will tell me. Do you understand?'

'Quite.' She forced herself to meet his eyes.

'We should return to the house.' He retrieved her straw bonnet and held it out to her.

She took the bonnet and set it on her head, her hands trembling as she tied the ribbons. When she finished and looked up again, he had his coat draped over his arm. 'Ready?' he asked.

'Yes.'

She hardly remembered the walk back to the villa. They walked without touching, neither of them speaking, until they reached the edge of the garden and Nico halted. He looked down at her. 'I am taking you through the side entrance. There is a small staircase you can use to reach your bedchamber without detection.'

'Thank you.' She could imagine nothing more mortifying than to meet the Duchess in her current state.

He led her through the side garden and to a side door. He halted. 'The staircase is just inside,' he said.

'Yes.' She made herself look at him. His face was cool and set. Any words she might say died on her lips. She brushed past him into the hall.

She reached her bedchamber unseen, slipped inside and closed the door. She pulled off her bonnet and sank down in one of the chairs near the window. What had she done?

No, she knew exactly what she had done. She had given herself to the Duke of Severin because he said he'd wanted her, needed her and, if she was honest with herself, she had wanted and needed him just as much.

But not so much she would marry him. How could she explain to him that she could not bear another marriage where the ghost of another love hovered between them? Nico might want her, even need her, but he still loved Angelina, just as Marco had loved Caterina. Why, why was it that she was the sort of woman men wished to marry, but did not love? Charles, Marco and now Nico. She feared that Nico, even more than the others, would tear her heart open. She could not, would not, risk that hurt again.

Chapter Thirteen

'Something is troubling you, I think.'

His mother's voice broke into Nico's thoughts. Dinner was over and they were in the salon. Minutes earlier, Cecily had gone up to bed. It had taken all his willpower to keep from running after Cecily and pulling her into his arms, demanding to know why she would not marry him, especially after their love-making. But her cool, strained manner at dinner had made it clear she would not welcome anything he had to say. He'd be damned before he forced his presence upon her again. Once they were in Venice, he would stay as far away from her as possible.

Exhaustion washed over him, a physical and mental tiredness he could not recall experiencing in an age. 'I must beg your pardon as well,' he said to his mother.

She regarded him with her clear intelligent gaze. 'But first, I must talk to you. Please, come and sit with me.' She indicated the place on the sofa that Cecily had vacated.

'If you would not object, I would rather any conversation between us take place tomorrow.' He doubted he could think clearly enough to hold a rational discussion.

'I do not wish to wait until tomorrow, for there will not be enough time before we depart for Venice.'

'Which is something I did wish to tell you before you retire for the night. I have decided to wait a few more days before travelling to Venice.'

'Because of Signora Renato?' Her worried gaze searched his face.

He hesitated, not knowing how to answer her. She placed her hand on his and continued to speak. 'I had hoped that perhaps there was an affection between you, that you would find the happiness with her that I have wished for you for so long. But I can see something is not right between you. Did you say something to distress her?'

He pulled her hand away from hers and rose. 'Apparently. I asked her to marry me. She refused.'

The shocked dismay that crossed her face made him wince. 'Why did she refuse?'

He shrugged. 'She does not wish to remarry.'

'But I am certain she cares about you. And you care about her, do you not? I have seen it in your face when you look at her. Did you tell her that?'

He could not remember for a moment, then recalled that he had told her that he held her in higher esteem than any woman he knew. And that he wanted her. 'She knows.'

Her eyes were still on him. 'Do you love her?'

'I...' He stopped. 'I have no idea. I like her more than any woman of my acquaintance. I admire and respect her. I wish to take care of her, protect her. I find her lovely. But I cannot say that I love her. Whatever that might mean.'

'I see.' She was silent for a moment. 'Perhaps it is for the best that she did not agree to marry you after all.'

He held out his hands, frustrated. 'Why? Why does it matter if I say that I love her? I have not found any other woman since Angelina that I've the least interest in marrying. I have offered to her everything that I have.'

'Not everything.' She rose. 'Angelina still holds your heart. You do not have that to give. Because of that, you have the power to greatly hurt any woman who might care for you. Including Cecily.'

When he said nothing, she pressed a kiss to his hand. 'Goodnight, my love. Think a little about what I have said.'

'Yes,' he said and watched her go.

Cecily tried to tell herself she was relieved that Nico had decided to delay his journey to Venice and, although he said something about estate business, she had no doubt it was because of her. The Duchess said nothing, however, on their carriage journey to Mestre.

Once in Mestre they left the carriage and stepped into the covered gondola, which would take them across the lagoon to Venice. Although the city was but two days' journey from Avezza, Cecily had never visited Venice. She would never forget her first glimpse of the city, with its turrets and domes shining in the sun that appeared to float on the water as if enchanted.

Her awe did not dissipate as they reached the city and entered the Grand Canal. She had seen paintings depicting various scenes, but none of them prepared her for the sheer wonder of gliding through the water past palazzo after palazzo with their exotic arches, graceful columns and elaborate balconies. Or the domed churches whose steps seem to rise up from the water.

The Duchess touched her arm. 'See, there is the Palazzo Cappelletti although we say Ca' Cappelletti for we consider the Doges Palace the only true palace in Venice.' The Duchess had explained as well that both her family's villa as well as their Venetian palazzo bore the family name of Cappelletti.

Cecily did not realise how nervous she was about meeting Mariana and Simon until she saw the façade of the Ca' Cappelletti. Three floors high, it was an imposing building with its row of arched windows separated by columns of white stone. Balconies of the same stone ran the length of the first and second floors above the canal level.

A servant appeared as soon as the gondola reached the stone steps in front of the water gate. He helped the Duchess and then Cecily from the craft. Cecily followed the footman and the Duchess across the patterned stone floor of the long *androne* to a staircase leading to the *piano nobile*. At the end of the *androne*, just before they started up the steps, Cecily caught a glimpse of an open courtyard.

They were shown to a spacious salon, which Cecily barely had time to notice before Mariana flew up from a sofa at one end of the room.

'Mama!' Mariana flung her arms around Cecily's neck. Cecily pulled her close, revelling in the feel of her slender, warm body.

Mariana finally pulled away. 'Oh! You do not know how worried I was about you! When no one knew where you were, only that you had left very suddenly and you were not to be found, I was so terribly frightened!'

'Just as I was frightened when you went away.' She touched Mariana's cheek, wanting to take the sting from her words.

'I am so very sorry. I did not think,' Mariana whispered.

Cecily glanced up and saw Simon had come to stand behind them. His expression was wary as he moved protectively towards Mariana. Cecily drew away from Mariana and held out her hand. They would marry and no purpose would be served by scolding him. She would not forget how her grandmother had looked at Marco with such cold disdain before informing them that they were never to see her again. She would not do the same thing to Mariana. 'Thank you for keeping Mariana safe.'

He took her hand after a moment. 'I would do anything for her,' he said quietly. 'I am only sorry that…'

She met his gaze. 'You do not need to say more. I will welcome you as my son-in-law.'

His eyes met hers. 'Thank you.'

He dropped her hand just as a young woman entered the room. 'Mama? You are here at last?' She was dark and pretty and Cecily had no doubt she was Nico's sister. She eyed Cecily with an almost haughty gaze that quickly turned to astonishment. 'You are Mariana's mama? Why, you cannot be much older than me! I quite expected you to be—' She stopped. 'I beg your pardon. You must think I am insufferably rude.'

'Eleanora!' the Duchess said with a reproving glance at her daughter.

'I do apologise. It was only that I expected you to be quite different.' Her appraising gaze travelled over Cecily and then she smiled and held out her hand. 'Welcome to Venice.'

'Thank you.' Cecily returned her smile. 'And thank you as well for looking after Mariana.'

'We are already quite fond of her.' She released Cecily's

hand. 'But where is Nico? Was he not to travel with you?' she asked the Duchess.

'He has decided to stay at the villa for another day or two.' Nothing in the Duchess's voice indicated she found that odd. 'I have no doubt Signora Renato is quite fatigued. She must go to her room and rest.'

'I have given her the room next to Mariana's.' Eleanora smiled quickly at Cecily. 'I thought you would wish to be next to her.'

'Yes, thank you.' Cecily was touched by Eleanora's thoughtfulness.

Eleanora said she would show Cecily to her room and Mariana insisted on accompanying them. The bedchamber was located on the floor above the *piano nobile* and, like the floor below, consisted of a large main saloon flanked by a series of smaller rooms on either side. Cecily was shown to one of these, a pleasant room with an old-fashioned bed in a small alcove. 'I will send my maid in to help you unpack and change,' Eleanora said. 'I will allow you to be private with Mariana. I am certain you have much to discuss.' She left the room.

Cecily found Mariana watching her, her dark eyes filled with concern. 'Is something wrong, Mama?'

'No, nothing is wrong.' She squeezed Mariana's hand. 'How can it be, now that I can see for myself that you are safe?'

'But you looked so sad.'

'It is only that I am rather tired.' She smiled at her daughter. 'I did not sleep well last night. I never do the night before I am to leave on a journey.' She sat down on the bed and patted the spot next to her. 'Come and sit. You must tell me what you have done this week while you have been in Venice.'

Mariana obligingly sat down and after a question or two, chatted quite eagerly about the many interesting things she had seen. As Cecily listened to her, she vowed to put Nico from her mind. Now that she was in Venice and reunited with Mariana she must keep her thoughts on the upcoming wedding. She could not allow her own affairs to interfere with Mariana's happiness.

Two nights later, Mariana entered Cecily's bedchamber and then stopped, her eyes widening when she saw Cecily. 'Mama! I have never seen you in such a gown before! I did not know you could look so…so beautiful!'

Cecily smiled, flushing a little at her daughter's mixed compliment. 'I have not worn such a gown before. And you!' Her heart caught a little at her daughter's appearance. 'Oh, Mariana, you look so pretty. And so grownup.' For, in her blue silk shot with gold, she no longer looked like a child at all but a young lady.

'It is a wonderful gown, is it not?' Mariana twirled in front of the looking glass. 'I am so glad you permitted me to wear a real colour. I do not think I will ever want to wear pale blue or that horrid shade of pink again!'

Cecily could not disagree, for the pastels deemed appropriate for young English ladies, which so well complimented many of their soft delicate complexions, only dulled Mariana's lovely olive skin.

'What necklace will you wear?' Mariana peered into Cecily's jewellery box. 'This one, I think.' She held up a garnet. 'The colours will looked splendid with the colour of your gown.'

She was right, of course. Mariana's instinct for such things was flawless. She helped Cecily fasten the necklace and then led her to the looking glass. 'See how perfect it is! And how beautiful you are!'

Cecily peered at herself. The gown and the necklace might have been made for each other. But as for the other, she hardly recognised herself. Eleanora had insisted on loaning her a gown for tonight—they had been invited to a *conversazione*. It was to be Mariana and Simon's first formal appearance as a betrothed couple. The gown was indeed lovely and certainly cast even her best gown in the shade.

Now that she was about to appear in company, she was beginning to wish she had insisted on wearing one of her own gowns after all. The bodice seemed to reveal too much of her arms and back and far too much soft rounded breast. Her hair was braided in a circle behind her head, a style Eleanora assured her was all the thing. She had no idea if she was as beautiful as Mariana said, for she looked so unlike herself she could not make a judgement at all.

She turned away. 'I certainly look different,' she said doubtfully.

'Beautiful,' Mariana corrected. 'If the Duke was to see you I am certain he would say the same thing,' she added with a teasing smile.

Cecily nearly dropped her fan. 'The Duke? Why would you speak of him?'

'I rather thought he liked you. Even Simon said so.'

'Indeed.' She prayed Mariana would not notice her suddenly flushed cheeks. 'We had best go downstairs. I dare say they are waiting for us.'

By the time they had been in Signora Fiori's elegant crowded salon for three-quarters of an hour, Cecily was certain she and Mariana had met at least half of Venice. Despite her absence of thirteen years, the Duchess seemed to be acquainted with everyone. They even met Mrs Hoppner, the English consul's wife, who greeted both her and Mariana very kindly.

Now Mariana stood with one of Eleanora's cousins, a pretty girl who was Mariana's age. Eleanora had just suggested that they take a turn around the room when someone said Cecily's name. Thais stood there in a pale yellow gown, smiling. 'I could not believe my eyes when I saw you! I thought you were in Padua. And Lady Eleanora! I had no idea that you and Cecily were acquainted.'

'Cecily is staying with us in Venice,' Eleanora said politely. She did not look particularly pleased to see Thais.

Thais looked momentarily surprised. Then she gave a little laugh. 'Indeed. How did that come about? I was quite certain you would be with Mariana in Padua.'

'Mariana is also here,' Cecily said.

'Mariana? Is she also staying with you?' Thais asked Eleanora.

'Yes. Perhaps you have not yet heard, but Signorina Renato and my cousin are betrothed.'

An odd expression crossed Thais' face. 'How delightful!' she finally said. 'Although I am certain it will be difficult for Cecily to have Mariana so far away.'

'We hope Cecily will return to England with us for a

visit,' Eleanora said. 'Signora Abruzzi has arrived. You have not yet made her acquaintance, have you, Cecily? Then you must excuse us, Lady Margate.'

'I had hoped to speak to Cecily for a little while before you take her away. You do not mind, do you?'

Eleanora glanced at Cecily. 'No, but you cannot have her for too long.' She gave Thais a little smile before walking off.

Thais watched her for a moment. 'She is pretty enough, but has such odd manners. But I do not wish to speak of Lady Eleanora, but of you. Let us go into one of the smaller rooms. And Mariana, of course. However did you managed to persuade Severin to allow the match? And Rafaele Vianoli? I presume he must have given his approval?'

'Of course. Both families are quite delighted.' Cecily bit back her annoyance at Thais' offhand dismissal of Eleanora.

'I am so pleased, as I am certain you must be.' Thais appeared genuinely pleased. 'So you will return to England? It would be very odd to return after so long, I would think.'

'I have not made up my mind.'

'I quite understand.' She looked over Cecily's shoulder, then placed a hand on her arm. 'Whatever you do, do not smile at the man who is approaching us. He has the most shocking reputation.'

Before Cecily could say anything, a man appeared next to them. He was heavyset and expensively dressed. 'Good evening, Lady Margate. You have decided to end your rustication and once again grace Venice with your charming presence?' He spoke English with an accent Cecily recognised as Austrian.

'For a little while. I will own I did not expect to find you here either. I have heard rumours that you bought a villa on the Brenta.'

'I did. It has been badly neglected, but the restoration is nearly complete and I will soon hold a little party in celebration.' He turned his clear, almost colourless gaze upon Cecily. 'But we are most inconsiderate to talk of these things when I have not yet been introduced to your lovely companion.'

'Then, Signora Renato, you must allow me to present the Baron Eberhart,' Thais said.

Eberhart took Cecily's hand. 'Enchanted, *signora*.' He raised her hand slowly to his lips, his eyes never leaving her face in a way Cecily found disconcerting. 'But you are not Italian?'

'I am English, sir.'

He finally released her hand. 'An English rose,' he murmured.

Thais tapped his arm with her fan. 'I have already warned her of your reputation, so you must not try to flirt with her. She is, as well, related to Rafaele Vianoli by marriage.'

'Indeed.' The Baron looked at Cecily even more closely. 'He is very talented. I had hoped he would be available to oversee the repairs to my villa, but alas he was not.'

'He has been very busy.' His praise of Raf softened her a little towards him. 'I must find my companions so I beg your pardon.'

'You are not with Lady Margate?' the Baron asked. 'For I had hoped to persuade you to stay to talk with me a little longer.'

'I am sorry, but I cannot.' She started to move away, only to find the Baron's hand on her arm.

'I am quite harmless, no matter what Lady Margate has told you,' he said.

She gave him a polite smile. 'I really must go.'

'But I must insist you stay.'

'And I must insist you release Signora Renato.'

Thais gasped and Cecily froze. Nico? The Baron dropped his hand away from her. 'Good evening, Severin. I assure you, I intended only conversation with the *signora*.'

'Against her will?' Nico regarded the Baron with cold eyes.

'I am beginning to think that perhaps I should be insulted.'

'Really, Severin!' Thais said.

Cecily forced herself to smile at Nico. 'I am quite certain the Baron did not intend to detain me, so there is no harm done. Perhaps you would not object to escorting me back to the salon. I wish to find Mariana. Have you yet spoken to her or Lord Ballister?'

'Not yet. My sister sent me to find you almost as soon as I stepped into the salon.'

'Then we most certainly need to go.'

'Yes.' His gaze fell on the other two. '*Buonanotte*, Eberhart. Lady Margate.' He held out his arm to Cecily. 'Signora Renato?'

His brusque cold tone made her heart sink. 'Yes, your Grace.' She placed her hand on his coat sleeve. 'Goodnight, Thais. Goodnight, Baron Eberhart.'

Nico barely gave them time to respond before whisking her from the room to the salon. He did not pause until they were near a table with a large vase of flowers. He stopped, and she pulled her hand from his arm. 'I would like to find Mariana, if you please.'

He scowled down at her. 'Stay away from Eberhart. He's dangerous.'

'Really? He seemed quite congenial.' She did not particularly care for the Baron, but she was even more irritated at Nico.

'He's a rake of the worst sort.'

'Are there better sorts of rakes than others?'

His mouth tightened. 'Yes. Where did you get that gown?'

'I suppose, your Grace, you intend to tell me you dislike it?' She met his gaze, her own defiant.

'I like it too much. Don't wear it in public again.'

'You've no right to dictate what I can or cannot wear.' She wanted to throw something at him. Or cry. Or both. 'If I wish to wear nothing, then I will do that as well!'

'Not unless you are with me, my sweet.'

She stared at him. 'That will never happen,' she said coldly and walked away from him.

Nico stared after her. What the hell had come over him? He'd planned to treat her with cool indifference, not quarrel with her in the middle of a *conversazione*. He'd arrived in Venice a short time ago, and, after changing from his travel clothes, had left for the Fiori palazzo. The first person he found was Eleanora, who wasted no time in informing him that Cecily needed to be rescued from Baron Eberhart.

As soon as he saw her in the damnable dress, beautiful and desirable and obviously not pining away for him, he'd lost all rational thought. Nor did it help that he saw his own feelings reflected in the Baron's gaze. He'd made a fool of himself over the dress because what he really wanted to do was pull her into his arms and kiss her into submission. Until she knew she had no choice but to marry him.

He thought of his mother's words after he said he did not know if he loved Cecily. *Then perhaps it is for the best that she did not agree to marry you after all.* Her words made no sense, for he could not see why it mattered whether he loved her or not. Cecily had not spoken of love at all—surely if she were in love with him, she would have accepted his offer. Perhaps that was why she refused his offer. She did not love him.

Which should make no difference at all to him.

But it did.

Chapter Fourteen

Mariana and Simon were married a week after Nico returned to Venice. The ceremony itself was quiet, with only family present, but the banquet held afterwards at the Ca' Cappelletti was a much more elaborate affair. After the lavish meal, a trio of musicians entertained the guests in the *piano nobile*.

To her surprise, Raf had managed to persuade Barbarina to attend. He had brought her from Avezza two days ago to stay with her cousin, Signora Gamba, although she insisted that Raf was to take her back to Avezza the day after the wedding. Now she was sitting alone on a sofa in an alcove of the salon in her customary black, an odd little figure among the colourful gowns of the other guests. As soon as she could politely do so, Cecily excused herself from the Contessa Alberti, the older sister of the Duchess, and made her way to Barbarina's side. She sat down next to her. 'I wanted to tell you how grateful I am that you are here. And that you have accepted Mariana's marriage to Lord Ballister.' She had been fearful that Barbarina would make some sort of fuss, but she had not.

Barbarina turned and fixed Cecily with her small dark

eyes. 'It is done, so what could I do? At least he is not a poor man, so she will not suffer in that way.'

'He loves her and she loves him. Is that not important as well?'

'Only if both love equally, otherwise it is worse than no love at all. You learned that, as I did.'

'Mariana and Simon will be happy.' She would not allow Barbarina to tell her otherwise. 'Would you like something? A lemonade? Or wine?'

'When will you return to Avezza?'

'I do not know. The Duchess has invited me to stay until Simon and Mariana return from their wedding journey. They are going to Lake Garda.' She had not made up her mind to do so. As much as she wanted to be here when Mariana and Simon returned, she did not think she could bear to stay under the same roof as Nico once they were gone. With the preparations for the wedding and the dinners given in honour of the forthcoming nuptials, she and Nico had managed to avoid each other. But with Mariana gone and the strain between them, she could not imagine staying on any longer.

'You have quarrelled with the Duke, no? So why do you wish to remain in Venice? It is foolish to hope he will love you as he did Angelina. It will be just as it was with Marco. You will love him and he will not love you.'

Cecily rose before she said something to Barbarina she would regret. 'Would you like something to drink?'

'A small glass of wine.'

Across the room in the corner she saw Thais with Nico. She managed to find a waiter and procured the wine and started towards Barbarina, careful to avoid Thais and Nico. Thais, however, met her before she could reach Barbarina.

'I have not yet had a chance to speak with you, Cecily. How beautiful and happy Mariana looks! You must be so pleased, but perhaps a little sad as well.'

'Yes, a little.' If she thought of Mariana's going away too much, she would probably burst into tears.

'Then I have the most splendid idea. You must come and stay with me after Mariana and Lord Ballister leave on their wedding journey. You do not need to give me an answer now, but please consider it.'

'You are very kind,' Cecily said, taken aback by the invitation.

'But I am not. I sometimes become quite lonely in my little palazzo, so I would quite enjoy your company. So you would be doing me a great favour.'

'I will consider it, then.' Cecily saw that Barbarina was now staring at them. What if she suddenly decided to join them and say some peculiar thing to Thais? 'I must take this wine to Barbarina now.'

'Most certainly. Poor creature, but she is so fortunate to have you to look after her.'

'What did she want?' Barbarina asked as soon as Cecily returned.

'Nothing in particular. I hope you will like this.' She handed Barbarina the glass.

'She is wicked beneath her smiles and rich clothes. You must not forget that.'

Oh, dear. She hated to think what Barbarina would say if she discovered Thais had invited Cecily to stay with her. Or worse, what she would say if Cecily accepted.

Nico glanced across the salon to where Cecily now stood with Bernardo. It was apparent from the way Bernardo

Parvatti hung on to every word that he was besotted. No matter that she was five years his senior. He found himself crossing the room.

'Good evening, Signora Renato. Bernardo.'

The smile faded from Cecily's face. 'Good evening, your Grace.' She spoke as if they were complete strangers, as if they had never been together as lovers. She turned to Bernardo with a charmingly sweet smile. 'I will leave you so that you and your cousin may converse. I hope we will have the opportunity to meet again.'

Bernardo looked as if he'd been offered a fortune. 'I...I would like that, *signora*.'

Nico reined in his temper. 'Actually, I want to talk to Signora Renato.'

'Ah, yes. I beg your pardon.' Bernardo executed a slight bow and then backed away, almost running into an elderly lady behind him.

Nico looked down at her. 'Are you certain it is sporting to give him false hopes?'

'What sort of false hopes would that be, your Grace? If you have come here to scold me about that, then you are wasting your breath, for I intend to walk away from you.' She spoke in a low angry voice and it occurred to him that she possibly hated him.

He felt completely out of control. Then he saw the distress in her eyes. Hell. 'We can go to the library. I promise I will behave as a gentleman. My mother and my sister will have my head if they think I've overset you. Especially today.'

The almost-smile that touched her lips made his heart thud. He wanted to kiss her. 'Will you come with me?'

'Very well.' She made a few polite comments as they left the salon, undoubtedly for the benefit of anyone who might be watching.

The library was shrouded in shadows; the only light provided by the full moon, spilling through the tall arched windows and across the marble floor. 'What is it?' she asked.

What did he want to say to her? His mind was blank; he could only think of how the moonlight shone across her hair and how much he wanted to take her into his arms.

'Your Grace?'

'I wanted to tell you that I plan to accompany Simon and Mariana as far as Mestre. To ensure that their carriage is ready and they are properly prepared for their journey.'

'Thank you. You are most kind. Shall we return to the salon?'

'I wish to apologise for my ungentlemanly behaviour after the *conversazione*.'

'We were both angry.'

'Yes.' He drew in a breath. 'Damn it, Cecily, why did you refuse my offer?'

She looked up at him, her face pale in the moonlight. 'Because you still love Angelina, just as Marco still loved Caterina. Her ghost would always be hovering between us. I have lived with one ghost; I cannot live with another.'

He did not know if he understood. 'I cannot help loving her.'

'I would not expect you to stop. But I would always be in her shadow. You would look at me and I would see that you regret that I am not Angelina. No woman ever will be, you know.' She sounded almost wistful.

'I hardly would expect you to be. For one thing, you look nothing alike.' The words did not come out as light as he had intended.

Her face clouded for a moment. 'No, I do not suppose we do. Everyone said she was beautiful.'

He had insulted her. 'But so are you. In a different way, of course. Is that it? You think I would compare your beauty to Angelina's?'

She moved a little away from him. 'No. Marco did not compare me to Caterina, at least not like that. But he had loved her since childhood. He adored her, worshipped her, and to him she was the embodiment of all that a woman should be.' She turned her clear gaze on him. 'But I was not.'

'He told you that?'

'No, he was too kind. But I could sense it. I could not be all that Caterina was. I cannot be all that Angelina was either.'

No response sprang to his lips. For the truth of what she said hit him with blinding force—he held all other women up against Angelina and found them wanting. Even Cecily.

She watched him for a moment. 'We had best return to the others,' she finally said.

'There is one more thing.' He did not move. 'Is there any chance you are with child?'

She shook her head. 'No. I...I knew that a few days after our...our encounter.'

'We were fortunate, then.' Instead of relief, he felt a sense of loss.

'Yes, we were.' She did not quite look at him. 'I must return to the salon. We must before someone notices we are gone.'

'Cecily...' he began and then stopped. Nothing he said would be of much use now.

* * *

Cecily waited until after Simon, Mariana and Nico left before telling the Duchess she planned to accept Thais' invitation to stay with her. 'Please do not think that I have been unhappy here, for that is not it at all. I—'

'You do not need to say anything more—I quite understand. My son told me that he asked you to marry him, but you did not accept his offer. You worry that it will be awkward for both of you if you stay.' She took Cecily's hand. 'He told me the night before we left for Venice and only because I asked him,' she said gently.

'I am sorry. It is not because—'

'You do not need to explain. I only wished to assure you that you will always be welcome under our roof whether we are in Italy or England.'

'You are much too generous.'

'No, I am only sorry that I will not have you for a daughter-in-law, but you are still part of our family, no?'

She looked at the Duchess's lovely, familiar face. 'I will miss you and Lady Eleanora very much. You have been so kind.'

'And we will miss you.' She leaned forward and kissed Cecily's cheek. 'If you decide that Lady Margate does not suit you, then you will come back to us. You must promise me that.'

'I will.' Cecily was quite certain she would not set foot in this house again.

A week later Cecily sat next to Thais in a carriage that was taking them to Baron Eberhart's villa. The Baron had invited Thais and her as well as a number of others to his newly renovated villa for a few days. Despite the clear blue skies and pleasing scenery, Cecily felt more than a little trepidation about actually staying under the Baron's roof.

During the week she had been with Thais, the Baron seemed always underfoot, escorting them one night to his box at Le Fenice, accompanying them to a dinner given by the Austrian governor another. He had even gone on a shopping trip with them and afterwards had insisted on taking Cecily and Thais to a small café for a light repast. He had always been courteous to Cecily, but she found the speculative way he sometimes looked at her unnerving.

'Georg looks forward to showing you the improvements he has made,' Thais suddenly said. 'You will be most impressed.'

'I am certain it is lovely,' Cecily said politely.

'Dear Cecily, you must guess that Georg is quite taken with you. I hope you like him a little?'

'I hardly know him well enough to form an opinion.' Cecily could think of no polite way to tell Thais she did not really like the Baron despite his impeccable manners and amusing conversation. She certainly did not like the way he persisted in referring to her as a 'delicate English rose' even after she had told him she did not like roses.

'Now you have a perfect opportunity to know him better,' Thais said. 'My dear, he is not so much a rogue that he will force you into anything. A little flirtation will do you good. You are still young and very pretty and, now that Mariana is married, you cannot hide yourself away with Signora Zanetti in that dull little town. Georg may be exactly what you need to take your thoughts from Severin.'

'I have no idea what you mean.'

'It is quite apparent that you have developed a *tendre* for him.' Her large blue eyes rested on Cecily's face.

'You are quite mistaken.'

'I do not think so, for I know the signs.' Her smile was not unsympathetic. 'It is quite natural for you to do so, particularly when he has not exactly been indifferent to you. You are quite the opposite of many of the women he meets, so it is not surprising he finds you rather intriguing.'

'He...he looks upon me as a relation. Which is exactly what I consider him. Nothing more.' Cecily spoke firmly and prayed the colour in her cheeks would not give her away.

'I hope not. He does feel quite protective towards you now that you are related by marriage, for he told me so. It would be easy for one to mistake his protective instincts for a warmer, more personal regard.'

'I quite suppose it would.' Cecily bit back a stab of hurt that he would discuss her with Thais. She glanced out of the window. Through the trees she caught a glimpse of a large square house with a classical portico. 'Is that Barbarigo?' she asked brightly.

'Yes.' Thais touched Cecily's hand. 'I did not mean to overset you, but I do not want you to be hurt as I was.' Her smile had vanished and she looked at Cecily with wide unhappy eyes. 'You see, I too was in love with Severin. I had hoped that we would marry, but he was to marry Angelina instead.'

Nico looked down at the letter the groom had just handed him. 'My lord, the Lady Eleanora says I must tell you that it is a matter most urgent,' the man added with an anxious look, as if he feared Nico intended to lay it aside. 'I am to tell you also that the Duchess is in the best of health.'

'I am relieved to hear that.' He glanced at the man, who still waited. 'I will open it while you go to the stables and see to your horse.'

'Thank you, my lord.' He bowed and backed out of the study.

Nico frowned for a moment, wondering what the devil was of such urgency that Eleanora must send a groom all the way to the Villa Cappelletti. Particularly when he was to return to Venice in the next few days. He broke the seal, quickly perused the contents and then swore.

If Eleanora was correct, then Cecily and Thais were, at this very moment, guests under Eberhart's roof. More disturbing, Eleanora reported that ever since Cecily had gone to stay with Thais, the Baron had been seen everywhere with them and it was rumoured a bet had been placed on how long it would take Eberhart to seduce Cecily.

He could not imagine Cecily a willing participant in any such scheme, but then why the hell had she agreed to attend this house party? And when he told her to stay away from Eberhart, she had replied that she found him 'congenial'. Cecily might not want him, but he'd abduct Cecily before he'd allow Eberhart to touch her.

If he left within the next hour, he would reach Eberhart's villa in time for dinner.

Chapter Fifteen

Cecily picked up her fan and wondered if Eberhart would suspect she was avoiding him if she pleaded a headache tonight and stayed in her room instead of going down to dinner. She had no real desire to see Thais either—the conversation in the carriage had disturbed her greatly.

Thais had been in love with Nico and expected to marry him? Had there actually been some sort of formal promise between them? Or had Thais only hoped there would be? She must have been in love with Nico that summer, but had anyone noticed? Perhaps not—Viola had described Thais as the sort of pale girl no one seemed to see. Despite living under Thais' roof for a week, Cecily did not feel she knew Thais much better than she had in Avezza, almost as if the pale unremarkable girl still lurked beneath her charming smiles and blonde loveliness.

Even the few confidences she had shared with Cecily did not, in retrospect, reveal much about her. She knew that Thais had been widowed twice, but Cecily had no idea if Thais had regarded either of her husbands with any sort of affection. She had numerous acquaintances, but none of them seemed to be a friend, at least not in the sense that Cecily considered Viola and, if circumstances were different, Lady Eleanora.

Certainly Thais had been hospitable and the week had passed in a whirlwind of social affairs, visitors and shopping, which had left Cecily in a sort of daze. She had scarcely a moment to herself except when she tumbled into bed at night and she was so tired she fell asleep with hardly a thought for Mariana and Simon. Or Nico. She felt as if she had left the Ca' Cappelletti a year instead of a week ago, for although they were in the same city, the only time she had glimpsed Eleanora and the Duchess was when the Baron had escorted them to the theatre. Thais had pointed out their box and Cecily had been taken aback by the jolt of longing that pierced her when she saw their familiar figures.

She was puzzled and a little hurt that neither the Duchess nor Eleanora had made any effort to visit her as they had promised they would. She thought that perhaps she had insulted them after all by leaving in the way she had.

Nothing seemed right. She walked to the window. Below were the formal gardens. Everything looked serene under the clear blue sky of an Italian afternoon. None the less, she felt on edge, as if she expected something unpleasant to happen. She would avoid Eberhart as much as possible but surely Thais was right and he would not do anything she did not want. She had worn one of her less becoming gowns tonight, a pale lavender silk, hoping he would consider her less of an English rose and more of an English thistle.

Someone rapped lightly at her door. She crossed the room, opened it and found Thais on the other side. She was dressed in a gown of delicate pink silk that emphasised her porcelain skin. Around her neck was a stunning necklace of diamonds.

'Dear Cecily, it is time to go down...' She stopped. 'Why are you not wearing the cerulean gown we had decided upon?'

'I found it had a stain.' The lie sprang quite easily to her lips.

'But this gown is so...so dull. Everyone will think you are someone's companion! And that necklace! It is so ordinary!' She pressed her lips together, dismay written all over her face. 'It is too late to do anything now. Perhaps if the bodice was arranged a little lower.'

'No! That is, I was feeling a trifle cold. I should hate to catch a chill.'

'It is too late for you to change, for we must go down. Tomorrow I will insist on supervising your dress.'

Cecily refused to feel guilty over deceiving Thais. She would have worn sackcloth and ashes if she thought that would help her escape Eberhart's attention.

Cecily followed Thais into the richly decorated salon where the guests gathered before dinner. Her hopes for an unobtrusive entry were dashed when the Baron's cousin and hostess, the Countess von Essen, spotted them and crossed the marble floor to their sides. Her cool grey eyes swept over them. 'A most charming gown, Lady Margate.' She turned to Cecily, a hint of surprise crossing her thin features. 'You are in mourning?'

'No, Countess.'

She looked a trifle puzzled. 'Come, my cousin most particularly wishes to greet you and Lady Margate.'

Cecily did not dare look at Thais as they followed the Countess across the room. She had the unpleasant sensation that several of the guests stared and whispered as they passed.

Eberhart stood with a heavyset man Cecily did not recognise. In fact, she realised she recognised none of the fashionably dressed guests she glimpsed as they crossed the room. The Countess excused herself, leaving Thais and Cecily with the men.

'Thais, my dear,' Eberhart said as he took her hand. 'As usual, you are the pinnacle of health and beauty. Another new gown, perhaps?'

'Will you scold me if it is?'

'Only if it did not become you.' He dropped her hand and turned to Cecily.

'Signora Renato,' he murmured. He possessed himself of her hand and brushed a brief kiss across the back of it. He impaled her with his strange colourless eyes. 'Welcome to my villa. I have anticipated your arrival since I learned you were coming.'

She forced her lips into a diffident smile and wondered how long he intended to go on holding her hand. 'Thank you.'

He finally dropped her hand as they were presented to his companion, Herr Schuler, who proclaimed himself in a heavy German accent delighted to meet such beautiful ladies. He too held Cecily's hand a trifle too long, his gaze a trifle too bold, before turning to Eberhart and speaking in rapid German. The Baron smiled and Cecily had the uneasy sense the Baron's comment concerned her.

The Baron started to speak just as a footman appeared at his side. He spoke to Eberhart in a low voice and the Baron frowned. 'You must excuse me, my dear ladies. An unexpected guest has arrived.' He left them with Schuler.

Schuler cleared his throat. 'I am most pleased to once again find myself in your splendid city.' His Italian was laboured as if he read from a schoolroom book.

Thais started to speak and then her attention riveted to something over Cecily's shoulder. 'Good heavens!' Pure dismay crossed her fact. She turned to Cecily and spoke in English. 'Dear Cecily, I fear I must warn you that Severin has just arrived.'

Nico? Cecily nearly dropped her fan. She slowly turned. Nico stood in the doorway. He seemed not to notice his approaching host as his gaze swept the room. Then his eyes fell on her with an intensity that was almost physical and she knew he was here because of her. She turned away and realised she was shaking.

She had no idea whether it was from anticipation, fear or relief. Or something else altogether.

Nico glanced down the table at Cecily. She was seated between Schuler and an elderly gentleman he did not recognise. Her profile was turned away from him as she listened to her dinner partner, her soft brown hair gleaming with bits of gold from the candlelight. Among the fashionable dress and glittering jewels of the others she looked like a poor relation in her drab gown, but that only rendered her more vulnerable.

His gaze shifted to the Baron, who laughed at a joke before gulping his wine. Although Eberhart was attentive to the lady seated at his side, his gaze frequently fell on Cecily with a speculative interest that raised Nico's hackles. He could not tell whether Cecily was aware of his interest, for she steadily avoided looking at the Baron. As she had steadily avoided looking at him since they had sat down to dinner.

'Are you certain it wise to stare at Cecily so often? Some might decide you are here because of her.'

He forced his attention back to Thais. She wore a little smile, but there was an edge to her voice he did not often hear.

'They would not be wrong.' He was in no mood to dissemble.

Slight colour stained her cheek. She stared at him and gave a little laugh. 'Whatever for? Really, I would think you must know by now that she finds you rather…well, intimidating. If you persist in this sort of thing, you will quite scare her.'

'I had not noticed that she finds me particularly intimidating.'

'Of course you do not! Men always assume that a woman who blushes and looks away from them is merely shy, but it is most often because they find the man too overwhelming. Contrary to what most men wish to believe, women do not in general like men who overwhelm them.'

He felt irked. 'You are speaking of women in general, or of Cecily?'

Her smile held a touch of pity. 'Have you not realised that Cecily wants nothing to do with you? Why else did she leave your house and come to stay with me?'

In that moment, he realised how much he disliked Thais. 'Perhaps, but what interests me is why you were so conveniently at hand to invite her to stay with you? More than that, my dear, I am quite curious as to why you brought her here, a place where most of the guests are no more respectable than their host?'

Her blue eyes widened. 'Dear Severin, I have no idea what you mean.'

'I think you do.' He held her gaze, his own hard. 'What game are you playing?'

Cold anger flickered across her face and then she gave a little laugh. 'Games? Why, none!' She looked away and picked up her wine glass.

What the hell was she up to? She knew exactly what she was doing when she brought Cecily here. He had no idea whether she deliberately intended to hurt Cecily or if Cecily was merely a pawn for some other nefarious purpose.

It did not matter—he intended to remove Cecily from this place as soon as possible.

The dinner was followed by a tedious tour of the Baron's collection of antiquities, which included two nude male statues. Eberhart chortled. 'I did not wish to offend the sensibilities of the ladies. Or make them dissatisfied with their current pleasures. Rather magnificent, are they not?'

A few crude comments followed, which only served to increase Nico's impatience.

Nico dallied, intending to allow the others to go ahead so he might fall behind and steal away to the salon. Eberhart usurped his plans by suddenly announcing they must join the ladies. He fell into step beside Nico.

'I am quite curious to know exactly why you decided to join my little party.' He glanced at Nico. 'Shall I guess? A certain lady, perhaps?'

'Yes.'

'I would hope you are referring to the delightful Lady Margate.'

'I am referring to Signora Renato.'

There was silence. Then Eberhart turned to look at him.

'I must ask you to turn your attention elsewhere. Perhaps you do not realise that I have an interest in the lady myself.'

'I have heard rumours to that effect. However, I have a prior claim.'

'Then I must ask you to relinquish it.'

'I am going to wed Signora Renato.'

Eberhart momentarily lost his bland expression. 'How very interesting, particularly since I had the impression from Lady Margate that the lovely *signora* had all but run from you.' He stopped in front of a painting. 'What do you think of my most recent acquisition? A present from an unfortunate Frenchman just before he was compelled to leave Italy.'

Nico looked up at the painting. 'Very nice. Which noble family did the Frenchman rob?'

'You are far too cynical, my dear Severin. If you insist on continuing in this vein, I might suspect you of harbouring radical sympathies.'

'My only interest is in Cecily Renato.'

The Baron began to walk again. 'Of course. I am curious if you have yet informed your intended bride she is to wed you.' He cast Nico a sly look. 'Because if you have not, then I still consider the lady fair game.'

'I suggest you rid yourself of that notion. Unless you want a bullet through you.'

'I would take offence, but since you are caught up in the throes of passion I will overlook your lack of gratitude for my hospitality. You would be wise to keep in mind, however, you are here only because I have allowed it.' They had reached the salon. Eberhart paused. 'We will make a little wager. I will give you until noon tomorrow to convince the *signora* to marry you. If she does not agree, then I will continue my pursuit of her without your interference. However, there is one more condition.'

'And that is?'

'If she agrees, we will announce it to the rest of the guests. To ensure that your intentions are honourable.'

'As yours are, no doubt.'

Eberhart smiled. 'Perhaps I am also in need of a wife.'

'You had best look elsewhere.'

'She is lovely, is she not, with an air of innocence despite her widowhood. One wonders if she has ever been brought to the height of passion. I have no doubt that, if properly tutored, she will be a most pleasurable bedmate. I am not certain if I wish to relinquish that task to you after all.'

Nico nearly lost his tight control then. 'The choice belongs to the lady,' he said coolly.

'Naturally. You will understand if I do not wish you success in your pursuit.'

'I do not intend to lose.' He stepped into the room.

Cecily was nowhere in sight.

Cecily had been glad to escape from the salon to the quiet of the bedchamber. But after the maid finished helping her into her nightclothes and left, an unexpected surge of homesickness washed over Cecily. Not for her house in Avezza, but for England. This room, with its silent marble floors and dark bed coverings, seemed huge and strange and she suddenly longed for the cheerful simplicity of her childhood room. For the first time in an age, she missed her grandmother. Lady Telford had been stiff and demanding and not very physically demonstrative, but when Cecily had been truly overset her grandmother would sit with her.

'You may cry for a while, but then you must dry your eyes and decide what you must do next,' Lady Telford told her many times.

After that she would gather Cecily into her arms, rather stiffly, and Cecily had known she was loved. Now, she felt an aching need for someone to hold her.

'Cecily.'

Her heart leapt to her throat. Nico?

'Cecily. It is Nico. Open the door.' His voice held a note of impatience. 'Now.' She did not think he would go away if she ignored him. She padded to the door.

She turned the key and opened the door a crack. 'I was about to go to bed.'

'Let me in before any of the guests find me shouting through the door.'

'Oh.' She stepped back. He brushed past her, closed the door behind him and turned the key.

She stared at the key and then at him. 'Whatever are you doing?' Her voice was a trifle too high.

'Locking the door. So our host doesn't disturb us.'

'Us?' Her voice squeaked.

'Yes. Us. We need to talk.'

'Could we not do it some other time?'

'No.' He folded his arms and leaned against the door, his eyes on her face. 'I told Eberhart I plan to marry you,' he said coolly.

Her heart thudded. 'Why did you do that?'

'So he would cease his pursuit of you.'

'You know of that?' How utterly humiliating.

'Yes, as do a good many others.'

'I see. You are most kind, but it was not necessary to tell him that—'

He stopped her. 'It was. I promised Raf I'd look after you. I'm not about to let you end up as Eberhart's mistress,' he said roughly. 'Or have your reputation ruined.'

'I am certain Raf did not expect you to go around telling people untruths in order to protect me,' she said coldly. So that was why he was here—to keep some sort of stupid promise to Raf.

'It is not an untruth. We are about to become betrothed.' His expression was grim. 'Eberhart will not touch you if you are under my protection. Furthermore, our betrothal will quell any rumours linking your name with Eberhart. There is one more thing. If Raf returns and discovers you have been compromised in any way, he will come after Eberhart. I doubt you would like to see Raf imprisoned or worse for killing an Austrian baron.'

'No, of course not, although I would hope he would be more reasonable.'

'Not where his family is concerned.' He moved away from the door. 'So you see, by agreeing to a betrothal, you will possibly spare Raf's life.'

'Surely things are not quite that dire!'

'They are.' He had come to stand in front of her and she resisted the urge to back up. 'Why did you leave my house in the first place? Was it because of me?'

'Only because I thought it would be awkward under the circumstances if I stayed.'

'Not because you are afraid of me?' He seemed to really want to know.

She gave a strangled laugh at this sudden change in topic. 'No, although when you stare at me in the grim way you are doing now I quite fear you are about to scold me or attempt to ride roughshod over me. But, no, I am not afraid of you.'

'I am glad.' Some of the harshness faded from his expression.

The air suddenly crackled with tension. She clutched her dressing gown more tightly about her. 'I think you should go. It is late…and…'

'I am spending the night with you.'

She took a step back, her pulse beating wildly. 'Spending the night with me? Whatever for?'

'To protect you from Eberhart. He has an unfortunate habit of roaming during the night. I should not want him to wander into your bedchamber and find you unprotected.' His voice was cool and matter of fact.

'But the door has a lock!'

'I doubt that will stop him. If he thinks we are spending the night engaged in passionate lovemaking, he is unlikely to stray into your room. Or question the veracity of our betrothal. He would like, I think, to discover I am only bluffing.'

'Oh.' She took another step back, crossing her hands over her breasts.

'I am not planning a seduction, if that worries you. I intend to sleep here.' He had crossed the room to one of the chairs near the mantelpiece.

'Th…there is a cot in the dressing room. It might be more comfortable.'

'I would prefer to be in the same room with you. In case, our host decides to investigate.' He had started to shrug out of his coat.

'Surely he would not do that! And if he did, he would think it equally odd if you are in the chair.'

He finished removing his coat. His hands stilled on his waistcoat. 'You are right, my dear. Then perhaps I should share the bed with you.'

She swallowed. Her eyes met his and even in the dim light of the room, she could not mistake the blatant desire in his eyes. The knowledge he still wanted her sparked the aching need for him she had tried to ignore. The strangeness of the day...everything whirled around her, everything but him.

Her gaze did not waver from his face. 'I think, yes, that would be the best thing to do.'

He stared at her. 'I beg your pardon.'

'I think we should share the bed.'

He looked incredulous and then gave a short laugh. 'My sweet Cecily, I was hardly serious. Sharing a bed with you would be disastrous.' He fumbled with the button of his waistcoat.

He was right. Even if his bluntness hurt. She sat on the edge of the bed and wondered how she was ever to sleep. Worse, the lost feeling had returned in full force. Having him in the room only intensified it. She sniffed, praying she would not start to cry like some missish creature.

'Cecily.'

Her head jerked up. He stood in front of her dressed only in his loose shirt and breeches. 'What is wrong?'

'Nothing is wrong.' She looked away. 'We...we should go to bed.'

He did not move. 'Do you really want me to share your bed?'

'N-not really. It...it would be st-stupid.' To her chagrin, her voice shook.

'Stupid. Dangerous. Disastrous. All of those.' He took her hands and drew her to her feet. 'Do you know why? Because I would want to make love to you. Over and over. All night.'

'Would you?' she whispered. She hardly seemed to be breathing.

'Yes.' He moved closer to her, imprisoning her between the bed and his body. She could feel the hard planes of his body against hers, feel the beat of his heart. His mouth was inches from hers and she could almost taste him. She reached up and tangled her hands in his hair and pulled his head towards her. Her mouth found his. He did not move while she explored his mouth. Her hands moved down from his head to his shoulders to the hard muscles of his back. He still stood motionless. She finally lifted her head. 'You do not like this?'

'Not like it?' His voice was ragged. 'My sweet, I can think of nothing more pleasurable than having you touch me. And if you continue, I will lose every vestige of control I possess.'

'What if I want you to?' She touched his cheek.

'Are you attempting to seduce me?'

'I...I think so.' She pressed closer to him.

He stilled. 'Are you certain you want this?'

'Yes. Will you kiss me?' She was beyond caring whether she made a fool of herself or not.

An odd light sprang to his eyes. 'Anything to oblige you.' And then his arms were around her, his mouth crushing hers in a kiss that sent her senses spinning. She clung to him; when he finally lifted his head, her legs nearly buckled.

'What else will please you, my lady?' His voice was husky with desire.

She managed to speak. 'Your shirt. I want it off.' Impatient, she fumbled with the buttons and then started to lift it over his head.

'Allow me.' He finished the task and stood before her. She had seen him partially unclothed before, but not like this, standing before her as a lover. She took him in, the broad shoulders and chest, the muscles, the dark hair on his chest, his narrow hips. He waited under her perusal, his eyes on her face. 'What else, sweetheart?' he asked softly.

She wanted to touch him everywhere. She swallowed and ran her tongue over her dry lips. 'I don't know.'

'It is my turn to make a request. Your shift must go.'

She thought she would explode when he undid the ribbon and then helped her from the garment. Then she stood naked before him. The heat in his gaze rendered her self-conscious for the first time and she crossed her hands over her breasts.

'Don't,' he said softly. He gently removed her hands and held them to her sides. His gaze seemed to burn through her as his eyes took in her breasts, her hips, the juncture of her thighs and her legs. He did not need to tell her he found her desirable; his sudden intake of breath was enough. 'Turn around,' he said hoarsely.

She did and then his arms circled her waist, pulling her back against him. He caressed the back of her neck with his mouth. He cupped her breast with his free hand and then moved down to her stomach, stroking the soft roundness in lazy circles. A whimper of pleasure and need escaped her and when his hand moved to the mound between her thighs, she shuddered.

He removed his hand. 'Come, we will continue this in the chair,' he said thickly.

'The chair?'

He took her hand and led her to the wing chair. He sat and pulled her down on his lap so she was facing him. He looked up at her, his eyes dark and sensuous. 'Kiss me, Cecily.'

She leaned forward, her hands bracing against his shoulders, and found his mouth. She kissed him, tentatively exploring his mouth, tasting him. He responded, his own kiss unhurried. The feel of the bare flesh of her thighs against the rough cloth of his breeches was unexpectedly sensuous and she found herself leaning forward and pressing into him. Her breasts fell forward and he cupped them. When he drew one nipple into his mouth, she thought she would die. She leaned into his caress, wanting more and then his hard length pressed into the sensitive nub between her legs. She shuddered with pure, hot desire.

He pulled his mouth away from hers. 'What next, my lady?' he whispered.

'I...' She was too far gone to think of propriety. 'Your breeches.'

He laughed softly. 'Of course. But we will need to stand for a moment.'

He rose, his arm around her. Her legs nearly buckled when she stood. In fascination, she watched as he undid the fastening of his breeches and then stepped out of them. But when he started to remove his small clothes, she averted her eyes. Whatever was she doing?

But he was drawing her to him. 'No need to be shy, *cara.*' He tilted her chin and kissed her mouth. 'Come and sit back down. This time properly. Or most improperly, as you wish.' He sat again, slightly sprawled, and she could not look anywhere but at his face.

A slight smile touched his mouth. 'Come and kiss me again. Just like before.' He held out his hand.

She took it and again was on his lap. She leaned forward to kiss him and this time he met her mouth with a hard, possessive opened-mouth kiss. Her head spun as his hand cupped her buttocks, lifting her slightly and then he was parting her thighs. She gasped as he slipped two fingers in her swollen opening. She clung to him as he explored, stroking and caressing the most sensitive places in her body until she was completely at his mercy. Her breath came in shallow gasps and when he finally withdrew, she thought she would explode. She opened her eyes. 'Please…' she begged.

'Lift your hips.'

She complied and then drew in a sharp breath when his hard length filled her. 'Lean forward and ride me,' he whispered.

She nodded and braced her hands on his shoulders and began to rock. Her body seemed to know what to do, moving and adjusting to seek the most pleasure possible. Her body was swollen and full, the movements only increasing her desire for release. He moved under her, matching her rhythm. She climaxed, wave after wave of sensuous pleasure crashing over her. His own climax followed and she collapsed against him, as her breathing slowed.

And sanity returned. She was sitting on the Duke of Severin's most private part after begging him to take her to bed. Except they hadn't even made it to the bed.

His hand brushed her cheek. 'Regrets already, my sweet?'

She opened her eyes. He watched her with a lazy, sensuous expression, but she felt as if he could read her soul. 'No. I...I don't know. I have never been like this.'

'Like what?'

'So...so...brazen.'

Slight amusement lifted his mouth. 'I feel more than complimented.'

'I suppose women often throw themselves at you.'

'But rarely with so much passion.'

She had no doubt this sort of lovemaking was nothing out of the ordinary for him. If his cool, slightly amused manner was anything to go by, he had not felt the same loss of control she had. 'Thank you for...indulging me.' She started to move backwards, only to find his arm trapping her against him.

'But I have not finished indulging you.'

'I really do not expect you to do any more.'

'Don't you? Then perhaps you will indulge me.'

'What do you mean?'

His smile held a hint of wickedness. 'This time I will tell you what I want.'

Her body was already tensing in anticipation. 'What sort of things do you...want?'

'This to start with.' He rose with her and pulled her to him for another raw kiss. He was already hard, his erection pressing against her flesh. He lifted his head. 'I think now we can go to bed.' He took her hand.

The pleasurable warmth of the body cradled against his slowly penetrated his sleep-fogged consciousness. She lay under his arm, her back to him, the soft roundness of her buttocks pressed against his stomach, one leg under his. He kissed the back of her neck and then pulled away. For the first time in an age, he was reluctant to leave a woman's bed. If he did not, however, they would be here for the rest of the day.

He half-turned, easing out from under her and bit back a groan as he moved his stiff arm. He managed to sit on the edge of the bed. His gaze was drawn to Cecily, to the curve of her cheek. One slender arm was flung over the covers. She looked vulnerable and soft, and innocent. Unexpected protectiveness surged through him—something he had not expected after a night of such wild passion.

As much as he'd wanted her, he had not expected to lose himself in her so completely that he no longer knew where he ended and she began. The pleasure had been nearly unbearable and, for the first time since his youth, he had lost control.

He'd never had such satisfying sex in his life.

He rose and found his shirt on the floor. He slipped it over his head, wincing a little. His breeches were flung over the chair where they had first coupled. The sudden hardness in his groin made him curse. He pulled up his breeches. When he looked up he saw Cecily was sitting, holding the bedcover up around her chest. Soft colour tinted her cheeks when she met his eyes and she looked away.

He walked over to her. Her hair was tousled about her bare shoulders and her mouth was soft. He wanted nothing more than to pull her back into his arms and entangle his hands in her hair, pulling the cover to reveal her breasts and make love until he lost himself in her. 'Once again, *cara*, we must talk.' He forced his voice to remain calm.

'I would like my shift first,' she said quietly. She did not meet his eyes.

'Of course.' He retrieved the garment from the floor and handed it to her. Then he walked to the window although the curtains were still drawn in order to give her privacy.

He waited until he heard her soft footsteps on the floor before he turned to face her. She stood at the foot of the bed, properly covered in the voluminous white gown, which did not render her any less desirable. But he was no longer a youth who could not control his desires. No matter what had happened last night.

'Sit down. Please,' he said.

She took a chair, not the one they'd made in love in. He had no idea whether she intended to avoid it or not. 'I hope you are not planning to beg my forgiveness for seducing me,' she said. 'In fact, I should beg your pardon for seducing you.' Her voice was calm, but the way she twisted her hands together told him she was not.

'Why? Because you regret it or you think I do?'

'I do not know.' She finally looked at him. 'You were here to do me a kindness and instead I…I took advantage of you.'

'My sweet girl, if I had not wanted to be taken advantage of, then there is nothing you could have done to, er…persuade me.' The conversation was not the one he had anticipated. He had never had a woman apologise for having her way with him. 'Will it ease your conscience if I tell you I have never been so enjoyably ravished in my life?'

She flushed. 'Oh.'

'Once we are married, we can repeat the experience any time you desire,' he said carelessly.

'Married? I thought…'

'You thought what?'

'That we were only to be betrothed. You said nothing about marriage.'

'I believe, my sweet, that in general marriage follows a betrothal. After last night, you do not have much choice. I've no doubt Eberhart knows we spent the night together and it is likely the others will suspect as well. Particularly after we announce our engagement today.'

'Today? Must we do it so soon?'

'Yes.' He scowled at her. 'Damn it, Cecily, marriage to me won't be that bad. I won't beat you.'

'I know,' she said quietly.

'Then why do you look as if you've just been sentenced to death?' He demanded.

'I…' She looked at him rather helplessly.

A cold fist slammed through him. She did not want to marry him despite the passion they had shared. It was possible Thais had been right after all, that for some reason Cecily feared him.

'Then we will consider the betrothal temporary. After a suitable length of time you may jilt me. For now, I had best leave your room and allow you to dress.'

'Yes.'

He tucked his shirt into his breeches and picked up his coat, then realised he'd forgotten to put on his stockings and shoes. He collected his shoes and stockings and sat down.

He finished and looked up. She stood near the window and he sensed it mattered not at all that the curtains were drawn, for her eyes seemed to be focused on something far away. Her shoulders drooped as if her thoughts gave her no pleasure. He rose and moved to stand behind her. 'Cecily.'

She turned, her expression rather confused as if she'd almost forgotten his presence. The forlorn look in her eyes tugged at his heart and he reached out to touch her cheek. She flinched and he dropped his hand. 'I am leaving now,' he said.

'Leaving?'

He supposed he should be gratified at the dismay in her face. 'Just the room. Not this villa. I would not leave you here.'

'No, of course not.'

'We will make the announcement before noon. After that we will leave.'

'Together?'

'Together, my sweet. Furthermore, you will return to my house. I will not allow you to go to Lady Margate so do not waste your breath in futile argument.' He did not wait for an answer. He turned and left the room before he could see her undoubtedly horrified expression.

Chapter Sixteen

Cecily rose from the bench. She could not spend the entire day in the villa's lush garden, as tempting as it was. She must return to the house and face the rest of the party. And Nico.

She had been beyond foolish to allow Thais to convince her to come here. The thought had never entered her mind that Nico would find out, much less come after her. Or that he felt such a…a stupid sense of honour that he would offer marriage to protect her.

Before they had made such passionate love.

Her whole body heated even thinking about it. Last night had been far different from the first time. Then, he had needed her and she had responded, but his lovemaking had held a certain desperation.

Last night had been something entirely different. He had made love to her, not out of need but out of desire. He had wanted her and she had wanted him back with a physical desire that had shocked her. Always slightly embarrassed by her unclothed body, she had stood naked before him, revelling in the knowledge he found her nude body beautiful.

She had run her hands over his body with an abandon she

had never shown with Marco, fascinated with the strong male hardness of his muscles, enjoying the feminine power she felt as he lay still beneath her hands, his breath coming harder and harder until she finished her exploration. And then…

No. She must put last night aside before she did something rash such as seduce him again. She must be completely depraved. Women, at least well-bred women, were not supposed to be thinking about such things. As much as she had enjoyed Marco's considerate lovemaking, it had never occurred to her to indicate she desired him.

She started up the path towards the house. She must face the others, including Thais. She only hoped Nico was wrong and no one would know they had been together last night.

She had nearly reached the lawn directly behind the house when she saw Nico coming around the side of the house. He paused for a moment and then he saw her. He strode towards her and there was no mistaking his black expression.

He halted in front of her. 'Where were you?' he demanded. 'No one could find you.'

'I was in the garden,' she said coolly. It was quite apparent he was not thinking about last night.

'Alone? What if Eberhart was to come upon you?'

'Well, he did not.' She must have truly lost her mind to think she would ever want to seduce this arrogant man. 'I am going back to the house. Are you coming, your Grace? Or were you about to visit the gardens yourself?'

To her great satisfaction, he looked as if he were about to explode. He did not. 'We are going back to the house where we will announce our betrothal,' he said through gritted teeth.

'Very well, your Grace.' She started to walk away, only to have him catch her arm.

She stopped and looked up at him. 'Is there something else you wished to say to me?'

'Yes.' He dropped her arm. His eyes still held an angry glint, but there was another emotion as well. 'This.'

He grasped her shoulders and pulled her into his arms. She was too startled to protest as his mouth covered hers. Her feeble attempts at resistance were swept away by his leisurely, seductive kiss and she melted into him, her mouth soft and pliable beneath his.

He lifted his head. 'We can go in now that you look well kissed. We would not want Eberhart to suspect we were quarrelling.' A little smile played about his mouth.

'And you do not appear to have been affected at all,' she said tartly, hoping to cover up her confusion. If he could look so calm and collected after ravaging her senses, then she would pretend the same.

A sardonic light leapt to his eye. 'In that, my sweet Cecily, you are quite wrong.'

Thais was the first person they met when they entered the house. 'Severin! Thank goodness you found her!' She grasped Cecily's hands. 'I was so worried you were not in your room and then no one knew where you had gone to!'

'I only wished to walk in the garden. I did not think anyone would worry.' Nothing in Thais' face indicated she guessed Cecily had been in Nico's arms a short time ago.

'You should have asked me to come with you. I adore walking in gardens. We can walk together tomorrow.' She smiled at Nico. 'I am certain you will not object if I steal Cecily away?'

'Actually, I do object.'

Thais stared at him, then gave a little laugh. 'Well, really! Then I will ask Cecily instead. I hope you will not go against her wishes!'

'Ah, so Signora Renato has not run away after all.' Eberhart had come up silently behind them.

'Of course she would not,' Thais said. 'But Severin refuses to let her out of his sight. I hope you will convince him he is being quite selfish!'

Eberhart's gaze raked over Cecily in a way that made her think that he guessed exactly how she'd spent her night. Her face heated, which brought a knowing smile to the Baron's full lips. 'You have pleasing news, I see.'

She glanced at Nico. His eyes were on Eberhart. 'You may congratulate us.'

'Most certainly.' Eberhart turned to Cecily. 'My dear, I must wish you all happiness.' He took her hand and brought it to his lips, his mouth lingering an instant too long, before releasing it. Nico's expression did not change, but he shifted closer to Cecily.

Eberhart turned to Thais. 'Lady Margate, do you not intend to congratulate the Duke and Signora Renato on their upcoming nuptials?' he asked blandly.

Thais had gone very still. For a moment, Cecily did not think she would answer. Then a strained smile crossed her face. 'Of course. I was just rather surprised, but I should have suspected something when Severin appeared last night.' She took Cecily's hand and kissed her cheek. 'I hope you will be happy, but it was very sly of you not to say a thing. In fact, I rather thought you did not care much for Severin at all.' She spoke in her light, teasing way.

'Thank you.' Why did Thais now say she thought Cecily

did not care for Nico when yesterday she had accused Cecily of being in love with him?

'There is only a quarter of an hour left until noon, so I suggest we make the announcement without delay. Unless, Severin, you wish to postpone it,' Eberhart said.

'I would prefer—' Cecily began. Everything was happening too fast.

Nico's hand closed around hers. 'We will make the announcement now.'

Eberhart smiled. 'Then let us proceed to the salon.'

Thais insisted on accompanying Cecily to her bedchamber so she could help Cecily pack. 'Although I think it is very bad of Severin to insist that you must stay with his family instead of me—I would have liked to have held a little party for you,' Thais said as they entered the room. Once inside, however, she closed the door and faced Cecily, the smile gone from her face.

'Perhaps I should not say anything, but as your friend I cannot remain silent.' She hesitated. 'Dear Cecily, are you certain you wish to marry Severin? I only ask because you do not seem happy. I worry that he has somehow forced you into accepting him.'

'Of course he has not.'

'Are you certain? He can be very overwhelming when he wants something. Particularly if he wants a woman. And it has been quite apparent from the very first that he has wanted you.' Her large eyes were filled with concern. 'Just as he wanted Angelina. Poor thing—he pursued her even though she found him quite intimidating. Everyone knew that she and Rafaele were to marry some day, but Severin did not care for that. He only wanted Angelina and would not allow her to refuse him. Sometimes I have wondered if her death was no accident, that perhaps she deliberately threw herself from the path rather than marry him.'

'That is a horrible thing to say.'

'Not if it is the truth.' Thais walked to the door. 'Do not make the same mistake Angelina did.'

Five days later, Raf was shown into the salon of the Ca' Cappelletti where Cecily and Eleanora were seated in front of the long windows facing the Grand Canal. Cecily looked up from the book she had been attempting to read, her pleasure at seeing him tinged with apprehension. 'Raf! What brings you to Venice? I thought you were in Vicenza!'

He smiled. 'You, of course.' He looked over at Eleanora, who had thrust the sketch she was working on under a paper. The smile left his face. '*Buongiorno*, Lady Eleanora.'

'*Buongiorno*, Signor Vianoli,' Eleanora said curtly. She stood, clutching the sketchpad to her chest. 'I am certain you wish to speak to Cecily in private, so I will leave you.' She brushed past him.

Cecily glanced at Raf, who regarded Eleanora's retreating back with a slight frown. She had no idea why Eleanora did not seem to like Raf.

Raf said nothing about her when he turned to Cecily. 'A few days ago I met an acquaintance who informed me that a certain Austrian baron has been pursuing you. He also mentioned you were staying with Thais Margate. When I called there today, I was told you were no longer with Lady Margate but were now here.' He regarded her, his face serious. 'Is any of this true?'

'As you can see, I am here.' She had hardly expected such news to reach him.

'I was referring to the rest,' Raf said.

She hesitated for a moment. No purpose would be served by dissembling. He would learn the truth soon enough.

'Cecily?'

'Yes. I went to stay with Lady Margate. I did not wish to stay here after Simon and Mariana left. It was too awkward.'

'Because of Nico?'

She flushed a little.' Yes. I met Lady Margate a few days before they departed and she suggested that I stay with her. I accepted.'

'Nico allowed you to go?'

'He did not know. He accompanied Simon and Mariana as far as Mestre and then went on to the Villa Cappelletti.'

'I see. What of Eberhart? Is this true as well?'

'Yes. He…he had an interest in me.'

He swore softly and she put her hand on his arm. 'But no longer. He invited Lady Margate and me as guests at a house party at his villa. Just before dinner Nico arrived.' She took a steadying breath. 'He told the Baron that we are to be married. But only to protect me,' she quickly added.

A peculiar gleam shone in his eye and then his lips curved. 'Of course. I should have known that Nico would not allow such a thing.' He took her hand. 'May I offer you my felicitations for your future happiness. I must call on him, however, since he did not ask my permission, although he can be forgiven under the circumstances.'

She gathered her wits together. 'We are not really to be married. The betrothal is only temporary.'

'Has it been made public?'

'I suppose, yes. The Baron announced it at the house party.'

'And did Nico object?'

'No, he quite wished the Baron to do so.'

'He means to marry you. He will not publicly humiliate you by breaking off the betrothal.'

'But he does not mean to marry me!'

'Then he is only trifling with your affections?'

'Raf!' She realised he was only teasing her, but she was uncomfortable none the less. 'No, of course not. I do not want to marry him, either.'

'So you intend to humiliate him?'

'No!' She took a deep breath before she lost her temper. 'I would never do such a thing. We mutually agreed that, after a suitable period of time, we would break off the betrothal. There will be no marriage.'

His mouth curved in a most wicked grin. 'But I have decided otherwise.' He brushed a brief kiss across the back of her hand 'It is time that I speak with your *fidanzato*.'

'Raf!'

But he was gone. She suspected he meant to tease her but she was not completely certain. Not that she was certain about anything to do with Nico. Since their return to Venice she had seen him twice. Both times in company and both times he had treated her with all the solicitousness of a devoted fiancé. Nothing in his manner indicated they had spent a night in each other's arms. She prayed nothing in her manner indicated how his impersonal touch sent her pulse racing and made her knees tremble. She would die if he guessed how much she wanted to throw herself in his arms again.

She feared she was very much in danger of falling in love with him.

***

Nico looked up from the letter he was attempting to write. He started when he saw Raf. 'What the devil are you doing here?'

Raf strode into the study. 'I heard rumours that Eberhart had been pursuing Cecily. She informed me that you had already dealt with the situation in a most admirable fashion.'

'Her words, I imagine,' he said drily.

Raf grinned. 'Of course. You have my blessing.'

'She does not want to marry me.'

'Do you wish to marry her?'

He stood. 'I have asked her twice. She has turned me down the same number of times.'

'Has she? I wonder why. She cares for you.'

He shrugged. 'Not enough to marry me.' He could not quite keep the bitterness out of his voice. She had given no indication since they had returned to Venice that she had been affected by their night together. When all he could think about was having her beneath him, while he made love to her again and again.

'Do you want to marry her? Or are you only doing what is honourable?'

'I need a wife.'

Raf merely looked at him. Nico folded his arms. 'Well?'

'You are in love with her, are you not?'

Nico stared at him. 'Why the hell would you say that?'

'I cannot fathom why you would put yourself to so much trouble if you were not. But it is more than that. Your face softens when you speak of her. You look at her the way a man looks at a woman he loves. You frown now and swear because you wish to cover your hurt that she has refused you.'

He wanted to shout and call Raf a fool, but the words died on his lips. 'I loved Angelina.'

'As did I. But she has been dead for over thirteen years. You cannot bury yourself with her.'

'I've hardly done that.'

'No?'

'No, damn you.' He eyed Raf coolly. 'I could fling the same accusation at you. For I do not see any indication you have fallen in love again.'

'Perhaps I have not met the right woman.'

Nico said nothing.

'Cecily is not Angelina. But then you are not the same youth who fell so wildly in love with her. I wonder—if you were to meet her now for the first time, would you still want her? Or if you would discover it was Cecily you wanted after all?'

He turned and left Nico.

Nico did not move. He should have cursed Raf. Mowed him down. Finished the mill they started at the inn that night.

For what? Suggesting he might not want Angelina at all? That he would choose Cecily instead? He should have thrown Raf's words after him, but he had not.

He had no idea why.

The letter arrived the next day. It was written in a thin, uneven hand that Nico did not recognise.

Cecily Renato will come to great harm if you do not end your betrothal. You must stay away from her.

He stared at it, his initial anger followed by a prick of fear. Barbarina. Of that he had no doubt, for the wording of the note bore too much resemblance to Barbarina's other dire warnings. How the devil had she found out about their engagement? The notice of their betrothal had been published only yesterday and few people had known beforehand. Except the guests who were present. Of those, only Thais knew Barbarina.

He frowned. He could think of no reason why Thais would take it upon herself to inform Barbarina. It made no sense.

He dismissed Thais; his greater concern was Barbarina. He had not thought much about Barbarina or the fête until now. Or the discussion with Raf and the possibility Barbarina had tried to harm Cecily.

Hell. Why had it slipped his mind? He stared down at the note, his expression grim. He had promised to look after Cecily and he'd failed when she had gone to stay with Thais. He would not make the same mistake again.

Chapter Seventeen

Eleanora turned to Cecily. 'Would you mind very much if we stop at one more shop? It is not very far from here. If you are not too fatigued, that is. I fear I can go on wandering for ever and never tire while my companions have nearly collapsed. I promise we will not get lost again.' They stood outside a small milliner's shop in one of the many narrow, fascinating streets winding through Venice.

Cecily smiled. 'Even if we did, I would not mind because it is such an interesting place in which to lose oneself.'

Eleanora smiled back at her. 'Oh, Cecily! I am so glad we are to be sisters! Have you tired of hearing that yet?'

'No, for I feel exactly the same.' She would not think about Eleanora's disappointment when she learned Cecily would not be her sister after all. For since her return to Venice nearly a week ago, she was more and more convinced marriage to Nico would lead to nothing but unhappiness for both of them. She shook off her uneasy thoughts—she did not want to worry Eleanora. 'Let us find your shop.'

Eleanora tucked her arm through Cecily's as they started

off, Giacomo, the footman, trailing after them. The small streets between the tall narrow buildings fascinated Cecily. As did coming upon the quiet canals where one must cross a bridge in order to reach the next *calle*.

The small shop was located in a tiny *campo*. Several women were gathered around the cistern in its centre to procure buckets of water. A few children and a dog chased after a hoop. They crossed the square towards one of the little shops. The sign proclaimed one could procure papers, paints and brushes.

Cecily turned to Eleanora. 'You are interested in art, then?'

'A little,' Eleanora said carelessly. 'I sometimes like to sketch or attempt a watercolour. We do not need to go in if you would rather not.'

She was not certain why Eleanora suddenly seemed so hesitant. 'I will look for a present for Mariana as she also enjoys drawing.' She stepped into the shop and after a moment Eleanora followed.

No one was in the shop. Eleanora looked around and then went to the display of paints. Cecily looked about her. 'It is exactly the sort of place Raf would like.'

'Raf?' Eleanora started. 'Of course. He is an artist, is he not?'

'Yes, although he does not paint much any more.'

'Oh.' She turned back. After a few moments, she chose a box of watercolours. 'This is all I want. Have you found something for Mariana?'

'Perhaps some paper and a new set of pencils. What would you recommend?'

Eleanora was soon engrossed in helping Cecily; by the time she stepped up to the counter to pay for the purchases, she was convinced Eleanora was more than an amateur artist, for she sounded exactly like Raf when Cecily had accompanied him to such a shop. Why then did Eleanora seem so reluctant to admit it? She held back her questions, not wanting to pry into Eleanora's affairs.

By the time they left the shop, Eleanora had reverted to her usual cheerful self. 'We can go over the Rialto,' Eleanora said as they crossed the *campo*. 'There is a little place where we can have an ice. It is not as grand as Florian's, but I must admit I like their ices better.'

Cecily was amazed how well Eleanora managed to find her way through the narrow maze of streets. Soon they were on the bridge that spanned the Grand Canal.

They slowly made their way up the shallow steps of the bridge through the crowds, stopping here and there to peer into one of the shops that lined the bridge. As they started down the other side of the bridge Eleanora's attention was caught by a display of books. 'I promise I will look at nothing else after this,' she told Cecily with a sheepish smile.

Cecily laughed. 'Should you promise that? There are certain to be more shops before we are home.'

'Yes, well.' Eleanora crossed to the display and picked up one of the books. 'Come and look, Cecily. Is this not an odd illustration?'

Cecily was about to move to Eleanora's side when she heard a shout. She looked up and froze in horror, for a small cart was careening down the steps towards her. Just in time she jumped away. Her foot caught on the edge of the step and then she was falling.

'Cecily!' Eleanora cried. She dropped beside Cecily. 'Thank God! I thought the cart was going to hit you.'

Cecily attempted to sit up and her head spun for a moment. She saw the cart lying on its side a few steps below her.

'*Signora!*' Giacomo suddenly appeared. Soon a crowd of fascinated, horrified onlookers surrounded them.

Giacomo helped her to her feet and to the inside of the nearest shop where someone procured a chair and insisted she sit. Her entire body hurt, she had torn her glove on one hand and, to her chagrin, she felt tears prick her eyelids.

Eleanora knelt next to her, her face worried. 'I have sent Giacomo for Nico. You cannot possibly walk home.'

Oh, dear. 'I am fine, really. Just rather shaken. It is not very far. I am certain I will be able to walk.'

'Well, I am not about to let you. Nico would strangle me.' Eleanora rose as a burly man, who appeared to be the proprietor, approached them. With him was a man wearing the uniform of an Austrian officer.

The officer introduced himself as Captain Guttman. He had seen the disturbance and had come to make certain the *signora* had not been badly hurt and to offer his assistance. After Cecily reassured him she had sustained no serious injuries, he offered to see them home.

'It is kind of you to offer, but I have sent for my brother, the Duke of Severin,' Eleanora told him.

'I will wait with you until he arrives,' Guttman said. He had a pleasant face and manner and Cecily had recovered enough to notice the admiration in his eyes when he looked at Eleanora.

Shortly after that, the proprietor announced the *signora*'s cousin had arrived. Expecting to see Nico, Cecily was stunned to see Raf instead.

She half-rose and then winced. 'Raf? Why are you here?'

He strode to her side. 'I was just leaving the Ca' Cappelletti when Giacomo arrived and said you were hurt. Nico was not home, so I came. Are you all right?'

'Yes, of course. Just a little bruised.'

Raf looked at Eleanora. 'What happened?'

'She was almost knocked down by a cart. She fell down the steps when she tried to get away.'

Raf's mouth tightened. 'Whose cart was it?'

'I do not know,' Eleanora said.

Guttman spoke. 'I would like to speak to you for a moment, *signor*.'

Raf turned to him. 'Captain Guttman offered to stay with us until Nico...or you arrived,' Eleanora said quickly. 'Signor Vianoli is a relation of Signora Renato,' she told Guttman. 'Oh, dear, I should have made a more formal introduction.'

'Under the circumstances this will suffice,' Raf said. 'You had something you wanted to tell me, Captain?'

'Yes. If you will step outside with me.'

Raf followed him out and they returned a few minutes later. Raf's mouth was set in a hard line, although his expression relaxed a little when he informed Eleanora and Cecily he would take them home now.

Guttman took his leave, bowing over Eleanora's hand a trifle too long.

It did not escape Raf's notice. 'You have an admirer,' he said.

'Hardly,' Eleanora snapped. She picked up her reticule and then Cecily's. 'Did you bring a gondola?'

'It is waiting near the bridge.' Raf looked down at Cecily. 'I will carry you.'

'I can walk perfectly well.' She rose, albeit rather stiffly. 'Shall we go?'

Raf did not argue, although she suspected he wanted to. The thought crossed her mind that Nico would have swept her up into his arms no matter what she said. Which was one reason she should be glad he was not here.

However, he was on the small dock outside the palazzo with its black-and-white striped poles. He helped Eleanora step from the gondola to the landing and then held his hand out for Cecily. Raf helped her to her feet and she grasped Nico's hand. She stumbled a little, her balance shaky, and then she was on solid ground, his arm supporting her.

'Thank you.' She drew away from him and managed a step before she swayed again.

He was at her side. 'I am carrying you to your room.'

She looked up into his cool, arrogant face. 'I suppose if I said I was perfectly capable of walking, you would completely override my wishes.'

'You are correct in your supposition.'

A strangled giggle escaped her. 'Then I will not argue.'

'Good.' He swept her up, his arms strong and safe around her. He looked down at her, and she saw the worry in his eyes. He was overbearing, but it was because he wanted to take care of her.

She closed her eyes before he could read the truth in her face.

She had fallen in love with him.

Raf whirled around when Nico entered the salon. 'How is Cecily?'

'She is bruised, but nothing more serious, thank God.'

Nico met Raf's eyes. 'Thank you for bringing her home.' He'd arrived at the palazzo minutes after Raf had left. Only his mother's calm reassurance that Eleanora was with Cecily and Raf would see her safely home kept him from going after her.

'I am only glad that I was still here when Giacomo arrived,' Raf said. 'It was not an accident.'

'How do you know?'

'An Austrian captain was waiting with Eleanora and Cecily when I arrived at the shop. He took me outside and told me that several witnesses claimed someone deliberately pushed the cart towards Cecily. A person in a black cloak and possibly wearing a mask.'

Nico's blood ran cold. 'I received a letter today. An anonymous letter. The writer said that if I did not end my betrothal to Cecily she would come to harm.'

'Do you still have the letter?'

'It is in my room.'

'I would like to see it.'

'Then come with me.'

Raf followed him to his room. He retrieved the letter from his writing desk and handed it to Raf. Raf read it and looked up his expression, grim.

'Do you recognise the handwriting?' Nico asked.

'I cannot say for certain.'

'Is it possible that Barbarina has returned to Venice?'

'I will call on Signora Gamba and see if Barbarina has returned to her. If she is not there, then I will leave for Avezza tomorrow—we need to know for certain if she has left Avezza and when.'

'And if she has not?'

'Then we will consider other possibilities. For now we must keep Cecily safe.'

'I will not allow her to leave the house unless I am with her. Or Giacomo. Once he understands what we want, he will guard her well.'

'How much do you want to tell your mother and sister? Or Cecily?'

'Not much until we discover Barbarina's whereabouts. I do not want to alarm them or Cecily unduly.'

'Very well. I will call on Signora Gamba now and let you know as soon as possible what I have discovered. I will show myself out.' Raf looked at Nico. 'I know you will keep her safe.'

'Yes.' He would. He had failed Angelina, he would not fail Cecily.

'You still have not decided what you wish to wear? Perhaps go as Brighella? A shepherdess? Or,' Eleanora said with a teasing smile, 'should we ask Nico?'

'Nico?' Cecily jerked her thoughts back to the topic at hand. 'Ask him what?'

'What you should wear to the masquerade. I do not suppose he has mentioned to you what he plans to wear.'

'No, he hasn't said a thing. I am certain I can think of something. For myself, that is, not Nico. I can always wear a domino and a mask.' She could only imagine what he would say if she attempted to choose a costume for him.

Eleanora made a face. 'You are as bad as he is! That is exactly what he always wears to a masquerade. I had hoped you might persuade him to actually wear a costume. I have a splendid idea. We can go out today and find masks. There is a little shop near San Marco that has the most interesting ones that I have seen. We can find one for Nico as well.'

'Find what for me?' Nico asked.

Cecily started and looked up, her heart pounding much more than it should. He stood in the doorway of the small salon.

'A mask. Cecily and I are planning to visit a shop today to find masks for the masquerade. I suggested we find one for you since you seem too busy to go yourself.'

'Are you certain Cecily is well enough for such an excursion?' He did not look at all pleased by the idea.

'Of course I am,' Cecily said, annoyed that he did not directly address her.

'I will go with you,' he said abruptly. 'When do you wish to leave?'

Eleanora and Cecily both stared at him. 'Well?' he asked impatiently.

Eleanora recovered first. 'As soon as Cecily and I are ready. Before you change your mind.'

Chapter Eighteen

It was not Nico who changed his mind, however, but Eleanora. An hour and a half later, Cecily entered the salon and found Nico there with the Duchess. 'Eleanora is not well, but wants you and Nico to go without her. She would like both of you to choose a mask for her,' the Duchess said.

Cecily glanced at Nico, whose polite expression conveyed no enthusiasm for the idea. 'I do not mind waiting until Eleanora is better. I am certain the Duke has other business to attend to.'

A gleam appeared in his eye. 'On the contrary, I am at your service.'

The Duchess smiled. 'Good. He can take you to Florian's for an ice for you have not yet been there. In fact, Cecily has not even seen San Marco, although it is not at all the same since Napoleon. He was a criminal, no better than the *banditti*.' She spoke with an angry passion that Cecily had not witnessed before. She quickly collected herself. 'But it is still beautiful, he could not destroy that. So Domenico will take you and you will enjoy yourselves and not think of these things today.'

By the time they reached the Piazza San Marco, Cecily wondered why he had agreed to accompany her—he had said very little on the journey through the canals. Once or twice, when they had accidentally touched, he had jerked away as if burned. Not that she had fared much better, for her pulse jumped every time he came close to brushing against her. She wished she had thought of developing a headache.

The shop was located in a narrow L-shaped *calle* several streets behind the Piazza San Marco. Nico pushed opened the door and Cecily stepped inside. It was a tiny shop and masks of every description covered the shelves and counters. A white-haired man emerged from a room behind the counter. Through the curtain Cecily could see half-finished masks spread across a worktable. 'May I be of assistance?'

'We are interested in your masks,' Nico said.

'For the lady or yourself or both?'

'For both of us,' Cecily said before Nico could answer. Eleanora had wanted him to get a mask so she would make certain he did.

'Very good, *signora*.' He came around the side of the counter. 'Do you wish to find a mask for the *signor* first?'

'For the *signora* first,' Nico said.

'Allow me to show you what I have.'

In a few minutes he had set out a bewildering assortment of masks. Some were plain white ovals; others were lavishly decorated with feathers or sequins. There were full masks and half-masks and Cecily hardly knew where to start. She finally picked up a purple one, all too aware of Nico hovering near her shoulder. 'We must choose one for Eleanora first.' She set down the mask and forced herself to concentrate on them instead of Nico. She finally found a silk half-mask in blue and gold. 'What do you think?' she asked Nico.

'I have no doubt she will like it.'

He certainly was no help. 'I will take this,' she told the proprietor. She turned back to the selection, finding she had very little enthusiasm for choosing one for herself. She picked up one of the plain white masks. 'This will do.'

'No.' Nico removed the mask from her hand. 'This one.' He picked up a mask. It was of green silk and exquisitely decorated with small jewels. He stepped back. 'I want to see it on you.'

She stared at it. 'It is very beautiful, but…'

'Turn around. I will tie the ribbons.'

She obeyed and he stepped close to her, his body almost touching hers. His hands brushed her hair as he tied the strings. He moved his hands to her shoulders and she had the sudden desire to lean back into his arms as she had that night at the Villa Barbarigo. Oh, lord, what was wrong with her?

'Let me see you.' His hands fell from her shoulders.

She slowly turned around and faced him, grateful the mask would hide her embarrassing desire. His gaze travelled over her in a way that brought heat to her face. 'I will buy this.' His voice was husky.

'The *signora* is beautiful, no? It is a very fine mask, made by my son.'

Cecily untied the strings. 'I cannot accept this,' she told him in English. 'It is not proper.'

'You are my fiancée, so it is quite proper. Don't argue. I am buying it for you and you will wear it.'

'Indeed. Then it is only fair that I choose one for you that you will wear.'

'I have a mask.'

'But I did not choose it,' she said with a tight smile.

An odd glint appeared in his eye. 'Very well, my dear. Find something for me.'

She turned to the shopkeeper. 'I wish to look at masks for the *signor*.'

'Of course.' He pulled several from a shelf and spread them out before her. While she examined them, he brought out more.

She finally found what she was looking for. 'This one,' she told him. 'I want you to try it on.'

'Only if you will tie the strings for me,' he said softly. He suddenly looked quite dangerous and she wished she had not made the offer. But it was too late and she refused to back down.

'Turn around. You will need to bend a little.'

As soon as her hands touched his thick, dark hair she knew she had made a mistake. Not only by her own pounding heart and trembling fingers, but by the way he suddenly stilled under her hands. She finished tying the strings and stepped back, her mouth dry.

'It suits the *signor*.'

The shopkeeper's voice startled her out of her trance. She glanced at Nico. 'Yes. Yes, it does. He will take it.' She hardly knew what she was saying. To her relief, Nico removed the mask himself. She pretended interest in a display of masks while the shopkeeper wrapped their purchases, every nerve in her body on edge.

Nico finally turned. 'Shall we go?'

She jumped. 'Yes.'

She followed him out the door, careful to avoid touching

him. Outside the shop, she paused. 'Perhaps we should return to the Ca' Cappelletti. I am certain your sister is eager to see our purchases.' She started to walk away.

He caught her arm. 'You are going the wrong way.'

'Oh.' She looked up at him and her heart pounded at the expression in his eyes. 'Then I had best turn around.'

'Damn it, Cecily, this is impossible.'

'What is?' She could barely form the words.

'This,' he murmured. He stepped towards her and then his mouth was on hers. Her eyes fluttered shut and she gave herself over to his kiss, hardly noticing when the package slid to the ground. He pressed her to him and her arms circled his neck, her hands finally tangling in his silky hair. His mouth was hard and demanding and she met him kiss for kiss.

A sense that someone watched them broke into her consciousness. She pulled away and he lifted his head, his eyes heavy with desire. He saw her face. 'What is it?'

She looked around. The street was deserted. 'I thought someone was here…watching us. I am being fanciful again.' She shivered. The high walls of the buildings seemed to close in on them.

'You were not fanciful last time. Come, we need to leave this place.' He retrieved the fallen package and then took her hand.

The grim set to his jaw alarmed her as he led her through the narrow street, around the corner and through the short passage to the streets that would take them back to San Marco. The crowded street was reassuring and when they finally entered the piazza, her uneasiness dissipated.

He dropped her hand. 'We can stop at Florian's before we return home.'

'Yes.' He led her across the piazza to the colonnaded row of shops. They sat down and she looked across at him. His face still looked grim. 'What is wrong?' she asked. 'Do you really think there was someone there?'

He looked over at her. 'I do not know…'

'Why such sober faces? I hope you are not quarrelling already!'

They both looked up. Thais stood next to them, a quizzical expression in her blue eyes. She was very prettily dressed in a canary yellow pelisse and matching bonnet.

Nico rose. 'Good day, Lady Margate.'

'Lady Margate? When have you become so formal?' She turned a smile on Cecily. 'How are you, dear Cecily? It has been quite dull without you. You cannot imagine how I have missed our little chats.'

'Perhaps you would join us,' Cecily said.

'If Severin would not object to sharing you. I suspect him of wanting to keep you solely for himself.' She cast a droll look in his direction.

'I do,' he said coolly.

'He is only teasing,' Cecily said hastily. 'Please sit down.'

'Thank you.' Thais took the chair opposite Cecily. After a moment, Nico sat down next to her. 'You have been shopping,' Thais said. 'What have you purchased?'

'Masks,' Nico said briefly. It was quite apparent he did not welcome Thais' company.

'Masks? For the Weston masquerade? How delightful! Where did you go?'

'In a little shop nearby which Lady Eleanora recommended.'

'I shall have to visit it myself for I have not yet purchased anything!' She looked up at the waiter who had returned to take her order and asked him for a coffee. After he left she smiled at Nico. 'I cannot help but think of Angelina whenever I visit the piazza. She so loved St Mark's. Do you remember how devastated she was when Napoleon removed the horses?'

Nico's face tightened. 'Yes.'

'I can only imagine the pleasure she would have felt upon their return!' She turned to Cecily. 'She was such a sweet girl, rather like your own Mariana. When I first saw your daughter I was quite reminded of Angelina. It is a pity you did not meet her, for I am certain you would have adored her, do you not think, Severin?'

A sick feeling rose in Cecily's throat at his bleak expression. She turned to Thais. 'I know I would have liked her very much.' She looked up and saw the waiter carrying a tray towards them. 'Our refreshments are here, thank goodness. I am starving.' She prayed Thais would be distracted by the cakes and coffee.

The waiter put the tray down on an adjoining table and set the plates and cups in front of them. After the waiter left, Thais took a sip of her coffee before speaking. 'Angelina always had a lemon ice when we were here. I quite forgot until now. Does this not remind you of the time the three of us came here? Except you are now betrothed to Cecily instead of Angelina.' She picked up her fork and calmly took a bite of her cake.

The thought darted through Cecily's mind that Thais meant to hurt Nico. She must stop her from saying anything more about Angelina. 'Have you yet decided on a costume for the masquerade? We have talked of nothing else.' She began to chatter about the various ideas Eleanora had suggested and when she had exhausted that topic began describing the plot of a novel she had just read in minute detail. Thais had no chance to do more than say a word before Cecily prattled over her. She was quite aware that Nico stared at her as if she had gone mad, but at least he had lost that horrible stricken look.

As soon as the bill had been paid, she rose. 'How nice to see you, Thais. But we really must return home.'

'I quite understand.' Her smile was guileless. She turned to Nico. 'I hope we will have the chance to speak of Angelina again. I miss her just as I know you do.' She walked off before he could reply.

Cecily touched his arm. 'We must go.'

He looked down at her as if he'd forgotten she was there. 'Yes. We must.'

He said little on the tedious journey home and Cecily had no idea if he even noticed her presence.

At the top of the staircase, outside the doors to the salon, he stopped. 'I will see you at dinner.'

'Yes. Thank you, your Grace.' She turned and left him. He had shut her out and she knew there was nothing she could say to help him.

Chapter Nineteen

Nico looked up just as Cecily appeared in the doorway of the small salon. He caught his breath. Ready for the masquerade, she was dressed as a lady from the preceding century. Her gown of embroidered cream-and-green silk emphasised her small waist and the soft curves of her breast. She wore a white wig, which was unexpectedly erotic, and he felt his groin tighten in response. For a moment she stared at him and he thought he glimpsed a similar awareness until her face closed. 'Good evening, your Grace. You wished to see me, I believe.'

He did not like the impersonal politeness in her voice. The same politeness that had been there since the day at San Marco. He had no idea how to bridge the gulf between them. He kept his own voice cool. 'I do. I have something to give you.'

'To give me?' She entered the room and stood a few feet from him.

He forced his eyes away from her lovely mouth and pulled the small packet from his waistcoat pocket. 'A ring.' He unwrapped it. 'Hold out your hand.'

She looked at the ring and then quickly up at him, dismay clearly written all over her face. 'But that is the ring the duchess wears.'

'It is traditionally presented by the Dukes of Severin to their intended brides upon their betrothal. My mother wished you to have it now.'

'It is lovely, but I cannot wear it,' she said quietly.

'Why?' He felt angry and frustrated. 'We are betrothed, are we not?'

'Yes.' She drew in a breath. 'It is only temporary.'

'Then you will wear the ring until we put a halt to it. It will look damnably odd if you do not. Hold out your hand.'

She did so. He took her slender hand in his own and slipped the ring on to her finger. He stared down at her hand now wearing the symbol of his family. He hadn't expected to feel anything, but the surge of possessive desire startled him.

She pulled her hand away. 'It is very lovely. I will take good care of it, your Grace.'

'Don't do that.'

She looked up at him. 'Don't do what?'

'Act as if we are strangers. No, worse, as if you can hardly stand to be in the same room with me.'

She lifted her chin. 'That is not true!'

'No? Ever since we have returned to Venice you have treated me with nothing but cold disdain.'

'I could accuse you of the same thing. You barely speak to me except when necessary and after that day we bought the masks you have hardly been around!'

'Only because you have made it clear you do not want me around.'

'This conversation is pointless. You do not want me

around and I do not want you around. It appears neither one of us is particularly fond of the other. I really think, your Grace, that perhaps we should end this betrothal now.' She started to tug the ring from her finger.

'If you do not want to marry me, then perhaps you will consider becoming my mistress.' He regretted the words as soon as they left his mouth.

Her head jerked up, the colour draining from her face. Her chin inched up a notch and she met his eyes. 'I would be most honoured to become your mistress.'

This time he was the one who started. 'You are bluffing, my sweet Cecily.'

'Only if you were bluffing when you asked me.' The little cool smile on her face did nothing to improve his temper.

'Not at all. I am leaving for the villa tomorrow. When I return we will negotiate the terms.' He had no idea what he was saying.

'You are leaving?' For a moment, her gaze faltered and then she recovered. 'I will look forward to discussing your terms.'

'Then let us seal our bargain. Properly.' He did not give her a chance to reply, instead he swept her into his arms and found her mouth. He finally lifted his head and released her. Her cheeks were flushed, her lips swollen, her breathing hard.

He stepped back, angry at his loss of control. 'You may slap me now if you'd like.'

'No. I do not think that will be necessary. The others are waiting for us. You are going to the masquerade, are you not?'

'Cecily.'

She swept from the room, leaving him staring after her.

He could no longer deny that he was falling in love with her.

* * *

Cecily stood with Bernardo and Eleanora in the salon of the huge palazzo leased by Sir Thomas and Lady Weston. Festoons of flowers and vines decorated the room and Chinese lanterns lent an exotic eastern aura.

'The musicians should arrive soon,' Eleanora remarked. She looked beautiful and quite intriguing in a flowing gown of dark blue silk.

'Then we should go to the *androne* now so we might have the best view.' The highlight of the evening was to be a barge of musicians arriving in front of the palazzo at midnight. Bernardo, dressed as Pantalone, held out one arm to Eleanora and the other to Cecily. Cecily smiled at him, determined she would not think about Nico. She had no idea where he was for Octavia had spirited him away shortly after they arrived.

Their parting before the masquerade had dashed any hopes she might have secretly entertained that something was possible between them. He'd asked her to become his mistress in anger and she had accepted in equal anger. She knew he regretted his words, the instant she saw his face after he'd kissed her. She was too numb to care, so when Bernardo appeared, a handsome troubadour, she found she had no trouble engaging in a mild flirtation with him. Perhaps her heart would not break after all.

Where was Cecily? Nico had lost sight of her among the crowd of masked guests. He finally spotted her with Bernardo and Eleanora heading towards the small hall that led to the stairs. He wanted to go after her, but he would hardly blame her if she refused to talk to him. Not after he'd insulted her. He felt a flicker of despair every time he thought of her face after he'd offered *carte blanche*.

'Severin, I must speak with you. In private.'

He turned and found a woman in a black half-mask and domino at his side. For a moment he thought he was staring at Barbarina Zanetti, then just as quickly recognised Thais Margate despite the black wig covering her curls. 'This hardly seems the time for a private conversation.'

'Please, I must talk to you before it is too late.'

She had an almost desperate note in her voice he had never heard before. 'What is it?'

'Not here. There is a room off the salon where we can go.' She placed her hand on his arm, her grip firm as if she had no intention of allowing him to get away.

Torn between curiosity and unease, he followed her across the crowded room and into one of the smaller rooms. Surprisingly enough, it was empty. She turned to face him, and even through the slits of her mask he felt the intensity of her gaze.

'What is wrong?' he asked.

'You cannot marry Cecily Renato. It is all wrong.'

'Why is it wrong?' he asked carefully.

'Because I love you. I always have.'

'Thais...' Shocked, he took a step back as she came towards him. He found himself backed up against a sofa.

'You must care for me at least a little.' She stood so close she was almost touching him.

Was she drunk? He caught her hand. 'Do not say anything more that you will later regret.'

She gave a peculiar little laugh. 'I only regret I did not

tell you this when you were so determined to marry Angelina. Would it have changed your mind?'

He released her hand. 'I loved Angelina.'

'You could not have. Just as you do not love Cecily.'

'You are wrong. I love Cecily. I am going to marry her.'

She stared at him. 'I will never let that happen.' She spoke in a cold, controlled voice.

'What do you mean?'

'I mean that you will never marry her.' She whirled away from him and before he could stop her had run from the room. He dashed after her, but she slipped past a trio of harlequins. A feeling of dread washed over him and he knew he must find Cecily.

He started through the crowd. Many of the guests were gathered in front of the tall windows facing the grand canal. Others were leaving the salon and starting down the stairs to the *androne*. The barge of musicians must be coming. He vaguely remembered Eleanora mentioning they would watch the barge from the *androne*. He crossed the salon and out of the corner of his eye saw a short dark figure in a black cloak. The hair on the back of his neck prickled. He pushed his way through the crowd, ignoring the indignant mutters at his rudeness, and reached the stairs. For a moment, he could see nothing and then saw the black-cloak figure was already in the *androne*.

He ran down them, shoving past a quartet of youths who were idling on the stairs. He had nearly reached the bottom when he saw Eleanora and Bernardo. They were nearly at the gates leading from the palazzo to the dock on the canal. At first he did not see Cecily and then he caught a glimpse of her green mask. He heard someone call his name, but he paid no heed.

He jumped down the last step and began to run across the marble floor through the crowd.

Cecily stood next to Bernardo on the small dock in front of the palazzo. Sounds of a Vivaldi concerto drifting out over the water heralded the approach of the floating concert.

The crowd pushed forward, hoping to glimpse the barge. A large nun jostled her way in front of Cecily, who stumbled a little. She righted herself and found Bernardo was no longer next to her. The mass of guests seemed to close around her and a sliver of panic shot through her.

A hand closed around her arm. She attempted to draw her arm away and found herself looking at a dark shrouded figure. A prickle of fear shot down her back, for there was something sinister and familiar about the figure. 'I think, sir, that you have mistaken me for someone else.'

'Good evening, Cecily.'

She nearly sagged with relief. 'Thais. You frightened me.'

Her grip tightened around Cecily's wrist and she pulled something from the folds of her garment. 'You cannot marry him, you know.' With sick shock Cecily saw a flash of silver and realised she held a dagger. Thais raised it just as the musicians reached the palazzo, the strains of the concerto echoing all round.

'No!' Cecily pulled away with all of her strength and stumbled. At the same time another dark figure burst through the crowd and leaped towards Thais. They both tumbled into Cecily and all three of them fell into the cold, dark water.

She went under for a moment and then clawed her way up, gasping and terrified. Her heavy skirts wrapped around her legs and she fought to keep from slipping into the chilly depths. There was a splash next to her. Strong arms grasped her. She flailed out, fearing it was Thais who meant to drown her.

'Cecily.'

Nico. She had no idea how he came to be there. 'Thais, she...she tried to stab me.'

'Don't talk, sweetheart. I need to get you out.'

He helped her to the edge of the dock. He half-lifted her as a man reached down and pulled her out. Her knees shook so hard she could barely stand and she was hardly aware of the voices and music around her. Someone draped a long cape over her shoulders. 'Come, *signora*, you must go inside.' She looked up and saw a man standing next to her.

'No. The...the others.' She realised Nico had not followed her out and in the dim light of the torches she thought she saw him swimming towards a black shape.

'Cecily. Thank God.'

Raf was suddenly at her side. 'Where is Nico?'

'In...in the water.'

He ran towards the dock just as Bernardo and Eleanora appeared. 'Cecily. Oh, dear lord, it was you.' Eleanora's face was pale. 'We must get you inside.'

'No. Wait.' For Raf had stooped to help another woman from the water. A woman whose hair was long and dark instead of blonde. He laid her on the dock and knelt beside her. Cecily ran towards her.

Cecily dropped down next to Raf. 'Barbarina!' Barbarina's eyes were closed, but she was breathing, thank God. She gripped Barbarina's hand. 'Barbarina, it is Cecily.'

Barbarina's eyes opened for a moment. 'You are safe. I tried to stop her…tried to warn you…warn him that she is wicked.'

'You must not talk.' She squeezed her hand and then quickly slipped the cape from her shoulders and covered Barbarina. 'She…she saved my life, Raf. We must take her inside. It is too cold.'

'I know.' He looked up and Cecily saw Nico standing next to them. Water dripped down his forehead and he was breathing heavily. 'How is she?'

'Alive,' Raf said. 'But barely. The other?'

'I could do nothing.'

Raf bent towards Barbarina. 'Barbarina. I will carry you inside.'

Her eyes fluttered open. 'No.' She looked past him to Nico. 'Must tell him…the Duke…' Her breathing was heavy. She closed her eyes.

'Nico?' Alarmed, Cecily looked up at him.

Nico dropped to the ground beside her. 'Signora Zanetti. Barbarina.'

With a great effort, she opened them. 'I saw her that day, when Angelina…'

'When Angelina what?'

'When she went to meet you. She followed…Angelina.' She paused, struggling for breath. 'She killed Angelina. I…I saw it in her eyes. At the fête, she…tried to kill Cecily.

Because of you.' Her eyes closed and she drew in one last shuddering breath.

Horrified, Cecily stared at Barbarina and then at the others. 'Nico?' she whispered. He looked as if he'd turned to stone.

Chapter Twenty

Cecily set her book aside on the bench and waited for Nico to cross the *androne* to the courtyard where she sat. Two days had passed since Barbarina's funeral; nearly a week since the nightmarish masquerade. Her heart sank a little when she saw his face—he still wore the remote expression of a man who was utterly unreachable, buried away in his grief.

'I wanted to tell you that I am leaving Venice for a while,' he said.

'When will you go?'

'Today. In a few hours.'

She would not let him see her dismay. 'Where will you go?'

'To a small villa near Vicenza.'

She stood. He was polite, none of the arrogance she so associated with him present. If only he would attempt to ride roughshod over her. Or scold her. But he'd done nothing but shut himself away since that night. 'I am sorry.' She could think of nothing else.

If anything, his expression only shuttered more. 'Why? You almost lost your life because of me.'

'You are wrong. I almost lost my life because of Thais. You saved my life. You and Barbarina.'

He said nothing. A sort of angry despair washed over her. 'Thais deceived all of us, even me,' Cecily said. 'I do not want to spend the rest of my life thinking that you blame yourself for what happened to me. I could not bear it. So for my sake, I pray you will not.' She picked up her book. 'I will say goodbye to you now. As always, I wish you happiness.' She waited for him to speak and when he did not, she left him. She did not look back.

Raf called just before Nico was about to step into the gondola. 'What do you think you are doing?' he asked Nico without preamble.

'I am leaving Venice.'

'Why? Because you blame yourself for Angelina? For Cecily?'

'I am about to leave. I would prefer to continue this discussion later.' *Or not at all.*

'Damn you, Domenico. We will have this discussion now.'

Nico had rarely seen Raf so angry. He suspected that, if he were to step into the gondola, Raf would follow. 'We cannot talk here. Come into one of the offices.'

Inside the office, Raf glared at him. 'What is it? You wish to take the guilt for Angelina's death upon yourself? You were not the one who pushed her that day.'

'No, but Barbarina spoke the truth; because of me Thais killed Angelina and tried to kill Cecily. I should have seen, should have known, what she was capable of doing.'

'None of us did. Do you think I have not blamed myself for the very same things? Thais did everything possible to convince me that Angelina was not happy with you—that Angelina loved me. I had some idea that Thais was jealous of Angelina, but it never occurred to me she would harm her. What of Barbarina? She suspected, but yet said nothing.'

'Thais did not have an obsession with you.'

'So that makes Angelina's death your fault? Did you encourage Thais?'

For the first time since that night, Nico felt a stirring of anger. 'No, damn it, but I should have made it clear I wanted nothing to do with her.'

'Do you think it would have mattered? She was not right; she was undoubtedly mad.' He looked at Nico. 'What of Cecily? You will leave her here by herself?'

'She is with my family. She has you if you are ever around.'

'She is betrothed to you, or perhaps you have forgotten that.'

'It is only temporary.'

'She loves you.'

He looked at Raf. 'Then she is a fool.'

Raf's fist balled. 'I should call you out for that,' he said softly.

'Choose your weapon.'

Raf stared at him for a moment. 'I am beginning to believe she is better off without you. She needs a man who will treasure her love, not trample it underfoot.' He strode to the door and then paused. 'Angelina is dead. And you have buried yourself with her.' He was gone.

Cecily looked around the bedchamber. The dressing table was bare; her fans and gloves neatly packed away in her bandbox. In another half an hour she would be leaving with Raf. She had decided she must return to Avezza. She had left a note for Nico with instructions it was to be given to him upon his return. She had left the ring with the Duchess.

'My dear, are you certain you want to leave us?' the Duchess asked. Cecily had not heard her enter the room. 'I do not like the thought of you returning to your home alone like this. You have been through a great deal in the past few weeks.'

'I will not be completely alone. Raf promised he will stay in Avezza for a few days.'

'Domenico needs you.'

She looked up at the Duchess. 'If anything, he has made it quite clear he does not. He would not allow me to give him anything. Not sympathy, not kindness. When I told him I was sorry he told me I did not need to be.' Just as Marco had refused to accept her comfort.

'My dear.'

'I can do nothing to help him,' Cecily whispered.

The Duchess was silent for a moment before speaking. 'He has not allowed any of us to help him, just as he did not before. In some way, for him, it is almost as if Angelina has died again. He blamed himself, you see, thirteen years ago, and I can only imagine how he must feel now. Not only about Angelina, but also about you. I have no doubt he feels he failed to protect you from Thais.'

'He is wrong. He did everything he could.'

'For him that was not enough,' she said gently. She took Cecily's hands. 'I cannot fault you for wanting to go, for you can do nothing for him unless he allows it. I only pray that he will open his heart before it is too late.' She bent forward and pressed a kiss on Cecily's cheek. 'It is time for you to go down.'

He had gone to the villa in the hills above Vicenza for a few days, but the solitude had brought him no relief. Instead his dreams had been restless and filled with imagies of Cecily and Angelina. He had given up and left for Treviso, the town where Angelina was buried.

Her grave was in the small cemetery near the villa that once belonged to her family. He found the marker easily enough, under the spreading shade of an old tree.

He thought of her dark laughing eyes set in an oval face, which she considered too long and which he found adorable, and her beautiful, curving body. She had enchanted him; he had wondered how any creature so exquisite and alive could adore him the way she had. He'd always had a sense she was not quite real; even their kisses tasted of magic, and he sometimes feared he would open his eyes and find she'd vanished like some enchanted creature.

In the end, she had vanished, leaving him bereft and empty-handed and wondering if his very attempts to capture her had somehow destroyed her.

In the end she had been destroyed because of him.

As Cecily had almost been.

Raf did not blame him. Nor did Cecily. He would never forget the look of despair on her face when she walked away from him, as if by holding himself responsible he was somehow hurting her as well.

Raf said Cecily loved him. He wondered if that was still true.

Raf was correct; he was not the same youth who fell in

love with Angelina. *I wonder—if you were to meet her now for the first time, would you still want her? Or if you would discover it was Cecily you wanted after all?*

For despite the hours he and Angelina had spent together, talking and laughing, and flirting, he could not recall one time when he had told her anything of substance. He had not spoken to her of the sorrow he felt over his father's ailing health. Or the apprehension he felt at the prospect of becoming the next Duke and finding himself responsible for his family's vast holdings and wealth and all those, family and employees, who would be dependent upon his goodwill and judgement. The few times he had brought such things up, she would tease him for his seriousness. 'You will become dull, Nico, if you continue to speak of such solemn matters!'

He could imagine telling Cecily those things. Just as he could imagine coming to her now when he needed her quiet understanding. Raf had asked him, if he met Angelina for the first time now, would he want her?

He had no idea if she would even want him, for he had changed just as Raf had said. He was no longer the young raffish marquis she had adored. He had a reputation for a cynical coolness she would undoubtedly find appalling and he spent more time on his estates than he did in London.

With cold clarity he suspected, if they met now, they might feel nothing more than a passing attraction for each other. If Cecily was with him, he doubted he would look at Angelina at all.

The realisation brought him no comfort. Tears sprang to his eyes. He bowed his head and for the first time since Angelina's death he was finally able to weep for her.

And allow her to rest in peace at last.

***

He decided to return to Venice that day. He must see Cecily. He had hurt her, trampled over her heart, just as Raf said he had. He had thought only of his own needs when he'd offered for her. He wanted her, but on his terms. He had not been prepared to give her all of himself, but he wanted all of her. He had not understood why, if she cared for him, she would refuse him.

He understood now. He would offer himself to her and pray she might forgive him.

Nico found his mother in the library. She was sitting on the sofa, a book open on her lap. She tore her gaze away at his approach. A warm smile lit her face when she saw him. 'Domenico. You are finally back.'

She set her book down on the sofa and rose. She held out her hands and searched his face. 'I think that you are better.'

'I am better. Much better.'

'I am glad.'

'So am I.' He pressed her hands. 'Where is Cecily?'

'She is not in Venice. She left for Avezza with Rafaele.'

He felt a stab of fear and then anger. 'Why? With Raf?'

She hesitated. 'She sent a note that she wished given to you when you returned.'

'Where is the note?'

'In your bedchamber.'

He released her hands. 'Then you will forgive me if I go to retrieve it now.'

'Of course.'

He found the note on the bureau. He broke the seal and quickly scanned the brief missive.

To His Grace the Duke of Severin,

I am most deeply grateful for your kindness in offering me the protection of your name so that I might be safe from the attentions of a man whom I find most repugnant. Under the circumstances I feel it is best that I return to Avezza and that we do not meet again.

As always, I wish you all happiness,

Cecily Renato

He cursed. What the devil did she mean by saying she felt it best they never meet again? He had intended to beg her for forgiveness and then insist she marry him. And why the hell was she with Raf? Common sense told him it was quite natural for Raf to escort her, but he remembered Raf's parting words—what if Raf had changed his mind and decided he wanted Cecily after all?

At the very least she could tell him face to face that she never wanted to see him again.

He went down the stairs and met his mother in the hall. 'I am leaving for Avezza,' he told her.

'What will you say to her?'

He stopped. 'I intend to ask her exactly why she found it necessary to leave Venice before I returned. I will also inform her that if she wishes to end our betrothal she must do it in person.'

'Perhaps she thinks it is you who wishes to end the betrothal.'

His brow snapped down. 'Why the devil would she think that?'

'What did you tell her when you left Venice?'

'I told her I was leaving for a few days. What else was I to tell her?'

'I do not suppose you told her that you love her?'

He could feel an unfamiliar heat rising to his cheeks. 'No.'

'Then I think you must.' She gave him a gentle smile. 'Go, then. I will inform Eleanora you needed to leave straight away. I have no doubt she will understand.'

Cecily found the leather-bound book under a pile of old shawls in Barbarina's room. She picked it up and saw it was a journal. How odd, for Barbarina did not seem the sort of person who would write down her innermost thoughts. She carefully opened it and saw the delicate, neat writing did not resemble Barbarina's spidery scrawl at all. The first page was dated 1 January 1803.

She rose and sat on the chair near Barbarina's bed. She turned to the last page: 15 August 1803. *I am going to meet Nico...*

Nearly an hour later, she slowly closed the book, tears streaming down her cheeks. Angelina had not believed Thais' lies; she had loved Nico up until the very end. She wanted to meet him that day, not to call off their betrothal, but to tell him she would marry him.

Barbarina must have read this as well; why had she allowed Nico to believe Angelina no longer wanted to marry him? But then Barbarina had done nothing to stop Thais; she had known about Thais' lies and had used them herself to attempt to drive a wedge between Nico and Angelina.

Because she hoped Angelina would marry Raf if Nico was gone. It was only after Angelina died that Barbarina realised how truly wicked Thais was.

She stood. Perhaps Nico wanted nothing from her, but she had one last thing she would give him before he returned to England. She had no doubt he would marry soon; most likely a proper English girl who would provide him with beautiful dark-eyed children...

How ridiculous. She could not think of such things. She would miss him. Terribly. She was grateful to him for so much. She had finally broken out of her self-imposed exile. She had written a letter to her grandmother and, for the first time in years, the burden of the anger she had carried towards her grandmother was now gone. She had even begun to think of visiting England.

She had loved again and, although he had not returned her love, it had not destroyed her.

Perhaps knowing that Angelina had loved him to the end would ease some of the pain he carried. She would give this to him, but it was not her gift...it was Angelina's.

Raf did not look surprised when she told him she planned to leave for Venice the next day or when she explained why. 'I will, of course, accompany you.'

'You do not need to.'

'It is what I wish. For you, for Nico and for Angelina.'

Chapter Twenty-One

They stopped at an inn the late afternoon of the following day. Cecily stepped down from her carriage and waited while Raf spoke with Figaro.

She started towards the inn and then her heart lurched when she saw the crest on one of the carriages standing near by.

It could not be. No, that was quite impossible. Perhaps she could inquire if an Englishman was staying at the inn. Then determine if he was dark and spoke fluent Italian and was a duke. If so, she would...

'Good evening, Cecily.'

She spun around, her hand going to her breast. The blood rushed to her head and for a dreadful moment she thought she would swoon.

He stood behind her, arms folded. He was hatless, the sun slanting through the trees onto his hair.

'I...I had no idea you were here,' she stammered.

'And if you had, you would have jumped back into your carriage and driven away as quickly as possible?'

'I do not know.'

He smiled, although it was not pleasant. She knew, then, he had received her note. He was angry.

Part of her was relieved. If he could feel angry, then perhaps there was hope after all. His gaze fell on something behind her and then his brow snapped down. 'Vianoli. What the devil is he doing here?'

'He is escorting me to Venice.'

'The hell he is.' He strode past her to Raf.

'Nico! Stop!' He looked as if he planned to knock Raf down. She hurried after him and caught his sleeve just as he stopped in front of Raf.

'What are you doing with my fiancée?' he demanded.

Raf's brow shot up. 'Is she? I was under the impression that your betrothal was of a temporary nature.'

'You are wrong. At least until she tells me to my face that she will not marry me.'

Raf glanced at Cecily. 'Do you wish to tell him that?'

'I...' She took a deep breath. 'This is ridiculous. We cannot stand out here and discuss this.'

'Then we will go inside,' Nico said. He took her arm. 'Coming, Vianoli?'

'Of course.' If anything, Raf looked slightly amused.

She glanced up at Nico. 'You can release my arm. I do not plan to run away.'

'I beg your pardon.' He dropped his hand away. They went inside to one of the vacant public rooms.

'Where are you travelling to?' Raf asked politely.

'Avezza.'

'Ah.'

'And why are you and Cecily going to Venice?'

'That is for Cecily to tell you.'

Nico turned to her. 'Why?' he demanded.

In an inn with Nico glaring at both her and Raf was not

how she'd envisioned telling him about the journal. She wondered why she had ever felt sorry for him, for he was in the stupid arrogant duke role that she detested. Why was it any of his business what she was doing with Raf? 'I would prefer to tell you at a time when you are not in such a disagreeable mood, your Grace. And when you speak to me in civil tones. For now I wish to go to my room.'

He stepped in front of her. 'At least tell me if you are in love with Raf.'

Her mouth fell open. She looked up into his dark eyes and the hard set of his jaw. 'At the moment, I do not think I am in love with anyone. Or ever want to be. Good evening, your Grace.' She swept past him with a feeling of satisfaction.

Nico turned on Raf as soon as she had left the room. 'Do you plan to let her walk away like that?'

'Do you?'

'She has made it clear she wants nothing to do with me.'

Raf merely looked at him. 'So why are you going to Avezza?'

'To see Cecily. To beg her to marry me. If it is not too late.' His gaze hardened a little. 'I will not let you have her without a fight if you have changed your mind about wanting her.'

'She is not in love with me. Nor am I in love with her. However, that does not mean I intend to let you have her. Not until I am assured that you will not walk all over her heart.'

'I love her,' he said quietly.

Raf eyed him for a moment. 'Then I suggest you tell her that.'

'If she will listen.'

'I will talk to her and ask her to dine with you. However, if she does not wish to hear you, I cannot force her.'

Hope was beginning to rise in his chest. 'I would not expect you to.' Not that he intended to allow her to refuse.

Raf smiled a little. 'One more thing—I would suggest you actually ask Cecily to marry you rather than telling her she will do so.'

Cecily gazed around the room. It was small but at least the bed linens appeared fresh and there were no unpleasant smells that would indicate a general lack of cleanliness. She sat down on the single chair in the room. She had no idea whether to laugh or to cry. Was it possible Nico was acting so oddly because he thought she was in love with Raf? That she and Raf were travelling together for some clandestine purpose? Just as Raf had accused her and Nico of the same thing?

They could be, at this very moment, fighting in the public room downstairs for all she knew. Not that she particularly cared. Perhaps they would knock some sort of rational sense into each other. At any rate, she was quite weary of feeling responsible for everyone else.

She bent down and was about to unlace her half-boots when someone knocked on the door. She straightened, feeling slight trepidation. *'Sì?'* She prayed it was not Nico.

It was Raf. She walked to the door and opened it. 'I would like to speak to you for a moment,' he said.

'Come in.' She stepped aside and allowed him to pass her into the room. 'You have no bruises,' she told him.

'What?'

'It is nothing. What do you wish to say to me?'

'Nico would like you to dine with him tonight. In private.'

She frowned at him. 'I really do not feel inclined to do so.'

He sighed. 'I am rather weary of playing matchmaker for both of you. He cares for you. You care for him.'

She shook her head. 'He asked me why, if I cared for him, I could not marry him. I told him I could not live with another ghost.'

'Caterina.'

'I never made Marco really happy. He always mourned her.'

'Barbarina told you that, no? She did not want you taking Caterina's place, but more than that, because her husband did not love her, she did not want Marco to love you.'

'It was not just Barbarina. I saw it when he looked at me.'

He took her hand. 'Listen to me, Cecily. He mourned her, it is true, but he loved you as well. He knew he was ill almost as soon as he brought you to Italy, but he did not know how to tell you. He worried about you and did not want to burden you with the knowledge he would not live very long.'

Tears sprang to her eyes. 'I...I did not know. He never said anything to me.'

'It was not always easy for Marco to speak of his feelings. Nico is much like him in that regard.' He looked at her for a moment. 'I think you should at least hear what Nico has to say to you. You did wish to give him the journal, no?'

'You could give it to him.'

'It will mean more if you do.' He closed her hand over her palm. 'At this moment, you hold his happiness here, in your hand. It is only right that you let him know what you have decided.'

'What if I do not know?' she whispered.

He brushed a kiss across her knuckles. 'I think you do.'

Cecily stood in the doorway of the small salon for a moment. Nico stood near the window and turned immediately. He stared at her for a moment as if she was an apparition. 'You came,' he finally said.

'Yes. Raf said you wanted to see me.'

He moved towards her. 'Come in.'

She stepped into the room.

'You are only here because of Raf?' he asked.

Certainly he did not look as if she held his happiness or fate or whatever nonsense Raf had said in her hand. 'Is there something you wished to say to me?'

'Why are you travelling to Venice with Raf? Particularly since you so recently left it.'

'I was coming to see you. Raf insisted on escorting me.'

Surprise flickered across his features. 'Indeed. I rather thought from your polite note that you had no wish to see me again. Except in the capacity of a relation. So were you coming to see me as a relation?'

'I have something to give you.'

'Indeed. Then it is most convenient that we met here. You will not need to travel all the way to Venice after all. What is it you wished to give me? It cannot be the ring—you left it in Venice.'

He was still angry. Because she had hurt his pride? She was suddenly very tired.

She held out the journal. 'I found this among Barbarina's possessions. I wanted you to have it.'

He took it from her and then opened the book. He stared

down at the page for a moment, then slowly looked up at her. 'It is Angelina's journal.'

'Yes.'

'Why did you bring it to me?'

'Because you loved her. And because, if you read her last entries, you will see that she loved you. She never had any intention of breaking off your betrothal.'

He looked back down at the book. She waited for a moment and then silently left the salon.

She had just reached the door of her room when she heard footsteps behind her. 'Cecily,' Nico said.

'What is it you want?'

He hesitated for a moment. 'I was going to Avezza to find you.'

She looked up. 'Why? To take me to task over the note I wrote? Or the ring? Perhaps I should have waited until you returned, but you were so distant and so cold that I did not think it mattered whether I was there or not. At any rate, I think we have said all that needs to be said between us.' She inserted the key into the lock, only to find his hand over hers.

'We haven't said all that needs to be said. At least, I have not,' he said quietly. 'Would you grant me a few moments at least? I vow I will not approach you again unless it is your wish.'

The arrogant duke had fallen away. Instead he looked almost desperate. 'Very well.'

'In your room or downstairs? I promise I want nothing more than to talk to you.'

Downstairs would be more circumspect, but she was too tired to think of going back down. 'My room, if you please.'

She managed to open the door despite her trembling

hands and stepped into the room. He followed her and she moved as far away from him as she could. He shut the door and leaned against it. He had Angelina's journal in his hand.

She tried to keep her voice calm. 'What do you want to say to me?'

'When I read your note, I was angry. But more than that, I was afraid.' His dark eyes were fixed on her face. 'Afraid I would not see you again. Afraid you would never agree to marry me.'

'I thought we had agreed we were not going to marry.' She clasped her hands together to keep them from trembling.

'I've changed my mind. I want you to marry me.'

'I have no idea why.'

'I love you.'

Her head spun for a moment. 'You cannot,' she whispered.

'But I do. I came to ask you to forgive me for hurting you. For wanting all of you without offering you the same in return.' He took a step towards her and set the journal down on the dresser. 'I am offering you myself. All of me. With no ghosts between us.'

'Nico…'

He took another step towards her, his eyes never leaving her face. 'You said you cared for me. Is there any chance you still do?'

'Yes. I—'

'Good.' He moved towards her and she found herself backed up against the dresser. 'Because I intend to make you fall in love with me.' A touch of his usual arrogance had returned.

She drew in a shaky breath. 'You do not need to make me fall in love with you.'

His body was nearly touching hers. 'Yes, I do. I intend to begin now.'

'You…you said you only wanted to talk.'

'I have changed my mind about that as well.' The determined look in his eye made her legs tremble.

'Nico…wait, there is something I must tell you.'

'Later.' He caught her into his arms and pulled her against him. His mouth sought hers. She resisted for a moment, and then her body melded into his as she gave herself completely to him.

Nico opened his eyes. The soft, warm body against his filled him with a lazy, peaceful contentment. He shifted a little, moving his arm out from under her so that he could turn and pull her more fully against him. He felt the stirrings of arousal, but he would control his urge at least for now.

He could not keep from nuzzling her neck, however, revelling in her clean, sweet taste and the faint scent of lovemaking that clung to her. She had responded with the same passion as before. She would succumb soon enough. Before they returned to Venice he intended to first take her to the small villa he owned in the hills above Vicenza where he would thoroughly and enjoyably compromise her.

She stirred. His groin tightened and he could not resist planting another kiss on the back of her soft neck. She half-turned, her breast brushing his hand and he nearly groaned. Her eyes fluttered open. 'You are still here,' she whispered. 'I was not dreaming.'

'No, *cara*.' He brushed the hair from her forehead. 'Nor were you dreaming when I told you that you are going to marry me.'

A half-smile touched her lips. 'You could ask me, you know.'

'You might say no. I would rather you had no choice.'

'I might say yes.'

His pulse quickened. 'Would you?'

'Yes. Yes, I think I would.'

'Only think? I want you to be certain.'

'But are you?'

He saw the doubt in her eyes. His first impulse was to kiss all her reservations away, but something in her expression stopped him. 'Why would you think I am not?'

She sat up. 'Where did you go after you left Venice?'

He sat up as well, the cover falling from his chest. 'I needed to tell Angelina goodbye.' He looked away for a moment. 'For the first time since her death I felt she was finally at peace. I knew she was finally gone.' He glanced down at Cecily. 'I left that day to return to you. I wanted to see you, beg your forgiveness. But you were gone.'

She caught his hand. 'I am so sorry. I did not think you needed me. Or wanted me. So I...I left. But then Raf came. He insisted that I return to you because you needed me. And because he needed a happy ending.'

'Raf is very wise.' He drew her against his chest. 'Promise me you will not run away again.'

'No. Yes, I promise I will not.'

He drew her against him. 'So, if I ask you to marry me, will you say "yes"?'

'Yes.'

His arm tightened around her. 'Will you marry me, Cecily?'

'Yes.'

'As soon as I procure the licence.'

'In the family chapel?'

He laughed and dropped a kiss on her forehead. 'No. Here. First, I've no intention of giving you time to change your mind. We can have a second ceremony when we return to England. We will spend as much time in Italy as you wish.'

'I think I would like to become reacquainted with England. I finally wrote to my grandmother.'

'Good. We will invite her to our wedding.' Although he was not paying much attention. The quilt had fallen away to reveal one pink-tipped breast and he could think of nothing but loving her again. He slid down and pulled her on top of him. 'But for now, I have other business to attend to. Such as making you fall in love with me.'

His hand cupped one of her rounded breasts, his finger and thumb tracing leisurely circles around the sensitive, hardened nipple.

Her little moan made him smile. 'In fact, I am considering holding you prisoner until you do.'

'Nico…' She gasped as his hand drifted down her stomach to the juncture of her thighs. 'Please…wait. I must tell you something.'

'Not now.' He had no intention of allowing her to change her mind. His mouth found hers, stifling any protest.

A fortnight later Cecily and Nico stood in the garden of the Villa. Their wedding had taken place that morning, a quiet ceremony that was attended only by their families. Raf had come as he promised, although he did not stay long. After the ceremony and the breakfast, Nico brought her outside to the garden.

He took her hand and she glanced at him, her heart swelling with tenderness and love. His face, which had always seemed so harsh, was now familiar, the hardness no longer quite so visible, particularly when he turned to smile at her as he did now. He looked happy and she was still amazed that she had that effect on him. She returned his smile and then took a breath.

'I have something I have wanted to say to you since we met at the inn.' For some odd reason, her hand was shaking.

His smile faded and he dropped her hand. 'It is rather late if you have suddenly changed your mind about wedding me.'

'Oh, no.' She caught his hand to hold it again. 'It is not that at all. I wanted to tell you that I…I love you.'

He looked rather stunned. 'You love me?'

'I tried to tell you at the inn. That you did not need to make me fall in love with you because I was already in love with you. You would not give me a chance to tell you.'

His laugh was shaky. 'I promise from now on I will give you as many chances as you want. I cannot think of a better wedding gift from you.'

She wrapped her arms around his neck and drew him to her. Their kiss was tender and unhurried, a kiss full of promise and, most of all, a kiss full of hope.

* * * * *